Fionn: Traitor of Dún Baoiscne

Also by Brian O'Sullivan

The Beara Trilogy:
Beara: Dark Legends
Beara: The Cry of the Banshee (forthcoming)

The Fionn mac Cumhal Series:
Defence of Ráth Bládhma
Traitor of Dún Baoiscne

Short Story Collections
The Irish Muse and Other Stories

Fionn: Traitor of Dún Baoiscne

The Fionn mac Cumhal Series - Book Two

BRIAN O'SULLIVAN

Irishimbas Books

ISBN: 978-0-9941062-8-5

ACKNOWLEDGEMENTS

Special thanks to Marie Elder.

Thanks and credit also to Chiaki & Nasrin (Chronastock) for the use of their image on the cover.

Many ancient Fenian Cycle texts were essential for the completion of this work. These included *Macgnímartha Finn* (The Boyhood Deeds of Fionn), *Acallam na Senórach* (The Colloquy of the Ancients), *Fotha Cath Cnucha* (The Cause of the Battle of Cnucha) *Aided Finn meic Chumail* (The Death of Finn Mac Cumaill) and many more.

Foreword:

This book and its characters are based on ancient narratives from the Fenian Cycle and in particular from the *Macgnímartha Finn* (The Boyhood Deeds of Fionn). The *Macgnímartha Finn* was a twelfth century narrative that attempted to collate a number of much earlier oral tales about the legendary Irish hero Fionn mac Cumhal and the Fianna. It was originally edited by Kuno Meyer in 1881 for the French journal Revue Celtique.

Many of the personal and place names used in this novel date from before the 12th century although many have common variants (Gaelic and English) that are in use today. **For those readers who would like to know the correct pronunciation of these names, an audio glossary has been developed and is available at** http://irishimbasbooks.com/. A more basic pronunciation guide for character names is available at the back of this book.

Prologue:

Ireland: 198.A.D.

Sárán an Srón smelled it as he emerged from the rock-strewn pass of Bealach Cam. Drifting in on a gentle breeze from the south, it hung heavy in the air around the rocky entrance, striking his nostrils with a meaty intensity that stopped him in his tracks.

Stew!

His body reacted immediately, from instinct, even as his head struggled to register the presence of a scent so alien to the Great Wild. Slipping into the shelter of the nearest tree, a tall holly thick with green fern and scrub about its base, he crouched in silence, scrutinising the surrounding terrain, as he subconsciously worked through the individual elements beneath the smell.

Some kind of meat. Wild mushrooms and onions. Herbs … but not any he immediately recognised.

His mouth watered as he turned his eyes to the south but beyond the rocky entrance to the pass there was little enough to see, nothing but a rough landscape choked in places with oak and pine. Despite his habitual caution on encountering strangers so far Out in the Great Wild, Sárán allowed himself to relax. There was no evidence of any immediate threat, he was well concealed and the smell was not one to provoke any particular sense of dread. It was not, for example, the putrid stink of urine and shit, the tang of adrenalin or the iron-tinged stench of freshly spilled blood, all distinctly foul odours he'd encountered in the past and which still had the ability to raise the hairs on the back of his neck.

A long period of time passed without incident and Sárán slowly rose to his feet, although he made sure to remain within the shadow of the holly tree. A big, shaggy-haired man of twenty-seven years, he had a muscular frame and a range of scars on his left cheek and shoulder that marked him as an experienced warrior. In his right hand, he carried a javelin with an easy grip that, although loose, allowed him to raise and cast the weapon at speed should the need arise. At the small of his back, tucked into his belt, he felt the reassuring weight of a small - but deadly - hand-axe. Three additional javelins were strapped to a wicker basket that hung from his shoulders. Intended to transport the game he'd caught, the basket was dispiritingly empty.

He tugged at a greasy moustache as he stood in the shadows, closing his eyes to better appreciate the scent of stew. Raising his hand, he wiped a gob of saliva from his lips for it did smell delicious.

He found himself drooling happily at the prospect of food. It had been over five days since Sárán an Srón had left his wife and two boys at Seiscenn Uarbhaoil, a settlement far beyond the eastern swampland. Since then he'd eaten nothing but hard tack and water cress, drunk nothing but river water. Such hardships would have been borne more easily with company but, on this occasion, he was travelling alone. Both his usual hunting companions had remained behind at Seiscenn Uarbhaoil, preoccupied with more pressing matters of their own. Domhnall Dubh, a keen hunter, was awaiting the birth of his first child. When Sárán had called on him to propose the expedition he'd looked longingly at his own javelins but his wife, an irritable woman rendered all the more ill-tempered from the pregnancy, had threatened him with no sex if he dared to leave.

Dalbach, his other regular companion, was also unavailable due to a twisted ankle obtained during a romantic tryst with a local girl on the rocks at Carraig. Flaunting his leaping ability, the warrior had slipped on one of the moss-coated boulders and fallen from a substantial height. He'd been lucky not to break his leg or worse but that hadn't stopped him moaning when Sárán informed him of his intention to go Out alone. He'd consoled his friend by promising to bring him back a haunch of venison. A big one.

Given his lack of success to date, that boast now looked overly optimistic.

Sárán scrutinised the southern forest once more, this time pleased to note a tendril of smoke rising up from the green canopy not too far to the south-east.

A campfire.

That would be the source of the smell. He stroked his nose, an overly large proboscis that had earned his nickname: Sárán an Srón - Sárán the Nose. Because of its size, many of the people at Seiscenn Uarbhaoil believed that he had sensory skills beyond that of ordinary mortals, that he could in fact 'sniff out' potential threats or dangers. Although he encouraged the stories because he enjoyed the attention, Sárán knew there was no truth in them. His sense of smell was no better, no worse, than most others at the settlement.

Staring at the distant plume of smoke, he frowned and scratched at the stubble on his jaw. He should be moving east, using the remaining sunlight to travel back in the direction of Seiscenn Uarbhaoil before he was obliged to set up camp for the night.

A dry camp.

With hard tack.

And cold water.

He sighed. Travelling alone as he was, he knew it would be wise to avoid strangers in the Great Wild, despite the fact that he was a fearsome

2

warrior, a fact that several opponents - now dead - had discovered to their detriment.

His stomach grumbled in counter argument.

Sárán mulled over the possibilities. He could always, he reasoned, scout out the source of the odour. If the people responsible for it looked in any way dangerous, he could simply slip away and continue his journey.

He stared to the south. The smell of the stew was delectable.

And he was hungry.

***

Once Sárán had reached the trees, he worked his way through the forest with the ease of an experienced hunter, carefully avoiding sections of woody debris where branches or twigs might crack beneath his feet and alert others to his presence. As he advanced, the smell of stew grew perceptibly stronger. Soon he was able to make out the muffled sound of a distant conversation.

Dropping to his stomach, he wriggled forward, working his way towards a heavily vegetated mound coated with a thick copse of ash trees and heavy foliage. As far as he could tell, the voices were coming from somewhere on the other side and this particular route offered both the best concealment for his approach and his possible flight, if that were required.

It was almost dark when he reached the crest of the mound. Shuffling sideways to one of the wider tree trunks, he cautiously eased his head around it.

Ah!

The campsite was located in a little grotto, part of a long gully carved out of the ground by some ancient waterway and still strewn with smooth, green boulders. That section of the grotto closest to Sárán's hiding place was relatively level and held a flattened rock that reached up to waist height. In the centre of this boulder was a deep depression full of rainwater from the previous night's shower. Beside the rock, an impressive fire was crackling. Sárán's eyes, however, were drawn less to the flicker of the flames than to the metal cauldron that dangled over it, the source of the delicious odour that now completely filled the air.

He licked his lips.

It was something of an effort to pull his eyes away to study the grotto's human occupants. All six were seated at the fire, three each in a single line on separate logs, facing each other across the flames. They were a strange looking group. Of the trio looking in his direction, two were big men, bald but stocky. Because of their size, both would have drawn the eye even if it hadn't been for the fact that they were completely identical. From the bald,

3

sunburned skulls, right down to the rough dark robes they were wearing, each was a perfect copy of the other.

A Man Pair.

Sárán bit his lip. He had heard of man pairs before but he'd never actually seen one. Apparently, there' been such a family at Seiscenn Uarbhaoil in the past. It had been before his time but people still spoke of the cursed mother who'd given birth to two sets of Man Pairs. On both occasions, the babies had died and, after the second pair, the woman had succumbed to fever. Grief-stricken, the father had wandered out into the Great Wild, never to be seen again.

The man seated to the left of the Man Pair, staring into the flames, was a skinny, old man. He too was bald but had countered the absence of hair on the back of his head with a thick growth of beard on his face that fell all the way to his waist.

Although he couldn't see the faces of the threesome on the closest side of the fire as they had their backs to him, they too looked quite odd. One of them, a cowl pulled tight over his head, looked to be extremely short and was probably a child. Seated beside him, another, taller, individual seemed all the taller for the shortness of his companion. He too was completely bald. On the far right of this trio, the final figure appeared to be of a more normal height but rather rotund given the tightness of the material around his girth and frame.

Sárán nodded in approval at their choice of campsite. It was a good location, one that provided shelter from the wind and which was well hidden. He himself would have bypassed it, completely unaware of their presence, if it hadn't been for the smell.

With this, his lips formed into a thin line. Despite their clever choice of location, this little group did not appear to have taken any other precautions. There was no-one standing guard and, as far as he could see, only two of them sported weapons – the two staffs carried by the Man Pair.

He gave a scornful shake of his head. Out in the Great Wild, death lurked behind every tree, lay waiting in every shadow for the unwary. Wolves and other predators prowled the land. If he had been a bandit, he could have snuck in and murdered them all without too much difficulty.

Reassured by this initial assessment and confident in his ability to deal with any threat that might arise from this particular group, Sárán got to his feet, stepped out of the trees and started walking down towards the fire.

Naturally, because they were facing in his direction, the Man Pair were the first to spot him. Startled, they quickly jumped to their feet, pulling their staffs up to hold them at the ready.

Sárán suppressed a smile. He could take both of them out easily with a javelin cast, leaving him with the hand axe to take care of the others.

And he was deadly with a hand-axe.

4

Seeing the Man Pair's reaction, the others had also turned about and quickly stood up to examine the unexpected arrival. Only the old man with the beard took his time, stiffly rising to his feet to face the newcomer.

Sárán raised a placatory hand. 'Hallo, Travellers,' he called out. 'I come in peace.'

The six strangers looked at one another. In the end, it was the bearded elder who finally stepped forward. He coughed and cleared his throat. 'I see you, stranger. I am named Rogein.'

'I see you, Old One. I am named Sárán ua Baoiscne.'

'Welcome to our campsite, Sárán ua Baoiscne. We are preparing our meal. Would you care to eat with us? There is not much but we are happy to share.'

The old man's voice sounded oddly brittle as though he'd done some damage to his throat in the past.

Sárán glanced at the steaming cauldron and nodded curtly, not trusting himself to successfully disguise his hunger for its contents. He advanced further into the little grotto and stood closer to the fire. 'I will join you,' he said, taking a seat on a small rock set back at an angle from the two logs on which the others were seated. As he sat, he made sure to keep his javelin close to hand. The men seemed harmless enough but he did not intend to take any chances. If necessary, the rock was sufficiently far from the group to allow him time to respond to any hostility.

And they will pay dearly if they tried.

If the old man noticed his caution, he showed no sign of it. Instead, he plunged a ladle into the little cauldron and scooped out a portion of stew which he slapped into a wooden bowl. He passed it to the big warrior who took it in one hand and held it under his nose. Briefly closing his eyes, he inhaled and savoured the aroma one last time before raising the bowl to his mouth and swallowing the contents whole.

'Aaah!'

He smacked his lips with relish. The food had tasted every bit as good as it smelled. He glanced at his empty bowl then back towards the cauldron but Rogein seemed to miss the hint. The other members of the group, meanwhile, were regarding him quietly as though unsure what to make of him. After a moment, they all sat down again.

'From where do you hail, Sárán ua Baoiscne?' asked Rogein.

'From Seiscenn Uarbhaoil. It is located to the east.'

'You are far from home.'

'I am on the hunt. Seiscenn Uarbhaoil is a growing settlement. The local forest has been hunted out.' He glanced at the other members of the party. 'Who are your friends?'

'Forgive me,' the old man answered. 'I am a poor host.' He pointed to the Man Pair. 'These are Futh and Ruth. They are brothers but you may have already noticed the family resemblance.'

Sárán considered them uneasily. Seeing them sitting there side by side was like looking at a reflection in still waters. It seemed unnatural. Despite his disquiet, he smiled politely and nodded a greeting which the two men returned. Rogein, meanwhile, had moved on to the corpulent man to Sárán's left. The warrior observed the fleshy face and pendulous jowls hanging below his jaw with silent censure. The folds of fat almost obscured a small tattoo of a spider on his right cheek.

'And this is Regna of Mag Fea,' said Rogein. 'He is the man who prepared the repast which you are enjoying.'

Sárán stared at Regna's stomach which protruded obscenely, pressing against the material of his robe like the belly of a pregnant woman. Although he'd never seen a man with so much useless bulk, he hid his distaste and nodded.

'This,' Rogein was indicating the extremely tall figure with the cowl, 'is Temle'. Temle lowered his cowl to reveal another bald head, a muted pair of eyes and a strikingly bulbous nose. Like Regna of Mag Fea, he too had a spider tattooed on his left cheek. Sárán glanced at the Man Pair and realised that they too had the spider marking although he'd missed it in the flickering shadows thrown up by the fire.

'And finally,' said the old man, gesturing towards the smallest figure at the far end of the log. 'This one is named Olpe.'

Sárán leaned forward in order to see the little shape more clearly.

'Hallo, little one.'

The figure turned to look at him but beneath the shadowed cowl it was impossible to tell if it was a boy or a girl.

The big warrior grinned. 'I have two boys about your age.'

With this a small pair of hands appeared from out of the sleeves and reached up to pull the cowl back. To his horror, Sárán found himself staring at the wizened face of a very old man. Like the others, he was completely bald.

Regna of Mag Fea roared with laughter. 'I very much doubt that!'

Sárán bristled, angered at being embarrassed in this manner. 'Who are you?' he demanded. 'Why does such an odd group travel Out in the Great Wild?'

Rogein quickly made a mollifying gesture. 'Forgive Olpe's little joke, Sárán ua Baoiscne. We are like you. Simple travellers.'

'I am not a traveller. I am a hunter.'

'Of course, of course.' He nodded. 'My comrades and I …' He paused. 'We too are hunters of a sort. Hunters of knowledge.'

'Hunters of truth.' Sárán could not hide the scepticism in his voice.

'Indeed. The stars reveal their secrets to us and we hunt their associated knowledge.'

Sárán continued to look at him blankly.

'If you can read them, the stars reveal many secrets. Some years past, for example, the stars told us that a great leader, a most powerful figure, had been born. Since then we have been travelling the land to seek him out.' He made a shrugging gesture. 'The problem is that although the stars tell us of such events, they do not tell us where they occur. That is why we travel now, seeking the one who was born.'

'Why would you seek out a baby?'

'To pay homage to him.'

Sárán struggled to keep the incredulity from his voice. 'To pay homage to a baby?'

'Yes.'

'How would you pay homage to a mewling infant?'

'Well, we are not wealthy men but we have gathered gifts of significance.'

'Oh?' asked Sárán with renewed interest.

'Temle.' Rogein looked to the tall man. 'Show our guest.'

With a sigh, the tall man reached down to open a little backpack resting on the log alongside him. Undoing the upper cord that sealed it, he withdrew three large clay pots and laid them on the ground before him. Removing the sealed lid of the first container, he tilted it forwards so that Sárán could see its contents: a large mixture of some papery bark, paired leaves, and flowers with white petals and a yellow or red centre.'

'Flowers. Very nice. I'm sure the babe's mother will appreciate that.'

'These are no ordinary flowers, Sárán of Seiscenn Uarbhaoil. They come from the lands far to the East and produce an alluring fragrance.'

Sárán ignored him, peering at the other containers. 'What else do you have?'

Temle opened the second pot. This was full to the brim with a powdery, reddish resin. Sárán leaned forward to examine it more closely only to draw back in alarm as he caught a whiff of the overpowering scent it gave off.

'This is another fragrance from the Myrrh trees. Again, they are found far to the East. And finally … '

The last clay pot was opened. Sárán stared. It seemed to contain a large collection of shiny metal disks.'

He looked at Rogein with a quizzical expression.

'They call this gold,' explained the old man. 'It is of great worth.'

'Of course, of course.' Despite his disappointment, Sárán supressed a great desire to roll his eyes. He had been hoping for more food of the quality of the stew, some weapons or even jewellery he could have appropriated to bring back to his wife in compensation for the lack of food. He tried not to laugh as he imagined the expression of the babe's family when this group arrived offering homage and pots of useless junk. The thought prompted his next question.

'You say you have been seeking this child for some time.'

'Yes. For some years. Although we know the child was born, we do not know where. Recently, we learned that he was to be found in a settlement said to be led by a woman.'

'A woman!' Sárán scoffed. 'What settlement would let a woman lead them?'

'It's true,' the old man conceded. 'It is difficult to believe but we were also told that this woman was a Gifted One and has received training as a *bandraoi* - a female druid. Have you heard of such a place?'

The warrior thought about that. 'I know of no such settlement in these parts but I have heard tales of a place far to the west, in the Sliabh Bládhma region. My sister's man once told me that it has links to *Clann Baoiscne* but I do not know what those links are.'

Rogein looked eagerly towards his companions who were now all whispering excitedly together. 'You see, brothers! Our informant did not fail us.' He quietened then as though absorbed in deep thought but after a moment he returned his attention to the warrior.

'You have our gratitude, Sárán. Can we offer you more stew as an expression of our appreciation?'

Sárán looked guiltily at the little cauldron. There did not seem to be enough for everyone but the flavours were still raging on his tongue, demanding more.'

'Very well.' He did his best to sound as though he was doing them a kindness accepting the reward that was his due for helping them in their bizarre search.

Rogein ladled another measure into his bowl and he immediately lapped it up, fearful that he might have to share. When he was finished, he wiped the leather sleeve of his tunic across his lips. 'Do not take this the wrong way, Rogein. It is not my intent to insult your hospitality but you are foolish to wander about in the Great Wild without protection. These lands can be very dangerous.'

As he spoke, he eased his javelin onto his knees and slowly, casually, allowed his left hand to drift behind his back to where his hand-axe waited. It was ungrateful of him, he knew, but he had come to the decision to rob this little company. They could keep their smelly pots but he intended to leave the camp with that cauldron. If they did not attempt to stop him, they did not need to die.

'I have a weapon,' said Regna of Mag Fea. The fat man held up a short boning knife that, although sharp, would have done little more than cause a gash in a real fight. 'And both Futh and Ruth have their stout staves.'

Sárán bit his tongue. These men were fools. Simple-minded idiots whose bones would inevitably litter the floor of the Great Wild's forests.

'You would not frighten a sand fly with such a knife. Staves are useful up close but they are no match for a sword or a battle axe. And they offer no defence against spear or javelin. You would require real weapons, Rogein.' He tapped his own javelin to emphasise his point. 'Something to strike fear into those who would attack you.'

Rogein looked at him in surprise. 'Why would anyone attack us? Apart from our gifts - which we keep concealed - we have nothing of value, nothing that anyone would want.'

Sárán glanced guiltily at the cauldron from the corner of his eye.

'You should fear travellers in the night,' the big warrior said. 'Death comes easily in the Great Wild.'

'We are six,' insisted Rogein. 'How can you claim to advise us when you are but a single man?'

'Because I am a warrior from Seiscenn Uarbhaoil. My blades are stained with the blood of many enemies. I am not one to be waylaid or interfered with. I am strong. I kill easily, without passion. You cannot compare us.'

There was a dull thump.

Sárán looked down to find that the wooden bowl had slipped from his fingers, hitting the rocky ground. He started to laugh and was about to make a joke of it but when he attempted to speak only a barely audible croak came out of his mouth.

Surprised, he raised his fingers to touch his lips and tried again. Once again, there was no sound but a croak.

Rogein was looking at him with mild curiosity. 'What is it, Sárán ua Baoiscne? Is the stew not to your liking?'

Sárán pointed urgently at his mouth and grunted.

'You cannot speak?' Rogein leaned forward and peered closely at his guest. Annoyed, Sárán opened his mouth wide, offering the old man a better view in the hope that he could see what was wrong.

After a moment, the old man pulled back and tugged thoughtfully on his long beard. 'I believe I know the cause. It will be the white root, an ingredient Regna of Mag Fea adds to his stews. It enhances the flavour, magnifies both the taste and the odour. Manipulation of scent is one of the many secret skills he learned in his travels through the Eastern Lands.'

Sárán glanced at the fat man who returned it with a smug smile then chuckled loudly. 'On occasion, it has the interesting effect of rendering an eater silent. A perfect antidote for boastful guests.'

Furious, the warrior made to reach for the javelin lying across his knees but found that his hand did not move. Alarmed, he tried to stand but found that his legs were not responding either.

'Ah, yes.' Regna of Mag Fea was stroking the smooth skin of his meaty jowls as he observed Sárán's efforts. He got to his feet, waddled towards the warrior and squatted down before him. 'That is another side effect. The more common one in fact. The white root causes a great lassitude of the limbs. It makes a person still and unmoving.'

He smiled at the growing alarm in Sárán's eyes. 'You are a man of sage advice, Sárán of Seiscenn Uarbhaoil. One should not travel without care within the Great Wild. It is a dangerous place. And it is a shame you are unable to follow your own counsel.'

Pulling the javelin from the warrior's knees, he tossed the weapon aside.

'I am glad you enjoyed our cooking. You were aware there was not much food but that did not stop you. Still, it can be said you enjoyed your last meal. The last visitor to our campfire enjoyed his meal just as you enjoyed him.

He nodded at the horrified comprehension in the frozen man's eyes.

'And now you see the truth of it. Yes, that is how we travel so light. When we are low on supplies we set our web at sites such as this valley entrance where travellers are, eventually, bound to pass.'

He pulled out the little boning knife and held it up in front of the stricken man.

'But you will forgive me, I'm sure. The night grows late and my companions grow hungry.'

Chapter One:

The butterflies were swarming, despite the early hour.

Sprawled across the moss-coated bough of a great oak tree, Liath Luachra watched the fluttering wave of orange, black and white wings drift across the pasture, settling like coloured rainfall on the wildflowers and trees to the south of the clearing.

The woman warrior stared in fascination. She'd always enjoyed the erratic movement of butterflies and, over the years, she'd seen many but never in such numbers and never swarming in such an unusual fashion. She looked again to where enormous clumps of the creatures were visible, hanging off the distant trees, the powdery undersides of their wings making them look like dusty clusters of some strange, grey fruit.

Liath Luachra chewed thoughtfully on the inside of her cheek. Although not one to ascribe a mystic explanation to events she didn't understand, she couldn't help wondering if this rare phenomenon heralded a prophetic occurrence, some dangerous consequence that she was unaware of.

Bodhmhall. I will ask Bodhmhall when I return to Ráth Bládhma.

Bodhmhall would know.

Pushing such thoughts aside, Liath Luachra stretched her limbs and yawned, focussing her attention on more physical distractions: the simple touch of sunlight on her skin, the lilt of birdsong, the busy hum of bees and crickets, the combined beauty of her surroundings. In her mind, all of these were good omens. Moreover, the softness of the morning promised a pleasant day, one that was all the more pleasant for being Out, back in the freedom of the Great Wild.

Situated at the centre of a large clearing known as An Folamh Mór – the Big Empty, her vantage point on the branches of the giant oak offered an unhindered view across a stretch of rough grass for several hundred paces in every direction. In the distant past, the trees on this spot had been felled by the Old Ones but for some reason they'd left a single, solitary oak standing in the centre. She had no idea why. It was hard to fathom the minds of the Old Ones, a folk that left impressive stone monuments in the strangest of places: on tops of steep hills, deep in the darkwoods, half-submerged in swampland.

Despite the intervening years, the forest had never fully recovered its grip on the land. The clearing had become a favourite spot for deer who enjoyed the sunlight and the sweet taste of its green pasture. Generations of the animals had regularly grazed the encroaching shoots sent out by the surrounding trees, preventing any reclamation.

Because of its position, the giant oak served as an ideal hunting platform. Its height, and the screen offered by its leaves, provided a perfect location from which to cast a javelin at those deer that wandered too close.

A soft breeze caressed the upper branches of the oak, stretching the thick wooden limbs to produce a series of drawn out creaks. A noisy crackling sound filled the clearing as bushy clumps of leaves brushed against each other.

Despite the idyllic setting, An Folamh Mór had its less favourable aspects. Earlier that morning, for example, the grass had been submerged by a thick, knee-deep mist that had hovered above the ground and showed no signs of dissipating. Up on her perch, Liath Luachra had fretted about that, aware of the deer's dislike of wet grass. Shortly after dawn, the situation had become even more complicated when a pair of grey timber wolves had detached themselves from the northern tree line, gliding quietly through the mist, the dark curves of their backs just visible above the brume.

Liath Luachra had observed their arrival with even greater trepidation for the wolves presented a potential encroachment more significant than the mist. If the animals remained in the area, they'd interfere with her hunt by scaring off the deer or, worse, competing with her for the kill.

After working through her options, the woman warrior had finally decided on a direct course of action. Grabbing two javelins, she lowered herself smoothly to the lower branches and dropped out of the tree, hitting the ground with an audible thump that caused the wolves to stop in their tracks. Two pairs of ears poked above the ghostly wisps and turned in her direction.

She made no attempt at silence as she moved forward towards them. In fact she did everything she could to make as much noise as possible: stomping and shuffling her feet, growling and cursing, banging the two javelin shafts together.

The two beasts weren't completely discernible until she was within almost ten paces of them and as soon as the grey forms congealed into something more substantial, she quickly drew to a halt. They were much bigger than she'd expected. They were also facing her, crouched low in preparation for attack. A bloodcurdling growl rumbled from the back of their throats as they bared jagged fangs, the skin around their muzzles drawn back in a vicious snarl. Liath Luachra responded with a snarl of her own, raising her arms to make herself look bigger as she brandished a javelin in either hand.

For several moments they'd faced one another, menacing and threatening, both attempting to intimidate the other and force them to back down. In the end, it was the wolves who'd conceded. Unwilling to risk engaging with such an undefined threat, they reluctantly relinquished their claim on the clearing, withdrawing back in the direction from which they'd first appeared.

Liath Luachra watched in silence as they slunk away, stopping occasionally to throw a vengeful glance back in her direction. She did not relax until they'd disappeared into the trees and, even then, she continued to keep an eye on the treeline. *Na mactíre* – literally 'sons of the land' – were not to be taken lightly. By themselves, the animals were relatively safe and could usually be scared off unless they were desperate or starving. When there was more than one, however, it tended to embolden them. The animals had a natural ability to work effectively against an opponent as a pair or as part of a pack. They could also be remarkably sly at times and moved with startling speed when the mood took them.

Satisfied that her competitors had truly departed, Liath Luachra allowed the tension to ease from her body and stretched repeatedly to relieve the stiffness in her neck and shoulders. In some respects, it had been foolish to confront them in the way she had. Wolves had a tendency to attack when threatened, particularly where approached within their own territory or at a place where they felt cornered. That had been the reasoning behind the initial commotion she'd made on dropping from the tree. By alerting them to her presence, she had allowed them ample opportunity to back away. As a general rule, she tended to avoid the animals and, indeed, would have done so on this occasion if they hadn't posed such a serious encroachment to her hunt.

The woman warrior returned to the oak, grabbed a low-lying branch and hauled herself back into the lower limbs then, subsequently scaled the trunk to the higher branches. Although unusually tall for her gender, she moved with impressive dexterity, slipping between the gnarled branches and curving around contorted angles with an ease that revealed impressive flexibility and upper body strength.

It took her surprisingly little time to regain the flat section she'd occupied since late the previous night. Making herself comfortable, she quietly rested the javelins alongside the reed basket that contained her supplies and settled down to wait.

She was used to waiting. Solitary by nature, she'd always tended to hunt alone, this habit of a lifetime broken only for Bearach, son of Cairbre, who she'd allowed to accompany her for a time. Somehow, the boy had won her over, undermining her austere personality with a disabling sense of humour she'd found herself unable to resist.

But Bearach's dead now.

She still missed Bearach's company and sometimes the simple memory of his laugh caused a twinge in her belly, like an old stab wound that had never properly healed. Six years had passed since the boy's death. Six years yet, even now, she sometimes found herself reaching to point out an object of interest or a view that he might have appreciated, only to remember that he was no longer beside her. At such times, she felt as though she'd somehow made a misstep, blithely treading off a steep height that she'd badly miscalculated.

With a grimace, she brushed all thought of the boy from her mind. She knew better than to dwell on black memories, traumatic occasions or events that she could not change. Such regrets were pointless. Best not to think of them.

Yet she knew that Bearach would slip back into her head.

To pop up with a grin when she was least expecting it.

***

It was a relief when the deer finally revealed themselves, their arrival dispelling the dark thoughts like morning sunshine on a bad dream. The first indication of their presence was a flicker of movement in the trees to the west. She'd expected that. The previous evening, she'd spotted substantial deer sign in that area, suggesting it was their usual route of approach to the clearing. Raising her head, she studied the movement of the nearer branches before nodding in satisfaction. The wind was coming from the west too. There was little risk of the animals catching her scent.

A large buck tentatively emerged from the trees and advanced onto the pasture. The animal came to a halt just beyond the treeline and stood there, waiting. Liath Luachra remained perfectly still. She knew the buck was surveying the area, relying on its exceptional hearing and sense of smell to alert it to any hint of danger. A long time passed before it finally relaxed and dropped its head to eat. When it did, four other deer emerged from the scrub to join it, picking at the lush grass with cautious gusto, regularly raising their heads to survey the clearing.

Liath Luachra released a deep breath as she studied the deer herd, pleased to see that they were healthy looking animals. All looked well fed and had shed their grey winter coats for the red of summer. The fingers of her right hand tightened around the haft of a javelin but she forced herself to relax and release her grip. The animals were still too far away to be certain of a kill. If the cast was not perfect, she would end up chasing a wounded animal through the forest until it bled to death. A poor outcome for all involved.

Slowly, tantalisingly slowly, the animals wandered closer to the oak. In minute, gradual movements, Liath Luachra raised the javelin, drawing it up to eye level then back in preparation for a cast. Her attention was focussed completely on the buck.

Closer, soft-eyed one. Just two or three steps closer.

Suddenly, the animal stiffened, raised its head and stared fixedly towards the north.

14

What ...?

And then it was off, bounding back across the pasture and into the shelter of the western trees, the rest of the herd immediately behind it. Up on the oak branch, Liath Luachra gnashed her teeth in silent fury as she stared at the now deserted clearing. The deer would not return. The entire morning had been wasted.

Despite her anger and a burning curiosity to learn what had spooked her prey, the woman warrior forced herself to turn slowly on the wide girth so the movement wouldn't draw any watchful eyes.

It wasn't long before the cause of the animals' flight became apparent: a distant crashing of bush to the northeast as someone made their way through the forest. As Liath Luachra watched, a figure surged out of the treeline, slowing abruptly on finding himself in such an open expanse after the tightness of the forest.

Liath Luachra studied the newcomer. The man was a stranger, slender with long, dark hair tied up in a knot at the back of his head. He had a short shaggy beard - more like several day's growth than a beard - and was dressed lightly in a loose fitting leather jerkin and leggings. A knife scabbard was tucked into a leather belt about his waist and he carried a spear in his right hand.

The stranger started running again, crossing the clearing at an easy pace but, even as he drew nearer to the great oak, she could tell that he was moving with a definite destination in mind. No hunter, then. And unlikely to be a bandit.

He makes for Ráth Bládhma.

She had no evidence to support this theory but, instinctively, she knew she was correct. The runner was headed in the right direction and out in this part of the Great Wild there was nowhere else he could be running to.

Putting the javelin aside, she grabbed a leather waterskin and swung herself to the lower limbs for the second time that morning. Quickly reaching the bottom branches, she dropped from the tree.

The runner skidded to a halt as she hit the ground several paces in front of him but he recovered quickly enough. By the time she'd regained her balance and stood up to face him, he was bringing his spear to bear. Liath Luachra considered the wicked looking spear head, impressed by its steadiness given the runner's obvious fatigue and the laboured attempts at recovering his breath. A strong odour of fresh sweat hit her as she raised her eyes from the weapon to the newcomer's face. Despite his beard, he was younger than she'd originally imagined, certainly no more than seventeen or eighteen years.

He has Bearach's face!

Liath Luachra stiffened for the resemblance was truly startling. This youth looked like an older version of her friend, the young man that Bearach would have grown up to be had he still lived.

She swallowed hard and examined the newcomer more closely. The beard was wrong of course. Bearach had favoured a wispy little moustache that he'd been ridiculously proud of. The eyes, too, were the wrong colour – green instead of blue – and sat slightly too close together. Otherwise, everything else was the same: the soft brown hair, the prominent cheekbones, even the laughter crinkles about his lips and eyes.

Not that this youth was laughing. His eyes were wide but that was a result of his shock at seeing her appear out of nowhere. She could see the internal struggle reflected in those eyes as he tried to work out how best to react to such unanticipated circumstances. Liath Luachra took a deep breath and pulled herself together.

'I see you, Running Man.'

Even to her ears, her voice sounded harsher than she'd intended. Bearach's ghost continued to stare back at her, nostrils flared, his breathing heavy.

She tried again. 'How are you named?'

This time she could see the young man weigh up whether to respond or not. Finally, he seemed to come to the conclusion that she didn't pose an immediate danger for the tension in his shoulders loosened and the spearhead dropped slightly. 'I am named Fintán,' he said. 'Of *Na Lamhraighe*.'

Liath Luachra looked at him blankly. This was another surprise. *Na Lamhraighe* were a nomadic tribe far to the north-east. To find one here, so far from his tribal lands, could not bode well. 'I know of *Na Lamhraighe*. Six years ago, Bodhmhall ua Baoiscne of Ráth Bládhma delivered a woman into the safekeeping of your leader, Gleor Red Hand.'

'The youth nodded in acknowledgment. 'I am bound for Ráth Bládhma. I bear news for Bodhmhall ua Baoiscne of Gleor Red Hand's imminent arrival with his company.'

Liath Luachra grunted softly to herself. This young man would be *Na Lamhraighe's* fastest runner, then. Travelling as a member of Gleor's retinue for the greater part of the journey, he'd have been dispatched ahead both to scout the trail for danger and to alert the settlement so they'd have sufficient notice to prepare the expected hospitality.

As these thoughts rolled through her head, she realised the youth was observing her with an oddly curious expression. 'What?'

'You are Liath Luachra, *conradh* – champion – of Ráth Bládhma. They call you "The Grey One".'

Liath Luachra shrugged. The epithet had been one assigned to reflect her preference for grey-coloured clothing and the colour of her eyes. 'I am.'

'You used to lead *Na Cineáltaí* – The Kindly Ones.'

'Long ago.' She tossed the water-skin to the youth, anxious to change the topic and disassociate herself from her days with that now discontinued mercenary band. 'You must be thirsty. Drink your fill.'

The youth had to release one hand from his spear to catch the leather container but he did so with surprising swiftness. Raising the water-skin to his mouth, he teased the stopper out with his teeth, spat it aside and tipped the contents into his mouth, swallowing greedily as it gurgled down his throat.

'Why does Gleor Red Hand travel to Ráth Bládhma?'

Fintán picked up the stopper and reaffixed it then tossed the leather container back to the woman warrior.

'He seeks counsel with Bodhmhall ua Baoiscne.'

'He comes a long way to seek Bodhmhall's counsel. Do *Na Lamhraighe* have no advisors of their own?'

The warrior looked embarrassed. He rested the base of his spear haft on the ground and tapped awkwardly at the earth with the heel of his foot. 'In truth, he was prompted to do so by his woman.'

'His woman?'

'Muirne Muncháem.'

The woman warrior was not one to openly display her emotions. When shocked – as she most surely was now – her immediate instinct was to clam up, to unconsciously suppress any emotional expression. Over time, she'd become aware that this reaction was misinterpreted as one of hostility and often made an effort to soften her expression but, in this case … 'Muirne Muncháem.' She repeated the name softly. Even after six years, the name left a sting like nettles in her mouth. 'Muirne Muncháem is with Gleor Red Hand?'

'She has been with him for five years.'

'I understood Gleor Red Hand already had a woman.'

'He did. She died of fever. Five years ago.'

'Uh,' Liath Luachra grunted again. Who would have guessed? She'd clearly read the omens wrong this morning.

The Flower of Almhu wastes no time lying in the hollow of another woman.

She knew she should feel no sense of surprise. Muirne Muncháem was a driven woman, desperately ambitious and with great political astuteness. It would have been a natural move for her to link herself to the lynchpin of power in whichever community she'd found herself. Nevertheless, the news disturbed her. Strife and death followed close in the footprints of Muirne Muncháem. *Muinntir Bládhma* – the people of Ráth Bládhma – had already paid dearly for their association with her. Bearach had paid dearly.

'And *Na Lamhraighe* are happy with this union?'

The young man said nothing. That didn't surprise her. Tribal members rarely revealed much on the inner workings and conflicts with people from outside the tribe. She continued to observe him, quietly pondering the ramifications of Muirne's return. Bodhmhall would not be pleased. That much was certain, particularly given her efforts to protect Muirne and subsequently secure her a hiding place where she could live in safety. When Muirne had left, there'd been a clear expectation they would not see her again. Given everything that had happened, the costs and the sacrifices made, nobody would desire her back. Liath Luachra certainly didn't.

And then of course there was Muirne's son to consider. Seeking advice from Bodhmhall certainly wasn't the true reason for this visit to Ráth Bládhma. Although Liath Luachra personally had no trace of maternal instincts, she knew enough to recognise the intensity of that bond between a mother and her child. Six years earlier, Muirne had been forcibly separated from her son in order to conceal and protect them both. She would be desperate to see him again.

Liath Luachra released a sigh as she looked at the youth with her dead friend's face. 'Ráth Bládhma is located in a narrow valley called Glenn Ceoch – Valley of Mists,' she said stiffly. 'It lies a good half-day's march to the southeast of where we now stand. You will only find the entrance by approaching the mountains from the west. Keep the steepest mountain to your right and the lower hills to your left. Otherwise, you will miss it. If you can run swiftly you will reach it by noon.'

'Muirne Muncháem has provided me with directions,' the youth responded with calculated smoothness. 'But are you not going to run with me?'

In some respects, his indignation was to be expected. When a messenger was encountered in tribal territory, it was considered good manners to escort him to his destination out of respect for the news he might carry. Liath Luachra, however was still smouldering at his unintentional disruption of her hunt. And then, there was the youth's unsettling resemblance to Bearach.

She shivered. She did not wish to run with a ghost. She needed some time in her own company to think things through and make sense of the matter.

The warrior woman considered the youth more closely again, carefully scrutinising his features to make sure she wasn't seeing something that wasn't really there. Discomforted by that rigorous examination, Fintán took a step backwards. 'Why do you stare at me in that manner?'

'You bear the features of a friend.'

'A close friend?'

'He was.'

'Then he is dead.'

18

She held his eyes. 'Yes,' she said flatly. 'He is dead.'

'What is that?'

She was surprised by the sudden change in topic but knew immediately that he was referring to the tattoo on the left side of her face where a thick, black line descended from the mid-point between her ear and her temple. On either side of that line, a number of smaller horizontal bars projected outwards from it at irregular intervals.

'It's a tattoo.'

'I know it is a tattoo. I am not a fool.' He frowned at Liath Luachra's provocative grin. 'I have not seen its like before. What does it symbolise?'

'Death.'

He looked at her askew, clearly wondering if she was mocking him but appeared then to take her at her word. He looked around the clearing, coughed and shuffled self-consciously. 'Would you flatten the grass at my side?'

Liath Luachra's response was a chilling silence.

'Well?'

'You wish to rut in the long grass?' She found her fingers running down the stitched leather edge of her knife sheath.

'Yes.'

'You feel untroubled by any burden of restraint?'

'I can run all day,' the youth boasted. 'I am full of *teaspaí* [energy – mischievous or sexual]. I could rut and then run for another day without need of rest.'

'I was not speaking of physical fatigue.'

Fintán looked confused. He clearly had no idea what she was referring to.

'You know my name,' she said. 'You know of my position at Ráth Bládhma.'

He nodded. 'Yes. You are Liath Luachra. *Conradh* of Ráth Bládhma.'

'So you must also know of my relationship with Bodhmhall ua Baoiscne.'

'*An Cailleach Dubh* – the Black Hag? Yes.'

'And this does not make you pause, even for an instant?'

'Aaaah!' He nodded in comprehension. 'You do not care to taste pleasure for fear *An Cailleach Dubh* would hear of it. His face split in a roguish grin and Liath Luachra winced inside for that expression was Bearach to the core. 'Perhaps *An Cailleach Dubh* would not know.'

'Oh, she would know,' Liath Luachra laughed, despite her discomfort. 'She would know.'

'That is a poor tale, then,' said Fintán. He nodded ponderously as though to give weight to his own words. 'Yes, a poor tale.'

19

Liath Luachra considered the youth with sudden insight. 'You are Gleor's son.'

Fintán looked at her then scowled. 'How could you know that? You do not know me.'

'Despite the offensive nature of that tactless beak, you are puzzlingly … undead. That means that within *Na Lamhraighe* you are either someone of importance or under the protection of someone important. You strike me as ill-suited for importance and you are too young to be Gleor Red Hand. Therefore you must be his son.'

The young man glowered. 'I am my own man.'

'Good. Then you will have no problem making your own way to Ráth Bládhma.'

***

Liath Luachra exhaled slowly as she watched Fintán depart, moving at speed across the clearing to disappear from sight in the tightly clustered treeline. The youth had left in a foul humour, embarrassed by her rejection and insulted by her refusal to accompany him to Ráth Bládhma. He had also been completely oblivious to how close to death his provocative missteps had drawn him, how close to her limits he'd actually pushed her.

Now that he was gone, Liath Luachra felt stricken by a bone-numbing weariness. Slumping onto the grass, she lay on her back, plucked a long stalk from a nearby clump and ground it aggressively between her molars.

It was the sight of Bearach's face that had thrown her. Seeing her friend's face on another had been bad enough but with Fintán's subsequent sexual advance, that uncanny similarity to Bearach had distressed her even further.

Because, for one moment, you felt a flush of desire.

Liath Luachra scowled then, frustrated by the situation and angry at her own reaction. She didn't understand where such a twisted desire might have emerged from or what had provoked it. Nevertheless, the incident had left her feeling soiled and corrupted and, worse, it had tainted the memory of her friend. She felt as though she had somehow let Bearach down and she despised the *Lamhraighe* youth for that.

The warrior woman closed her eyes as though that might somehow banish the sensations she was feeling. Throughout her life, she'd always struggled to make sense of her emotions, a task that few others appeared to find as difficult. The only emotions she truly felt she could distinguish with certainty were the affection she felt for Bodhmhall and the spiralling fury that had formed so much of her earlier life. She was aware that much of the latter had to do with her exceptionally violent upbringing but *Na Cinéaltaí* had almost certainly exacerbated the problem. During her time leading that

20

mercenary group, she'd ingested vast quantities of potions, hallucinogens and other mind-altering substances. Sometimes these had dulled the fury, other times they'd simply intensified it and the consequences were significant. To this day, there were great swathes of time and events she couldn't recall with any clarity.

When she'd first come to Ráth Bládhma, that internal fury had eased, its intensity dampened by a new life of relative peace. Then the settlement had come under attack and it had flared into being once more. In the six years since the *fian* attack, that internal rage had dissipated and she'd truly believed that it was gone for good. Now, this simple encounter with a vainglorious youth had demonstrated how easy it was to topple her from her pillar of calm, how close beneath the surface the dark killer lurked.

'GAAAAAAAAHHHHHHHHHH!'

The great roar erupted from deep within her but it still took her by surprise. Her body was shaking violently and she was sweating as she got to her feet. Around the clearing, the silence swelled as the sound of birds, bees and crickets around An Folamh Mór instantly, fearfully, ceased.

I must run!

She knew that much. She was thinking too much and too much thought never led anywhere but dark places that were difficult to escape. She needed to move, to flatten the anger inside her, to push herself physically to such an extent that she could no longer feel, no longer think.

And emotion was extinguished.

A sudden noise from the southern edge of the clearing prompted her to turn in that direction. There, as though in response to her ululation, the butterflies were swarming again. Swelling up from the wildflowers in a great, vivid cloud, they quickly transformed to a quivering veil of colours that was twice the height of a normal man. It started to drift across the clearing towards her.

She exclaimed in surprise as the unnatural wave drew closer. Just as it loomed above her, she closed her eyes then felt it wash over her, the gentle scrape of a hundred-thousand wings against her arms, her face, legs, anywhere where skin was exposed. The sensation was strange but not entirely unpleasant. It was like being gently stroked by many, tiny hands.

The experience lasted for several moments and when it finally faded, she opened her eyes and turned about to find that the swarm had floated past her and was now headed for the giant oak. As she watched, the butterflies washed up against this mighty obstacle and, bizarrely the cloud seemed to break apart. Almost instantaneously, it dispersed into several hundred smaller clouds of undulating colour all made up of many, many individual insects, flickering and tumbling about the clearing.

Or a hundred thousand concepts converging in her head.

Slowly, the smaller clouds drifted away into the surrounding forest and soon An Folamh Mór was empty once again. Liath Luachra stared around the clearing, unsure as to what she'd actually witnessed, unclear as to how she felt, but knowing, instinctively, that she should leave immediately.

My javelins.

She cursed then with the realisation that she'd left her javelins in the upper section of the oak. There was no question of leaving without the weapons for she'd spent far too much time and effort creating them. She wasted no time lamenting the fact but ran for the giant tree, jumped up to grasp one if its lower limbs and proceeded, once again, to climb. It didn't take long to regain her original position where the weapons were tucked safely into a hollow in the moss-coated bough. Retrieving them, she attached them to the wicker backpack with a long strip of fibre and slung it over her shoulder. Just as she was about to descend, she caught a flutter of colour from the corner of her eye.

Another butterfly.

Liath Luachra regarded the insect with curiosity for it'd become ensnared in the sticky fibres of a spider web that spread from the trunk of the tree to the lower section of the branch on which she'd been sitting. As she watched, she could see how the butterfly's feeble struggles to escape sent vibrations along the radial threads. A moment later, a hairy spider appeared on the upper section and quickly scuttled down the silken threads towards its entangled prey.

Without thinking, the woman warrior grasped the butterfly by the wings and softly prised it from its silken trap. Releasing it into the morning air, she watched it tumble briefly between the branches before abruptly disappearing around the trunk and out of sight. Glancing down at the web, she saw the spider sitting there, unmoving, emanating an almost stoic dejection.

Enough! Leave this place.

Anxious to depart, she slid down the tree somewhat faster than she should have but she reached the ground without incident. Even as her feet hit the soft grass, she knew that she wouldn't return to Ráth Bládhma. The prospect of encountering Fintán or Muirne Muncháem again was not only repellent but, in her current state of mind, she couldn't guarantee that she wouldn't attack them. No. She would remain Out, wait until they had departed. Then she would see.

***

Liath Luachra left An Folamh Mór at a rapid pace, initially following the same route taken by the *Lamhraighe* youth. As she ran along the trail, she crossed sign of his passing on a regular basis, every ten paces or so, and her

22

lips compressed into a tight line. Confident in his ability and fleetness of foot, Fintán was making no effort to cover his tracks, a potentially lethal oversight in the hostile lands of the Great Wild.

The trail she followed was a natural track from the low hills where An Folamh Mór was situated. Several hundred paces south of the clearing the forest faded into a stony flatland that resulted from the poor topsoil and the rocky terrain which she knew as An Slí Cráite – the Tormented Path. This rough flatland extended towards the south-east, spotted with occasional clusters of trees and scrub. Although Liath Luachra didn't like being out in the open, on this occasion her desire to get away from An Folamh Mór meant that she was willing to compromise safety for speed.

As she progressed further south-west, the forest gradually began to close in again on either side and An Slí Cráite grew more and more constricted. Further on, she knew, it would reduce to little more than a narrow passage through the forest before, eventually, petering out.

Soon she reached a natural fork in the path where a new trial branched off to the south-west along the remains of an old river bed. This turn-off marked the point where her shared route with Fintán ended for it was her intention to follow the south-westerly trail. Throwing one last look at An Slí Cráite, she veered off to the left.

And came to a complete stop.

Slowly turning about, she backtracked to the fork in the trail and stared down at what had caught her eye.

A footprint.

Dropping to a crouch, she reached around to the wicker basket on her back and slid a javelin free. After carefully scrutinising the surrounding scrub, she shuffled forwards on all fours and lay on her stomach in front of the track to examine it in more detail.

It was an impression of a bare foot. No boots, no moccasins. No missing toes either from the look of it. It was an adult size, big enough to assume it'd been made by a man but whoever it was, he'd been travelling light for the imprint wasn't deep. The footprint was also pointed in the direction of the north-east, the direction Fintán had taken.

Snapping a dry spine off a withered blackthorn bush beside the track, she used it to poke the imprint gently on its outer side. It did not crumble.

Recent then.

She frowned. Very recent. In this heat, the shallow imprint would have dried out very quickly and the brittle remnants crumbled apart at the slightest poke.

But it hadn't.

Studying the surrounding trees with care, she rose to her feet and cautiously advanced along An Slí Cráite once more. Sure enough, now that she was actively looking for it, she found another, similar, imprint several paces further on from the first. This one lay in the shade of the treeline where the soil was still soft, untouched from the sun.

A few paces on from that she found another and now she was able to see that the tracks were quite widely spaced. The person who had left them was running, apparently in a hurry. Unlike Fintán, this individual had made some effort to hide his passing but given the speed at which he was travelling he couldn't avoid leaving some trace, like this imprint, behind.

So why is he hurrying?

She frowned and chewed thoughtfully on her inner cheek, an old habit of hers when she was absorbed in concentration.

A stranger travels on An Slí Cráite. He is hurrying, trailing Fintán who also travels at speed.

She frowned. Perhaps she was being too suspicious. This new stranger might simply be on the same trail. It happened.

Except she didn't believe it. Her instincts were telling her that this was not right. In terms of timing, this person would have had to come across Fintán's track after he left An Folamh Mór and before she herself had left. Besides, as a general rule in the Great Wild, people tended to avoid contact with strangers and, when an unfamiliar track was encountered, would often take a more circuitous route to their destination to avoid any kind of engagement.

She bit her lower lip.

No. Whoever this person was, he was following Fintán. She was convinced of that. Given the freshness of the tracks, she was equally convinced that if she backtracked to An Folamh Mór, she'd find similar tracks somewhere along the edge of the clearing. This person had probably been watching while she'd been talking with the youth and then followed him directly once he'd departed.

A good thing there was no rutting in the long grass.

Liath Luachra cursed quietly under her breath. Once again, Fintán was unconsciously interfering in her plans. Despite her dislike of the youth she could not ignore the fact that someone was following him and possibly intended harm.

She considered her options a little further.

She'd directed him to Ráth Bládhma via the longer route that circled about Ros Mór and brought him into Glenn Ceoch from the west. She herself could return much more quickly via a route through the secret pass at Gág na Muice. Her directions for the slower Ros Mór passage had not been given out of spite so much as from simple necessity. The Gág na Muice route was a secret known only to the members of Ráth Bládhma and she didn't want it spread further than that. The western route was also more practical and easier for a stranger to find. If the youth strictly followed the topographical bearings she'd provided, he would find his destination. If he did not, he might wander the forests for years, despite the directions that Muirne Muncháem had given him.

If she moved fast, she could reach Glenn Ceoch before him and intercept him – and his pursuer – in the woods at the entrance to the valley.

She sighed as she replaced the javelin.

It was time to run.

Chapter Two

'Think carefully before committing yourself. Impetuous acts generally carry unforeseen consequence.'

Bodhmhall ua Baoiscne, leader of Ráth Bládhma, looked across the square *fidchell* board to where Demne, her fair-haired nephew, was studying the pattern of black and white pegs with quiet absorption. The six year old raised his head to look at her and frowned. As always, she was bemused by the intensity of his regard, an expression more suited to a cynical old man than a young boy barely out of babehood.

'Imagine,' she suggested, 'that you are a *laoch,* a warrior seeking to work your way across a bloody field of combat. How would you cut through your adversaries to achieve your objective, the other side of the board?'

She was amused to see the boy's forehead crinkle in concentration as he focussed once more on the pegs. Martial comparisons always seemed to work with boys.

Satisfied that he was fully engaged in the task she'd set him, Bodhmhall raised her hands to remove the bronze clasp that held her full, black hair in place. The released mane dropped like an oil spill over her back and shoulders. With her generous mouth, smooth, oval face and prominent cheekbones, Bodhmhall was considered a handsome woman by most people she encountered although, for some, the penetrating intelligence of her brown eyes had a tendency to intimidate. This effect was further exacerbated when she rose to her feet for at full height, with the exception of Liath Luachra, she stood almost a head above the other women at Ráth Bládhma.

As she waited for her nephew's response, she tapped the edge of the board with her fingernail and mused sadly at the solid wooden sound. The board game had originally been a prized possession of Cairbre, Ráth Bládhma's previous *rechtaire*. Following his death, it had been inherited by his eldest son Aodhán but, preoccupied with activities of a more physical nature, the warrior had passed it on to Bodhmhall. Although she lacked Cairbre's passion for the game, the *bandraoi* had been pleased with the gesture for the board prompted happy memories of his attempts to educate her in tactics, something she was now doing her best to replicate with her nephew.

Despite all Cairbre's teachings, Bodhmhall knew that she remained a mediocre player at best. She understood the permitted movements of the pegs, the almost infinite number of sequential patterns that could be utilised but, to her mind, those patterns were too limited, too prescriptive.

When developing a plan, she preferred to utilise a more organic approach, combining experience and intuition, amended to suit each particular set of circumstances. She also knew that she was most effective in clarifying her thoughts by discussing them with others. Although he may never really have appreciated it, Cairbre had acted as an excellent foil in that regard, considering her proposals then subsequently offering up his own dry and detached observations to tighten those initial plans.

But Cairbre is gone. And Conchenn. And Cumhal.

Looking at the child, she felt a great surge of affection well up inside her. Demne was her only remaining link to her brother Cumhal but she loved him as if he were her own. Although everyone in the little settlement contributed to his upbringing, over the last six years, it had been Bodhmhall who'd acted as the boy's principal guardian, care-giver, advisor and teacher and ... mother?

She regarded the tussled mop of blond hair bent over the *fidchell* board. 'So, have you a proposal for me?' she asked.

To her surprise, the boy looked up and nodded enthusiastically. Reaching forward, he plucked one of his black pins from the board and, tapping his way through a complex trail of pin holes, demonstrated how he would weave a path through her white-pegged defence.

Bodhmhall watched in silence, her astonishment increasing with each movement Demne made. The pattern of the boy's attack not only accorded with the rules but did so in a surprisingly elegant manner, breaching what she had considered a stalwart defence with a fluidity that made it look effortless.

She was still staring gobsmacked at the board when the leather flap of the roundhouse brushed aside with a noisy flutter. The two players looked up at the slim woman in a sleeveless tunic who stood silhouetted against the bright square of daylight in the doorway behind her. The newcomer's long black hair was tied up but she reached up to brush a loose strand from her face as she entered the roundhouse.

'Morag?' The *bandraoi* was surprised. Generally, people respected her desire not to be interrupted during the instruction periods with her nephew.

'Bodhmhall. A *techtaire* – a messenger– has come.'

Bodhmhall returned the younger woman's worried expression with one of surprise. Isolated in the vast loneliness of the Great Wild, Ráth Bládhma rarely received visitors. In the nine years since the current settlement had been established on the ruins of the original colony, it had never received a genuine *techtaire* of any kind.

'Who sends this *techtaire*?'

'He says he bears a message from Dún Baoiscne. From your father.'

Bodhmhall dropped her eyes and sighed.

27

***

When she emerged from the glum interior of the roundhouse, the intensity of the mid-day sun made Bodhmhall shut her eyes against the glare. She stood outside the doorway like this for several moments, torn between the desire to enjoy the simple pleasure of sunlight upon her skin and the necessity to talk to the mysterious messenger.

Needs must.

Opening her eyes, she squinted as she looked about the *lis*, the circular interior of the ring-shaped settlement that had been her home for the past nine years. Ráth Bládhma was typical of most *ráth* or 'ringforts', a circular hamlet surrounded by a deep external ditch and a high, inner earthen embankment created from the upcast of that ditch. Combined, the two provided an effective defence against all but the most determined of assaults. Nine years earlier when Bodhmhall's little party had first arrived to establish a settlement on the ruins of the original *ráth*, Liath Luachra had insisted on strengthening those defences further by embedding an additional barrier of wooden pilings along the top of the embankment. Three years later, this foresight had enabled them to survive a violent attack by a mysterious *fian* – war band – sent to capture her nephew.

Ráth Bládhma had, surprisingly, thrived since that deadly attack. Despite the losses they'd sustained, *Muinntir Bládhma* had absorbed survivors from the surrounding settlements to increase their own population to ten adults and seven children. To deal with the extra numbers, two additional roundhouses had been constructed within the *lis*, increasing the total number of dwellings to four. The need to secure the livestock inside the *ráth* at night, however, meant that the settlement had no space for further expansion. The roundhouses were now hemmed in closely beside the internal herd pens and one of the inner lean-tos formerly used as a wood store had already been dismantled and moved outside to free up additional space.

The dairy herd, Ráth Bládhma's principal food source and a measure of its wealth, had also expanded, now numbering nineteen cows and a bull. Admittedly, that bull would soon have to be replaced to ensure untainted blood lines for the future. Bodhmhall frowned. Yet another challenge to be addressed.

Although the settlement had grown a little stronger over the years, Bodhmhall was not so confident of their security to ever drop her guard. In the vastness of the Great Wild, theirs was still very much a precarious existence. As a community, they had no-one to call on for aid and since the attack of the *fian*, and the destruction of their closest neighbours, no-one with whom they could trade for essential equipment or supplies. In addition to this, they still had no idea as to the identity of 'The Adversary' –

28

that unidentified opponent who'd instigated the attack against them. Despite the peace of the previous six years, Bodhmhall remained convinced that their enemy was still out there, biding his time for another attempt on her nephew.

'Does this bode poorly for us?'

Bodhmhall turned to consider Morag. The younger woman had followed her out of the roundhouse and now stood beside her with an anxious expression on her face. Bodhmhall clicked her tongue. Although exceptionally competent, there were times when Morag's lack of exposure to the world beyond her old settlement of Coill Mór meant that she could be naïve when faced with an unfamiliar situation.

'In my limited experience of *techtaire*,' said the *bandraoi*. 'I do not recall one ever being the bearer of good news.'

With this, she turned to traverse the *lis*, her bare feet hitting noisily on the hard earthen surface. Normally soft and muddy from rainfall and the regular movement of livestock, at present it was solid and baked firm from the intense heat of the sun.

Reaching the southern section of the *ráth*, she scaled a wooden ladder resting against the inner embankment wall and climbed up onto the rampart, a curving platform of beaten earth inside the pilings that had been overlain with flat slabs of wood. The rampart provided a good outlook over the narrow V-shaped Glenn Ceoch – Valley of Haze – in which the settlement was situated. Set at the extremes of *Clann Baoiscne* territory, it was a beautiful place, enclosed on either side by two steep, tree-coated ridges that converged east of the *ráth* to form a steep and impassable barrier. Up in the lower slopes of this formidable buttress, pooling in a small pond of clear water, a sparkling spring fed the stream – *Sruth Drithleach* – that emptied down onto the valley floor and flowed out towards its western entrance.

Bodhmhall paused for a moment to glance longingly towards the *lubgort* – the vegetable garden lying close to the eastern side of the *ráth*. Because it was mid-summer, that period of greatest passion between the Sky and Earth, her garden was flourishing. Unfortunately, the increased resource within the settlement also meant a wider range of issues that needed to be dealt with and, consequently, Bodhmhall was finding it harder and harder to spend time in the garden she loved so much.

As Morag clambered up the ladder to stand beside her, the *bandraoi* sighed, consoling herself with the possibility that she might get to the *lubgort* later that afternoon. Instead, following the curve of the rampart around to the west, the two women made their way towards the bulk of the stone gateway, the sole point of entry into the settlement. The granite structure had been built by the original inhabitants of the *ráth*, long before Bodhmhall had established her own colony there. Facing west towards the entrance of Glenn Ceoch, it was accessed by a narrow causeway that traversed the ditch to a constricted passage, penetrating the lower level of the gateway to the interior. Despite its impressive bulk, the structure had not saved the original settlement from slaughter, which was why Liath Luachra insisted on the presence of a sentinel at all times. On this occasion, the gateway was manned by both the woman warrior Gnathad and the red haired Ferchar and Bodhmhall was pleased to see that although there was but a single intruder to the valley, the substantial barrier designed to obstruct the passage had been erected and locked in place.

Gnathad and Ferchar were leaning against the rampart, gazing down at the *techtaire* who was sitting on the grass just beyond the narrow causeway. The messenger was a muscular man with a round face, a small mouth and a sharply crooked nose that looked as though it'd been broken and reset many times. Seeing the two women arrive onto the upper gateway, he quickly got to his feet, his eyes bright as he stared up at them.

'I see you Bodhmhall ua Baoiscne,' he called in an unusually gravelly voice.

The man was guessing, Bodhmhall assumed. He wouldn't have known which of the two he was addressing although, possibly, he'd recognised her because of her height.

'I see you, stranger. But I do not know you.'

'I am named Cargal Uí Faigil.'

Bodhmhall nodded, recognising the tribal name. The *Uí Faigil* were a small tribal grouping from the coastlands far to the east of Dún Baoiscne, the *Clann Baoiscne* stronghold. An offshoot of the *Uí Muirde* clan – strong supporters of *Clann Baoiscne* – theoretically they were also allies to *Clann Baoiscne* because of that linkage. Apart from their name, however, Bodhmhall knew little else about them. During her childhood at Dún Baoiscne they'd had almost no influence or presence there.

'You bear a message from my father?'

'I do.'

'Very well, then. Relay the heart of his words.'

The *techtaire* regarded her with a pained expression. 'Out here? In the open? The sun is hot and I have travelled far. Some cold well water would soothe my parched tongue. Some food would comfort my empty belly.'

'Of course. Food and drink is already being prepared.' She looked to Morag who, taking the hint, nodded and quickly descended to the *lis* using the ladder by the gateway.

'While we wait, perhaps you can share the news from Dún Baoiscne.'

The *techtaire* did not look impressed. 'Is this, then, the hospitality of Ráth Bládhma? A welcome that greets a loyal messenger with closed doors and levelled spears? I have travelled long distances through dangerous territories to locate you here.'

30

Bodhmhall frowned at that for the man *had* appeared to find the settlement with remarkable ease. Secreted away in the secluded Glenn Ceoch, Ráth Bládhma's best defence was the very fact that it was so hard to find in the vastness of the Great Wild. Although it was true that, as an old *Clann Baoiscne* colony, Dún Baoiscne would almost certainly have provided any messenger with exact directions, the idea that they could be found so easily after the horror of the *fian* attack was unsettling.

The *bandraoi* stared down at the *techtaire* and did her best to repress her instinctive antagonism towards the man. Although carrying out her father's bidding, the messenger was not her father. He was also due the normal terms of hospitality.

Bodhmhall fretted as she tapped a foot against the base of one of the pilings. There was a responsibility for hospitality but then there was also a responsibility for the settlement's safety. Given past events and her ongoing dread of the Adversary, she remained reluctant to trust any face she did not know. That situation was further exacerbated by the absence of Ráth Bládhma's core fighting force. Liath Luachra had departed two days earlier to hunt the western lands. Aodhán, his brother Cónán and the eccentric warrior Tóla were hunting somewhere off to the north-east. Admittedly, Gnathad and Ferchar were capable defenders but, in her estimation, they formed an insufficient force to risk the presence of any strangers – even a single individual – within her walls.

She forced a placatory smile.

'This is the caution of Ráth Bládhma. Our hospitality is reserved for our friends and precious few of them remain. Besides, I do not know you, Cargal Uí Faigil.'

'You know my clan. And now you know how I am called.'

'I know how the bitter storm winds of winter are called. I also know how the dark wolves that prowl the woods are called. That does not mean I treat either with any less caution.'

The messenger grew red-faced, offended at her suspicion.

'I have been entrusted with my message from your father. I was hand-picked by Tréanmór himself for this undertaking.'

'So then you know of the strained relations between us.'

'I do. And all the more reason for you to let me in and hear my message. Your father seeks reconciliation. He seeks to make peace with his daughter.'

Reconciliation! Now?

Bodhmhall did her best to hide her distrust. 'So, why would he send a man who is unknown to me? A clever man would send a friendly face, someone whose features would reassure me, encourage me to drop my guard. And my father is a clever man.'

31

'Your father could not –' He stopped abruptly. 'I am here on a secret mission.'

'The *bandraoi's* forehead furrowed. 'Go on.'

'I can say no more. My words are for the daughter of Tréanmór's ears alone.'

Exasperated, Bodhmhall felt her hands tightening into fists.

'Bodhmhall.'

The *bandraoi* turned to Ferchar, glad of the interruption to such an irksome conversation. The red-haired warrior was pointing westwards, up the valley to where a distant figure could be seen running smoothly in the direction of the settlement. Both of them stared, studying the newcomer's lope but it was not one that either recognised. Observing their reaction, the messenger turned to see what they were looking at. From the startled expression on his face, he was equally as surprised by this new development.

Everyone watched in silence.

The approaching figure took some time to make it all the way up the valley, allowing ample opportunity to observe him. He appeared to be a young man, dressed lightly and fit and trim as a deer. It was only as he drew closer and Bodhmhall was able to make out his face that the familiarity of those features caused her to gape in surprise.

The runner finally came to a halt just beyond the causeway. He stood there, puffing and struggling to catch his breath as he gazed curiously at the closed passage then glanced across at the brawny *techtaire* who was observing him with suspicion.

Bodhmhall considered him in silence as she waited for him to recover, quietly wondering how Aodhán and Cónán would have responded if they'd been present to confront this older version of their brother.

'Bodhmhall ua Baoiscne, I see you.'

'I see you stranger. You know how I am named?'

'Your name and features are familiar to me. I was present when you visited my father's lands some years past. He remains one who counts your friendship dear.'

The *bandraoi* arched one eyebrow in curiosity. 'Your father?'

'Gleor Red Hand of *Na Lamhraighe*. He has tasked me to bring his greetings and to seek hospitality for him and his company at the hearth of Ráth Bládhma.'

Cargal Uí Faigil, who had been listening with increasing agitation, finally exploded. 'What's this? I was here first! I bear a message from Tréanmór, *rí* of Dún Baoiscne. It is my right to enter Ráth Bládhma and be heard before you.'

Startled by this emotive interruption, the youth glared fiercely. 'I care little who sent you. I represent the intent of Gleor Red Hand, *rí* of *Na Lamhraighe*.'

Up on the gateway, Bodhmhall considered the visitors with a bemused expression. No *techtaire* for nine years and then, suddenly, two at once. And both arguing for her attention, puffing out their chests and crowing like cockerels in an attempt to gain the rather sad prestige of entering first. She glanced over at Ferchar who was grinning wickedly, greatly amused by the situation.

'Is this the baying of flea-ridden curs or two old crones bickering over their looks?'

The arguments ceased abruptly with the sound of that voice. Up on the gateway, Bodhmhall watched with interest how the *Lamhraighe* youth's jaw dropped as all eyes turned to the lithe figure strolling around from the western side of the *ráth*.

Liath Luachra had returned.

***

With the reappearance of her *conradh*, Bodhmhall felt a great burden shift from her shoulders. Liath Luachra's presence greatly improved her confidence in the security of the settlement, sufficiently so that she was prepared to allow their 'guests' to enter the *ráth*. Before the barrier to the gateway passage was removed, however, she drew Gnathad to one side and whispered in her ear.

'Gnathad, Demne is within my roundhouse. Once the visitors have been escorted to Morag's hut for refreshment, take the boy to the hunting booth and remain there with him.'

The warrior looked at her, her brow furrowed beneath the leather headband holding the great tangle of blond hair in place. Bodhmhall did not need to guess what she was thinking about, the same thing she was always thinking about: the safety of her own children.

Prior to joining *Muinntir Bládhma*, the young woman had been married to a landowner of Ráth Dearg, a neighbouring settlement destroyed by the *fian*. With her husband dead and her home destroyed, she had fled to Glenn Ceoch with her two girls and a number of other refugees only to find herself under attack once more as the *fian* descended on Ráth Bládhma. Through courage and sheer good fortune, the settlement had miraculously survived but her sense of powerlessness and inability to protect those she loved had preyed heavily on her.

Soon after the settlement's eventual recovery, Gnathad had approached Liath Luachra seeking instruction in the martial arts and, to Bodhmhall's surprise, the *conradh* had agreed. Ever since, she'd rigorously trained the woman in the use of spear and sword, weapons they had in surplus from the dead *fian* warriors.

Despite her faith in her *conradh*, Bodhmhall had watched developments with a somewhat pessimistic eye. Woman warriors of Liath Luachra's ilk were the exception rather than the norm and it was generally recognised that those adults like Gnathad who'd received no early training in weapons rarely, if ever, become completely proficient.

In hindsight, of course, Liath Luachra's decision had proven the correct one. Under the *conradh*'s tutelage, Gnathad's confidence and sense of wellbeing had increased substantially. Ráth Bládhma, meanwhile, had obtained an additional resource to protect its walls. Although it was true Gnathad would never be the most skilled of warriors, Bodhmhall was not so cynical as to ignore the fact that anything increasing the settlement's defensive capacity had to be a positive thing.

'Your children are in no danger, Gnathad. It is just my preference that these strangers do not see my nephew.'

The blond woman nervously twisted the haft of her spear between her fingers before nodding with some reluctance. 'Very well, Bodhmhall. I will do as you ask.'

With this, Gnathad descended to the *lis* to help Ferchar detach the barrier obstructing the passage. A thick slab of oak reinforced with metal strips, it was fixed in position by four iron rungs set into the gateway and a wooden brace that wedged firmly against a large boulder. It took several moments to roll the boulder away and lift the barrier free.

Cargal Uí Faigil was the first to push his way through the newly cleared access way, determined to be the primary dispenser of news within the settlement. Following in the irritable *techtaire's* footsteps and muttering softly to himself, came Fintán mac Gleor. Entering the *lis*, his grumbles trailed off as he looked around the little settlement with evident interest. A nomadic tribe, *Na Lamhraighe* had several settled areas where they spent specific parts of the year but none of these would have been anywhere near as established as Ráth Bládhma.

Last to enter the *ráth* was Liath Luachra, strolling in with that familiar haughty, feline stride. As the *bandraoi* watched her cross the *lis* to the settlement's central hearth, her inclination was to rush over and embrace her. For formality's sake, however, she restrained that impulse, moving instead to address the visitors. Greeting the ill-matched pair with words of welcome, she quickly dispatched them with Morag to receive the food and drink that had been prepared, promising to speak with them shortly.

As their visitors followed the young woman into the nearest roundhouse, Bodhmhall approached the hearth where Liath Luachra had seated herself on one of the many reed mats surrounding the stone ringed fire-pit. Taking a seat beside her, she reached over to squeeze the Grey One's muscled shoulder.

'You return sooner than expected.'

Liath Luachra's response was one of those rare half smiles that softened the formidable severity of her habitual expression.

'I missed you, Grey One. The nights are darker each time you leave.'

Never one to speak easily of her feelings, Liath Luachra pulled a wooden ladle from a nearby water bucket and drank deeply. When she'd emptied the container, she adroitly turned the discussion to other topics. 'I crossed trails with Gleor Red Hand's son at An Folamh Mór so I know why he is here.' She dropped the ladle back into the bucket. 'But that other *techtaire*. The grumpy one. Is it true he comes from Dún Baoiscne?'

'That is his claim.' Bodhmhall sighed. 'It appears that Ráth Bládhma will be the host for many visitors tonight.' She glanced at Liath Luachra, noting the solemnity in those deep grey eyes. 'What worries you?'

The woman warrior took a moment to choose her words carefully. 'It seems to me that the last time Ráth Bládhma merited such attention was six years ago.' She paused for a moment but Bodhmhall didn't need to ask to know that she was thinking of the *fian* attack. 'When are Aodhán and the others due to return?'

'Tomorrow.'

'We may have need of Aodhán's keen eye. And his casting arm.'

Bodhmhall looked at her, the gravity of the *conradh's* expression prompting a growing unease. 'Why?'

Slowly, the Grey One told her of the mysterious trail she'd discovered and her subsequent return to Ráth Bládhma, recounting the events and her suspicions with her usual directness. As the *bandraoi* listened, she could feel the tension tighten her shoulders and by the time the Grey One had finished, she was forcibly holding her hands in her lap so as not to scratch her palms. 'What is your advice?' she asked in a voice that sounded gratifyingly level.

'I think ...' Liath Luachra's voice trailed off as her gaze snapped across the *lis* to where Gnathad was hurrying towards the gateway passage, Demne in tow behind her. The blond woman didn't glance in their direction but the boy saw them and waved. Bodhmhall felt a lurch of fear for the child and when she turned back to Liath Luachra she found the woman warrior regarding her with questioning eyes.

'They go to the hunting booth,' the *bandraoi* explained. 'We have two visitors within the *ráth*, both of whom are unknown to me. I do not intend to take any chances.'

Liath Luachra held her eyes for a moment then abruptly nodded her approval. 'The hunting booth is well concealed. They will be safe there as long as they remain hidden and do not move about or leave tracks.' She thoughtfully played with the ladle in the bucket for a moment. 'I think it best that the cattle are brought inside. Early. We should do this now. And bar the passage. We should remain within the *ráth* until Aodhán and the others have returned. Then we can consider the matter further.'

As she listened to her conradh's advice, Bodhmhall could feel her heart sink.

It's happening. It's happening again.

The warrior woman had clearly sensed her concern for she reached over, took her hand and squeezed it. 'Do not despair, Bodhmhall. We are simply taking safeguards. Those tracks may well have been nothing more than curious strangers passing by.'

'Perhaps,' Bodhmhall agreed. Although her response lacked any conviction it did, at least, serve to stir a renewed sense of determination. 'Let us talk to our visitors,' she suggested. 'Once we learn what ill winds their news blows our way, we will be better placed to know where we stand.'

***

They met first with Cargal Uí Faigil, given that they already knew the reason behind Fintán mac Gleor's presence. It was also obvious that the *techtaire* was anxious, almost desperate, to relate the message that had been assigned him.

While Fintán remained with Morag, it was Lí Bán – the eldest of the women within the settlement – who escorted the messenger to the roundhouse shared by Bodhmhall and Liath Luachra.

He entered their dwelling with tentative steps, looking around the circular living area with curiosity once his eyes had grown accustomed to the internal gloom. His gaze passed over the central fire-pit, the two roof support poles adorned with clusters of dried herbs for Bodhmhall's remedies, the wooden frame holding Liath Luachra's red leather battle harness and weapons. They lingered longer than necessary on the large sleeping platform layered with heather and furs.

The two Ráth Bládhma women, seated on wicker mats by the fire pit, noted this inspection but said nothing as Cargal advanced towards them. Although the base of the fire pit had been layered with tinder and dry wood, the fire had not been set alight given the balminess of the evening. The *techtaire* took a seat facing them.

'So,' Bodhmhall began. 'You bring a message from my father.'

Cargal Uí Faigil looked at her, then pointedly turned to stare at Liath Luachra before returning his attention to the *bandraoi* once more. The meaning was clear. He did not wish to speak in the presence of the warrior woman.

36

Bodhmhall ignored the unspoken suggestion and continued to hold the *techtaire*'s eyes. As the silence extended, his brazen gaze wavered and he started to scratch the back of his left hand, a nervous tic of some standing given the abraded condition of the skin.

'Very well,' the *techtaire* conceded. 'If it is truly your desire to receive the message in company then I have no option but to comply. It was, however, your father's desire that you hear his words alone.'

With this, he sat up straight and cleared his throat and puckered his fleshy lips. Raising his head, he closed his eyes and opened his mouth to commence *An Dord Rúnda* – the Secret Drone – that vocal technique used by the more talented *techtaire* to both memorise and deliver their messages. Bodhmhall held up one hand. 'Stop.'

The *techtaire* blinked and stared at her in incomprehension, bewildered by the interruption.

'You are overeager to divest yourself of your responsibility. You have neglected to provide us with *an t-urra* – the surety.'

'*An t-urra!*' The messenger slapped his hand against his forehead. 'Of course, of course.' His eyes dropped to the floor, embarrassed by the gravity of his omission.

As he should be.

Bodhmhall was unimpressed. Prior to the delivery of any formal message it was customary for the *techtaire* to provide confirmation of the sender's identity in order to guarantee the authenticity of the message. Habitually, this was provided through the sharing of a confidence, a secret that only the recipient and the sender would know but other variations and codes were also used.

The *techtaire* was silent for a moment as he gave *an t-urra* he had been provided with. 'The surety is as follows,' he said at last and his eyes fixed on Bodhmhall. 'You broke one of two at three. You broke one of only one at sixteen.'

Bodhmhall returned Cargal's stare with a frosty expression but she made no response. The *techtaire* shifted uneasily under that hostile scrutiny. '*An t-urra* is not accepted?'

Bodhmhall made no response for several heartbeats. Finally she dropped her head for a single nod but the gesture seemed to lack enthusiasm. '*An t-urra* is accepted,' she said in a dull voice.

Relieved, the *techtaire* nodded. Closing his eyes, he took a deep breath and, once again initiated the low hum that would slowly build up to the full-blown chant used to relay his message. Soon, the hum was a steady drone consisting of a throaty rhythmic breathing, powered from the *techtaire*'s chest prior to the initial intonation.

'Hear the words of Tréanmór, grandson of the great Baoiscne, rí of Dún Baoiscne.
His speech is untainted, unchanged in tone or sense.'

37

The words dropped away but the drone continued, the messenger's torso swaying slowly backwards and forwards in time with the deep sounding rhythm.

The walls of Dún Baoiscne ring loud with silence.
My sons and daughter are absent, their places sit empty.
No one laughs at the feasting table.
Tréanmór grows old and sees the long night draw close.
He seeks the company of his remaining children for one last meal.
Come to Dún Baoiscne by the second day of the next full moon.
There are many truths to be shared.
Tréanmór grieves but seeks the closeness of family.

Once again, the words ceased although the *techtaire* maintained the deep throbbing chant. Bodhmhall waited, her curiosity mounting. After three further cycles, the final part of the communication came forth.

Children of Tréanmór, beware the wolf in the mist
The light foot in the night.
The merchant of loyalties.
The betrayer of Clann Baoiscne secrets,
Trust no-one.
Only through Bearna Garbh does safety lie.

Bodhmhall continued to watch the *techtaire* but the chant was slowly but surely spiralling down. His message was coming to a close. After two more cycles, both decreasing in volume, it puttered out and stopped.

Cargal Uí Faigil wheezed and slumped forwards, suddenly looking completely exhausted. Bodhmhall studied him with interest. During her instruction at Dún Baoiscne, the druid Dub Tíre had always told her that once a *techtaire*'s message was conveyed, it was erased from his memory. She'd always had her doubts about that. Although visibly tired from his travels and the focussed effort of relaying the message accurately, the *techtaire*'s eyes remained bright and vigilant as he awaited her response.

Bodhmhall caught a movement from the corner of her eye as Liath Luachra turned to glance at her but she remained focussed on the *techtaire*, absently tapping her lower lip with the tip of her index finger.

'Who advises Tréanmór now?'

'Who? What …?' The *techtaire* fumbled, momentarily thrown by the unexpected direction of the question. He had clearly been anticipating either a direct response to the message or a question of a more clarifying nature. He licked his lips uneasily but under Bodhmhall's tenacious stare, finally responded to the question.

'The *rí* of Dún Baoiscne receives advice from many people,' he suggested with careful diplomacy. 'But, in the end, as leader he would make up his own mind.'

'But he will have a key adviser,' Bodhmhall insisted. 'Who advises him now that Dub Tíre is no longer about?'

This time the messenger regarded her in alarm. It was common knowledge that Dub Tíre, druid at Dún Baoiscne, had died by Bodhmhall ua Baoiscne's hand. This, indeed, was the generally accepted reason for her expulsion from the Baoiscne fortress some nine years earlier. To have the subject of the druid raised so blithely, visibly put him in great discomfort.'

'Well,' she pressed.

'Becán,' he said at last, the name grudgingly offered up with a voice that was stiff and muted.

'Becán,' the *bandraoi* repeated. She mulled over this item of information for a moment before addressing the *techtaire* again. 'The last words you spoke were words of warning.'

A stiff nod.

'Of treachery.'

'Yes.'

'This is the matter you did not wish to speak of openly?'

A quick twist of the eyes to Liath Luachra and back again. Cargal shuffled uneasily. 'Your father has learned that the battle of Cnucha where your brother Cumhal died was not an opportunistic skirmish. It was a pre-arranged ambush. *Clann Morna* were informed of the route the *Clann Baoiscne* men were taking.'

Bodhmhall stared at him, her face growing pale at the ramifications of what he was telling her.

'There is a traitor at Dún Baoiscne?'

Cargal Uí Faigil nodded. 'Your father has not identified the traitor but he is convinced of his existence and does not trust even those closest to him. This is why I, as an independent *techtaire*, was summoned and entrusted with the message for you. The 'friendly face', you expected might not truly have been so friendly.'

Bodhmhall's continued to stare, her head spinning. Someone in the clan, probably someone she'd known as a child had betrayed everything; family, friends, clan, to the *Clann Morna*, *Clann Baoiscne*'s long-time enemies.

Dark days. Oh, dark days.

It took her a moment to pull herself together but she disguised her consternation by quietly staring at the floor of the roundhouse as though in deep thought.

'Cargal Uí Faigil,' she said a last. 'You have my gratitude for conveying this message. Food and other supplies will be prepared for you before you depart tomorrow but, for tonight, please accept the hospitality of Ráth Bládhma.'

Cargal acknowledged her gratitude and hospitality with a nod. 'Do you have a response for your father?' he asked.

'Not at present. I will require time to think on this. You will receive my answer before you leave in the morning.'

'Very well.' The *techtaire* stood up to leave.

Bodhmhall also rose to her feet and accompanied the burly man to the doorway. Passing through the leather flap to the *lis*, they found Lí Bán waiting outside. The old woman glanced at Bodhmhall but said nothing as she'd been instructed earlier.

'Lí Bán will take care of you.'

Cargal nodded his thanks once more and, escorted by the grey haired women, walked off to the roundhouse to which he'd been assigned.

Returning inside, Bodhmhall joined Liath Luachra by the fire pit and sat quietly pondering the *techtaire*'s message while she stared into the ghosts of the flames. Finally she turned to her *conradh* who'd pulled a short branch out of the kindling and was twisting it silently between her fingers. 'Do you have history with the *Uí Faigil*? Anything from your days with the Kindly Ones?'

The woman warrior shook her head. 'They are a small grouping. They lack enemies powerful enough to warrant attention from those such as *Na Cinéaltaí*.'

'The *techtaire* says he is of *Uí Faigil*.'

'You do not believe him?'

A shrug.

'What do your instincts tell you?'

'My instincts scream to slit his throat and cast him from the *ráth*.'

Liath Luachra considered her, impressed by the vehemence of that response.

'*An t-urra* was not satisfactory?'

'It seemed satisfactory.'

'Your reaction did not suggest that.'

Bodhmhall frowned. 'The surety was a riddle. Only my family and close family advisors would be aware of my love for riddles. Besides, this particular riddle makes reference to events only they could know.'

Liath Luachra tapped the branch against one of the fire pit stones but made no comment.

She sighed. 'I broke one of two at three. I broke my leg when I had three years on me.'

Liath Luachra thought it through then nodded, impressed. 'Clever. And one of one at sixteen?'

'My sixteenth year marked the end of my love for Fiacail mac Codhna. A broken heart. And our wise ones always tell us that we have but a single heart.'

'Oh,' said Liath Luachra simply.

Bodhmhall shot her a subtle sideways glance, attempting to gauge her reaction but the woman warrior sat motionless, giving nothing away. She picked up a clay pot from the side of the fire pit and idly started to roll it in her hands. It wasn't difficult to guess what was going through the Grey One's mind. The reference to Fiacail mac Codhna would not have pleased her. Even at the best of times there was no love lost between Liath Luachra and the brash *Clann Baoiscne* warrior. The additional complexity of Bodhmhall's history with Fiacail would probably not have helped although Liath Luachra had always been adamant that wasn't something that disturbed her.

'So, the surety appears valid,' she continued. 'Despite this, in my heart I struggle to believe that such a message could come from my father.' Her fingers beat a rapid cadence along the side of the little pot. 'If I knew with certainty that it did come from my father, I would probably trust the message all the less.'

Liath Luachra observed her in silence. 'Well,' she suggested at last. 'We have *Na Lamhraighe* to deal with, of course, but both Cargal Uí Faigil and Fintán mac Gleor will be billeted in Aodhán and Cónán's dwelling tonight. I will watch over their door to ensure there is no treachery. With Gnathad at the hunting booth, Ferchar will have to guard the gate alone tonight but we should be able to manage one night until the others return.'

'Another reason for resentment then. I would have preferred you by my side tonight.'

'There will be other nights, *a rún*. Many other nights.'

'Mmm.' The *bandraoi* nodded distantly. A moment later, she turned back to look at the woman warrior. 'That young man, Gleor Red Hand's son. When you first appeared around the *ráth* he looked shocked, then very angry at you.'

'I believe I may have broken his heart.'

Despite herself, Bodhmhall smiled. A joke from the Grey One, no matter how vague, was a rare occurrence. 'You do not find him pleasing to the eye?'

'His face is not unpleasant.'

'He has Bearach's face.'

'Does he? I had not noticed.'

Bodhmhall curled one sceptical eyebrow. 'Do not parry half-truths with me, Grey One. I know you too well.'

For a moment Liath Luachra remained silent then, suddenly, the branch she was holding snapped in two. She tossed both pieces back into the fire pit. 'Yes! Yes, he has Bearach's face. It burns me to see his features on such a fatuous youth when my friend lies cold in the ground. It burns me when he makes advances using Bearach's voice and mannerisms.'

Astounded by this new revelation, Bodhmhall could only stare back at her. The other woman growled.

'Forgive me, Bodhmhall. My anger bites. Fintán mac Gleor is but a child, a clumsy young bull who crushes the spring flowers. He has no idea of the damage he leaves in his trail.'

Bodhmhall regarded her with fresh concern. Following Bearach's death during the *fian* attack on Ráth Bládhma, Liath Luachra had steadfastly refused to discuss the issue. In the six years following the attack, although she had calmed, the warrior woman had also grown ever more … contained. She placed a comforting hand on the other's knee.

'These things happen, Grey One. It is not uncommon to see familiar features on another's face. I know that when Cairbre was younger he lived north for a time in *Na Lamhraighe* territory. It's possible he left a portion of his seed there. Even Conchenn, Bearach's mother, passed some time in that area. It is just … unfortunate.'

Liath Luachra acknowledged what she was saying with a sharp dip of her head but her posture remained stiff and tense. She attempted to shrug the topic off. 'It's not important. We should prepare for *Na Lamhraighe*. They will be here later this evening.'

At the mention of their forthcoming visitors, Bodhmhall felt a great weariness settle over her. On the footsteps of the Dún Baoiscne message and the disconcerting information her *conradh* had just shared with her, the additional burden of organising hospitality for visitors was almost more than she could handle. 'Strangers,' she growled. 'They bring us poisoned words and deeds of ill intent. We might do just as well to slit their throats and bury their bodies deep in the forest.'

Turning, she found Liath Luachra regarding her with a strange expression.

'What troubles you?'

The Grey One hesitated for a moment before responding. 'The Bodhmhall ua Baoiscne I have always known would never speak such words. Even in jest. My blood burns to think others have troubled you in such a manner.'

'Given all that we have had to endure, I think that now I would seriously consider any and all responses. I have responsibility for protecting the settlement, protecting Demne. I will *not* let anyone take my nephew away. I will …' Her voice trailed off as she heard the intensity of emotion in her own voice.

She took a deep breath and sighed deeply. 'This time, perhaps, it is on me to apologise. Cairbre once told me that the leaders who prevail are those who can act with ruthlessness and brutality. Individuals who can make harsh decisions and sacrifice their people without conscience. That advice has always haunted me. It disturbs me to think that I could change, could harden to become such a person. Yet this may be what is required for my nephew and my people to survive.'

'You have no need to justify your actions to me, Bodhmhall. Your leadership meant Ráth Bládhma and its people survived when other settlements were destroyed. We've all changed since that day. We saw our friends butchered. Such violence has the power to change a person for the worse. I know that better than most.'

Bodhmhall silently considered the woman warrior's words. 'Perhaps,' she said simply, although she did not sound convinced. 'This day has been a poor day. Let us be grateful it will soon draw to a close and cannot become any worse.'

Liath Luachra reached up and took the *bandraoi*'s face gently in both hands. 'It pains me to tell you this, *a rún*,' she said. 'But, it can get worse. Muirne Muncháem returns to Ráth Bládhma.'

Chapter Three

The *Lamhraighe* party appeared in Glenn Ceoch late that evening, just as Fintán had foretold. Predicting their arrival with remarkable accuracy, the youth was waiting on the gateway with Ferchar and Bodhmhall when they first emerged from the trees to the west and started up the flat pasture of the valley towards Ráth Bládhma.

Bodhmhall watched the little party advance for several moments before glancing back into the *lis* to make sure everything was in readiness. Bamba and Bran, the settlement's two eldest children, had already brought the cattle inside and locked them securely in their pens. Now both were helping Lí Bán at the hearth spit, turning the two pigs that Ferchar had slaughtered and gutted that afternoon. Morag, Cumann and the remainder of the children, meanwhile, were laying out pitchers of cool stream water, baskets of girdle cake, fresh bread and steamed watercress on a rough table constructed specifically for the occasion. Several paces off to the side of the table, beds of heather and fern had also been made up in preparation for their guests.

Lifting a hand to shield her eyes against the glare of the dying sun, the *bandraoi* peered down the valley. The group was still quite far away and although she could now make out nine individual figures, they were still too far away to identify.

Muirne Muncháem returns.

For Demne.

The *bandraoi* struggled to suppress the sickening tightness in her stomach. That afternoon when Fintán had identified himself and brought news of Gleor Red Hand's imminent visit she'd instinctively feared the worst. When Liath Luachra had subsequently confirmed those fears, it had provoked an intensity of bitterness she'd never thought herself capable of.

She bit her lip as she recalled the last time she'd set eyes on Muirne Muncháem. That had been more than five years ago, at the outskirts of Gleor Red Hand's summer encampment when she and Fiacail mac Codhna were leaving to return back to Glenn Ceoch. Several hundred paces from the camp, some instinct had prompted Bodhmhall to turn and look back and she'd spotted the Flower of Almhu standing alone at the edge of the camp, long hair whipping furiously in the gusting breeze. She'd felt a brief flush of guilt at deserting the woman, for leaving her alone in a strange place without friends or family, but the sensation hadn't lasted long. Bludgeoned by memories of the death and destruction the younger woman had brought on Ráth Bládhma, those feelings of sympathy were extinguished.

She looked again at the approaching party and thought of that forlorn figure and the baby she'd been forced to leave behind.

She will never forgive the separation from her son. She will smile, she will be polite but she will never forgive.

Taking the ladder back down to the *lis*, Bodhmhall busied herself, helping with the final preparations until, all too soon, the first formal call from the visiting party could be heard over the walls of the *ráth*.

'I see you Muinntir Bládhma. I see you, my son Fintán.' The voice was loud, harsh but friendly.

'I see you *Na Lamhraighe*,' Ferchar responded in turn. 'You are welcome to Ráth Bládhma.'

Bodhmhall took up position several paces back from the passage entrance and brushed some dried mud from her tunic as Morag and Bran started to remove the barrier. Young Bran, one of the refugees from the Ráth Dearg settlement, had now grown into a slim *óglach* – an unblooded young warrior – of about thirteen summers. Despite his slender frame, the boy was strong, removing the barrier with little difficulty before hauling it aside with Morag's assistance to clear the passageway.

The first person to enter the *ráth* was a tall, bearded man with a savage red scar down the right side of his face. The eye set in the centre of this thick mutilation was a mass of scar tissue and the skin around it had fleshed over badly. Dressed in a leather battle harness, he stopped at the end of the passage and used his sizeable bulk to obstruct it as he stood eyeing the *lis* for any potential sign of danger. Finally, satisfied, he stepped inside, throwing a nod to Bodhmhall as he took up position beside the gateway. The *bandraoi* returned the nod with one of her own, recognising him from her brief stay with *Na Lamhraighe* six years earlier.

Marcán Lámhfhada, bodyguard to Gleor Red Hand.

The warrior's fearsome face was not one to be easily forgotten. Gleor's right hand man for almost twenty years, time had left unmistakable traces of grey in the dense growth on his face. Despite his age, however, he was still an impressive warrior and carried himself with the easy, physical swagger of a fighting man. Wrapped in a leather sheath strapped across his back was the large double handed sword that had earned him his name: *Marcán Lámhfhada* - Marcán of the Long Arm. The sword was substantially longer than most other weapons and, because of the extra weight from its length, required a man as big as Marcán to wield it properly.

Bodhmhall glanced over to the roundhouse where Liath Luachra was standing, arms folded, eyes keenly assessing that weapon. According to her *conradh*, she and Marcán had once fought on opposing sides in some long distant battle although they'd never directly confronted one another on the battlefield.

Six other warriors followed Marcán inside, the scars and battle tattoos identifying them all as battle-hardened fighters. Clearly, Gleor was taking no chances in his travels.

When the last warrior had entered the *lis*, the passage remained empty for several moments then, suddenly, Muirne Muncháem was standing there. She stepped into the *ráth*, followed immediately by Gleor Red Hand himself.

Although not a big man, the *Rí* of *Na Lamhraighe* cut an impressive figure, carrying himself with an almost regal air of authority. With his closely cropped black hair, sprinkled with silver, he looked the epitome of dignified leadership for great wisdom and conviction of purpose were chiselled into those handsome, venerable features.

'I see you, Gleor Red Hand.'

'I see you Bodhmhall. It is a glad sight for these tired eyes to rest on the contours of your form.'

'Old honey-mouth.'

He chuckled and she reached out to embrace him, feeling the soft prickle of the old chieftain's beard against her cheeks as he hugged her close. Gleor had more than forty-nine summers on him; the same age as her father, in fact. At one time, the two men had been close friends but many years earlier they'd fallen out over some matter she'd never really been privy to.

Finally, she turned to face the single female member of the *Lamhraighe* company: Muirne Muncháem, the Flower of Almhu. Six years, it seemed, had served only to make the young woman more beautiful. She looked taller, her frame had filled out to more pronounced curves, and her blue eyes sparkled with intelligent resolve. Her face and cheeks, no longer gaunt, now radiated a demure beauty. Blond hair, thick and sleek, was tied up with a beautifully handcrafted silver brooch. The years had also added to her confidence it seemed, for the woman who stood before her returned Bodhmhall's stare with a stately assurance that had little in common with the frightened girl who'd emerged from the Great Wild all those years ago.

'Hallo, cousin.'

'I see you Bodhmhall ua Baoiscne,' Muirne replied, falling back on the more formal greeting.

'You are back.'

The Flower of Almhu smiled: a brief, coy, tightening of the lips. Bodhmhall's gaze dropped to the bronze torc that hung in a wide glittering arc across her breastbone, then down to the beautifully decorated fur robe. The robe was a work of art that would have taken someone of talent months of effort to create.

Bodhmhall softly clicked her tongue. Muirne had taken time to clean up and dress herself in these precious items before presenting herself to Ráth Bládhma. Evidently, she did not wish to be remembered as the ragged, exhausted urchin who had thrown herself on their mercy some six years earlier.

With this, the *bandraoi* could not help but glance down at her own drab, handspun dress and she had to fight to prevent her lips from curving into a self-deprecating smile. Despite her amusement at her visitor's efforts to impress, the presence of such quality possessions in a nomadic tribe revealed much about Gleor's feelings for the woman. Evidently, the *rí* of *Na Lamhraighe* treated her not with love so much as with deference.

Her gaze dropped to Muirne's belly.

'And you are once more with child.'

The younger woman's composed demeanour cracked and she stared at Bodhmhall in shock. Suddenly, she shook her head and chuckled loudly. 'Of course! *An tíolacadh.* The *Gift.* I had forgotten you could see equally as well inside as out.'

'What? What's this?' Gleor looked from one to the other, eyes hungry for clarification.

'It is Bodhmhall, *a Rí.* She is a Gifted One.' Muirne placed one reassuring hand on the older man's arm. 'Her *Gift* is that she can perceive the life-light of all living beings. Our friend not only has the ability to discern a man concealed in the middle of a fog bank, but to distinguish the life flame of the child growing inside me as well.'

Gleor stared at her open mouthed then switched his gaze to Bodhmhall as though seeking confirmation of what he'd just heard. The *bandraoi* ignored him as she continued to study the yellow glow of life inside the other woman's belly. The pregnancy was very early yet, the weak glow of the unborn child barely distinguishable against the more intense life-fire of its mother.

Bodhmhall frowned as she examined that miniscule glow more intently. Six years earlier she'd seen the life-light of her nephew inside that very belly but the unique blaze of Demne's flame had greatly surpassed what she was seeing now.

'Come inside,' she said at last. 'Some things are best discussed in quiet surroundings and refreshment has already been prepared for you. Your men can remain here in the *lis.* My people will ensure that they're well taken care of.' With this, Lí Bán and Morag started to carve slices of meat from the roasted pig while Cumann and the other children distributed reed panniers of roast tubers.

Muirne, Gleor Red Hand and his persistent shadow, Marcán, followed Bodhmhall into the roundhouse where they found Liath Luachra waiting, having surreptitiously slipped away during the greeting ritual. She'd seated

47

herself beside the central fire pit which now contained a low, crackling fire. Several bowls and other containers had been arranged in the ashes to keep their contents warm.

As Bodhmhall and her visitors took their places around the fire, Bamba entered the dwelling and started to serve them, handing out individual wooden plates loaded with slabs of pork and placing two water-buckets and ladles between them to be shared by all. Bodhmhall regarded the freckled, red-haired girl as she bent down to pull a bowl of steaming tubers from the ashes and arranged them on a fresh plate. Another refugee from Ráth Dearg, Bamba now had fourteen summers on her and had adapted well to her life in the settlement. Of all the children at Ráth Bládhma she was, without doubt, the most vocal and Bodhmhall was relieved to see that, tonight, she was taking her hospitality duties seriously and remaining silent while serving.

Shuffling into a more comfortable position, the *bandraoi* watched Muirne look around the little roundhouse. The woman's expression was terse and she was staring quietly at the spot beside the fire where Bodhmhall had found her sleeping that first time she'd arrived at Ráth Bládhma. Intrigued, Bodhmhall continued to observe her, wondering what must be passing through the young woman's mind, what memories were being provoked by these familiar, if unloved, surroundings.

With a sharp shake of her head, the Flower of Almhu appeared to dispel those unpleasant memories. She glanced over to where Liath Luachra was staring into the fire, chewing glumly on a piece of dry bread. 'I see you Liath Luachra.'

The woman warrior looked up and stared back at her coldly. Observing the obvious tension between them, Gleor placed a protective hand on his woman's knee and quickly attempted to fill the hole left by the hostile silence.

'You are Liath Luachra? Defender of Ráth Bládhma?'

With a visible effort the warrior woman pulled hostile eyes from Muirne and turned to face the leader of *Na Lamhraighe*. 'I am Liath Luachra,' she growled.

Muirne has told me much of your bravery, how your saved the settlement and your friends through a somewhat unique feat of valour that –'

'I didn't save my friend. He's dead.'

There was another awkward silence. Gleor looked at her with some discomfort but also with evident irritation, clearly unaccustomed to being interrupted in such a manner. Beside him Marcán casually rested one hand on the hilt of the sword which lay on the mat beside him.

Bodhmhall stared nervously around the little group, using both her natural talents of perception and her *Gift* to assess her guests' reaction.

Muirne and Marcán's internal glow showed no real change. Both radiated a constant yellow-blue hue. Although he disguised it well, Gleor's heightened internal fire indicated that, in truth, he was very angry. The Grey One's characteristic yellow fire simmered, as always with intense little flecks of red, a small flame that could transform to a conflagration at a moment's notice.

'Let us eat,' the *bandraoi* suggested quickly in an attempt to diffuse the situation. 'Our hunger strains our mood and words settle better on a full stomach.'

Everyone seemed willing to disperse the tense atmosphere. The food and drink was distributed and they began to dig into the meal in earnest. At first, there was little discussion, no sound except the tearing of meat, the chomping of jaws, the licking of lips. After a time, the mood had mellowed enough for polite conversation, one that focussed on harmless topics such as *Na Lamhraighe*'s uneventful journey to Ráth Bládhma.

Finally, when most of the meal had been consumed and young Bamba had departed from the roundhouse, Bodhmhall turned the conversation to that area which most interested her.

'Why have you come here, Muirne?'

Taken aback by the directness of the question, the Flower of Almhu blinked then slowly turned a wry smile to her husband. 'As ever, *An Cailleach Dubh* does not mince her words.'

Bodhmhall ignored the veiled insult in her use of the diminutive term. *Cailleach Dubh* – 'the Black Witch' or 'the Black Hag', depending on the context, was a nickname introduced by Muirne herself when she'd first arrived to Dún Baoiscne as Cumhal's wife and had identified the *bandraoi* as a potential competitor to her influence. Thanks to Muirne's efforts the name had stuck but, over the years, Bodhmhall had grown accustomed to it. Nowadays, she felt a certain sense of pride in the title, considering it something of a badge of honour for challenges faced and overcome.

'Our shared history gives cause for forthrightness. It is not my intent to cast insult but your presence places us all at risk. I delivered you into the lands of *Na Lamhraighe* – she threw an irritated glance at the older warrior who had the grace to look away in embarrassment – 'to secure you in a place of safety where no-one could find you.'

'Alas, Bodhmhall, it appears that someone did find me.'

'What do you mean?'

'She means,' interrupted Gleor, 'that someone learned of her presence with us. This, despite our frequent wanderings to seek fresh pasture for our herds.' He glanced at his woman. 'On the last full moon, we received a *techtaire* at our spring camp. He came from Dún Baoiscne.'

'Dún Baoiscne?' Bodhmhall almost choked on the dry tuber she'd just placed in her mouth. Putting it back on the wooden board that served as a plate, she took a deep breath. 'Dún Baoiscne?' she repeated, as nonchalantly as she was able.

Muirne looked amused by the reaction her news had provoked. 'The *techtaire* was dispatched by Tréanmór himself. In his message, your father specifically requested my company at Dún Baoiscne.'

'It would seem you have a way with old men,' muttered Liath Luachra.

Gleor cast the woman warrior a glance that was hot with anger. Muirne, however, ignored her, all attention fixed on Bodhmhall. 'Tréanmór says that if I return to Dún Baoiscne, I will be welcomed, treated with the respect due the wife of his son Cumhal.'

Bodhmhall nodded slowly, giving no indication of her true feelings on the matter. Muirne was clearly preoccupied by the reputational and political capital such recognition from the leader of *Clann Baoiscne* might offer. She considered her words with care before responding.

'With respect, this is not the proposal my father intended these six years past. With Cumhal's death he was of a mind to hand you over to *Clann Morna*, an act that would have meant certain death for Demne. That is, you may recall, why you came to seeking sanctuary at Ráth Bládhma.'

Muirne nibbled on a morsel of meat before daintily putting it aside. 'That was a time when your father had little choice. *Clann Morna* had decimated his fighting men at Cnucha. Now the threat of *Clann Morna* is diminished.'

'The threat of *Clann Morna* is never diminished.' The *bandraoi* stared at the burning embers of the fire, trying to decide how much she could share with her visitors. She raised her eyes. 'We too have received a *techtaire* from Dún Baoiscne, an *Uí Faigil* who remains with us tonight. His message contained a similar invitation from Tréanmór but the messenger made no mention of you.'

Muirne made a dismissive gesture. 'I know nothing of any other messenger. Our *techtaire* was also *Uí Faigil*, a tall red-haired man but he was dispatched to Dún Baoiscne prior to our departure. It was my decision -'. She quickly corrected herself. 'It was my husband's decision to respond with confirmation of our agreement.' Muirne regarded her shrewdly. 'It may be that your father is putting his affairs in order.'

Bodhmhall looked at her but said nothing. A similar thought had passed through her own mind but she had no intention of revealing anything to her old rival.

'Tréanmór has also asked to see his grandson.'

And so we come to the nub of the matter.

Although she'd been anticipating this all afternoon, Bodhmhall still struggled to conceal her consternation. 'I hope you gave no answer in that regard.'

50

Muirne's eyes flared in anger. 'The answer I gave was that my son would accompany me to Dún Baoiscne to meet his grandfather.' One hand raised involuntarily to clutch the bronze torc hanging around her neck. 'You cannot keep my son from me, Bodhmhall. I am his mother. Neither can you prevent your own father from seeing the boy if he demands it so.'

'Taking Demne to Dún Baoiscne will expose him to danger. Have you given no thought to the Adversary?'

'It has been six years, Bodhmhall.'

'Time means nothing to those with evil intent.'

Irritation flickered in Muirne's eyes. 'You fixate on this imagined Adversary. Just as the twisted jackdaw fixates on shiny metal. Her hand dropped from the torc. 'That danger is passed. If there ever was an Adversary he died here in battle six years ago.'

Bodhmhall silently recalled the tall, hatchet-faced man who'd appeared to lead the *fian* attack on the settlement. After the battle they'd never found his body but then it had been a time of great upheaval and it was always possible the wolves had dragged his body away.

She just didn't believe it.

'Our enemy still lives to threaten us. And my people still rest in their graves for trying to protect you and your child. By taking Demne away you insult the sacrifice they made and play straight into the Adversary's hands.'

This time both Muirne's eyes and inner flame flared with anger. 'This Adversary is nothing more than an excuse to keep me from my son. An excuse I no longer believe. I have come to reclaim him.'

Bodhmhall silently considered the other woman; the set jaw, the fierce determination in those eyes. Blinded by the prospect of retrieving her child and lured by the call of Dún Baoiscne, Muirne could not see the danger she was facing. Her intentions were set and there was nothing – nothing – the *bandraoi* could do or say to change them.

She glanced at Gleor, hoping to find some support from the knowledgeable and practical leader. To her dismay, the *rí* of *Na Lamhraighe* was staring at the ground, refusing to participate in this particular argument.

Bodhmhall sighed, resisting the desire to let her shoulders slump from the overwhelming burden. She had no choice. She could not deny Muirne the right to see her own child. 'Very well. Liath Luachra will take you to see your son once we have finished our meal.'

'I would prefer to see him now.'

Bodhmhall took a deep breath and held it tight in her lungs as she regarded the antagonistic young woman.

Oh, she's changed all right! The old Muirne Munch, would not previously have dared such rudeness in my domain.

'As you wish,' she said, although she could taste the acid of spite on the tip of her tongue. 'I have lost my appetite, in any case.'

'I haven't.' This from Liath Luachra who was noisily munching on a steaming, white-skinned tuber. Noting the *bandraoi*'s warning glance, she sighed, tossed the remnants onto the plate and reluctantly got to her feet.

'Wait,' said Gleor Red Hand. All eyes turned to the grey-haired *rí* who'd been so silent up to this point. He focussed his gaze on Muirne Muncháem. 'Marcán will accompany you.'

Surprised, the hostess and her guest turned to assess Liath Luachra's reaction but the warrior woman simply shrugged. 'As you wish,' she said with distant grace.

The ill-matched trio quickly left the roundhouse. With their departure, the little dwelling grew quiet, the heavy silence broken only by the woody crackle of the fire. Bodhmhall considered the dancing flames with mute resignation.

'You do not speak to me, Bodhmhall?' asked Gleor.

Bodhmhall raised her head. 'You wish me to speak to you? Very well. Perhaps I will pose a question you might answer to my satisfaction. Who now rules in the lands of *Na Lamhraighe*?'

Gleor scowled, unhappy at the insinuation.

'Do not provoke me, Bodhmhall. You are dear like a daughter to me but I will brook no insult to my leadership. I still rule *Na Lamhraighe* with a steady hand.'

'A steady hand does not spill water from the cup it is holding. You are a dear and trusted friend, but you are also a lusty old goat. You lie with Muirne Muncháem, the very person whose safety I entrusted you with.'

Gleor glared at her, his face growing evermore contorted as a great rage stormed through him. Finally, just as it looked as though he was about to roar, the tension drained from his face and he began to chuckle softly. 'Your words have always had the impact of the mallet,' he conceded. 'Even as a child. But I cannot deny they consistently strike true. Yes, I am a lusty old goat.' He gave a great snort of good humour, grabbed a cup of water and threw the contents down his throat.

He wiped his face with the sleeve of his tunic. 'They say that age brings wisdom Bodhmhall, but I tell you that sometimes it allows the luxury of foolishness. I know Muirne weaves me about her fingers but I trade that for the pleasure of her body warming my bed of night. And she carries my child. My future son.'

'You already have a son.'

'I have a single son. If anything were to happen to Fintán, my line would be cut to a withered branch. The more sons I have the more chance that my line will survive.'

'What will you care? You will be dead.'

'I care. All men care of such things. Believe me, Bodhmhall.'

The *bandraoi* accepted this with silent acknowledgement. 'Then it is your intent to support Muirne in her plans, to escort her to Dún Baoiscne.'

'It is.'

She has moved her fidchell pieces well.

Bodhmhall grunted softly. 'Why would you wish to go to Dún Baoiscne? I had believed you and my father were no longer on friendly terms.'

'It's true. We are not allies, nor are we friends but neither are we enemies. This journey is for Muirne and her son. If they receive the recognition deserved from Dún Baoiscne, she may yet have a foothold in the future *Clann Baoiscne* leadership.'

'Which places Na *Lamhraighe* in an advantageous position.'

'I do not deny it.'

Bodhmhall toyed momentarily with a pork bone on her plate. 'When will you leave for Dún Baoiscne?'

'If your hospitality remains willingly granted, we will rest here for another night before continuing our journey.'

She looked at him, surprised. 'So soon?'

'Tréanmór's instruction was to attend him at Dún Baoiscne by the second moon. We must travel with speed to reach the fortress by then.' He paused. 'There was an underlying urgency to your father's message. Have you … have you received word of his health? Of his intentions? It may be that he has limited time.'

Bodhmhall slowly shook her head. Gleor Red Hand gave a shrug. 'It matters not.'

'You intend to take Demne with you?'

'Yes. I regret to say so. I know this will cause you grief but it is Muirne's right to reclaim her son. You know this.'

The *bandraoi* nodded reluctantly. 'Yes. Yes, I do. But there is … there is a complication.'

'A complication?'

'It concerns your son, Fintán.' She paused to make sure the *rí* of *Na Lamhraighe* was listening. Sure enough, the older man was regarding her intently, a single furrow across his brow.

'Liath Luachra encountered your son during her hunt in the Great Wild. They went separate ways but on her return to Ráth Bládhma, she crossed tracks that trailed those of your son.'

Bodhmhall paused to stack the dirty plates into a small column which she set to one side of the fire. 'Liath Luachra has an insatiable curiosity. When she has a question in her mind, it cannot be dislodged until she has satisfied herself with an answer. This is why she decided to follow both sets of tracks. She discovered that those of your son's pursuer eventually converged with the tracks of two other strangers. All three continued to follow Fintán.'

The *bandraoi* was satisfied to see that Gleor was staring at her, clearly intrigued by the tale.

'Liath Luachra recognised none of the footprints but she was convinced that the strangers were following Fintán. Not offering any threat, simply observing and trailing him to Ráth Bládhma. Satisfied that he was in no immediate danger, she returned to Glenn Ceoch by another route to alert us but it is likely that we are now being watched by those strangers.'

Gleor continued to regard her. He was frowning and clearly thinking through the ramifications of this new information. The old man may have been besotted with his new wife but he was no fool.

'Bandits?' he suggested.

'Possible,' she admitted. 'But they followed Fintán for a considerable distance without attacking him.'

'Perhaps they simply wished to see where he was going, to find a camp or settlement that they could potentially loot in the future.'

'Again, that's possible but bandit groups don't tend to be so patient or strategic in their thinking. They followed him for a significant distance without action of any kind. That behaviour is unusual.'

Gleor Red Hand rubbed his bearded chin. 'It is unusual. I thank you Bodhmhall for this warning. Nevertheless, this does not change our plan.'

'You are determined to push ahead? Even with an unknown threat on the trail?'

'They may not be on our trial,' he reminded her. 'No. We will take suitable precautions of course but I have Marcán, Fintán and six of my strongest warriors with me. That is a formidable force they would be foolish to tangle with.'

Bodhmhall considered this in silence for several moments. 'I will accompany you,' she said at last.

'What?'

'I will accompany you to Dún Baoiscne. As will Liath Luachra.'

'You wish to travel to your father's fortress with us?' Gleor did not sound particularly enamoured by the proposal, no doubt thinking of the fractious relationship between the three women.

'We have already received a summons to Dún Baoiscne. It would make sense to travel the route together. And Liath Luachra knows these lands like no other. She can guide us on a safe course.'

'And what of Ráth Bládhma?'

'Our warriors return tomorrow. With their presence and a cautious footing they will keep the settlement safe.'

The old man considered her suggestion for a long time as Bodhmhall fed the hungry fire. 'Very well,' he said at last. 'It does make sense to travel together but I warn you, you must not make trouble with Muirne. You must not complicate matters with your affections for her son or torment her with talk of the Adversary.'

'And yet I believe the Adversary behind all of this.'

Gleor winced. 'Do not make me regret my decision.' He looked at Bodhmhall closely. 'Do you know the tale of the Cowardly Rabbit?'

Bodhmhall offered him a glare of indignation. The tale of a Cowardly Rabbit was one of the more common tales of instruction told to little children by their parents.

'I will tell you the tale in case you have forgotten,' the grey-bearded man insisted. 'There once was a Cowardly Rabbit. He lived in a burrow with his friends in the middle of the forest. One night, while they were sleeping, the rabbits were woken by strange noises outside the burrow. As they huddled together and stared at the burrow entrance, a stick poked through the hole and struck the Cowardly Rabbit on the side.

The next morning, all the rabbits left the burrow with the exception of the Cowardly Rabbit who was too scared to leave his place of safety. "Come," his friends told him. "Come eat the fresh grass and breathe the clean air." But the Cowardly Rabbit would not go.

The next day, the same thing happened. And the day after that. The Cowardly Rabbit remained in his burrow and grew thinner and thinner while his friends grew fat on the summer grasses. After a time, Cowardly Rabbit grew weak and died.'

Gleor gave a wide grin. 'I'm sure you've heard this tale many times as a child but the instruction of the lesson remains valid. You should respect danger but you should not fear it. Life is full of peril and that is a fact to be accepted. Your choice is to live your life or hide away in fear which is another kind of death. So it is with your Adversary.'

He sat back, satisfied by this expression of wisdom. Bodhmhall stared at him, clearly vexed. 'I too have a tale of the Cowardly Rabbit,' she said. 'But my version differs.'

'Oh, yes?' asked Gleor.

'Yes. In my version, the tale starts off in a similar manner. The rabbits are huddled in their burrow at night. They hear a noise that wakes them. But when the stick pokes the Cowardly Rabbit in the side, he becomes enraged and leaps out to bite the hand that holds the stick. That hand beats the Cowardly Rabbit, but the deepness of the wound from the animal's bite is such that the blood becomes tainted. Eventually, the hand rots and dies.'

Gleor looked at her, bemused by this interpretation. 'This is hardly a tale of instruction. This is a tale of humour. It has no lesson.'

'Oh, it has a lesson,' Bodhmhall answered. 'The lesson of my tale is "Poke the Cowardly Rabbit at your peril".'

When they left the roundhouse, Liath Luachra had Ferchar and Bran open the gateway passage and quickly exited the *ráth*, followed closely by Muirne Muncháem and Marcán Lámhfhada. Although it was late, the sky retained some vestige of light, sufficient at least for her to guide them around to the south of the *ráth* then towards the dense woods to the east of the settlement.

It was a short distance and it did not take long to reach the trees but on entering beneath the heavy canopy, it immediately grew darker and harder to see. Off to their left they could hear the gush of a flowing waterway where the high spring waters poured down from the steep mountains.

Muirne Muncháem stopped suddenly and turned to confront the woman warrior. 'I have travelled this path before. This is the trail that leads to the escape route from Glen Ceoch.'

Liath Luachra glowered at the young woman, angry that she'd reveal such a secret in front of the big warrior beside her. 'That is not the route we take.'

'Then what is the route?' demanded Muirne. 'I have followed this trail. I know it ends at the cliffs by Gág na Muice.'

'This trail continues to Gág na Muice but we turn off before then. Here.' She raised her hand to indicate a narrow opening in the trees, a gap so tight and difficult to see in the dim light that they'd have walked right past it had the woman warrior not specifically pointed it out. With a huff, Liath Luachra squeezed in through the thick bush, leading them further into the wood where it was increasingly difficult to move due to the constricting thickness of the trees.

After advancing a distance of twenty or thirty paces they came to a small clearing that was wide enough to hold slightly more than double their number. Liath Luachra cupped two hands around her mouth and called deeper into the trees. 'Gnathad! It is Liath Luachra. I bring Muirne Muncháem and another with me.'

The three stood in silence. The shadows between the trees slowly grew denser. Suddenly a grey shadow seemed to detach itself from the darkness and stood in the little clearing before them.

'Muirne Muncháem. There is a name I did not expect in this valley again.'

Muirne and Marcán stared at the woman warrior. Although it was difficult to see her clearly in the encroaching darkness, the glower of ill-concealed hatred was evident, as was the spearhead pointed directly at Muirne's stomach. Slowly Marcán edged in front of the shaking woman, putting himself between the weapon and his charge.

Gnathad sighed and lowered the spear, resting the base of the staff on the ground so that she could lean against it for support. 'My man died because of you, Muirne Muncháem.'

'I had no connection to the *fian* that attacked Ráth Dearg,' the Flower of Almhu protested. 'You know that-.' She stopped talking. The blond haired warrior woman had walked past them, back into the woods in the direction from which they'd just come. Infuriated by the insult, Muirne turned to direct her resentment instead at Liath Luachra. 'Bodhmhall mentioned your training of Gnathad. I see now that martial skills were not the only instruction you passed on. If you think-'

'You will find a small hunting booth twenty paces directly ahead,' said the warrior woman, abruptly cutting her off. 'It is a small shelter we use to stockpile food and water in case the Gág na Muice route needs to be used. Your son is sleeping inside.'

The Flower of Almhu woman glared at her, lips quivering in fury. Liath Luachra could see the conflicting desires in that face: the ferocious drive to confront the warrior woman and the urgent yearning to find her son.

In the end, she opted for the latter. With an angry sweep of her cloak, she stepped forward into the trees. Marcán made to follow her but a curt instruction thrown back over her shoulder instructed him to remain where he was.

The two warriors waited, listening to the stumbling noises and the crackle of broken twigs as the woman advanced further into the trees. Finally they heard a little sigh, an exclamation that could have equally been either happiness or despair. A moment later, a soft crooning sound floated through the night air. Liath Luachra cocked her head to one side, straining to make out the words but the only sentence she could make sense of was a repeated refrain:

> Sleep in peaceful slumber
> Sleep, sleep
> In peaceful slumber

As the song finally drew to a close, Liath Luachra and the one-eyed warrior exchanged stares, measuring each other in silent assessment.

'You have a unique catch to your sword sheath,' the big man said at last, breaking his silence. He spoke slowly, almost ponderously, with a deep, harsh voice. He pointed to the leather thong on her sword hilt designed to hold her weapon in place within its sheath. 'It secures but it also allows the sword to be drawn with speed. That is good.'

Liath Luachra stared at Marcán, surprised by the unexpected compliment. The warrior wasn't actually looking at her, she realised. He was staring off into the trees, into the surrounding darkness. His face, even

57

from the side, was unreadable, obscured by a shadow cast down by an overhanging branch. She stood there for a moment, trying to think of a suitable reply. 'Yes,' she said at last.

'How is your blade named?'

'*Gléas Gan Ainm,*' she answered. Weapon Without A Name.

Marcán grunted but she was unable to tell if it was amusement or a simple acknowledgement.

'And yours is named *Lámhfhada.*'

'It is.'

'The name is … apt.'

Another silence.

'Liath Luachra.'

'Yes?'

'I know of your reputation, of your skill on the battlefield. I have heard tales of your time with *Na Cinéaltaí* but also of the battle you fought here in Glenn Ceoch. People name you Defender of Ráth Bládhma for you fought a much greater force of invaders and you survived. I respect that.' He lapsed into silence once more.

'But ...' she hazarded.

'But I have also seen how you look at Muirne Muncháem. If I observed you walk into the woods with the Flower of Almhu it would not be my expectation that both of you returned.'

'Come to the nub of what you wish to say. You start to bore me.'

'I am saying that I have been directed by my *rí* to protect Muirne Muncháem, to sacrifice my own life for her if need be.'

'You would sacrifice your life for Muirne Muncháem?' The woman warrior was genuinely shocked.

'Not for her but for my *rí*. If he instructs me to do so then I will do so.'

'Then you're a fool.'

Although she couldn't see him in the darkness, Liath Luachra sensed the big man stiffen. 'And you,' he countered, 'know nothing of loyalty.'

'I know to offer loyalty to those who deserve it. You are an innocent calf, licking the hand of those who wish to fatten you, oblivious to that fact that one day you will end up on their plate.'

The darkness between them suddenly seemed laden with compact hostility.

'As long as you understand,' the harsh voice said. 'If you raise a hand against the Flower of Almhu you will need to deal with me.'

Chapter Four

Liath Luachra listened carefully.

The remnants of the morning chorus had long since faded but the surrounding trees still clamoured with birdsong. Sometime earlier, she'd heard the distant grunt of a wild pig from further inside the trees but since then, nothing. To all appearances, the forest was safe, benign, clear of danger.

Or those dangers were very well hidden.

Where are they?

Lying face down in a massed carpet of *coinnle corra* [bluebells], Liath Luachra was doing her best to ignore the increasing pressure against her bladder, a pressure that had slowly grown from prickling irritant to an all-consuming physical necessity. She pushed her face into the thick growth, distracting herself with the dewy scent of the crushed flowers. It was unusual to find *coinnle corra* flourishing so late in the season but she was grateful for the concealment the fleshy flowers provided.

With great care, she allowed herself a controlled squirm that wouldn't set the flower stalks shaking and, thereby, signal her presence. The movement did, however, produce a muted creak from the battle harness.

She was dressed for battle. Her hair was tied up into two tight braids, she was wearing her red leather harness, the colour now bleached to a muddy brown that was ideal for slinking through the woods of Glenn Ceoch. In her hand, she gripped her favourite javelin, a short, iron-tipped missile that she knew would fly straight and true when cast. Two similar missiles were sheathed in a leather quiver strapped to her back.

Her short iron sword, *Gléas Gan Ainm,* was also sheathed, lying in the scabbard sewn into her belt through a stiff leather fold and further secured by a flax tie at its tip. Tucked inside a smaller scabbard on the opposite side of the belt was her knife, *Blas na Fola* – Taste for Blood. She'd spent the better part of the night honing that particular blade to a fine sharpness while watching the door of the roundhouse where Fintán and Cargal Uí Faigil lay sleeping.

The thought of the swarthy *techtaire*, his thick tongue and greasy lips, provoked a sting of antipathy. His proposed departure from the settlement that morning was the cause of her current predicament. During the night, she'd belatedly realised that his route would take him through the valley entrance where the mysterious trackers of Fintán mac Gleor were believed to be concealed. With a sick feeling in her stomach, she knew that she had no choice but to secure the area in order to ensure his safe passage.

Just before dawn, with much ill will, she'd slipped over the ramparts of the *ráth's* eastern embankment, clambering across the ditch by means of a long wooden plank angled down to the earth on the far side. Reaching the ground safely, she'd watched Ferchar slowly draw the plank back inside. Low cloud had obscured the moon and stars, smothering the valley in darkness but she'd had the vague impression that he'd given her an encouraging wave from the safety of the pilings before disappearing from sight.

The grey tint of dawn was already staining the eastern sky so she'd wasted no time circling around to the north of the settlement then crossing the pasture at a run to reach the trees at the base of the northern cliffs. Pausing to catch her breath inside the shelter of the treeline, she'd peered towards the west. Unable to distinguish anything through the gloom, she'd nodded to herself, satisfied that her own departure had not been observed.

When she was sufficiently rested, the woman warrior had worked her way towards the valley entrance. Nearing the western tree-line, she'd come to a halt and waited for the visibility to improve. Up to this point, she'd been able to move through the northern woods through touch alone because of her great familiarity with the topography but a certain amount of noise was unavoidable. Given the possibility of enemy scouts, it was simply too dangerous to proceed any further until she could clearly see where she was going.

In time, the absolute blackness within the valley had given way to a sickly grey that, although very dim, was sufficient for her purposes. Moving carefully into the treeline of the western forest, she'd advanced on a course that ran perpendicular to her earlier trajectory, finally reaching the area where *Sruth Drithleach* entered the forest. She'd followed the northern bank of the stream for about thirty paces or so until the waterway broadened, breaking up into numerous individual rivulets that gradually drained deeper and disappeared into the increasingly boggy earth. Before the ground became too soft, she waded across the shallow waters that reached just above her ankles.

On the southern bank, Liath Luachra paused to throw a troubled glance back in the direction from which she'd come. Had she continued due west instead of crossing *Sruth Drithleach*, her route would have taken her further into An Talamh Báite – *The Drowned Land*. A large section of swampy flatland, this continued further westwards and became increasingly deforested until it eventually reached the bog island of Oileán Dubh. This was where, six years earlier, Bearach had lost his life in the battle against the *fian*.

Don't think. Forget that. Focus on the task at hand.

With a grimace, the woman warrior had turned her face to the south-west and moved forward at a crouch. The route into Glenn Ceoch was close now and any enemy scouts would almost certainly be stationed nearby. The trail itself was a tight path, wedged between the forest and the base of the valley's southern ridge. Leaving Glenn Ceoch, it ran parallel to the ridge for a distance of several hundred paces before branching out and subsequently merging into the flatland forest beyond the Sliabh Bládhma hills.

She was still some distance from the trail when she'd come to a wide clearing where many of the trees used for the reconstruction of the *ráth* had originally been felled. The empty space was slowly being reclaimed by the forest but the growth was still restricted to the thick mass of *coinnle corra*, numerous saplings and the occasional, scattered ash tree. The woman warrior wasn't happy about traversing such an exposed area but the woodland on either side, clogged with dry scrub and debris, was impassable without making a significant racket.

She'd started across the clearing at a crawl; her face, the breast of her battle harness and the knees of her leggings quickly saturated from the heavy dew that coated the high-stems of the flowers. She'd made it almost half-way across when a sudden cough made her freeze and press herself flat against the earth.

For the first few moments, Liath Luachra had been convinced she'd been spotted and the tension was unbearable as she'd waited for javelins to come arching up out of the trees towards her. As time stretched on and no attack was forthcoming however, she'd realised that her luck had held. Whoever had coughed had not seen her.

Since that initial cough, she'd lain stationary in the *coinnle corra*, waiting for the morning breeze that almost invariably swept through the valley just after dawn.

It will come soon.

As she lay enveloped in the wet mass of flowers, she struggled to control her mounting nervousness for her position was a precarious one. Although it concealed her well enough in the glum light of dawn, she'd become much easier to spot as the visibility improved, particularly if anyone stepped into the clearing. Using the tip of the javelin, she made a parting in the fronds directly in front of her and studied the view ahead: twenty paces or so of open ground to the green cover of the trees that were tantalisingly out of reach. She winced, her disquiet exacerbated further by the knowledge that the *techtaire* would leave the settlement shortly.

And she still hadn't identified the location of the silent watchers.

Fortunately, the much anticipated westerly chose that very moment to appear. Liath Luachra felt the sudden drift of air as it brushed over her, stirring the tops of the flowers and the higher grass stalks. All around her, the forest creaked as its great boughs were stirred and stretched.

Now that the shivering of flower spikes and stems from her own movement could no longer be distinguished from the wind's caress she wasted no time. She began to drag herself forwards through the blue-green cluster, still damp and slimy from the heavy dew. The tops of the flowers barely reached above her head but she continued to crawl, aligning her movement – as far as she could – to the irregular breeze that swished overhead.

When she reached the tree line she breathed a silent sigh of relief and immediately huddled close to the mossy bulk of a solitary oak set in the middle of the beech and elder trees. Screened from view from the west and northwest, she remained crouched as she listened for anything that sounded out of the ordinary.

A long time passed.

There was no noise but the usual bustle of the forest: the creaking of trees; the rustle of wind through the leaves; birdsong.

Nothing else.

Maybe they've moved on.

Either way, she had other priorities. Remaining at a crouch, she leaned her javelin against the trunk, yanked her leggings down and pulled her loincloth aside. She had to bite back a sigh of relief as the pressure finally eased.

Wiping herself dry with a fistful of leaves, she was in the process of tugging her leggings up when there was another cough, this time much louder and significantly closer. Startled, she almost fell over onto the damp patch she'd just created but managed to grab the rough girth of the tree trunk to keep her balance. Her heart pounded like the attack rhythm of a war drum. The sound had been close, far too close. And, for a moment, she'd been completely defenceless.

Foolish! Foolish!

She worked to control her breathing, to calm the surge of adrenalin coursing through her veins. She'd been taken by surprise a second time but the length of the cough, and the lack of any effort to mask it, suggested that whoever it was, he had no idea how close she was.

Unless it's a trap.

The thought provoked a frown. She didn't think it was a trap. If they knew she was there, they'd have pinned her with javelins when she'd been exposed in the clearing. No. She nodded unconsciously, convinced by her own logic. Whoever was there, she was certain he was unaware that he had company.

Slipping the javelin back into its quiver, she slowly pulled *Blas na Fola* from her belt. She didn't know for sure how many opponents she was facing and a javelin cast in such circumstances was too risky to ensure a silent kill. Any confrontation would have to be up close and bloody.

Lying on the ground, she placed her cheek against the detritus of leaves and twigs on the forest floor then quickly poked her head around the tree trunk, scanned the route ahead and pulled back again immediately.

Hmm.

She plucked a twig from the ground, popped one end in her mouth and chewed on the hard material as she mentally reviewed what she'd seen. The woods stretched onwards on every side except towards the south where they thinned as it approached the trail. She'd seen no sign of movement but that didn't mean anything. The Coughing Man was out there and she was relatively certain that he was situated in the thick stand of beech she'd spotted forty paces west of her current position. It was from this direction that the sound had seemed to originate and, enclosed by deadfall as it was, it provided both a good shelter against the wind and a potential refuge against any passing wolves. It would have been her choice of campsite had she spent the night in these woods.

Dropping to her stomach once again, she shuffled forwards, crawling parallel to the tree line for more than fifty or sixty paces before circling around in a wide arc that brought her back to the stand of beech from a south-westerly direction. She managed to get within thirty paces of her objective, when she finally spotted him; the Coughing Man.

The subject of her scrutiny was a skinny individual, bearded, with a tangled blond mane that hung long and lank around his shoulders. Seated at an angle that looked away from her, he was leaning back against one of the trees and had a heavy cloak wrapped around his shoulders. From his posture, she could tell that he was awake although he didn't look particularly alert. Gazing, as he was, in the opposite direction to the clearing, she now understood why he hadn't seen her. Her lips compressed in disapproval. His carelessness had probably saved her life but she still found herself irrationally vexed by such a lax attitude out in the Great Wild, where death was always so close.

Always so close.

Placing the blade of *Blas Na Fola* between her teeth, she amended her direction, edging slightly to the right so that she could approach him from behind, hidden by the very tree he was leaning against. Slowly, she worked her way closer, pausing every few moments to listen, observe and make sure that nothing had changed. She was about six or seven steps from the beech stand when she finally got to her feet behind one of the fallen trees. The scout's bare legs were visible now, poking out from the side of the tree he was using as a leaning post. Taking the knife from her teeth, she slid soundlessly over the fallen beech and crept forwards.

The incompetent scout was taken completely by surprise. In the middle of a loud yawn, he was tilting his head back when Liath Luachra snapped forwards, clamping a hand about his mouth as she carved through the front of his throat. There was a brief, desperate struggle but it was weak and short-lived, waning rapidly as his lifeblood gushed out onto his lap. Releasing him, Liath Luachra pulled back behind the tree again as he slumped sideways onto the ground. The body gave several brief, involuntary spasms and there was a stink as it voided its bowels. She ignored it, scanning the surrounding forest for any sign of movement.

When she was certain that no-one else was present, she slid back around the tree trunk and examined the dead scout more closely. It was hard to tell with the bushy beard but she didn't think he could have had more than eighteen or nineteen seasons on him. The face wasn't one she recognised but then that was hardly unusual. She did notice that it bore several decorative scars on the upper cheeks, a swirling design she was unfamiliar with.

Beneath the heavy cloak, the dead man's clothes were caked with mud but serviceable and well made. They also looked two sizes too big for him, suggesting that he'd either stolen them or borrowed them, a theory supported by her subsequent discovery of a well-made iron sword with traces of rust along the blade. The weapon was of too good a quality for the original owner to willingly allow it to be neglected in such a manner.

A bandit?

She clucked her tongue. It was possible. Perhaps Gleor Red Hand had been correct after all.

Using a short branch, the woman warrior lifted the front of the dead man's bloody tunic to reveal a pale stomach underneath. Repelled by the stink of sour sweat and shit, she was about to drop it again when she noticed an ugly pendent hanging from a leather thong at an angle down the left side of his rib-cage. The ornament was a circular bronze disc with designs engraved on one side. She stared at it, intrigued but not quite sure why. There was something familiar about the design but she couldn't work out what it was.

A harsh caw caused her to lift her head. She stared up at the branch above where a solitary rook was sitting, small black eyes regarding her with cool disdain.

'I see you, Dark Crow.'

The bird deigned to respond but the warrior woman continued to regard him with interest. *Na rúca* – the rooks – were interesting birds with a reputation for intelligence and trickery. Although they usually tended to mate for life, this particular one appeared to be alone, content to sit watching her rummage through the slain scout's possessions.

This is a brazen bird.

'Tell me your secrets, Dark Crow, you who see everything from your silent perch.'

Once again, the bird returned her stare with blank eyes. She regarded the metallic black-blue sheen of its feathers, the greyish white base of its silver beak. She noticed that the bird had an unusual white fleck on its breast.

'Do you bring me a message, handsome one? They tell me *na rúca* are messengers of the Gods. Is that not so?'

No answer.

She chuckled softly to herself. 'You are no friend of mine, then.'

Suddenly, with a raucous flutter of black wings, the crow took to the air. Alerted, Liath Luachra spun around on her right knee, hand dropping for her sword.

She heard the whistle of the missile as it came whirling out of the trees but didn't see it before it struck. With a sudden smacking sound there was a javelin embedded in the tree just behind her head, its shaft quivering from the force of the impact. She made to turn and face her attacker but a sharp yank at the side of her head prevented her from doing so. It took one horrible moment to work out what had happened. The javelin had missed her but had pinned one of her braids firmly to the tree.

She reacted without thinking, bringing *Blas Na Fola* up to slash through the braid then scurrying around to the far side of the trunk as another javelin slammed into it with a heavy wooden *thunk*. Heart pounding, she got to her feet and pushed herself up against the coarse bark. The girth of the trunk was three times her width which meant she was safe for a few moments. Dropping the knife back into its scabbard, she withdrew two javelins from the quiver and paused to listen. She couldn't hear anything.

Moving to her left, she poked her head out, pulling it back too swiftly to make a target. Nothing was moving out there, as far as she could see. Whoever they were, they were well hidden.

The trees groaned and the leaves rustled as a fresh gust blew through the woods. Jamming the javelins under her armpit, she wiped the sweat on her palms against the rough material of her leggings. Her heart was pounding and she had to make a conscious effort to resist the urge to flee.

A twig snapped somewhere off to the left but when she threw a quick glance in that direction she saw nothing.

A diversion!

She quickly edged over to the other side of the tree and threw a cautious glance out there as well.

Nothing.

Taking a deep breath, she forced her mind to slow, to think through her predicament. Judging from the tracks she'd seen the previous day, there was one, possibly two, of the scouts still out there. They knew where she was hiding so they were, more than likely, working their way towards her, probably around to her flank where they could get a clear cast.

Which meant that she had to remove that advantage, confuse them as to her location.

Shifting around, she pressed her back against the trunk and plotted an escape route from her current position. First, over the fallen beech tree. It was four or five long paces away and lay at waist level across her path but, once she got over it, its bulk would shield her and allow her to crawl to the clump of bushes near the uprooted end. Although the former provided no shield against a javelin, they were wide and bushy enough to provide a minimal screen while she made a break for the deeper forest, a distance of ten or twelve paces.

Her lips twitched at that. She'd be quite exposed for that last burst, an open target for one or two javelin casters.

It'll have to do.

Replacing one of the javelins, she braced herself against the tree, preparing to push herself off and use the momentum to increase her speed.

One, two -

Suddenly a horrific scream rang through the forest. It quavered, caught and was abruptly cut-off leaving a terrible stillness hanging in the air. Alarmed, Liath Luachra pulled back even closer against the coarse surface of the tree. She swallowed, shuffled nervously to the right and tossed a quick glance around the trunk. Once again, she saw nothing.

The techtaire!

The thought made her shiver. Could she have left it too long? Had Cargal Uí Faigil been attacked on the ...

She allowed the thought to trail off. Surely, she'd have heard him running if he'd come along the trail. It also seemed unlikely that the remaining scouts would have broken off their attack on her to focus on the *techtaire*.

She chewed thoughtfully on the inside of her cheek.

It doesn't matter. Still have to move.

With that, she turned and launched herself towards the fallen beech. Without slowing she dived over the hefty obstacle, hitting the ground in a roll then kicking herself back into the shelter of the trunk. Moving on her hands and knees, she shuffled along to the exposed roots that splayed out like the hair of a demented old woman. Remaining in its shadow, she stared across the open ground to the denser forest. It suddenly looked much further than it had when she'd looked at it earlier. Taking a deep breath, she prepared to launch herself forwards when a loud, high-pitched whistle pierced the silence.

That's not right!

Consumed by curiosity, she twisted around and quickly poked her head over the trunk. She pulled it back down again almost immediately but not before spotting something unexpected. Leaning calmly against the tree that had so recently served as her refuge, was a scrawny old warrior with a tangled beard and hair streaked with grey.

Tóla!

She was rising cautiously to her feet when the frantic wings of a passing starling caused her natural reactions to kick in and she dropped to her knees again. A raucous howl of laughter rolled over the bulk of the tree trunk. Scowling, Liath Luachra stood up and stared at the gaunt warrior.

'That scream,' she called. 'That was you who killed the other scout.'

Tóla's response was a wide, gap-toothed grin.

She scrambled back over the fallen tree and retraced her steps to the stand of beech. Tóla watched her approach, his grin as wide as ever despite the sunken cheeks. As she drew close, he held up a javelin with her pigtail embedded in the metal tip. She halted, looked at it then looked at him. With a grudging nod of thanks, she plucked it from the javelin point and stuffed it down the front of her battle harness.

Tóla turned away and started muttering excitedly, if incomprehensibly, to himself as he pointed to where the dead scout was lying. To her surprise, Liath Luachra saw that there was now a second body there, lying prostrate next to the first. Her lips turned down.

No chance of asking who sent them now.

She turned to face Tóla. 'Why did you drag him all the way over here?'

He looked back at her with as much expression as the rook she'd seen on the tree before the skirmish.

'Did you see a third man?'

Tóla regarded her blankly then suddenly lunged forwards to tap her twice upon the shoulder. Liath Luachra regarded him uncertainly. Communication with Tóla was a frustrating experience at the best of times. Although he clearly understood what people were saying to him, any reciprocal engagement was never quite as clear cut.

Ever since the grizzled old warrior had come to Ráth Bládhma in the company of Fiacail mac Codhna, six years earlier, he'd shown a marked reluctance to talk, restricting any communication to his kinsman, the warrior Ultán ua Feata. Following Ultán's death during the battle with the *fian*, he hadn't uttered a word for several weeks, a situation that remained unchanged until Ferchar had emerged from the coma-like state caused by a head injury received during that same battle.

For some reason, known only to himself, Tóla had decided to open up to the young, red-haired warrior. He'd also developed a disconcerting habit of sidling up to him at the oddest of times to whisper urgently in his ear. When questioned as to what the old warrior was actually saying, Ferchar – clearly bemused by the situation – insisted that the whispers consisted mostly of complaints about the food. The only other time Liath Luachra

67

had ever seen him vocally animated was when he held great, silent arguments with some silent friend that no-one else could see.

Tóla again tapped her twice on the shoulder.

'What?' she demanded. He sighed then suddenly jerked his head towards the west. Turning to gaze in that direction, Liath Luachra saw two slim figures emerge from the trees and finally understood what the warrior had been trying to tell her.

Two men. Aodhán and Cónán. Coming in from the West.

She confirmed her understanding with a sharp inclination of her head. With that, they ignored each other and watched in silence as the brothers approached, their movements hampered by the heavy flax baskets carried on their backs. As they approached, she saw that Aodhán was also carrying a second basket, held tightly in his arms.

Tóla's.

As the brothers entered the beech stand, both glanced briefly at the bloody corpses. Ignoring them, they approached their comrades and, although aware that Liath Luachra didn't enjoy close physical contact, insisted on embracing her. Because they were her people now, she let them.

'You're back,' she said with convincing understatement.

Aodhán nodded. Tall, slim and downy haired, he looked more and more like Cairbre with every passing year. As of late, the young warrior had also taken to growing his beard out in the style favoured by his father, making the resemblance that much stronger. Cónán, by comparison, took after their mother. Short and dark-haired, he also carried his mother's heritage in the darker toning of his skin.

'We're back,' the elder brother agreed. 'We were crossing the slopes towards Sliabh Bládhma when we found two sets of tracks leading directly for Glenn Ceoch. All of them unfamiliar. We came as fast as we could but I sent Tóla on ahead to scout the land and observe what was happening. He glanced at the bloody corpses. 'A fortuitous decision, it seems.'

Liath Luachra sniffed. 'Everything was in hand.' She poked the second body – the one that Tóla had inexplicably dragged there – with her foot. 'The party that these two formed part of, had a third person. Did you come across any sign of him?'

Cónán shrugged off his heavy backpack. 'There was a single set of tracks leaving Glenn Ceoch that matched one from this group. But they were older. Probably from yesterday.'

Liath Luachra sighed. That was not good news.

'Grey One, what takes place in Glenn Ceoch? Who are these warriors? They were not linked to the first party for they were all travelling separately.'

'We believe that this group were sent by the Adversary. The other group is a *Lamhraighe* company. They were escorting Muirne Muncháem to Ráth Bládhma.'

Seeing the disbelief on their faces, the woman warrior proceeded to explain the events of the previous day and answered the subsequent questions as far as she could. Aodhán and the others were, unsurprisingly, disturbed to learn that the *ráth* was full of *Lamhraighe* warriors. They were even more disturbed when Liath Luachra informed them of Bodhmhall's intention to accompany Demne to Dún Baoiscne for an unspecified period of time.

That unwelcome piece of information upset Aodhán most of all for not only was the young boy dear to him but he knew that responsibility for leading the settlement would fall to him while they were away. The woman warrior watched him swallow his anger, impressed by how he took the time to contemplate a response before articulating it. Most young men his age would have blurted or blustered without even thinking it through first.

'Both of you are leaving?' The son of Cairbre shook his head. 'What is a creature without a head?'

Liath Luachra stared at the young man in confusion. Was this a riddle? Was he responding with a riddle? If so, he was better off talking to the *bandraoi* for she really had no head for such matters.

She turned her gaze away, repressing a quick twinge of guilt. Looking at the young warrior had sent her thoughts wandering to Bearach, and by association, Fintán mac Gleor. She gave her head a sharp shake as though to dislodge the memory.

'It is a corpse,' Aodhán answered his own question, oblivious to the woman warrior's internal consternation.

Liath Luachra shrugged, the intellectual nature of his argument sailing over her head.

'Bodhmhall is no fool, Aodhán. She's working on a plan. Besides, you have five warriors and much wisdom amongst the others to draw from. I've taught you well enough to defend the *ráth*. I know *Muinntir Bládhma* will remain safe under your leadership until we return.'

'But you are taking part of *Muinntir Bládhma* away with you, Grey One. Demne is *Muinntir Bládhma*. He belongs here. Not at Dún Baoiscne.'

There was an uncomfortable shuffling amongst all of those gathered. Liath Luachra glared at him, unsure how to respond. As on many other, similar occasions she wished she had even a portion of Bodhmhall's fluency with words. She knew the warriors liked the child and that the prospect of losing him to Muirne Muncháem – someone for whom they had little love – made them angry enough to gnash on metal. She liked the boy too although, accustomed to loss, she'd always made a point of keeping him at arm's length.

69

'Let us bury the dead strangers,' she suggested. 'We do not want the bodies to attract wolves. When we're done, we can return to *Ráth Bládhma* and Bodhmhall will explain her intentions.'

Aodhán looked at her as though he was about to argue but the unexpected sound of running feet in the distance distracted him. The four warriors gazed towards the trail where the thump of heavy footfalls echoed out from the cliffs of the southern ridge. They caught a brief glimpse of Cargal Uí Faigil's muscular form as he ran between the trees, moving at impressive pace.

Noting Liath Luachra's apparent lack of concern, Aodhán cast her a curious glance. 'Who is the stranger?' he asked. 'Is he one of the visitors?'

Liath Luachra looked down to the two dead scouts and slowly shook her head. 'He is a rook,' she said and sighed. 'Bearing ill news from the Gods.'

***

On the hunting party's return to Ráth Bládhma, Bodhmhall took everyone by surprise by calling an immediate council for the adults of *Muinntir Bládhma*. The abruptness of the announcement and the timing – so early in the morning – allowed Aodhán and the others little respite from their days of hard travel. From her expression, however, it was obvious that for Bodhmhall at least, time was not a luxury she could afford.

While the others gathered to talk in the roundhouse, Liath Luachra remained outside, sitting by a log at the central fire pit. From her earlier discussions with Bodhmhall, there was nothing else she could add to the conversation and she was keen to clean the blood from her hands and feet.

And there was a lot of blood. Although standing behind the scout when she'd cut his throat, it was impossible to escape the blood spray from such a wound.

Before she started, she paused for a moment to rest her head in her hands. Fatigue lay heavy on her, the sleepless night and the after effects of the battle adrenalin combining to wear her down. From experience, she knew that she could force herself to remain alert for a while longer if necessary but, at some stage, she would need to curl up in a dark corner and sleep.

Using a ladle from the rainbucket, she poured water over her feet. The liquid was already tepid from the morning sun and its touch briefly reminded her of the moment the blood had spurted over them. That sticky warmth of spilled battle blood was a distinct sensation that wasn't easily forgotten. There was really no other feeling like it. Even the slaughter of animals was different for it lacked the heady intoxication of violence, the overpowering sensations of desperation and relief.

She wiped the remaining stains away with her hands, watching the pinkish liquid dribble off her skin and onto the surface of the *lis* where it was immediately absorbed by the dusty soil.

Another offering to the Great Mother.

She felt no remorse at the taking of the scout's life. The scout and his comrades had posed a threat to those she held dear and she was very clear about where her priorities lay.

A dark shadow slid across the earth in front of her and she looked up to find Demne standing before her, staring down at the pink stains with a troubled expression.

'The blood of your opponent,' she said. 'Always better than the blood of your friend.'

She spoke quietly for most of the *Lamhraighe* warriors were still dozing in the makeshift beds off to the far side of the hearth. Demne too had slept with the visitors, his mother insisting on removing him from Lí Bán's roundhouse, where he usually slept with the other children, to spend the night with her and Gleor.

The boy nodded sagely, acknowledging the wisdom of her words although he couldn't possibly have understood the context behind what she was saying.

'You do not remain with your mother?'

'She sleeps.' He sniffed and looked up towards the sun as though to verify that it was still up there. 'The old man is tired. He snores.'

'Uh-huh,' Liath Luachra grunted sympathetically. The news came as no surprise. The *Lamhraighe* party had travelled a significant distance in a very short time. Anyone would have been taxed by such a hike. And Gleor was not a young man.

'You do not like my mother.'

Liath Luachra looked at the boy, surprised by such intuition in one so young. 'No,' she admitted and looked down, her attention focussed on scrubbing the last of the blood from her hands and feet.

'Why?'

'Your mother is … untrustworthy.'

'Un-trust-wor-thy,' he pronounced the word out in four distinct syllables. 'What does that mean?'

'It means that she is scant with the reason of things. She does not always tell the full truth.'

'Do you always tell the full truth?'

This time she stopped what she was doing and raised her eyes to consider him intently. Demne could be an odd one at times and had the annoying habit of switching from the temperament of a gregarious child to that of a worldly old fogy without any warning. 'Usually,' she admitted. 'Unless I have strong reasons not to. People who lie are fearful of others or

71

fear repercussions for their actions. I have been close to death too often to truly fear the Dark Leap anymore. When you do not fear, you can tell the truth and when you tell the truth you make any problem belong to someone else.'

'My mother says I am to leave Ráth Bládhma, that I will live in a fortress far from Glenn Ceoch and never see you or Bodhmhall again. Is she telling the full truth?'

Liath Luachra returned to scrubbing her feet. 'She is probably telling the full truth as she sees it.'

Demne went very quiet and stared down at the ground. The woman warrior glanced sideways at him and saw that he was trembling and his face had gone very pale.

With a grunt, she got to her feet. 'Perhaps this is a good time to give you something.' She started across the *lis* in the direction of her roundhouse, trailed by Demne's haunted eyes. Her flax backpack lay against the wall by the entrance way and as she knelt to rummage through it, she could hear Bodhmhall and the others arguing inside. The voices were heated and full of emotion, not anger so much as concern and fear.

Ignoring them, she pulled an object wrapped in dock leaves from the basket and returned to where the boy was waiting. His face was still pale and his lip quivered but his eyes held an unmistakable trace of curiosity. She held out the package. 'This is for you.'

Demne looked at it and then at her. 'What is it?'

'A weapon.'

'A weapon?' His eyes widened.

'You are no longer a child of the hearth ashes. Tomorrow you go Out. You travel in the Great Wild so you will need a weapon of your own, something more threatening than the wooden sword we practise with.'

Face bright with suppressed excitement, he took the package and started to rip it apart, tossing the torn leaves aside until the contents were exposed: a hand-woven flax cradle attached to two separate lengths of braided flax and a small leather bag.

'It's a sling.' The boy's voice was flat.

Liath Luachra scowled. 'Do you want a weapon or do you not?'

'I want a real weapon. A man's weapon.'

'You're too small to fight with a full-grown man's weapon. You need something you can use from a distance. Something that's accurate and fast but allows you to flee if you miss.'

The boy's eye brightened at that. 'I could use a javelin. Or a harpoon. Like Aodhán.'

She shook her head. 'No. You're too small. Your cast would lack force.'

'Bran's small. And he casts javelins.'

'He's bigger than you. And he's had practice casting javelins for many years.' There was no give in the woman warrior's voice. For her, at least, the subject was closed. She picked up the leather bag, undid the leather string that bound the opening. 'Hold out your hand.'

Demne did as he was told and she poured a number of smooth, pigeon-egg sized stones into his palm. Each individual stone had been painstakingly decorated with small carvings, basic but creative depictions of wild-fern curls, bird's wings, or badger claws.

Demne stared at them, intrigued and suddenly looking more impressed. Noting his expression, the woman warrior put the leather pouch aside. 'These stones ... They are not playthings, do you understand? They are carriers of death and should be respected as such.'

The boy reluctantly dragged his eyes away from the stones and glanced up to give a half-hearted nod before his attention turned once more to his gifts.

'The sling carries no name for it does not draw blood. It is the stones – the bullets – that do that.' Liath Luachra took the sling from his hand and hefted its weight in hers. 'Don't underestimate this weapon. The fools do, the loose-mouths who brag about close quarter fighting. Close quarter fighting's all hack and cut. It doesn't matter how skilled you are. It all comes down to brute force and strength and it's only a question of time before you get cut.'

She grew silent for a moment, haunted by some distant memory until she realised, with a start, that Demne was waiting for her to continue. She drew herself up straight. 'With practice, a good sling cast can hit a man at seventy paces and kill him dead. Even if he's wearing leather armour the blow from a stone will break him on the inside.'

She reached over to pluck one of the bullets from his hand and dropped it into the cradle. 'The sling stone is placed in the cradle, like so. You see how I have cut a slit. That allows the flax to fold around the bullet to hold it more securely.'

Demne peered closely. 'I see, Grey One.'

'Put your middle finger through the loop at the end of this length of flax. The other length has a release tab that you hold between your thumb and forefinger, like so. When you're ready, you swing your sling to build up speed, then flick your wrist to release the tab and the bullet flies out to hit the target.'

The woman warrior got to her feet. Turning towards the southern embankment, away from the sleeping *Lamhraighe* warriors, she slowly started to swing the sling in a vertical loop, adjusting her position until she was facing the lean-to where firewood, tools and other items were stored. To the left of the lean-to was a wide, flat section of wood used as a base for chopping wood. Standing on top was a solitary wedge of firewood.

73

'You see the wood there, waiting to be split?'

Demne nodded.

Using the momentum of the arc, Liath Luachra snapped the sling upwards, releasing the tab at the exact same time. The discharged bullet flew through the air, smashing the firewood backwards off the base. Demne clapped enthusiastically, his earlier sorrow forgotten. Off to the side of the *lis*, one of the *Lamhraighe* warriors cursed and turned on his side, angrily drawing his cloak tight over his shoulder.

The woman warrior bent down and started to wrap the sling about the boy's forearm. 'This way,' she explained, 'you can carry your weapon at all times.'

Demne looked up at her shyly. 'Thank you, Grey One. This truly is a wondrous gift.'

He moved as though to hug her but the woman warrior quickly shifted backwards. 'The sling extends the strength and the length of your arm,' she said hurriedly. 'That means you can cast your shot farther and faster than you would if you tried to throw it by hand. If you cast from higher ground you can increase that range. If you have enough comrades you can create a hailstorm of stone that no force will resist.'

Demne stared at her, confused and unsure how to respond to the woman warrior's sudden coldness. Liath Luachra, meanwhile, continued with her awkward lecture. 'You might wonder why the flax cords are braided. That would be a good question. It's because the braiding stops the flax from twisting when it's stretched. It improves the accuracy of-'

'Liath Luachra.'

Taken by surprise, the woman warrior turned to find Bodhmhall standing beside her.

'The Council is done,' the *bandraoi* told her. 'But we should talk.'

Liath Luachra frowned, annoyed at being taken by surprise.

Bodhmhall reached up out and ran her fingers through the woman warrior's hair where she'd slashed it with the knife. 'What have you done?'

'It's only hair.'

The other woman looked at her but it was difficult to guess what she was thinking. 'Yes. Aodhán informed the Council of your engagement with the scouts following Fintán mac Gleor.' She sighed. 'You should have told me what you had planned, *a rún*. I could have convinced Gleor to send some men with you.'

'By the time I'd decided to go out it was too late and you needed rest for your dealings with Muirne. Besides, Gleor's men would only have got in the way.'

Bodhmhall responded to that with a brief, infuriated look but from her body language it was evident that she was going to concede the point, on this occasion at least. 'Aodhán says that one of the watchers was not there. That he had already departed.'

'Yes.'

'That is ... unfortunate.'

Bodhmhall took a deep breath, and turned her gaze to Demne. Preoccupied with his gifts, the boy was oblivious of her examination. The *bandraoi* returned her attention to Liath Luachra. 'We should go inside. We have plans to discuss.'

'Very well. Let me just -.' The woman warrior stiffened.

Bodhmhall, perceptive as ever, picked up on her reaction almost immediately. 'What? What is it?' She turned, following Liath Luachra's gaze to the eastern side of the *ráth* where a single rook was perched on one of the pilings, staring down into the *lis*.

The woman warrior swallowed, her eyes fixed on the distant bird. 'I saw that rook earlier today. Before the engagement with the scouts.'

'You are certain it is the same? These birds are much alike.'

'It's the same. I recognise the white spot on its breast.'

Liath Luachra continued to stare. For some reason, the rook's reappearance unsettled her, put her on edge. 'I do not like this, Bodhmhall. I do not like that Muirne and our so-called allies have come to take your nephew. I do not like that we are to venture through unknown lands to a fortress that bears us no love. And, most of all, I dislike the portents the Great Wild offers me.'

Bodhmhall looked at her, saying nothing but her concern plain on her face. 'Demne, go and help Lí Bán and the other children prepare breakfast for our guests.

'Aah, *a Aintín* ...' His voice was plaintive as he looked up to plead his case. Seeing the expression on her face, he stopped dead. He had seen that face before. He knew there would be no discussion.

***

'You should not push him away.'

Unstrapping her belt and sword, Liath Luachra stared blankly at the other woman.

'Demne,' the *bandraoi* explained. 'You should not push him away. He likes you. He respects you.'

Liath Luachra turned away with a bleary lack of enthusiasm. Shaken by the sight of the rook and worn with fatigue, she was in no mind for such discussions. She said nothing as she stripped out of her battle harness and hung it on the wooden stand she'd constructed specifically to support it. With a stab of frustration, she saw that several small traces of blood still stained the leather.

'We have plans to prepare, Bodhmhall. That should be our priority.'

The *Cailleach Dubh* sighed. 'Very well. But lie down, dear one. You look spent. We can talk while you rest.'

The woman warrior needed no further persuasion to climb onto the sleeping platform and lie on her stomach across the furs. As she lay there, she listened to the *bandraoi* bustle about at her 'herb' shelf before joining her on the bed, a bowl of scented oil in her hands. She heard the quiet 'slurp' as Bodhmhall dipped her fingers into the bowl, the slick crinkling noise as she moistened her palms, then her hands were on her shoulders, massaging deep into the muscle tissue. Liath Luachra sighed and closed her eyes, giving into the sensation. This was an old and familiar routine between them, a comfortable intimacy she'd never shared with anyone but Bodhmhall.

'If one of the scouts has departed,' the *bandraoi* said suddenly, 'we can assume that whoever sent them will soon know of Muirne's presence here. And subsequently, Demne's.'

'That would seem to be the way of it.' Liath Luachra's confirmation was muffled so she raised her face out of the furs. 'Bodhmhall, have you thought through the wisdom of leaving the protection of Ráth Bládhma?'

As though in response, the *bandraoi*'s fingers delved down into a tender spot under her left shoulder blade – an old injury – expertly locating the knotted muscle hidden beneath her skin. Liath Luachra hissed but swallowed the pain.

'I have. These events – the invitation from my father, the visit from Muirne, the secret watchers in the forest – they all come about at the instigation of the Adversary. His interest lies solely with my nephew. If Demne is no longer present at Ráth Bládhma, then our home will no longer draw his enmity. It will remain safe.'

'But we will not. Out in the Great Wild, we're exposed to whatever machination the Adversary prepares. We will not have the walls or the javelins of Ráth Bládhma to protect us.'

Bodhmhall did not respond for several moments, focussed on kneading the tension from the woman warrior's back. When she finally did speak again, her voice was laden with evident distress. 'Grey One, you know as well as I that we won't survive another assault like the *fian's*. The walls and javelins of Ráth Bládhma are not enough to protect us this time.' She grunted briefly, fingers probing deep into Liath Luachra's shoulder muscle. The woman warrior winced but remained silent, allowing Bodhmhall to continue.

'No. This time, the fight takes place beyond Glenn Ceoch and our best option is to travel to Dún Baoiscne. If we accompany the *Lamhraighe* party, we not only stay close to Demne but make use of the additional protection from Gleor's warriors.'

'And when we get to Dún Baoiscne?'

'Dún Baoiscne is the weakness of my plan.' Bodhmhall's admission was reluctant but characteristically forthright. 'With the Adversary's previous attack, we knew at least what we were facing: a direct assault from the *fian* and the Tainted One. This time, his approach is much more subtle, his manoeuvers too unclear to counter. The prospect of returning to Dún Baoiscne, no matter how unpleasant, allows us to change the placement of the pegs on the *fidchell* board. It is the only scheme I can think of to destabilise his intent while giving us the opportunity to learn more of the threat we face.'

The Grey One twisted her head to look up at the *bandraoi*. 'The message from Tréanmór. The timing could not be more suspect. My every instinct tells me that …' She lapsed into silence.

The *bandraoi* allowed her hands to drop to her side. 'I share your misgivings, *a rún*, but the same reasoning still holds true. We can protect Demne more effectively if we travel with Gleor and Muirne. That way, at least, we have allies by our side if there is any attempt at treachery. But,' she paused. 'My father is many things but subtle he is not. He is not one who would play machinations. If he truly had an interest in Demne, he would be forthright and demand to take him.'

Her face took on a distant expression as her thoughts drifted inwards. After a moment, her eyes cleared once more and she turned a sad smile to Liath Luachra. 'To be honest, I'm unclear as to the true nature of the influence we have over the child. At Demne's birth my *Gift* revealed his linkage to the future of *Clann Baoiscne* so we cannot avoid what is inevitable. My hope is that we can at least sway the lines in which it is played out.'

Liath Luachra allowed herself to be pushed gently back onto the furs. As the *bandraoi* massaged her legs and thighs she gradually allowed herself to relax. Silence swelled within the dwelling and the air, already warm, grew even warmer as the small blaze in the fire pit fire crackled and burned. Liath Luachra found herself becoming drowsy, only vaguely conscious of Bodhmhall's hands mapping the contours of her spine.

At some point she must have drifted off for she was roused by the sound of the *bandraoi* placing the wooden bowl onto the floor. Peering through her eyelids, she saw that the fire had all but died and the room was almost dark, although a crack of daylight still glowed warm and yellow beneath the leather flap at the entrance. Bodhmhall had stopped kneading her back muscles but she could feel her fingertips trail the crusted lines of scar tissue running from the back of her neck to the curve of her left hip.

'Why do you like me, Bodhmhall? I am so very broken.'

'You're not broken, *a rún*. Beaten perhaps. Or poorly used. But not broken.'

'I feel that I'm missing many pieces.'

The *Cailleach Dubh* gently caressed her shoulder. 'We are all missing some part of ourselves, dear one. I believe these are mostly the pieces of the person we aspire to be. You know you are dear to me as you are. You are tough and quiet and as beautiful as the smoothest river stone. Your presence by my side gives me courage and makes me better than I am.'

Liath Luachra kept her eyes closed but the *bandraoi's* words caused something to twist inside her. She gave a sad laugh.

'There is something else, Grey One. I can tell something weighs on your heart.'

The warrior woman stiffened and rolled over to look up at her with an expression of wounded apprehension.

'I am *An Cailleach Dubh*,' the *bandraoi* intoned with mock solemnity. 'The Black Hag. I see deep into the souls of all and read their innermost thoughts.' Observing the troubled look in Liath Luachra's eye, she paused. 'It is not the *Gift*,' she reassured her. 'I do not need *An tíolacadh* to know when something troubles you.'

Liath Luachra continued to regard her with a wary eye. The *Cailleach Dubh* sat back on her haunches, hands in her lap, waiting.

After a moment, Liath Luachra sighed and sat up too. She avoided the *bandraoi's* eyes as she pulled a light tunic on over her head. When she was dressed she coughed and cleared her throat, delaying the response that had suddenly proven much more difficult than she'd expected. 'I see things out in the Great Wild,' she said at last. 'Not just the rook but other things as well.'

Bodhmhall held her eyes but said nothing, allowing her the space to continue in her own time.

'Two days ago – the same day I met Fintán mac Gleor – I saw something, something I've never seen before. With the arrival of the *techtaire* and everything that's happened since, I've not had opportunity to speak of it to you.' She paused, opened her mouth to continue then closed it again.

'What did you see?' asked Bodhmhall.

'Butterflies.'

'Butterflies?'

'A swarm of butterflies. So many of them they blotted out the sun.'

The woman warrior proceeded to describe her experience at An Folamh Mór, outlining the events in detail from her first sight of the swarm to its subsequent dispersal against the great oak. When she'd finished her tale she stared bleakly at the *bandraoi*. 'I don't know what it means, Bodhmhall.'

Bodhmhall chewed on her lower lip and was silent for a time. Liath Luachra could see that she was thinking through what she'd been told so she forced herself to remain patient until the *bandraoi* had completed her deliberations. After what seemed like an insufferably long period of time, she finally raised her head to face the woman warrior.

'There are two possible interpretations.'

Liath Luachra studied the *bandraoi*'s face, wondering why her voice sounded so hesitant, so guarded.

'The first interpretation is that it means nothing at all. What you saw is simply the Great Mother doing as she must do. Despite all our travels and our so-called accomplishments, the truth is that we're little more than fleas on the Great Mother's hide. We catch glimpses and scraps of what the Great Wild contains but we understand even less of it.'

'So you ascribe no significance to their behaviour.'

'I wouldn't say that. I ascribe significance to it but I think its significance has more relevance to the butterflies than to the person who observes them. The activities of butterflies mean as little to us as our behaviour means to them. We tread different worlds, different levels of interaction and awareness.'

'But the *draoi*, the druidic order ... They say that the actions of one world is reflected in another.'

Bodhmhall nodded. 'They do say that,' she said quietly.

'You do not believe them.'

The *bandraoi* took several moments to construct her response. 'The *draoi* say many things, some of which is true, some of which I know to be completely false.'

Liath Luachra scowled. She knew that Bodhmhall would never lie to her but her past experiences with the druidic order meant that she could be extremely cynical of their assertions, the contentions and concepts that most others accepted as fact. Such questioning of the established foundations made one's comprehension of the world that much more difficult. 'And the second interpretation?' she asked.

'What?'

'You said there was a second interpretation.'

'Ah, yes.' To her surprise, Bodhmhall reached over and took her hand, stroking the calloused palm with those strong, dextrous fingers. 'The other interpretation is one told to me by Dub Tíre.' The *bandraoi* could not help grimacing at the use of her old teacher's name. 'You know I have reason to doubt much of what I was taught by the *draoi*. I cannot tell you if it is true or not and I do not wish to offer false comfort.'

'Yes?' Liath Luachra found herself growing increasingly curious at the other woman's obfuscation.

'Dub Tíre told me that butterflies act as messengers, similar to the way that rooks are said to deliver messages from the Great Mother.'

'Messages?' Despite the warmth of Bodhmhall's hand, Liath Luachra felt an inexplicable shiver run down her spine. 'Messages from who?'

Bodhmhall looked her straight in the eye. 'From those who have taken the Dark Leap. Our ancestors and those who have gone on before us.'

Liath Luachra gave her a blank stare. 'I don't understand. You are saying the dead are sending me messages. What does that mean? Why would the dead communicate with me in that manner?'

Bodhmhall sighed. 'It would mean,' she said with obvious lack of enthusiasm 'that someone you once loved, someone who has moved on, is sending you a greeting.'

'Bearach!'

The *bandraoi* winced. 'I cannot say, dear one. This is an interpretation and it would be best not to leap to those conclusions that make us feel better.'

The woman warrior ignored her. 'What would he be saying?'

Bodhmhall regarded her with anxious eyes. 'He would be saying,' she said, her voice laden with a reluctance that made it sound even deeper than usual. 'He would be saying "Do not be sad", dear one. He would be saying "We are happy. Do not mourn us."'

The warrior woman gasped and clutched the *bandraoi*'s fingers. Slowly she began to weep.

Chapter Five

At daybreak on the following morning, Bodhmhall assembled in the *lis* with Liath Luachra, Demne and the various members of the *Lamhraighe* party. The settlement was a bustle of activity as preparations were made to depart, the travellers packing up the last of their belongings and supplies, securing flax baskets and, of course, eating their final hearty meal for some time to come.

The full complement of *Muinntir Bládhma* was also up and about, gathered to offer the traditional hospitality expected of them but, more importantly, to bid farewell to Demne. The little boy had been crying since early that morning, finally comprehending that it was all actually happening, that he was leaving Ráth Bládhma and, in all likelihood, would never see most of these people again.

Beside the stone gateway, Bodhmhall gritted her teeth at the sight of the boy weeping as his friends approached in turn, to hug him, offer a small gift or a blessing. Although not a person normally roused to anger, the *bandraoi* was angry now, incensed by the political machinations of a self-centred woman and the impact they were having on someone she loved. Struggling to hide her emotions, she turned her gaze upwards to the slate-coloured sky. The drawn out farewells, already mournful, had been rendered even more despondent by a slick, grey drizzle that had eased in overnight and now dampened everything it touched with a fine mist.

'Bodhmhall.'

Pushing the anger down into her belly, she turned to find Aodhán, Morag and Lí Bán standing beside her.

My three lynch pins. The three I count on most to keep Ráth Bládhma safe while we are gone.

'Bodhmhall, we will miss you more than I can say. We ...' Lí Bán raised both hands in a despairing gesture as her words trailed off. Her eyes were red-rimmed and watery.

She looks tired.

The *bandraoi* kept her thoughts to herself but her *Gift* showed her that the older woman's internal flame had grown pale and subdued, very different from the brightness it'd exuded when she'd first come to Ráth Bládhma. She was jaded, worn down by a fatigue that was not only physical.

While she embraced the older woman, she caught a glimpse of Aodhán reaching over to clasp Morag's hand in his. That simple, intimate gesture stirred a melancholy warmth inside her. The Ráth Bládhma warrior and the youthful Coill Mór girl had been a couple for over five years – ever since the *fian* attack, in fact – and the great affection between them was evident.

She sighed as she stroked the older woman's hair. Everyone had coped with the consequences of that savage assault in a different way. Lí Bán with her children, Aodhán with Morag and the badly wounded Ferchar with the blond haired Cumann of Ráth Dearg. Traumatised by the savage attack on her home and the massacre of her kin, the latter had lost her voice and her reason for a long period of time. Although she'd recovered her wits for the most part, due to the kindness of her red haired warrior, to this day she remained unable to venture beyond the safety of the *ráth* without experiencing severe bouts of anxiety.

We are all survivors. All of us. Pieces of flotsam drifting in the water after the storm. That is Muinntir Bládhma

As she looked around at her people, her friends, the *bandraoi* felt an icy trickle down her spine. This journey to Dún Baoiscne would be her first major trek in almost six years. Following the destruction of the nearest neighbouring settlements, there had simply been no-one to visit for friendship or trading missions.

As for Dún Baoiscne …

Since her expulsion from the fortress some nine years earlier she'd never felt any desire to return. Even now, the thought of going back to her childhood home filled her with dread.

She kissed Lí Bán on the cheek. 'Be strong, Lí Bán. The children need you. They are your legacy.'

The old woman nodded and drew back. Glancing to one side, Bodhmhall saw that Na Lamhraighe were all a-bustle, loading baskets onto their backs, the warriors gripping their weapons, lining up to leave. To her surprise, she saw Gleor take a stand on one of the logs in the centre of the *lis*, Muirne by his side, and address the small crowd.

'We give you thanks, *Muinntir Bládhma*. For your bounteous hospitality, for your generosity but more importantly for the warmth of your friendship. We will not forget how you have welcomed us into your home and I tell you this; with Na Lamhraighe you will always have friends to the north.'

There was a subdued cheer from both the hosts and the visiting party then Marcán was abruptly rallying his men forward, urging them towards the gateway to exit the *ráth* in single file.

As Na Lamhraighe passed through the passage beside them, Aodhán drew close and threw his arms around her, hugging her tightly to him. When he finally released her, Morag, conspiratorially, pulled her to one side and whispered in her ear. 'There is something I should tell you, Bodhmhall.'

'You are with child. Yes, I know.'

The slender woman looked at her in surprise then comprehension registered in those dark blue eyes. 'Of course. *An tíolacadh*.' She nodded slowly. 'Sometimes I forget, Bodhmhall.'

Morag wrung her hands in the rough apron knotted about her waist. 'Lí Bán says that my pregnancy will run its course and that the birth will take place in mid-winter.' She hesitated and Bodhmhall winced inside. Morag and Aodhán had already lost one child through miscarriage and although she'd been present there had been nothing that she could do, nothing but look on helplessly as the baby's flame fluttered and died inside its mother's womb.

'Can you come back, Bodhmhall? To be with me. I think that if ...' Her voice trembled. Behind them the last of the *Lamhraighe* warriors disappeared though the gateway and Bodhmhall caught a glimpse of Demne, hand gripped tightly in Muirne Muncháem's, staring desperately in her direction.

'Bodhmhall! Bodhmhall!'

'Torn, the *bandraoi* quickly reached over to place a reassuring hand on Morag's arm. 'If you truly need me, Morag, I will be here. On that you have my word.'

She looked once more around the *lis*, ingraining the sight in her memory, each physical feature, the face of every individual. Her heart was breaking. 'Take care of my *lubgort*,' she said and followed the others through the gateway.

***

Led by Liath Luachra, the party travelled quickly, taking the trail out of Glenn Ceoch then turning north towards the rough forest country of Tobar Íseal. The resolute warrior woman led them at a demanding pace, keen to make as much distance from the settlement as possible. Bodhmhall could tell that she was worried about the surviving scout. Given their numbers, it would be tough to disguise the evidence of their departure and their trail would not be difficult to follow.

The *bandraoi* gnawed on her lower lip as she followed the warrior ahead of her. She was of two minds about that, unable to decide whether it was a good thing or a bad thing. Although keen to draw any threat away from Ráth Bládhma, the prospect of being pursued through the rough terrain of the Great Wild did not appeal either.

A fresh shower sprinkled over the Company but it was light and did not last long. They were fortunate in that the cloud kept the worst of the sun's heat at bay while the intermittent drizzle did little more than cool their faces.

At the edge of Tobar Íseal, the party entered territory for which they had no name, crossing the narrow waters of the fast-flowing river that *Muinntir Bládhma* considered a natural boundary for the majority of their interaction with the Great Wild. On the far bank, Liath Luachra split the party into three groups, instructing each to make their separate ways up the forested slopes to a meeting point on a distant hill. Moving slowly, the reduced numbers would allow each group to work more effectively at concealing the traces of their passing.

Bodhmhall travelled with Demne, Muirne and Marcán who did most of the work to cover their tracks. They progressed slowly towards the meeting point. It was arduous work and Bodhmhall knew the success of the ploy would, to a large extent, depend on the tracking skills of their pursuers – if indeed, there were any pursuers. The lack of certainty was frustrating. Nevertheless, Liath Luachra felt the precaution was worth the effort and she was not going to second guess her *conradh* on such issues.

At a rocky crest on top of the hill, they rested briefly, chewing on hard tack and dried fish. A short time later, they recommenced their journey in a westerly direction, following difficult, roundabout trails that only Liath Luachra was in any way familiar with.

That night they camped in a deep cave set in the cleft of a steep hill. The cave was fronted by a wide semicircular clearing, surrounded in turn by a thick stand of beech trees. Bodhmhall had camped there in the past with Liath Luachra on three separate occasions and because of its veiled, inaccessible location she felt confident that it was a safe site to pass the night.

Settling into the cave, they set up a campfire in a circle of small stones just inside the entrance, laying its base on the charred remnants of other campfires, many of them extremely ancient. Regarding the age-old cinders and stubs of burnt wood, Bodhmhall strongly doubted that anyone had passed this way or set a fire there since the last time she'd passed through.

Two of the *Lamhraighe* men set a small pot over the fire and started to cook up a stew using fat strips of pork and tubers provided by Ráth Bládhma that very morning. They worked with quiet efficiency and soon a mouthwatering smell wafted about the interior of the cave.

Marcán took responsibility for the Company's security, detailing two of his warriors to stand guard outside the wide cave entrance while the others ate. During the meal, Bodhmhall noticed the big man rise on three separate occasions to go outside and check with his men, staring intently at the surrounding forest before returning to the fire.

As daylight began to wane and sleeping rolls were laid out on makeshift beds of heather and fern collected from the clearing, Bodhmhall led Gleor deeper into the cave to show him the ancient cave paintings she'd discovered there on her previous visit. To her surprise, Muirne insisted on accompanying them.

Using a flaming torch constructed from oiled rags wrapped about a hard wooden baton, she had them follow her closely through the shadows, stepping carefully in the flickering light until they arrived at the large rock wall that marked the inner limits of the cavern. Bodhmhall raised the torch, brought it close to the vertical slab and heard Gleor gasp at the sight of the colourful paintings revealed in the wavering glow of the flames.

Many of the images were simple designs, bright red tracings of splayed hands, abstracts lines and circles daubed onto the rock in vibrant ochres, startling whites and fiery orange. Others – more complex – depicted small figures holding spears or animals, some familiar, others of a type that none of them had ever seen before.

It took them some time to examine the paintings for there were a substantial number spread not only all over the vertical slab but on the nearer rock faces as well. While they worked their way around, Muirne tapped her foot impatiently with the unsubtle suggestion of a return to the campfire. To her frustration, however, Gleor was displaying an almost reverential fascination for what he was seeing and insisted on remaining until he'd examined each individual image in detail. 'Have you seen such paintings before, Bodhmhall?' he asked the *bandraoi* in a voice that was tight with excitement.

Bodhmhall nodded. 'Yes. There were similar designs at a sacred cave in the hills near Dún Baoiscne. The druidic order forbade the people from entering but I saw them briefly during my initiation with Dub Tíre. They weren't as detailed or as vibrant as these paintings, though.'

'And do you know what those creatures are?' He pointed to an image of a ferocious looking creature with great claws and teeth and a very long tail.

She shook her head. 'No. I've heard stories of such animals in the hot lands across the seas to the south but I don't know if there's any truth to such tales.'

'They have a fearsome appearance.' Gleor tapped his lower lip repeatedly with the tip of his right forefinger as he stared at them. I would not like to encounter their likes out in the Great Wild. It would be a great - ?'

'We should return,' interrupted Muirne. 'Demne needs to rest. We have another long trek tomorrow.'

Bodhmhall looked at the woman in surprise. From her lips, such maternal concerns sounded both false and affected.

Gleor, too, did not appear to appreciate the interruption for he glared at her in irritation. 'Do not try my patience, woman. I have watched the boy march today. He carries no pack and he showed no sign of fatigue.'

The Flower of Almhu lapsed into resentful quiet and Bodhmhall did not need her *Gift* to recognise the intensity of offended fury she nursed in that silence.

When Gleor's curiosity with the cave paintings was finally sated, the trio returned to the campsite. There they found the sun was starting to descend behind the mountains to the west. The two warriors who'd been on watch were now taking their turn to eat, finishing off the remainder of the pork. Craon Dranntánach [Craon the Grumbler], a skinny warrior with red eyes and a constant frown proved to be well named for he complained incessantly about food growing cold. Tutal Caol, the second warrior and the youngest member of Gleor's bodyguard, simply scratched two circular tattoos on his upper arm and shrugged, completely inured to the complaints of his comrade.

Some moments later, Marcán entered the cave to join them and glanced curiously into the pot. 'That'll be the last of the fresh meat,' he remarked with a rueful expression. 'Unless we hunt game on our travels to Dún Baoiscne.'

'We'll have little enough time for hunting at the pace we travel,' muttered Craon Dranntánach. Nobody else said anything but Bodhmhall noticed one or two of the other *Lamhraighe* warriors nod in silent agreement.

Moving out closer to the cave entrance, she took a seat on a smooth rock that overlooked the clearing and sat there rearranging the contents of her basket. On leaving Ráth Bládhma, the container had been laden with meat but as a result of the meal, it was now much lighter, something she knew she would be grateful for when she hoisted it on her back the following morning.

'It is a pleasant evening.'

Bodhmhall looked up, startled, as Muirne Muncháem settled down on the rock beside her, a small leather pouch clutched in both hands.

What does she want?

She regarded the younger woman and forced herself to maintain a neutral expression. The two women had barely acknowledged each other's presence over the course of the day and then only at times when the presence of others required them to be civil. Despite her resentment towards Muirne, the *bandraoi* knew she had to put her animosity to one side. A long and dangerous trail lay ahead of them before they reached the safety of *Clann Baoiscne* territory. Like it or not, she knew they'd be obliged to work together to survive that journey. It would also be critical to maintain some form of relationship with Demne's mother if she wanted to retain access to her nephew at Dún Baoiscne.

'Yes,' she said. 'It is very pleasant.'

'I offer you my earnest gratitude, Bodhmhall.'

The *Cailleach Dubh* raised her head and stared at Muirne with undisguised scepticism.

'For taking care of my son,' the other woman explained. 'I am not so foolish to believe you did this out of love for me but I cannot fault you on your rearing. The boy is polite and clear-spoken. You have raised him well.'

Unsure how to respond, Bodhmhall settled for acknowledging the compliment with a simple dip of her head.

'I had feared you would poison him against me,' Muirne continued in a low voice. 'But you did not. My son treats me as a stranger which is to be expected. But not as an enemy.'

Bodhmhall sighed and put her basket to one side. 'Demne has wisdom beyond his years. He would work out his own mind in years to come, in any case.'

'Wisdom beyond his years?'

'Yes.'

Muirne gave a soft grunt. 'Then, I will gladly accept credit for that. After all, he takes after my side of the family.'

Bodhmhall scratched her nose and smiled at the joke.

'You've never spoken much of your family. I know the fortress of Almhu is much admired and your father is said to be a powerful lord but its distance from Ráth Bládhma meant there was little interaction between our peoples when I was a child. Do you have many brothers and sisters?'

'None.'

Bodhmhall looked at her in surprise. If Muirne had no siblings that meant Almhu had a single female heir. She could imagine the intense interest such a situation must have provoked amongst the neighbouring tribes. Not to mention the potential for internal power struggles it would have created within Almhu itself.

Tréanmór's great yearning to align my brother to their house makes that much more sense now.

'Does that situation not concern your father?'

Muirne pulled some colourful flowers from her leather pouch and arranged them in a row on a flattish rock in front of her. 'It has never previously caused him concern. My father has always assured me that he will retain ownership of Almhu. Long after I have died.'

Astounded, Bodhmhall simply stared at her.

Tréanmór was clearly ignorant of that particular piece of information.

'No doubt he intends to live forever.' Muirne's voice held a distinct trace of bitterness.

An energetic whoop from Demne caused both women to look up and stare across the clearing to where the boy was preparing to engage in mock combat with Liath Luachra. Both had taken up position on opposite sides of a broad oak tree and held a wiry ash plant stripped of leaves.'

'What are they doing?' Muirne's voice had hardened, the ease of the previous moments fading faster than the sunlight.

Observing Demne's huge grin of pleasure beneath that crown of golden hair, Bodhmhall felt a gentle sadness run through her. 'Soft now, Muirne. They are playing.'

'Playing?'

'It is a game. A game Liath Luachra created to train your child in martial skills. The goal is to chase your opponent around the tree and slap him on the buttocks with your weapon – the ash plant.'

The tension in the Flower of Almhu's stance did not ease. 'How does such an exercise teach martial skills?'

'Liath Luachra says it teaches flexibility and balance. Apparently, it also helps to control the risks of overextending one's weapon. In any case, it's amusing to watch. Quiet, now. We will observe and you can see for yourself.'

With evident effort, Muirne sat back, her hands in her lap and stared gravely at the two opponents. '*Réidh,*' they heard Liath Luachra call, her voice surprisingly soft in the dappled evening air. Ready.

'*Ar aghaidh!*' Go!

She lunged and, at the same instant, Demne took off around the girth of the tree. The Grey One was immediately after him, moving in a tight circle as she attempted to catch up with the boy. Because of his smaller size, Demne had the advantage of being able to circle the tree with less momentum and, subsequently, more control. Liath Luachra, however, with her natural athleticism, was also very fast.

As the light bleached and dulled, they continued to chase each other about the tree and although Liath Luachra got the majority of strikes in, there were several instances where the boy managed to strike her buttocks as well and not always because she let him.

Finally, exhausted, the boy fell to the ground with a groan.

'Enough, Liath Luachra.' His groan was surprisingly loud. '*Tá tuirse orm.* I'm tired.'

'Is the bear tired on the hunt?' was the woman warrior's response. 'Is the wolf tired when he chases his prey? If the wolf is tired, does he eat?'

'No.' A softer, slightly sullen admission.

'Well, then.'

'Demne!'

The boy and the woman warrior turned to stare at the cave. Focussed on the pair's activities, Bodhmhall too was taken by surprise. Beside her, the Flower of Almhu had risen to her feet and was standing stiffly, glaring out at her son.

'Come, Demne. It is time to sleep and you wear yourself out. Lie here by me.' She pointed to the bedroll she had laid out alongside her own.'

'Muirne,' said Bodhmhall hurriedly. 'This is not necessary. You can-.'

The Flower of Almhu whipped around on her. 'You are not his mother,' she snapped.

Across the clearing Demne regarded them in alarm, his face pale, his expression terse. Muirne transferred her attention to the woman warrior. 'Liath Luachra, I must ask you to leave my son be. Demne is tired and does not need these … games.'

Bodhmhall was suddenly aware of the silence within the cave. The *Lamhraighe* Company had gone very quiet and were watching the interaction intently. She threw a glance towards Gleor who was sitting on a rock by the fire, sharpening his sword. Catching her glance, he slowly shook his head.

Head down, Demne grudgingly turned towards his mother. Entering the cave, he went to his bedroll and wordlessly lay down, turning on his side to face the rocky wall. Bodhmhall looked out to where Liath Luachra was still standing by the oak tree, glaring at Muirne with an expression of utmost contempt. Without a word, she turned to walk into the trees and disappeared from sight. Furious, the *bandraoi* spun around to confront the younger woman.

'You did not need to do that. You do more harm than good.'

'I have told you once. You are not his mother.

'But I am his aunt and I have raised him quite well, as you saw fit to mention just a moment ago. What you are doing is wrong.'

'I must do as I believe fit. I am simply attempting to fulfil my duty as a parent.'

'No,' said Bodhmhall. 'You are acting out of spite, out of fear at Liath Luachra's influence with the boy. To make matters worse, you were also trying to establish your own dominance.' She got to her feet, intent on following the warrior woman. 'If you truly wish to make an enemy of your child, Muirne, then you are well on your way to achieving that goal.'

***

The following morning the Company set off later than Bodhmhall would have expected but she was grateful for that for she'd passed a restless night. Her efforts to locate Liath Luachra the previous evening had proven fruitless and when she'd finally managed to fall asleep a strange and disturbing dream concerning a solitary standing stone was rendered even more upsetting with fearful images of the woman warrior in distress and danger.

She awoke before dawn to find, much to her relief, that Liath Luachra had finally returned. The Grey One sat quietly by the fire, munching a breakfast of cold porridge and ignoring the others as they woke and started to pack their belongings. It was only as they prepared to depart that she finally spoke, and then only to insist they delay their departure until the sun had risen higher in the sky.

When they eventually left the cave and entered the forest, they were headed in a northerly direction and the reason for the Grey One's delay soon became apparent. Less than a hundred paces into the trees, the forest was already dark and coated in shadow, the visibility hampered by the closeness of the trees and the dense canopy overhead. If they had left earlier, Bodhmhall realised, they would have struggled to see anything. As it was, what little sunlight penetrated the trees was filtered to little more than a mildewed greenish hue.

Moving carefully, Liath Luachra led them along a deer trail so narrow that they were obliged to walk single file, constantly brushing back the slimy branches and damp undergrowth that threatened to choke what little space remained. Bodhmhall sniffed the air for it was dank and moist, heavy with the smell of rotting wood, mould and other odours she couldn't clearly distinguish.

Over the course of the morning the travellers followed the woman warrior, their world constricted to a constantly weaving tunnel of green-brown walls, occasionally relived by short stretches of uneven trail coated with layers of decayed leaves. It didn't take long for an uneasy silence to settle over the Company. The claustrophobic nature of their surroundings was hardly conducive to conversation and it was difficult to talk with the person in front or behind while trying to avoid the tree roots and other obstructions. Nevertheless, the forest was not a silent place. Bodhmhall could hear the regular drone of insects, the never-ending chatter and chirp of birdsong and, occasionally, the startled movement of larger animals scurrying unseen behind the dense foliage on either side. At one point, curious, she drew on her *Gift* to examine her surroundings and her sight revealed a world that glittered and sparkled with lifelight more furious and more numerous than the stars in the night sky.

After a time, the sun became a distant memory above the impenetrable canopy. Bodhmhall found herself retreating further and further inside her own head, absorbed in her thoughts as her body automatically – almost hypnotically – followed the movement of the warrior in front of her.

Around mid-day, Liath Luachra, out of sight at the front of the column, called a halt and the weary travellers sank onto the damp forest floor to chew on some pre-cooked tubers and slices of smoked eel. Despite the respite from walking, the constrained surroundings meant that it was impossible to group together easily so the few, subdued conversations that started quickly reduced to a whisper before dying out altogether.

Once they had eaten and rested, the Company were quick to restart their journey. Everyone was feeling cowed by the oppressive surroundings, keen to make their way out as quickly as possible.

It was late afternoon when the path finally widened and the walls on either side began to thin, allowing some welcome sunlight to reach the weary travellers. Although the forest was still too thick to see far beyond their immediate surroundings, the additional brightness cheered their mood immensely and they advanced with a lighter step. As they continued onwards, Bodhmhall noticed that it was taking more of an effort to maintain the pace, as though they were climbing a very gradual incline. These suspicions were confirmed much later when the forest unexpectedly opened out onto sheer sky and the party found themselves standing at the top of a cliff overlooking a wide river.

The sheer impact of blue from the unclouded sky stretched out before them was, quite simply, spectacular. On the opposite bank of the waterway below, a thick stretch of woodland was compressed between the flowing waters and a steep hill where the forest diminished, tapering off into a number of individual clusters, set between patches of broken, stony ground. Beyond that there was nothing but unrestricted sky.

Bodhmhall and the others collapsed onto some boulders set several paces back from the edge of the precipice. A refreshingly cool wind snatched at her hair and wrinkled the thin material of her sleeveless dress. She sighed at the coolness of it for she hadn't realised how hard Liath Luachra had been pushing them. Her dress was glued to her back and she was breathing heavily. Undoing the tie that held her hair in place, she allowed it to fall free, whipped about by the wind for several moments before she bundled it back and replaced the tie once more.

Off to her right, she noticed Murine glance in her direction and scowl, one protective hand clasping Demne's knee. Since the previous evening's altercation, she'd avoided the *bandraoi*, making every effort to keep at least two warriors between her and her son at all times. The little boy threw a plaintive, almost desperate glance towards her but she could do little more than offer him a reassuring smile before sadly turning away.

'Bodhmhall.' She looked up to find Gleor by her side, a leather waterskin held out towards her. She accepted the container gratefully, gulping down several mouthfuls of the tepid liquid before handing it back.

'Thank you, Gleor.'

The grey-haired leader nodded as he reaffixed the plug. 'Your *conradh* drives us hard.'

'She will have her reasons.'

As though on cue, the woman warrior wandered back from the cliff edge to join them, lowering herself onto a smooth rock next to the one on which Bodhmhall was seated. She glanced from one to the other then slapped at her bare arm where a midge had drawn blood. 'We should continue on.'

The *rí* of *Na Lamhraighe* sighed. 'Our legs tremble from exertion, Grey One. We must rest a spell. Recover our strength.'

Bodhmhall watched as the woman warrior shook her head and Gleor frowned in response. 'Grey One, we have accepted you as our guide because Bodhmhall assured me your knowledge of the land would save us several days of travel. You do *not* lead this party.'

Liath Luachra's grey eyes hardened. 'I do not care to lead *Na Lamhraighe*. This is an issue of timing.'

'What are your thoughts, Grey One?' Bodhmhall interjected quickly, her *Gift* revealing the intensifying glow to Gleor's smouldering lifelight.

'We should follow the trail to the bottom of this cliff and ford the river. We can set our camp on the far bank and pass the remainder of the evening in rest.'

Gleor looked at her, his anger momentarily checked by his surprise. 'You wish to halt so soon?' He glanced up to check the position of the sun. 'The rays of gold stretch far. They will not fade for some time yet. We can still cover some ground before night falls.'

Liath Luachra shook her head again, this time pointing to the hill across the river. Although lower than the cliff where they were sitting, its bulk was still high enough to prevent them from seeing what lay beyond. 'The marshlands lie on the other side of that hill and stretch for a great distance. The traverse is slow and treacherous and we would not make firm ground before nightfall.' She sniffed and wiped her nose with the back of her hand. 'Crossing those marshes in the fading light is not something you would wish to attempt.'

Gleor considered her with a stony silence. 'Very well,' he said at last. 'Your reasoning seems sound and you make good sense. We will defer to your judgement.' He scratched absently at his beard. 'Was that the issue of timing you were referring to?'

'It was one. There was another.'

'And what was that?'

The woman warrior reached down to pick a yellow wildflower from the earth and began to pluck the petals from it, one by one. 'I set a pace that would bring us here before dark. That gives us the best opportunity to rest before we traverse the marshlands. By camping on the far bank tonight, we can leave, refreshed, at first light.'

Gleor nodded. 'Yes. Good.'

'Any pursuers on our trail are likely to arrive too late or too early to make the traverse. Either way, they will lose more ground than us working out the right time to cross.'

'Our pursuers.' Gleor Red Hand took a deep breath and subjected her to his most vexed look.

The woman warrior returned that look with one that could have been interpreted as downright disdainful. Bodhmhall was relieved she had the wit to hold her tongue.

'You remain convinced that some enemy wishes to bury a battle-axe in our heads. And yet there is no sign to support that.' He shot an exasperated glance at Bodhmhall, knowing that she shared this conviction.

'There are the scouts who followed your son,' the *bandraoi* reminded him.

'Who are more likely to form part of a bandit group.' The *rí* of *Na Lamhraighe* held her gaze with quiet certitude. 'Unless, of course, you have seen something that would convince me?' He transferred his gaze back to Liath Luachra. 'How about you, Grey One? You've been Out more than any of us. Have you come across any tracks? Any campfires? Anything that would give you cause to believe we are at risk?'

Liath Luachra glowered. 'They're probably still some distance behind us.'

Gleor rolled his eyes, causing the warrior woman to bristle. 'They will catch us eventually if we are not smarter than them.'

The grey-haired *rí* gave a long-suffering sigh. 'So you have nothing. Then my earlier words still hold. Even if any such pursuer exists – which I most strongly doubt – they would be foolish to menace us unless they have a substantial force. My warriors are battle-hardened, more than a match for anyone who would raise their hands against us.'

Liath Luachra shrugged and looked away. Bodhmhall leaned forward and presented the older man with her most intense regard. 'Gleor, the *fian* that the Adversary sent against us comprised almost forty men. You do not get more substantial than that.'

Gleor looked at her in exasperation, clearly irritated by her ongoing preoccupation with the Adversary. 'Bodhmhall, I love you like a daughter but on this issue I question your judgement. It is fear of losing Demne that puts dark shadows in your head. If you look into your heart you will see that this is true.'

***

That evening, after crossing the river, the Company camped on the far bank as Liath Luachra had suggested. The Lamhraighe party already had an established routine for the nightly camp preparations. Everyone had their assigned tasks and duties and did them without discussion or argument. Invariably, Marcán set a pair of sentinels in place while two others prepared the campfire and the utensils for eating. Each person was responsible for setting out their own bedrolls, most preferring to stay close to the fire, more out of habit than out of any real need of warmth in such calm conditions.

That evening, Fintán and one of the other warriors waded into the river and successfully speared a number of the many trout swimming in the shallows. These were steamed in leaves and the Company dined well on fresh fish washed down with river water.

While they were eating, Demne came to sit beside the *bandraoi*, ignoring his mother's angry looks. For a little while they were able to sit and pretend that nothing had changed, that they were simply chatting by a campfire as they had so often, discussing some of the sights they had seen during the day and wondering what those back in Ráth Bládhma would have made of them.

Although pleased to spend such time with her nephew, after a while the *bandraoi* felt obliged to send him back to Muirne to avoid the inevitable confrontation were he to remain by her side. The boy did so with great disinclination, a fact not missed by his mother.

Distressed, Bodhmhall retired to her bedroll under an elm tree removed from the rest of the Company. She sat there in bitter contemplation watching the darkness slide in to smother their surroundings. Liath Luachra had not yet returned from scouting the route towards the marshlands and, removed from her usual work and responsibilities at Ráth Bládhma, she felt isolated and helpless. Unfamiliar with the *Lamhraighe's* effective evening routines, she could not assist with even the most menial duties without getting in the way and, unlike Liath Luachra, she added little value in terms of defence or guidance. She had not trodden these lands and was as unfamiliar with them as her allies. Even with the reference of the sun and the stars, she had no more than a vague idea of their current position and absolutely no idea of the route they would have to take to reach their destination.

Contemplating her situation, she picked up a slender branch that lay beside her bedroll and absently tapped it against the side of her foot as she stared across at the campfire. Demne and his mother were engaged in conversation and their earlier enmity appeared to have been forgotten. Surprisingly, both looked at ease in each other's company. Watching Muirne reach out to stroke her nephew's head, she felt an immediate swell of jealousy, a great knotting of tension deep in her chest.

It is fear of losing Demne that puts dark shadows in your head.

She tapped her foot with the branch once more. Was it really that fear which put shadows in her head, she wondered. Was there a genuine risk to her nephews' safety or was she merely striking out at shadows as a result of some unconscious desperation?

She exhaled slowly.

94

It was true that she had no concrete evidence, that she was reacting to events based on instinct. In the years following the attack on her home six years earlier, she also knew those instincts had been pushed, gnawed at by her increased apprehension and suspicion.

She glowered at her nephew and his mother. They were laughing together now, responding to some joke from a beaming Gleor Red Hand who was amicably slapping Demne on the back. Muirne looked extremely content with her son. This despite the fact that, only a short time before, she'd sent him the evil eye for consorting with his aunt.

With a sudden surge of frustration, she tossed the branch aside.

No! It is deeper than that.

Muirne's growing closeness to the boy undoubtedly provoked a great bitterness but her conviction that danger threatened Demne was not derived from any emotional or intellectual provocation. Since their departure from Ráth Bládhma she'd been dogged by an unshakeable sense of menace. This more intense sense of foreboding was very much different from her normal fears for her nephew, possibly a premonition subtly induced by her *Gift* or even by sheer gut instinct. Whatever it was, she remained convinced that out there, in the Great Wild, they were treading towards the lip of a treacherous precipice. She did not know what danger threatened them and all she could do was share the anxiety of the smith's anvil.

Waiting for the hammer to fall.

'Bodhmhall.'

She jolted upright, alarmed by the unexpected voice even as she recognised it for Liath Luachra's. Without warning, a pair of arms encircled her waist from behind and two hands pressed firm and tight against her stomach.

'Grey One!' The *bandraoi* was startled, her annoyance at been taken unawares overtaken by her relief at the woman warrior's safe return and the prospect of distraction from her own melancholic musings. Reaching down to one of the hands on her stomach, she grasped it, entwining her fingers with those of the woman warrior's. 'You're late. I was concerned.'

'It pleases me that you still worry for me. Even after all these years.'

The *bandraoi* chuckled and the tightness lifted from her chest. She lay back against Liath Luachra's chest, tipping her head back as the woman warrior kissed her on the neck and hugged her close.

'I missed you.' The Grey One's voice was a whisper in her ear; husky, surprisingly needful. Bodhmhall felt the touch of warm breath against her cheek, the brush of lips down the nape of her neck. She shivered involuntarily as a tongue flicked out to lick the lobe of her ear.

A warm wind shifted around them and she could smell the Grey One's faint musk, the sage oil in her hair. The woman warrior's free hand pulled upwards then slid inside the armhole of the *bandraoi*'s tunic to cup her right breast, caressing the nipple between thumb and forefinger.

Bodhmhall's eyes flickered nervously towards the campfire, around which the body of the *Lamhraighe* party had gathered: Gleor, Muirne and Demne included. The sunlight had all but faded but she worried sufficient light remained that they could be observed. 'Too many eyes, Grey One.'

A warm breeze brushed over them, showering them with the scent of oak trees and fire smoke.

'Eyes that are blinded by the fire. They see nothing.'

Bodhmhall could feel her body tense, not only from desire but also by the prospect of being seen. An intensely private person, the thought of having her carnal pleasures witnessed by strangers was terrifying.

And yet she knew she needed it, the intimacy and the pleasure that would counter those feelings of despair.

I need it now.

She released Liath Luachra's other hand and felt it drop then ease up beneath the lower skirts of her dress. A warm palm slid over the tautness of her belly then dipped into the softness between her thighs. Here the hand paused momentarily over the thin material of her underclothes before slipping inside to form a cup around the heat of her mound. Bodhmhall stiffened, unable to prevent herself responding to the warrior woman's touch. She gave a soft gasp of pleasure, followed by a sharp intake of breath.

The *Gift* kicked in then as it always did, heightening her sensitivity to every physical sensation, magnifying her arousal to the touch of skin, the soft whisper of cloth, the catch of air in her throat as she responded to the Grey One's. Her back arched as she pressed back against the warrior woman's chest, clenching her teeth at the delicious swelling of pleasure. A hundred thousand fireflies burst inside her core and she shuddered, still held by the firm strength of Liath Luachra's hand.

***

For a long time after the heat of pleasure had faded, they lay together. By then, most of the Company had retired for the night, the campsite had grown silent and dark.

As she rested in the woman warrior's arms, savouring the lingering afterglow, Bodhmhall felt swathed in a lethargy, physically and emotionally at ease for what felt like the first time in many months. Danger awaited them ahead. And heartbreak. This much she knew. But, for now, such issues lay far away. For this moment, there was nothing she could influence, nothing she could do, nothing she had to respond to and that, in itself, was an unfamiliarly blissful situation.

96

Finally, pushing the woman warrior's arm aside, she sat up and got on her knees to fumble with the clasp of her backpack. Disturbed by the muted bustle, the woman warrior opened one eye and peered at her. 'What are you doing?'

'I'm preparing for the morning. I assume we leave at first light again.'

Liath Luachra remained lazing on the bedroll, one arm strewn across her forehead, brooding quietly as Bodhmhall packed the last of her belongings with the exception of the bedroll and her cloak which she'd sort the following morning.

The *bandraoi* turned, drawn by a soft mutter from the woman warrior. 'What did you say?'

'I said, this is an unpleasant undertaking.'

Bodhmhall gazed at her, struggling to make out the other woman's face in the darkness. 'What do you mean?'

'Our company is an unhappy one. Demne is weighed down by sadness. Muirne nurses her internal poisons and regards us with hatred. We travel an uncertain route to an unclear goal, pursued by an enemy we know nothing about.' She released a tight breath. 'And to make matters worse, the *Lamhraighe* resent both the route and the pace I suggest.'

'Gleor doesn't resent the route you set. He said as much on the far cliffs.'

'On that occasion, yes.' Liath Luachra made a dismissive gesture. 'But Gleor's judgement is swayed by his blood horn for Muirne Muncháem. And his own sense of self-importance. He's spent too many years commanding weaker men to wipe his arse.'

'I do not think Marcán a weak man. And from their looks the other warriors appear equally hardened.'

'Oh, they're hard. But they are on Gleor's leash, Marcán most of all. They follow his commands without question or challenge and thus are easily manipulated. They are weak men.'

'Do not dismiss Gleor so easily. He is a good man, a canny man. You do not lead your people on the nomad path without a clear head and sharp intellect.'

Liath Luachra said nothing but she was clearly unconvinced. They sat in silence for a time, the woman warrior's hand flat against the *bandraoi's* back.

'Could we have got it wrong, Bodhmhall?'

Despite herself, the *bandraoi* smiled. 'You are gracious, *a rún*. You mean, could I have got it wrong.'

'I do not doubt your judgement. I have never doubted your judgment.'

'Then you should, dear one. I am not infallible. I too need to be challenged. Otherwise are you not a Marcán to my Gleor?'

The woman warrior chuckled, a rare sound that filled Bodhmhall with fresh courage.

Silence fell again and they listened to the sounds of the night: the crackling of the camp fire, the breeze through the branches of the elm tree overhead. Somewhere in the distance an owl hooted.

'These marshlands mark the end of the territory familiar to me,' the woman warrior murmured softly. 'But I believe if we veer to the north on the far side of the marsh, four or five days of travel will bring us to the mountains where Bearna Garbh lies.'

Although Bodhmhall made no response, the woman warrior's words gave her pause for thought. If Liath Luachra had felt a need to articulate these facts out loud, it meant that she was genuinely uneasy about the route they were taking. Not that she'd never admit to that directly.

'You know the pass?'

'I know of it. From what I've heard, it is well-named. An Bearna Garbh – the Rough Pass. It's little more than a cutting on the saddle of a hill that's wide enough for fewer than ten men to stand abreast. The problem is that it's accessible from the west only through An Glenn Teann, a narrow valley that's said to run long and steep.'

Bodhmhall frowned, instinctively realising what bothered the warrior woman. 'Tréanmór's instruction to take this pass rather than the more familiar route concerns you.'

Liath Luachra shrugged. 'If there truly is a traitor at Dún Baoiscne the instruction makes sense. Any traitor would expect us to come from the easterly route and could effectively lay an ambush there.'

Bodhmhall sat quietly for several moments, mulling over the woman warrior's comments. 'It seems to me,' she said at last, 'that our party is most exposed to attack on this side of An Bearna Garbh. If we traverse the pass, we are that much closer to *Clann Baoiscne* territory and the risk to our pursuers is much greater.'

Liath Luachra nodded her agreement.

'So, if we can evade or hold our pursuers at bay until we reach the pass then our chances of delivering Demne safely to Dún Baoiscne are improved.' She lifted her eyes to regard the woman warrior intently. 'Is that a task that can be accomplished, Grey One?'

The warrior woman displayed no reaction, but Bodhmhall's familiarity with her habitual restraint allowed her to discern the other's disquiet.

'You do not know what you ask, Bodhmhall. I know nothing of the force that may be arraigned against us. I am ignorant of their strength and the nature of the threat they might pose.' She sat up, shifting uneasily on the thick wool of her bedroll. 'The task you set me is one that's hardly possible.'

And yet you achieved the impossible once before.

But at what a cost.

98

Bodhmhall reached over to place a hand on the woman warrior's shoulder. 'Forgive me, *a rún*. It is unreasonable to place such a burden on your shoulders. It would be unreasonable to place such a burden on any person.' She turned to stare out into the darkness and shivered. 'And yet I fear the task may fall to you alone to save us.'

Chapter Six

Three days after leaving the marshlands, Liath Luachra caught her first glimpse of the mountains. A distant flash of grey and blue against the horizon, they lay framed between a pair of tall oaks on the hill she was climbing.

Continuing up the forested incline, she followed a twisted path between the trunks and thick foliage, seeking a section of open ground that would allow her an unobstructed view of the surrounding countryside. After a frustratingly long period of time, she eventually located a site on the western slope sufficiently clear for her to get her bearings.

The mountains formed a solid smudge to the northwest, poking above an expanse of rocky flatland. The flatland stretched westwards from the edge of the forest, just visible from the clearing. It would take the Company about two days to reach the mountains, she estimated. Once they hit those slopes, however, they'd have to follow them south until they found the entrance to An Glenn Teann.

Taking a seat on a nearby boulder, Liath Luachra reached inside her tunic and withdrew a morsel of dried fish wrapped in green leaves, a residue of the previous night's meal. She popped the smoked flesh into her mouth, chewing half-heartedly on the gritty texture as she stared at the view spread out before her.

I should go back.

Despite this conclusion, a deep-rooted fatigue prevented her from rising. She tapped the heel of her foot idly against the smoothness of the boulder. She was tired. Very tired. Since taking on the responsibility for protecting the Company from attack, she'd spent increasingly long periods of time scouring the landscape ahead, then subsequently circling back to check for any sign of pursuit. Fortunately, because of the slower pace imposed by Muirne and Demne, she was able to move much faster than the main party, however the physical effort of continually covering so much ground was taking its toll.

With a growl, she flung the remnants of the fish deep into the forest canopy below her.

A key part of her concern stemmed from the fact that she could not depend on *Na Lamhraighe*. She had no faith in their ability to successfully defend themselves or, more importantly, to protect Bodhmhall and Demne.

Perhaps I am too harsh.

Hmm.

She mulled over that possibility for a time. She could not deny that Marcán and his men were experienced warriors. They comported themselves as fighting men should, always keeping their weapons to hand, always on their guard and ready to respond to attack.

No.

Even as she chewed on the flavour of that particular argument, she knew she didn't really believe it. She wasn't being too harsh. For all their combat experience, *Na Lamhraighe* lacked any kind of strategic appreciation of the risks associated with this particular trek. In a combat situation, the best fights were those you successfully avoided or manipulated so that they took place on ground of your choosing at the time of your choosing. This was how you gained the advantage and seized control of the combat's outcome.

Gleor Red Hand however, blinded by the possible advantages of a formal association with Dún Baoiscne, was placing too much faith in Tréanmór's guarantee. As a result, both he and Marcán seemed unwilling to entertain the possibility that a military force of any consequence could be preparing to align against them. On the two occasions she'd raised the possibility, they'd laughed at her concerns, confident of their ability to deal with any threat.

Na Lamhraighe operated in a very reactive manner, probably because that's what had always worked for them in the past. Unfortunately, this Company was not moving as a nomadic tribe through well-known territories, but as a small group through unfamiliar lands with a threat of untested strength lurking in the shadows.

As a result of her own history as leader of *Na Cinéaltaí* and her position as *conradh* for Ráth Bládhma, Liath Luachra was accustomed to making her own martial decisions and having those decisions put into effect. Her current standing within *Na Lamhraighe's* party, therefore, was galling in that she obviously had all the influence of a lowly shield basher. The previous evening, disgruntled and despairing, she'd attempted to convince Bodhmhall that they should take Demne and slip away into the night, leaving Gleor and Muirne to their own devices. They could, she'd argued, make their own way to Dún Baoiscne and be that much safer for it.

Bodhmhall, unfortunately, wasn't having any of it. She'd already thought the issues through before leaving Ráth Bládhma and although her final decision conflicted with Liath Luachra's thoughts on the matter, the woman warrior had to acknowledge that the *bandraoi's* rationale made sense. The *Cailleach Dubh* was a rarity in that she was able to think beyond the immediate threats and risks of this particular journey, to incorporate the strategic alliances and long term consequences associated with their arrival at Dún Baoiscne. Liath Luachra knew that, for her part, she was limited to the present. All she could do was continue scouting around the Company, trying to locate and nullify the threat before the threat found them.

With a sigh, she got to her feet.

It really was time to go back.

***

Leaving the clearing, she started back in the direction of the Company's previous campsite. She'd left well before dawn that morning but she knew that by now Bodhmhall and *Na Lamhraighe* would be well on their way, following the signs and indicators she'd left along the trail to guide them. Given their more restricted pace, she was confident that if she hurried, she could intercept them before noon.

But she was in no mind to hurry.

Striking back downhill, she caught a flash of sun striking a body of water some distance off to the north-east, a useful topographical reminder of the river she'd spotted earlier from the northern slope of the hill. Amending the angle of her downward trajectory, she veered towards it. Her waterskin was almost empty, her mouth was dry from the smoked fish and she hadn't seen any other major water source since leaving *Na Lamhraighe*.

She hit the river when she emerged from the forest, several hundred metres from the foot of the hill. That particular section of water was quite narrow but it ran swift and deep, the silver current surging furiously towards the west. Despite the force of the torrent, she could tell that the water level was much lower than normal. The main flow had retreated far from its outer banks, exposing large spreads of stones and silt on either side.

Clambering down the grassy northern bank, Liath Luachra crossed the gravelled surface to a point where a small mound of shale dipped into the waterway. There she crouched and refilled the waterskin. When the container was full, she stood and followed the stony surface towards a rocky promontory where the waterway curved around and out of sight.

She approached the outcrop with one eye scouring the gravel riverbed for stones that might potentially be used as slingshot. She also glanced up repeatedly to watch for movement on the terrain further along the bank. It was a movement on the opposite side of the river however, that caused her to stop in her tracks and stare.

Directly across the river, six strangers were standing quietly, gazing steadily back at her. Startled, her hand dropped to *Gléas Gan Ainm* but it was an automatic, unconscious reaction. Even as her hand touched the leather-thonged hilt she knew she was in no immediate danger because of the deep waterway between them.

The strangers immediately struck her as an odd grouping, all different shapes and sizes yet wearing similar grey, hooded cloaks that looked too heavy and uncomfortable for the heat of the day. Her eyes automatically scanned them for signs of danger, her gaze drawn initially to those who looked to pose the most significant threat. At first glance, this was a heavyset Man Pair who carried simple but solid-looking staves. Almost immediately she discounted them, her focus switching instead to the older, grey-bearded man and the more corpulent figure to the far right. Both of these individuals carried themselves with an air of assurance that distinguished them from their comrades. Even in this unusual encounter, the body language of the others suggested that they deferred to these men.

The distance between the two banks of shale could not have been more than twenty paces, within easy hailing distance. Despite this, none of the six uttered a single word, continuing instead to scrutinise her with a disturbingly dispassionate intensity. A shiver trickled down her spine. There was something odd about this group, something very, very wrong. The way they just stood there looking at her, it was as though ... as though ...

And then she had it. They were observing her with predatorial interest, their expressions eerily similar to that of a wolf eyeing up a solitary ewe.

One of the men – the tallest one – pulled his hood down to reveal a pale, bald pate. Ignoring her own scrutiny, he gazed judiciously up and down his side of the river bank as though seeking a ford where they could cross the water without danger. Completing his assessment, he raised his head to look her straight in the eye and, despite herself, Liath Luachra shuddered and felt a sudden instinctive urge to turn and flee.

Keeping a careful watch on the strangers, she took two steps backwards, the motion immediately prompting all six on the other bank to step forward in unison, advancing until they were at the edge of the bank.

She was suddenly extremely grateful for the torrent of water between them.

Liath Luachra felt as though a claw was being scraped down her insides. These men didn't look particularly dangerous but their menacing behaviour belied that impression and her instincts were screaming at her to get away.

Turning on her heel, she sprinted for the bank, the stones beneath her heels skittering and clattering in her wake. Clambering up onto the bank, she lunged for the tree line, feeling an immediate sense of relief as the forest closed in about her. There, crouched in shadow amongst the reassuringly familiar smells and noises, she finally felt safer.

With her flight, the six individuals appeared to lose interest for after a few moment's discussion they turned and headed, single file, along the bank in a westerly direction. She continued to watch them as they walked away, her focus unwavering as they approached that point where they'd become obscured by the promontory on her own side of the bank.

The first to disappear from sight was the old man, then the little one and the Man Pair. The corpulent one was next and then, just as the tall man was about to pass from view, he stopped and turned to look back in her direction. Despite the distance between them and the fact that he couldn't possibly have seen her, Liath Luachra hissed under her breath and pulled back, deeper into the shadows. The tall man continued to stare for several moments then, abruptly, turned and vanished from sight.

***

It was early afternoon when Liath Luachra reunited with the *Lamhraighe* party. By chance, the group had just stopped to rest on a craggy hill-top overlooking the land back to the south-east. As a result, she took the opportunity to sit with them and chew on cold hard tack as she described the terrain ahead and gave her opinion on the best route through the wilderness.

Gleor, as usual, questioned every detail of her report but even he seemed cheered to learn of their proximity to An Bearna Garbh. In fact, this news lifted everyone's spirits for now there was clear evidence of progress having been made and a potential end to their journey. According to the *techtaire*'s original directions, *Clann Baoiscne* territory was less than two to three day's trek from the far side of the pass. From that point, it wouldn't take more than a few day's travel to reach the fortress of Dún Baoiscne.

Before the woman warrior had finished eating, Bodhmhall approached and drew her aside, anxious to learn if she'd seen any sign of the Adversary's forces, any evidence she could bring to Gleor. Once again, Liath Luachra was forced to admit that she'd found nothing although she did describe her strange encounter on the riverbank.

Bodhmhall was nervous, not so much by the description of the six strangers but by the absence of any sign of a pursuing force. Taking a seat alongside the woman warrior, she poked half-heartedly at a small stone by her foot. 'It doesn't make sense,' she murmured to herself after a moment or two. 'The Adversary must surely attack on this side of the pass. The closer we get to *Clann Baoiscne* territory, the more precarious such a venture must become for him.'

Her statement led to a brief discussion on their options but neither woman was able to come up with an alternative to what they were currently doing. Eventually, their conversation was brought to a close when Demne approached, keen to show the Grey One the progress he'd made with his sling.

To humour the boy, the two women sat and watched as he completed one cast after another, pitching the bullets at a largish rock little more than

104

twenty paces away. Although the majority of his casts went wide, it couldn't be denied that his accuracy had improved over the course of the trek. Urged by Bodhmhall's unwavering stare to acknowledge the boy's progress, Liath Luachra nodded and awkwardly patted him on the back. 'Well done,' she said. 'That was well done.'

Delighted with her praise, Demne beamed and his smile was bright enough to challenge the sun.

***

Liath Luachra decided to remain behind when the Company finally moved on. The hill crest gave a rare uncluttered outlook over the path that *Na Lamhraighe* had taken that morning and any pursuers within striking distance, by necessity, would also have to follow that trail. If they did, the advantage of elevation would allow her to discern them from afar, long before they had any chance of seeing her.

When she told the others, only Marcán seemed surprised at her departure from the routine so rigorously adhered to over the previous days. Justifying her decision on the basis that she'd already marked the route the party should follow, she also hinted at a longing to obtain some fresh meat, something she could potentially achieve before catching them up later that evening.

Gleor, for his part, clearly suspected her true reasons for remaining behind. Refraining from comment however, he settled instead for a disapproving shake of the head as he passed her by.

She waved the Company off as they headed west and it wasn't long before the thick forest on the lower ground swallowed them up from view. Her last sight of them was of Demne waving furiously back at her before a hand grabbed him and dragged him into the trees. For a long time afterwards, although she couldn't see them she could hear the sound of their voices in the still air, punctuated by an occasional guffaw or a bark of laughter from one of the *Lamhraighe* men. With a sigh, she moved onto a flat ledge of rock that protruded out over the lee of the hill and settled down to wait.

She sat silent and unmoving, enjoying the caress of the wind against her face and through her hair. With nowhere to go and no immediate task to fulfil, she was free to breathe easily and savour the spectacular view of baggy white cumulus rolling ponderously across the sky. As ever, the Great Wild provided endless distraction for one who cared to watch. A falcon plunged out of the blue with startling speed to strike a passing wood pigeon, knocking it to the ground to be devoured at leisure. On a clearing below her vantage point, a family of hares played together, ignorant of the fox closing in through the high grass. Such was the conflicting nature of the

Great Wild, she reflected. Peace and beauty switching to violence and death at a moment's notice.

A sudden noise from the direction in which the Company had departed caused her to rise in one swift movement, hauling back a javelin in preparation to cast. As the noise – the shuffling of footsteps – continued, she relaxed and lowered the weapon. Whoever was coming did not seem to be a threat for he was certainly making no effort to mask his progress.

She was unable to repress a groan when Fintán mac Gleor emerged from the trees. The unenthusiastic response was not lost on the youth for he stood blinking at her, his brash assurance foundering on the cold, hard reef of that stony expression. For a moment, it looked as though he might turn about and disappear back into the trees but, ultimately, ego must have won over discomfort, for he stepped forward with fresh resolve.

'Liath Luachra.'

The woman warrior regarded him but did not respond. Despite his presence at Ráth Bládhma and their subsequent status as travelling companions, there'd been no single occurrence when the two had been alone together since their original encounter at An Folamh Mór. That situation hadn't been one that the woman warrior had gone out of her way to engineer but, at the same time, neither had it been one that initially displeased her. She was still smarting at the youth's clumsy advances and remained distinctly discomforted by his close resemblance to Bearach.

'I thought you might take pleasure from company.'

Liath Luachra shook her head. 'No.'

Her response had all the impact of a child's wooden sword on a metal shield. Seemingly oblivious to her frosty appraisal, Fintán held up a small leather pouch and shook it between his fingers. 'I bring a treat to tempt your taste buds.' With this, he opened the pouch and poured a pile of tiny, intensely dark-blue berries into his palm. 'Na fraocháin. [Billberries]. The full succulence of ripened summer.'

'My hunger is sated.'

This time her coldness could not be ignored. Fintán coughed as he poured the berries back into their pouch then slid the leather container inside his tunic. Shifting his weight awkwardly from one foot to the other, he shifted the topic of conversation just as gracelessly. 'You stay behind to ensure our party is not pursued?'

The woman warrior sighed. If someone like Fintán had worked out what she was up to, then it was highly likely her intentions were common knowledge amongst the others as well. She could feel her earlier calm evaporate, upended by the interruption of her solitude. 'Yes,' she answered through gritted teeth. 'If someone pursues us from our tracks at Glenn Ceoch, this is the route they must take. The Great Wild is vast but the easier routes of passage are surprisingly limited.'

'When we first met you directed me to Ráth Bládhma by an extended path although you knew of an easier route.'

Liath Luachra shrugged. 'As I recall it, you insisted you had sufficient directions from Muirne Muncháem.'

'She did not have your in-depth knowledge of the land. Or the other route.'

There didn't seem much point in continuing that particular line of discussion so Liath Luachra didn't. The youth waited, growing increasingly uncomfortable at the absence of any further response. 'I wish good relations with you, Grey One.'

She continued to regard him in flinty silence, wondering where he was taking the conversation.

'I … I like you. I would spend time with you.'

She considered Gleor's son with growing disbelief. Over the years, she'd had her fair share of male attention, ranging from the bawdiest of ballads to the more common drunken crotch grab. Never before however, had she been subjected to such a clumsy attempt at seduction.

'Fintán, I have relations with Bodhmhall ua Baoiscne.'

'But she is a woman!'

'And so?'

He stared at her in complete bewilderment. 'That makes no sense. I am attempting to offer you a taste of male companionship.'

She laughed at that, a reaction that took them both by surprise. She did not laugh often but for all that she had a surprisingly soft and lilting laugh. 'You believe me so ignorant of the pleasure wrestle?'

'I don't know,' he admitted. 'But I would happily share the warmth of your bed.'

With this, she stiffened, the fleeting humour in her eyes abruptly transformed to ice. 'There is no warmth to share.'

Confused by the oblique response, the *Lamhraighe* youth stood uncertainly, scratching his chin. 'You are difficult to read, Grey One. You say little and your eyes do not reflect the thoughts in your head.'

She returned his stare with impassive stillness, her apparent indifference concealing her incredulity. Could this youth truly be as foolish as he appeared? Flirting in such a manner with the partner of a close ally was an inevitable route to conflict, particularly where it was so clearly undesired. She shook her head in mute disbelief. When she'd first encountered Fintán at An Folamh More, his actions had reminded her of Fiacail mac Codhna. Now she could see that such a comparison was not entirely accurate. The Seiscenn Uarbhaoil man was a tomcat, a braggart and a wastrel but it couldn't be denied that he was an excellent fighter and a capable battle leader when he wasn't tripping over his own cock. Fintán by comparison, despite a similar swagger, had distinctly less credible competence.

Growing increasingly ill at ease from her continuing silence, the young man's forehead crinkled in frustration. 'It is a grand thing,' he said, 'to know the strength of a man's arms about you, the scent of a male filling your nostrils in the morning hours.'

Liath Luachra momentarily considered unsheathing her sword to terminate this inept conversation. Somehow, she managed to stifle that temptation. There was already enough tension within their Company without adding to it by killing the leader's only son.

You've changed. In the old days you wouldn't have worried about such consequences.

She placed her palm over the hilt of *Gléas Gan Ainm,* as though to prevent it from leaping out of the scabbard of its own accord. 'This is something you recommend from personal experience?'

'I have received no complaints,' he answered, the sarcasm whizzing, untouched, overhead.

The unexpected naivety of that response prompted a sudden surge of insight. The woman warrior folded her hands, cocked her head to one side and assessed him coldly.

'You are untasted.'

'What?'

'You are untasted. Fresh, green tree sap. You have not felt the brush of flower blossom lips, the touch of a smooth hand, have you?'

The young *Lamhraighe* warrior stiffened, straightened his back and glared at her. Undeterred, Liath Luachra continued to study his face, noting how his nostrils flared with each anxious, aggravated breath.

Fortunately he spared them both the embarrassment of a denial. Instead, turning on his heel, he walked away, back down the trail towards the forest. He reached the thick treeline surprisingly quickly, plunging directly into the bushy vegetation to disappear from sight.

He did not look back.

Liath Luachra continued to stare at the trembling foliage for some time afterwards, unsure if she was feeling regret at the bluntness of her words or satisfaction at having dampened the youth's unwanted attention. In the end, consoling herself with the knowledge that she had resolved the situation with unusual diplomacy, she retraced her steps to the lookout point, brushed the matter from her mind and settled down to wait.

While she was absent, the Great Wild seemed to have become surprisingly calm, displaying a restraint not normally seen until just before the fall of darkness. Down in the clearing, there was now no sign of the rabbits although she could just make out a smear of blood across the grass that hadn't been there earlier. The hawk too was nowhere to be seen although she did hear an avian squawk somewhere in the distance. A breeze fluttered the leaves down the path where Fintán had disappeared but on the route taken by the Company that morning there was no trace of movement.

Gathering her long black hair up into a tight pair of plaits, Liath Luachra chewed on the inside of her cheek, watching where the trail faded into forest.

'Where are you?' she wondered.

***

The Company reached the edge of the forest late the following morning. It was the wind that initially alerted them to its proximity. A heavy, shower-soaked gale had been blasting the land before dawn and although the thickness of the canopy spared the travellers from the worst of it, they could feel the gusts grow stronger as the vegetation dwindled and the forest thinned. Beneath their feet, the mossy, leaf-strewn surface progressively coarsened with increasing expanses of rock or stone.

They halted at the ragged treeline marking the start of the flatlands and there Liath Luachra awaited them, huddled in the shelter of a fallen tree with her grey cloak wrapped tight about her. The woman warrior watched the travellers arrive impassively, noting how most of them paused to stare towards the low mountains off to the west. She cast a curious glance at Fintán but the youth stood stiffly with the other warriors, glowering angrily and refusing to meet her eyes. His father, however, suffered from no such sensibilities. Accompanied by his *conradh*, he marched boldly up to the woman warrior. 'Your report, Grey One?'

Annoyed by his presumption, Liath Luachra was tempted to ignore him but a warning shake of the head from Bodhmhall prompted her to rein her temper in. 'We should keep moving.' She could not help responding with more than her usual brusqueness. 'Make as much distance as possible before dark.'

Marcán stared unhappily at the exposed terrain. 'There will be little shelter against the gusts.'

The woman warrior laughed out loud at that. 'Do *Na Lamhraighe* fear a shower and a stiff breeze?' Her grin grew wider as Marcán bristled. The one-eyed warrior was surprisingly easy to bait.

Gleor intervened before the conversation could grow more volatile. 'Calm, Marcán. I for one am satisfied with the fact that we can now, at least, see the mountains where An Bearna Garbh is situated. Is it far Grey One?'

'A full day's march. We'd be obliged to set camp on the flatlands but it's not as barren as it appears. The terrain conceals wide dips and great depressions full of grass and scrub.'

Gleor continued to stare ahead in silence. 'Very well. Let's proceed without delay.' He turned to his bodyguard. 'Marcán, rouse the men. They sit too comfortably and we have a route to make.'

The older warrior reached up to pick at a loose piece of scab from the spot where his left eye should have been. With the other he subjected Liath Luachra to a heated if somewhat ineffective glare. 'Very well,' he muttered shortly and stalked off to where the warriors had settled.

The Company set off once more, wrapped in thick cloaks, hooded heads hunched resolutely against the force of the blustery showers. Shortly after leaving the forest behind, the rain mercifully weakened and, a little later, cleared altogether, although there was no respite from the wind.

At first, the travellers looked up occasionally, intrigued by the rocky environment so at odds with the topography to which they were accustomed. Soon however, this novelty was eroded by the wind and the effort of walking, and the Company trudged on with heads bent.

Fortunately, the presence of the mountains eased their plight, the visible headway they were making helping to raise the group's flagging morale. Their enthusiasm was also buoyed by the discovery that the terrain *did* undulate dramatically, dropping at times into expansive basins containing pasture and substantial woods, dotted like scattered seeds between the higher stretches of grey stone. These undulations did nothing to increase the speed of their progress but it did, at least, offer occasional relief from the incessant wind.

Because she'd already scouted the terrain ahead and the route – for the most part – was self-evident, Liath Luachra remained with the Company on this occasion, walking beside Bodhmhall and, at times, Demne, when he managed to break free from his mother. She was with them both that evening when they came upon a broad hollow cut into the lower curve of a steep hill that hadn't been visible from the edge of the forest.

In shape, the natural indentation resembled a giant bowl that had been sliced in half. It contained a small stream that emptied out from a narrow gash in the central curve of the half-bowl and was marked at the entrance by an enormous standing stone that loomed twice the height of a man.

The decision to establish camp there was hardly a difficult one. The site not only provided a fresh source of water but the curvature on the hill created sharp ridges on either side that sheltered them against the prevailing wind. Relieved to be off the exposed rockland, Liath Luachra started to follow the others deeper into the hollow then paused to glance back at the *bandraoi*. Bodhmhall had not moved from the standing stone and remained there now, consumed in her examination of the faded designs on its roughened northern face. The woman warrior's lips gave a wry twist as she watched the other woman.

It is little wonder the druidic order wanted her.

Age-old structures such as the standing stone had always held a fascination for the *draoi*, obsessed as they were with the long-lost knowledge and skills of the Ancient Ones. In this respect, at least,

Bodhmhall was no exception for she too had always been intrigued by the remnants of their mysterious predecessors. Where the *bandraoi* differed from her contemporaries, however, was in her motivation. Bodhmhall's interest in such objects was driven by an inquisitive mind, an intellect that sought simply to understand the purpose and design behind their construction. For many of her druidic brothers and sisters, however, that interest stemmed from an obsessive desire to control the potential powers of such age-old knowledge. Liath Luachra herself had seen the jealous manner in which the druidic order restricted access to such sites, claiming that they were potentially dangerous without the intercession of an experienced *draoi*. Bodhmhall, with typical cynicism, had always been sceptical of such assertions. By her account, the *draoi* actually understood a lot less than they claimed, often substituting sober ritual and ceremony where genuine understanding or insight was lacking.

As she watched the *bandraoi*'s intense scrutiny of the monolith, Liath Luachra experienced a rare swell of emotion, a combined sense of affection and pride. Shaking her head, she turned and followed the others out of the wind.

Within the hollow, *Na Lamhraighe* initiated the campsite rituals with their usual efficiency; Marcán set his sentries, two of the warriors laid the campfire while the others prepared a layer of heather on which to lay their bedrolls. As usual, Liath Luachra set her own bedroll at a distance from the others.

'Grey One.'

She looked up to where Marcán was observing her, his earlier enmity apparently forgotten.

'Yesterday you indicated a craving for fresh venison. Is it your intention to hunt when you scout ahead tomorrow?'

She nodded slowly. 'It would make sense to do so. If I travel to the southern ranges, I can …' Liath Luachra's voice trailed off for the scarred warrior had frozen, his attention no longer fixed on her but locked on some point directly over her left shoulder.

Turning, she followed his eyes and was startled to see a thin pillar of smoke that hadn't been there earlier, rising up from somewhere deep within the core of the hill. Almost immediately, her gaze slid down to the shadowed gash from which the small stream issued, a silver-white ripple on the black rocks where it flowed at a gentle angle into the bowl. Given the steepness of the ridges on either side, this seemed the most likely access to wherever the source of the smoke was located.

'Congal. Lonán,' Marcán snapped at the two closest warriors. 'Come with me. The rest of you, see to Gleor and his woman.'

'Hold your swords.'

All eyes turned in surprise to stare at Bodhmhall. The *bandraoi* had abandoned her position at the standing stone, quietly sidling up beside them while they'd been staring at the smoke. 'That fire poses no threat to this party. The site in which it lies is sacred to *Na Draoi*.'

Liath Luachra buried her immediate disquiet beneath several layers of apparent indifference. Although equally as surprised as the other members of the party, she knew better than to question the *bandraoi* while they remained nearby, despite her certainty that Bodhmhall had never been to this site before. Marcán was not so easily assuaged. He screwed up his eyes and stared sceptically at the *bandraoi*. 'A site sacred to the druids?'

'Yes. And as such, you know you are forbidden from entering.'

Marcán frowned and glanced uncertainly towards his *rí*, unsure how to respond to the subtle warning. Gleor, for his part, considered the *bandraoi* for several moments before dipping his head in assent. 'I defer to Bodhmhall on such matters. Our interests do not lie inside that hill and I certainly have no need to antagonise the druids.'

His words were followed by an uncomfortable silence as the other members of the Company glanced uncertainly at one another.

'I suggest,' said Bodhmhall with surprising authority, 'that you settle here and continue preparations for the night. Liath Luachra will accompany me to investigate the source of this smoke.'

There were a few disgruntled mutters but none of the *Lamhraighe* appeared willing to argue with her on matters of a druidic nature. Instead they watched in apprehensive silence as Bodhmhall made her way towards the gully, the woman warrior following closely at her heels.

Liath Luachra waited until they were out of earshot. 'What game do you play, Bodhmhall?' An angry whisper from the corner of her mouth.

The *bandraoi* continued walking and didn't turn her head but when she responded her voice was low and very terse. 'This place, Grey One. I've never been here and yet I recognise it from my dreams.'

Keeping pace with her, Liath Luachra frowned. 'I don't understand.'

'In my dreams I am standing before that very same standing stone. Then I'm walking with you into that gully just ahead. Just as we are doing now. Once inside, we work our way up to the first bend and then …'

'And then?'

'I don't know. The dream always stops at that point.'

Liath Luachra grunted as they drew up next to the cleft. That seemed typical of *draoi* visions. They always alluded, tempted, teased. They never seemed to provide the critical knowledge you actually needed.

She studied the water course with attention. The gash in the rock where the stream flowed out was actually a gully little more than the width of three people standing close beside each other. The walls of the inner passage looked to be relatively flat although they were pocked and cracked in parts and coated extensively with some kind of sickly, green moss. The crack in the outer face spread upwards above them for over a hundred paces and remained open at the top. Enough light filtered inside to distinguish how it stretched back into the rock for ten paces or more before twisting sharply to the left.

Turning sideways, Bodhmhall stepped into the ankle-deep current and edged her way carefully through the narrow passage. With great misgiving, Liath Luachra followed her, wincing at the coldness of the water against her bare feet. Glancing back over her shoulder she saw Gleor, Fintán, Marcán and the others watching with faces tight with tension. Muirne was biting fretfully at her lips. Demne simply looked intrigued.

Moving against the flow, they slowly made their way up the passage, grasping the black granite walls on either side to keep their balance. The bed of the stream was slippery due to a thin layer of some white, mucous-like material but was made even more precarious by its slight gradient. They rounded the bend to find that it made up but one of a whole series of bends through which the water meandered in its slow flow out of the hill.

It took time to navigate the twisting passage, splashing and shivering in the icy water but, at last, they rounded one final bend to a straight stretch that continued for over thirty paces. At the far end of this section, the light was perceptibly brighter and they were able to make out a large body of water which fed the stream in which they were standing. Liath Luachra hissed in surprise. It was a lake! A lake right in the very heart of the hill.

At the end of the passage, they emerged onto a water-covered ledge to find themselves at the edge of an enormous open crater holding a lake with water so dark it barely reflected the greying sky. Some distance off to the left and several paces out from the edge of the crater wall, a low islet was visible. A narrow path cut into the rock curved around from where they were standing and ended abruptly at the water's edge. A short series of stepping stones continued outwards, providing access to the island.

Liath Luachra stared in amazement. This place was unlike anything she'd ever encountered before.

The thick plume of smoke they'd spotted from the campsite could now be seen to rise from the island. The two women glanced briefly at one another, then slowly started along the tight path towards it, treading the slick surface with care.

Reaching the end of the trail where the black rock touched the lake's edge, they looked across the water and saw that the islet had a small, cascading waterfall on its eastern end and, despite its enormous rock base, a thick coat of vegetation on top. Ten or fifteen paces in from the little waterfall, Liath Luachra could make out a thatched hut surrounded by a ring of colourfully painted stones and wooden totems from which strings of feathers and yellowed bird skulls were dangling. A large fire pit set in front of the hut was responsible for the thick tendrils of smoke that drifted directly upwards. Close beside it was the source of the water for the waterfall, a pool of bubbling dark water, obviously a spring.

Sitting on opposite sides of the fire were two women: a surprisingly dark-skinned woman with long, curly black hair, and an ancient grey-haired crone wrapped in a deerskin blanket. Catching sight of the newcomers, the dark woman yelped and took off on all fours, scampering around the black pool to conceal herself ineffectually behind some low rocks to the rear of the islet. The crone raised her head as though sniffing the air then turned her head in their direction. Liath Luachra bit back a hiss. The woman's eyes were milky white. She was completely blind.

To Liath Luachra's dismay, Bodhmhall started forward, stepping lithely onto the glistening stones and crossing with ease to the larger body of rock. With an aggrieved sigh, the woman warrior hurried after her. As they drew closer, the woman warrior saw that several trout had been hung over the fire on a wooden frame, in the process of being smoked. Several others had been wrapped in leaves and placed in the ashes.

The old woman, seated on a clump of loose reeds, stared in their direction with impressive accuracy, despite the whiteness of her eyes. Her hair was a wild tangle of matted clumps and scraggly knots interspersed with raw bald patches. She offered them a toothless grin as they stood before her.

'I see you, Old Mother,' said Bodhmhall.

'Welcome strangers.' The woman answered with a strong voice that took the warrior woman by surprise, given how at odds it seemed with the frail figure beneath the cloak. As if sensing the intensity of her visitors' scrutiny, the crone tightened the cloak about her. 'Welcome to Tobar na Guthanna.'

Out of the corner of her eye, Liath Luachra saw Bodhmhall balk. She shared the *bandraoi*'s trepidation for she too had heard the tales of Tobar na Guthanna – the Well of Voices – the ancient spring that revealed the secret futures of those who made an offering. Given the fantastical nature of the stories, she'd always believed the place to be little more than a tale the old women told to scare the children at night. Now …

Bodhmhall recovered her equilibrium with remarkable self-possession. Smoothing her dress, she settled down on a mat facing the old woman with all the aplomb of an honoured guest at a banquet. She threw a curious glance to where the dark girl crouched, cringing behind her hiding place. 'Your companion fears our company.'

'Bah!' The hag spat, an impressively solid chunk of phlegm that hit a nearby rock with a wet splat. 'That one fears everything. She has the body of a woman but her mind is possessed by a rabbit.' Another cough brought up a fresh lungful of phlegm that ended up the way of the first. 'But she is a good rabbit. She brings me fish and chews the flesh to tenderise it so that I can eat. Shall I get her to gnaw up some food for you, travellers?'

Visibly repelled by the offer, the *bandraoi* shook her head then, remembering the woman couldn't see her, said, 'We have already eaten.'

'Too bad, too bad. The fish here is tender. So fresh and tasty.'

'What is this place, Old Mother?'

The old hag reached down and started to scratch aggressively at some dry skin on the inside of her thigh. 'It is Tobar na Guthanna. A sacred site of the Ancient Ones.'

'And you live here?'

She snorted. 'My people lived in the hollow outside. But they're all gone now. Done their Dark Leap. I am the last of them. The last, yes.' She nodded slowly to herself and Liath Luachra wondered what those sightless eyes were seeing. 'We used to have visitors, travellers who'd come to make an offering and hear their foretelling. Now, there is no-one. No-one visits anymore.'

'I have never been here, Old Mother. But I know this place. I've seen it behind my eyes when I sleep.'

The hag lolled backwards and forwards. 'When you sleep,' she repeated. 'When you sleep.' Suddenly, she seemed to straighten up, filling up the inside of her cloak. 'Then you are Bodhmhall ua Baoiscne, *An Cailleach Dubh.*'

Bodhmhall stiffened, her mouth open but no words coming out. Behind her, Liath Luachra shuffled uncomfortably.

'Like knows like, Bodhmhall ua Baoiscne. One hag knows another.' The crone seemed to find this statement highly amusing for she started cackling, a harsh noise that sounded like rocks scraped against each other. Suddenly, she turned her head to peer at the Liath Luachra, somehow knowing where to locate her, despite her evident blindness. 'But you there, Little Sister. You I do not know.' She paused and sniffed the air several times. 'I do not know you but I can smell the stench of spilled blood on your breath.'

Liath Luachra's breath caught in her throat but, fortunately, a fresh intervention from Bodhmhall distracted the crone from further scrutiny. 'How do you know me?' *An Cailleach Dubh* asked.

'I just told you. Like knows like. I am a Gifted One. Just like you. *An tíolacadh* – my Gift – enlightened me of your arrival.' The numerous wrinkles on her face congealed into a fluid frown. 'But it did not tell me when. I have been awaiting you these many, many years. Waiting for that encounter I knew I could not avoid. Your visit marks the last of my foretellings. When you have departed I can take the Dark Leap and find my rest.'

'You have foreseen this visit?'

The crone made a dismissive whistling sound. 'You make it sound so mysterious. Anyone can see the future if they open their mind and their eyes. One day soon it will rain. Then there will be sun. The sun will rise and cross the sky, the sun will fall and sleep. There will be death, there will be births. The Great Mother will continue on with as little regard for us as she ever had.'

Bodhmhall regarded her with an odd expression. 'The *draoi* tell us that the Great Mother cares for us, intervenes for us.'

The old crone laughed. 'And what do you think, Bodhmhall ua Baoiscne?'

The *bandraoi* bit her lower lip but did not answer the question. 'What did your vision show you?'

'That you would come to Tobar na Guthanna to make an offering and taste its waters.'

'Why would we want to taste its waters?'

'I have no knowing of your motivations, *Cailleach Dubh*. I know only that you will. Perhaps you are simply thirsty.'

'And once I have tasted the waters?'

'Then you will let me taste your future for in doing so it will save your life.'

The *bandraoi* glanced towards Liath Luachra but the woman warrior shrugged. This was not something she had any confidence to advise on.

'All this because you have seen it, Old Mother.'

'With these dead eyes,' she cackled. 'Yes. But now, before you taste the waters of Tobar Na Guthanna, what do you offer the well in exchange?'

Liath Luachra watched as the *bandraoi* stared helplessly at the older woman, knowing that, apart from the clothes on her back, Bodhmhall had nothing of value with her. The few valuables she owned remained back at Ráth Bládhma.

Silently, she stepped forward and pulled her knife from her belt. 'I will make the offering. If you say it will save her life then it is a small price.' Catching the hag's wrist, she guided the gnarled fingers to the handle of the weapon. The old woman's limb felt dry and brittle to the touch, weak as a rotten branch.

The hag's hand tightened about the hilt. Holding the weapon up in front of her, she sniffed at it then tentatively touched the flat of the blade with the tip of her tongue and ran it carefully upwards until it reached the point. Lowering the knife, she licked her lips. 'Hmmph. A blooded blade. A much blooded blade. You have been busy, Little Sister.' She nodded. 'This offering will do.'

With this, she turned about and tossed the weapon into the pool. There was a brief splash, a small fountain of silver in the air as the black waters swallowed the weapon. A moment later the surface was flat and calm again

116

apart from the gentle bubbling of the spring, as though it had never been disturbed.

With surprising alacrity, the hag pulled a metal cup from beneath her cloak and leaned off to the left, scooping up a portion of water in one smooth movement that suggested a lifetime of repetition. She handed the vessel wordlessly to Bodhmhall. The *bandraoi* took it in one hand and swallowed the contents in a single draught.

'Very good, *Cailleach Dubh*. How was it?'

'It was cold,' Bodhmhall answered bluntly.

'Let me taste you.'

'What?' Bodhmhall pulled backwards. 'What do you mean?'

'Foolish child. Your *Gift* allows you to *see*. My *Gift* permits me to *taste*. Let us waste no more time. Bend down and let me proceed.'

With obvious lack of enthusiasm, the *bandraoi* rolled forwards onto her hands and knees, crouching down so that her nose was touching that of the older woman. The hag sniffed, turned her head to rest one wrinkled cheek against Bodhmhall's then poked out her tongue and ran it slowly along the skin under the curve of the *bandraoi*'s jaw, drawing it upwards until she reached the bottom of her earlobe. Liath Luachra looked on, repulsed and fascinated in equal measure.

Slowly, the hag pulled back to rest on her haunches and chewed her gummy lips as though trying to identify some unusual flavour. Her white eyes made it impossible to work out what she was thinking.

'This is ... strange.'

'What is strange?'

'I can taste you suckling a large child. And yet I have tasted no birth.'

Bodhmhall and Liath Luachra exchanged stunned glances.

'Your child,' the old woman continued, pausing to chew repeatedly. 'It hungers. It thirsts. It is insatiable. It will use you to quench its need.' She paused abruptly, alarm spread across the rumpled features. 'The child is corrupted. It is a Tainted One. It turns. It sees me!' She sounded shocked. 'It sees me!' The old woman's whine grew into a genuine screech of alarm. Grabbing the *bandraoi*'s cup she scooped up another cupful of water and used it to wash her mouth out. Frightened, the two Ráth Bládhma women stared helplessly on.

To their great relief, the hag released a great sigh and her shoulders sagged, released of all tension. Slowly she turned her eyes to Bodhmhall and gave her a wide, gummy grin. 'I have just saved your life, Bodhmhall ua Baoiscne. Do you believe me?'

The *bandraoi* stared back at her, unable to speak. Oddly enough, Liath Luachra did believe the crone's claim but she too found herself unable to speak.

117

As though sensing her consternation, the crone whirled her wrinkled face around, effectively targeting her once again. 'And what of you, Little Sister? Do you have courage enough to let me taste your future?'

'I carve my own future. I have no need of you to set it for me. Besides, I have nothing else to provide as an offering.'

'The task I set you would be offering enough.'

Liath Luachra looked at her in curiosity. 'A task?'

'I would have you kill my pretty rabbit.'

There was a stunned silence. Liath Luachra glanced over to where the dark woman was still cowering, head down behind the rocks. 'That would not be a task I'd fulfil.'

'I have tasted my pretty rabbit's future. The act would be a kindness.'

Liath Luachra shook her head. 'Enough,' she declared. 'Your voice is a midge's buzz in my eardrum. I want no more to do with you.'

Without warning, the hag reached down and yanked the woman warrior's hand towards her mouth. She managed a quick lick of her index finger before the outraged woman warrior yanked it back with a snarl. 'Do not touch me! I will cut you!'

Easing back onto her haunches the hag chewed on her gums with a wrinkled grimace. 'Oh, Little Sister, you are full of Dark. So full of Dark it burns my tongue. She turned her head and spat, then stuck her tongue out and wiped at it feverishly with the fingertips of both hands.

'You taste of death.'

'And you smell of death,' the Grey One retorted. It was true. Up close to the old woman she'd picked up a sickly sweet scent of decay.

The hag started to cackle. 'Your tongue is not as sharp as your blade, Little Sister. My life song is almost sung. That much I already know so your insult bounces off this wrinkled hide.'

With that, she seemed to sink inside herself, shrinking to half her original size inside the deer cloak. All of a sudden she looked completely defeated, ancient and very, very weary. With obvious effort she raised her head to face her two visitors once more. 'You should go now. You have a future to fulfil.'

Chapter Seven

'So that is An Glenn Teann.'

Gleor Red Hand raised one hand to shield his eyes as he squinted towards the valley entrance. In the glare of the morning sun, the route was marked by a dark shadow where it cut through the treeline on the lower foothills.

Liath Luachra considered the distant trees and the mountains behind with edgy ambivalence. After a restless night pondering the events at Tobar Na Guthanna, she'd risen early, leaving before dawn to travel west and assess the lay of the land. As a result, she'd already scouted the terrain stretched out before them. She had, in fact, penetrated beyond the flush curtain of beech trees to the wide defile of the inner valley.

That inner section of rough pasture and grassy tussocks bordered by craggy cliffs was exceptionally beautiful in its own bleak and austere way. That morning unfortunately, she wasn't in the mood to appreciate its splendour. Prior to locating the entranceway, she'd also spent time scouring the land around Tobar Na Guthanna but her efforts had revealed no sign of human activity less than several years old. And even that was scant.

This bothered her more than she cared to admit. By now, the pursuers should have made their move, at the very least sent scouts ahead to confirm *Na Lamhraighe's* location. To her complete bafflement however she'd found absolutely no evidence of either.

She'd made no mention of her growing unease to Gleor Red Hand. The *Lamhraighe* leader would have used the absence of any sign against her, citing it as further evidence of her – and Bodhmhall's – excessive paranoia.

And that would not do.

Liath Luachra had endured constant danger throughout her life and survived. Her instincts were telling her they were being shadowed and she trusted her instincts implicitly.

In contrast to the woman warrior's uneasy restraint, the *rí* of *Na Lamhraighe* was in an ebullient mood, greatly pleased at the sight of An Glenn Teann, the key milestone on their journey to Dún Baoiscne. He regarded Bodhmhall with an expression of almost paternal tenderness, eager to share his contentment with her. 'And you, dear Bodhmhall. How do you feel now that we've reached this pass without incident?'

The *bandraoi* was seated on one of the many rocks strewn about the flat where they'd stopped to rest. She'd removed her moccasins – now almost worn through from the relentless travel – and was in the process of rubbing a homemade herbal liniment into the sole of her foot. Wiping her hands on the hem of her tunic, she raised her eyes to reflect on his question. 'I feel relief, Gleor,' she said after a moment. 'I will feel even greater relief when we are safe at Dún Baoiscne.'

'Of course, of course.' He nodded benevolently and redirected his gaze to Liath Luachra, his good humour overruling his usual stiffness with the woman warrior. 'And you, Grey One. You have surpassed all expectations in locating our route so swiftly. You have our gratitude.'

Liath Luachra gave guarded acknowledgement to the compliment with a curt dip of the head.

'Do you know how long it will take to reach the pass proper?' Gleor asked.

'Half a day. Perhaps less.'

'And you say the trail continues to steepen?'

'That's what I've been told. The valley runs flat at first but as you progress further into the mountains the slope steepens. The sharpest gradient is located three-quarters of the way up the trail, supposedly denoted by the presence of an old stone circle. They say a waterfall flows from the northern wall at that point as well.'

She glanced sideways at Bodhmhall for the *bandraoi*'s head had picked up at the mention of the stone circle.

Gleor nodded absently as he looked around at the members of his company. Many, like Bodhmhall, were sitting on the plentiful boulders, others were sprawled on softer patches of grass between the rocks. 'You seem remarkably well informed for someone who's never travelled this path.'

The woman warrior regarded him coolly. 'In my previous life, I fought with men who travelled … far.'

Gleor responded with an ambiguous toss of the shoulders. Comprehending the reference to her days with *Na Cinéaltaí*, he didn't press her further. He turned again to regard the valley entrance for a time. 'This route shows great wisdom on Tréanmór's part,' he informed them with fresh conviction. 'Within the confines of that valley it'd prove a hard task for any enemy to take us by surprise.'

'Perhaps.' Liath Luachra was more ambivalent. 'I was also told that as you proceed into the mountains, the valley becomes increasingly constricted with stands of trees. Detecting an enemy in such terrain would prove more difficult.'

Nothing, however, could dampen Gleor's expansive mood on this particular morning. 'I grant you we should take precautions, Grey One, but as ever you are overcautious.'

'Very gracious.' Gleor missed the tinge of sarcasm in her voice but she noticed Bodhmhall cast an admonishing glance in her direction.

120

'It is simple fact. Any pursuing force would have to actually catch us before we reach the valley.' He looked at her, gave a tolerant chuckle and shook his head as though admonishing an errant child. 'Which they do not appear to have achieved. Besides …' He pointed towards the distant cliffs, barely visible beyond the treeline. 'Any such ghostly pursuers would have to outflank us, an impossible feat within such a restricted space. To my mind, the threat from any pursuing force has come and gone now that we are almost within the valley. Do you not think so?'

She shrugged but gave no answer, unwilling to acknowledge the truth of his words.

He laughed softly at her consternation but had the grace to refrain from rubbing the logic of his argument in her face, diplomatically choosing to change the topic instead. 'Will you scout ahead now, Grey One? As you've done so frequently these past days.'

Liath Luachra shook her head. 'I would spend some time to the rear of the column this afternoon, one last appraisal of the flatland.'

Gleor shrugged. 'Very well. As you must. We will await you in Glenn Teann, further up towards the pass.' He glanced up at the sky and she could see him mentally estimating the travel distances possible within the remaining daylight. 'We'll set camp by the stone circle you spoke off,' he said at last. 'You will find us there on your return.'

With that, he beamed happily at her. Liath Luachra returned his look in silent confusion for the grey-haired leader seemed to be expecting some kind of confirmation. Unsure how to respond, she simply muttered 'I will prepare,' turned on her heel and hurried away.

It was only when she reached the shade of the trees where she'd left her bedroll and a light food pack for her travels that she realised, with a start, what Gleor had been expecting.

Gratitude.

***

When Liath Luachra left them, the Company was headed in a loose line towards the foothills, preceded by Marcán and Tutal Caol. Following close behind was the main column comprising Fintán and two additional warriors, Gleor, Demne, Bodhmhall and Muirne. This was trailed in turn by the four remaining *Lamhraighe* warriors.

Disturbed by the unusual bustle within their territory, a flock of rooks scattered from the trees at the Company's approach, their outraged squawks ringing in the stillness of the late morning air. Liath Luachra halted briefly, trying to spot the rook with the white fleck, but the birds were too far away and flying too erratically to make out in any detail.

With a sigh, she turned south, maintaining a loose lope that would allow her to eat up distance without tiring too quickly. The route she had in mind was a wide semi-circle. Curving from a point south of her current position, around to the site of the previous night's campsite at Tobar Na Guthanna, it then continued back to the mountains south of the valley entrance. In essence, she was applying the most basic of tracking techniques, an approach used specifically for finding tracks bound for a specific destination – in this case the entrance to An Glenn Teann – when the point of origin was unknown. Anyone following the Company would have to cross that virtual arc at some point and if they'd done so over the previous half-day, she would intercept their trail.

Back in the forest, she'd attempted a similar approach on several different occasions but each time her efforts had been frustrated by thick vegetation that not only hampered her ability to follow an accurate semicircle but made it extremely difficult to discern any tracks. Here, on the flatter land, she felt confident that she could complete her circuit with greater certainty, that she could confirm, once and for all, if someone was on their heels.

For the remainder of the morning she ran, using the position of the sun and the features on the landscape to guide her movement. On the flatter sections, she moved quickly for she was able to scan the ground with ease. When she entered large dips or encountered other features of the natural topography that made tracking more difficult, she slowed to a walk and moved more cautiously. Despite the great stretch of terrain scoured over the course of the morning however, she again found no tracks, no sign of human activity whatsoever.

Sometime before noon, she spotted the low hill marking the location of Tobar Na Guthanna. The first arc of her intended semi-circle was almost complete. Shortly afterwards, the tall standing stone at the entrance to the half-basin slid into view and she drew to a halt to rest and fill her belly before continuing the journey.

Sitting on a grassy hummock close to the imposing monolith, she pulled a bloodcake from the inside of her tunic and ate it in silence as she stared into the hollow. The dark mouth of the narrow gully leading into the hidden lake looked grim and ominous despite the brilliant sunshine. She shuddered as she thought of its strange, wizened inhabitant and her idiot disciple.

Evidence of the Company's recent occupation was evident throughout the basin: charred remains from the campfire, depressions in the earth where the various members had laid their bedrolls, chaotic footsteps scattered all over.

She frowned and stared more closely.

There are a lot of tracks.

Pushing down a growing undercurrent of concern, she got to her feet and walked deeper into the hollow, closely examining the ground ahead. Approaching the gully where the stream emerged, she noted how the ground on either side of the waterway had been severely scuffed and trampled. A large number of people had been milling around that entry point.

And it hadn't been *Na Lamhraighe*.

Liath Luachra reached down to grasp a handful of the disturbed soil and rubbed it between her fingers. It was dry and brittle to the touch suggesting that it'd been exposed to the warm air for some time.

Tossing the dirt aside, she stood quietly, trying to decide on her next course of action. Finally, with a heavy sense of foreboding, she stepped into the chilly water. Proceeding deeper inside the gully, she worked her way through the dank passage, eventually reaching the long passage that opened onto the secret lake.

Hidden in the shadows at the foot of the passage, she studied the distant islet, the only area offering any kind of concealment on that expanse of black water. After a long period of scrutiny that revealed no sign of human activity, she took a deep breath and pulled a javelin free from the sheath on her back.

Scurrying around the narrow pathway, she reached the water's edge and rapidly traversed the stones. Stepping onto the little island, she found no flames blazing in the fire pit although she did locate the Hag of Tobar Na Guthanna in front of her hut. The woman was dead, pinned to the ground with a spear through her belly.

Moving forward at a crouch, Liath Luachra examined the old woman's corpse. The deer blanket had spread open and the crone was naked underneath, the ancient body wrinkled and skeletal beneath the crumpled covering. She attempted to wrench the spear free but whoever had made the thrust must have been exceptionally strong for the weapon was wedged fast into the earth, the barbed metal head entangled in whatever root system grew beneath the soil. The Hag's killer had clearly been unhappy at the loss of the spear for he'd gone to some effort venting his frustration, removing her head – a serious and insulting taboo – and impaling it on one of the nearby totem poles. The ancient crone's dead eyes now stared even more sightlessly out at the circle of water that had been her home for so many years.

Your visit marks the last of my foretellings.

Liath Luachra chewed thoughtfully on the inside of her cheek. In that respect at least, the old woman's prediction had proven undeniably accurate. She wondered briefly if the Hag had 'tasted' the nature of her own demise then intentionally brushed the reflection aside. It seemed an overly disturbing and morbid concept.

Following the Hag's unpleasant mutilation, the invaders had proceeded to ransack her hut in search of any items of value or hidden treasure. The floor had been dug up in several places, holes had been poked in the walls and her few pathetic belongings lay strewn on the ground, discarded amongst the resulting clutter.

Leaving the rude dwelling, she wandered around to the eastern side of the islet and it was here that she found the dark-skinned woman. Close to the little waterfall, it was the dark hands she spotted first. Firmly lashed to two wooden poles set into the earth, they were tied in a raised position and, from a distance, it looked as though she'd been praying to the heavens.

With growing apprehension, she approached the body. In death, the little woman looked even smaller. Sprawled naked on her back, her legs were gracelessly splayed and a puddle of blood had pooled and dried on the earth between them.

Liath Luachra bit her lip as she studied the woman's remains, coldly noting the scorch marks and blisters round the skin of her breasts and the inside of her thighs. From the bruises on her face, it looked as though she'd been repeatedly beaten and then, finally, strangled. A leather thong was fastened tight about her throat. Her mouth was open and her tongue protruded foolishly.

Liath Luachra stared at the still form for a long time, her heart beating rapidly. She struggled for some sense of empathy, of connection with the dead woman but it was as though the reality of what she was seeing simply couldn't fit inside her head.

A sudden nausea overcame her and she felt an overpowering need to leave the bloody site. Driven by sensations she couldn't clearly articulate, she left the bodies where they lay and ran back towards the stepping stones. The women were dead. There was nothing meaningful that she could do for them and she had more pressing concerns for those who still lived.

She crossed the stepping stones two at a time and dashed frantically back along the narrow path to the rocky passage entrance. Here, recognizing how close to panic she actually was, she forced herself to stop and pause, to regain her equilibrium. Taking a deep breath, she stared back across the black body of water, to the little streak of green where the two dead women rested. The sight now provoked an overwhelming sense of loss and rage. Instinctively, she knew that something wonderful had been squandered in this lonely place. Brutal acts had irreversibly tainted its beauty and its sanctity. Now, over time, like the memory of the two women, all knowledge of the Well of Voices too would fade, all last vestiges of both disappearing as though neither had ever existed.

***

The tracks the raiders had made entering – and leaving – the hollow were located just a short distance beyond the standing stone, not far, in fact, from where Liath Luachra had originally stopped to eat. Although every instinct urged her to get back to Bodhmhall and the others as quickly as possible, she forced herself to follow the trail for a short distance. She needed a better understanding of the group's make-up if they were to successfully oppose it.

In some respects, she found their sign similar to that of the *Lamhraighe* party; the members were moving in single file and consisted predominantly of fighting men, somewhere between ten and fifteen, at a guess.

A fian then. A war party out for blood.

Unburdened by a young child and the measured pace of their quarry, the pursuers should have been moving quickly, increasing their pace to catch up with *Na Lamhraighe*. Reading the tracks, however, it seemed that they were intentionally holding back, restricting their progress to a relatively leisurely gait.

But why would they do that?

She pondered the strange behaviour for a moment but was unable to come to any firm conclusion. Putting such considerations aside, she veered off the *fian*'s trail and started for the mountains. Depending on how far ahead the *fian* had progressed, she might still have a slight advantage. The war party was following the trail left by *Na Lamhraighe* but the latter had been headed due east when they'd left the basin, unaware that the entrance to An Glenn Teann was actually much further to the south. If she made a straight run for the entrance while the *fian* followed the less direct route, there was a chance she could reach the valley before them.

She started running.

As the sun traversed the sky, she careered across the flatlands in the opposite direction. Unlike the *fian*, she did not hold back, running flat out without pause to catch her breath. When she eventually reached the shadowed treeline marking the entrance to An Glenn Teann, she was coated in sweat and gasping for breath but, to her immense relief, she could see no evidence of the *fian*'s presence. Staggering to a halt in the shade from the overhanging boughs, she wearily examined the ground to make sure she hadn't missed anything. Finally, after a few tense moments, she relaxed and released a long, drawn-out sigh. The only tracks to be found were those made earlier that afternoon by the *Lamhraighe* party. The *fian* were behind her.

The woman warrior flopped onto the ground beneath one of the beech trees, drawing great whooping draughts of air into her lungs while the rooks cawed angrily overhead. Disturbed by the volume of the bird cry, she looked up, astounded to - once again - find a rook, with a white mark on its breast, perched on of the branches above her. Shaken, she stared at it incredulously. Could it truly be the same bird she'd seen back at Glenn Ceoch? It seemed to her that this bird was somewhat larger but she couldn't be certain. 'Bearach?' she asked, her voice trembling with fatigue and emotion. 'Is that you?'

The bird's beady eye displayed no visible reaction. Liath Luachra waited. A long time passed. Finally, Liath Luachra sighed tiredly, grasped the trunk of the tree and pulled herself to her feet.

Bodhmhall was right. I am being foolish.

With a loud squawk and a flutter of wings, the rook took flight. The warrior woman gravely watched the departing bird gain height then slowly circle towards the north, a far-off flutter of wings against the blue backdrop of the sky. Liath Luachra felt emotion as a sudden, heavy weight in her stomach.

A movement to the north distracted her from such concerns. Peering intently, she was able to make out a single line of warriors ease into view over a distant rise.

They come!

With a curse, she pushed off the tree trunk, using the momentum to propel herself forwards, deeper into the valley. She didn't know how far ahead the Company had managed to travel but they needed to be warned of the approaching danger.

And she needed to increase the distance between them before they spotted her tracks.

She ran.

For a long time she was conscious of little else but the pounding rhythm of her heels against the soil of the valley floor, the chest-numbing thump of her heart and the ongoing curve of the trail, deeper into the mountains. After a time, she noticed that her view of the path ahead was becoming blinkered, constrained not only by the grey shades of exhaustion at the edge of her vision but by the gradual encroachment of the valley walls on either side. After what seemed an eternity, she also became aware of a different sound, a hollow background roar that offset the heavy throb of her own heartbeat.

The waterfall.

Sure enough, after pushing herself onwards for another three hundred paces, she rounded a long curve to an area where the ridges closed in abruptly. Further up the valley a torrent of water gushed from a V-shaped gash in the southern cliffs and tumbled into a deep fissure that cut across the valley floor. The resulting torrent flowed down at an angle towards her until veering sharply in the direction of a wide breach in the northern ridge more than fifty paces in width.

It was at this point that the waterway plunged from the northern cliffs and into another valley below. A great cloud of spray partially obscured her view but Liath Luachra caught a brief glimpse of two heavily forested ridges and a great white river flushing between them.

Struggling to remain upright, Liath Luachra stumbled to a halt and blearily examined the surroundings through her own cloud of exhaustion. On the opposite side of the waterway, a faint path led up from the waterfall to a wide flat with the remains of a large stone circle at its western edge. The ancient structure, consisting of twelve separate upright slabs, looked relatively intact, although the stones were worn smooth from erosion and one of the slabs on the northern side was missing. Regarding the water channel directly in front of her however, she discovered that missing slab now stretched between the banks of the surging waters, a narrow but solid and very functional bridge.

The Company had set up camp on the far side of the stone circle, away from the noise of the waterfall. One or two heads looked up at her approach but her own eyes immediately locked onto Bodhmhall's familiar form. Crouched over some herbs by the treeline further up from the campsite, the *bandraoi* must, somehow, have sensed her arrival for she looked up sharply. The broad smile of pleasure that crossed her face quickly faded when she saw the woman warrior's exhausted and harried state.

With one last, great effort, Liath Luachra stumbled forwards, across the makeshift bridge and up past the stone circle where she tottered into the campsite and sank to her knees beside the blazing fire. Various members of the Company quickly clustered about her as she crouched on all fours, wheezing desperately in an attempt to draw air into her lungs. Someone passed her a wooden bowl of water but she was too sapped to accept it so it was placed untouched on the ground at her side. She sensed rather than saw the *bandraoi* at her side and heard her name being spoken. Before she could answer, two indistinct shapes came to stand directly in front of her, blotting out the remaining rays of sun and shrouding her in shadow. Gleor and Marcán.

'A *fian*,' she managed to gasp. 'Eleven men. On our trail.'

'A *fian*?' exclaimed the *rí* of *Na Lamhraighe*, his voice tight with disbelief.

Unable to respond, the woman warrior simply nodded. An uneasy silence persisted for several moments. 'Are you sure they're following us?' asked Marcán at last.

She panted a little longer before she could answer. 'Following ... following tracks from last campsite.'

The two *Lamhraighe* men exchanged glances. Gleor made a harsh guttural sound that was half-grunt, half-exclamation. 'It seems you were right all along, Grey One.' He turned his gaze to Bodhmhall. The *bandraoi* had dropped to one knee beside the exhausted woman warrior, holding her trembling shoulders with both hands. 'Forgive me, sweet Bodhmhall. I should have trusted your judgment.'

The *bandraoi* looked at him coldly before returning her attention to Liath Luachra.

Vexed by her reaction, Gleor's expression darkened. 'This is not a situation to distress us,' he objected, although it seemed obvious his response was directed more at his own people than at the Ráth Bládhma women. 'We are not overly outnumbered and our men are a match for any force. Besides, we hold the advantage with this location. Two men with javelins could hold this bridge against a much more substantial force. If this *fian* truly lack the nous to curb their blood lust and insist on attacking they will rue -'

'They will not attack.'

'What?' The *rí* of *Na Lamhraighe* glanced down at the woman warrior in consternation. 'What do you say, Grey One?'

Ignoring him, Liath Luachra now reached out and grabbed the bowl of water. Raising it in one hand, instead of drinking she poured the contents over her head, sighing at the sensation of cold mountain water against the heat of her skull. Tossing the empty bowl aside, she struggled to her feet and looked him straight in the eye. 'They will not attack.'

'What nonsense is this?' interjected Muirne Muncháem, her voice brittle and shrill with tension. 'First you tell us they are at our heels and now you say they have no intention of attacking.'

Liath Luachra eyed her old antagonist with cold disdain. 'They will not attack,' she said, 'because that is not their goal.'

'And what then is their goal?' Gleor's voice remained composed but the angry glint in his eye revealed the true extent of the anger he was holding in check.

'To contain us. They've been holding back, keeping their distance all this time. That is why I've been unable to find evidence of their pursuit. Even now they remain at the mouth of An Glenn Teann. They made no effort to catch me.'

Gleor and Marcán looked at her blankly.

'They do not care that we know of their presence,' she explained. She watched Marcán, noting how his fingers unconsciously gripped the comforting solidity of his sword hilt. 'I don't understand,' the old warrior growled. 'If they've kept such a distance how could they have caught up with us so easily?'

'Because they've always known where we were headed.'

This time Gleor Red Hand finally yielded to the strain of his curbed frustration. 'You make no sense!' he roared. 'How could they know where we were headed? No-one was familiar with this route except Tréanmór and he ...' He paused in mid-sentence, sudden doubt evident in his eyes.

Liath Luachra continued to hold his gaze but when she spoke again her voice too was tainted with several layers of palpable resentment. 'You allowed yourself to be deceived with sweet promises. Our enemy's objective has always been to lure us to this isolated place. By entering this valley, we have walked into a trap. The *fian* remain stationed at the eastern entrance to prevent us from leaving. They are the stopper in the flask. The main force is most likely situated further up the pass.'

There was a stunned silence and then, a moment later, it started: the protests, the angry exclamations of disbelief, the forceful refutations. Tired and dispirited by their refusal to face the reality of their situation, Liath Luachra did what she always did when she knew words had no worth. She walked away.

There was an immediate tirade of yells demanding her return but she ignored them all. Tottering with exhaustion, she clumsily stumbled down towards the waterfall. Soon both hostile discourse and Gleor's bellows for silence faded behind her, swallowed up by the roar of the tumbling water.

Hurried footsteps at her back alerted her to Bodhmhall's approach so she was not surprised when the weight of the *bandraoi's* hand come to rest on her shoulder.

'Liath Luachra, I ...'

The *bandraoi's* sentence hung unfinished in the air. Liath Luachra shrugged in understanding. There was simply nothing to say.

The woman warrior continued onwards, down the stony path to the wide ledge that extended to the lip of the cliff where the rushing water thundered from the cliff top. The flat rock glistened, lashed by the spray being driven backwards by the wind. She was breathing heavily, her bronzed skin shiny with sweat, dark hair plastered against her forehead. Stripping out of her clothes, she stumbled forwards onto the ledge where she was immediately enveloped by the heavy spray and mist.

She stood there for some time, pushing against the wind as she washed the sweat and grime from her body, the stain of Tobar Na Guthanna from her mind. The force of the spray was fierce and stung more painfully the further she advanced towards the edge of the precipice. Despite the discomfort, she continued. The noise of the waterfall at this point was deafening but there was a distinct relief – almost a comfort – from a roar so powerful it drowned out all rational thought. Blinded by the spray, she held one hand over her eyes in an attempt to look down and far below the cliff she caught sight of a deep pool of churning froth and a white-water river surging off down the narrow valley.

When she finally pulled back from the edge of the cliff and emerged out of the saturating mist, her ears were ringing but she felt significantly calmer. Making her way back to the spot where she'd discarded her clothing she found that the battle harness and leggings were gone, replaced with the spare tunic and another pair of leggings from her satchel. The clothes had been folded in a little pile, placed on a rock and covered with her cloak to shield them from the moisture.

Bodhmhall.

It was growing dark when she retraced her steps back up the path to the flat. At the far side of the stone circle, she moved around the campsite to avoid contact with *Na Lamhraighe*. From the gloom she could see Gleor and his men arguing by the campfire and found that she didn't envy the grey-haired *rí*. His men were furious and resentful at the lack of foresight and the treachery that had brought them to this valley. He had a significant challenge ahead of him attempting to mollify them.

She found the *bandraoi* further up in the trees beyond the campsite, reclined on the bedrolls laid out beside the moss-coated buttresses of a particularly twisted oak. With a loud groan the woman warrior collapsed onto the woollen blanket beside her. Saying nothing at first, she closed her eyes and massaged her temple with the fingers of both hands.

'The Hag is dead, Bodhmhall. I returned to Tobar Na Guthanna and found her body.'

Despite the fact that she was looking away from the *bandraoi*, Liath Luachra could tell that she had gone rigid with shock. 'The *fian* killed her,' she continued bitterly. 'They killed her. And the little, dark woman.'

She turned to find Bodhmhall struggling to affect an outward calm. Despite her best efforts, it was several moments before she was able to assemble a response. 'Perhaps it was a mercy. The Hag was dying. Without her the dark woman would have faced a long and lonely death on her own.'

'It wasn't a mercy.' The uncharacteristic harshness in the warrior woman's voice caused the *bandraoi* to wince. 'They staked her out on the ground, Bodhmhall. They raped her and they tortured her and once they'd had their fun, they killed her.' Liath Luachra stared furiously down the darkening valley, her hands clenched so tight her knuckles shone white through the skin. 'It would have been a mercy had I done what the Hag asked of me.'

'You cannot blame yourself for that, *a rún*. You could hardly know what was to happen.'

Absorbed with her own efforts to contain the great fury flaring up inside her, Liath Luachra did not answer. But then, she noted in grim realisation, she hardly needed to. Bodhmhall's *Gift* would display the true extent of her inner turmoil, her internal flame dazzling the *bandraoi*'s night vison with an intense clarity that her own inarticulate mumbles could never hope to equal.

She gazed mutely down at the stone circle where *Na Lamhraighe* remained huddled about their campfire. The camp was silent now. Even the arguments had ceased. The usual camaraderie, the jokes and laughter she normally associated with the end of a hard day's travel, were markedly absent.

They're afraid.

She ran one fingertip down the left side of her face, tracing a rough edge along one side of her tattoo. The *Lamhraighe* response was understandable. She, too, was afraid. At a complete loss what to do next.

She flinched as Bodhmhall placed a hand on her knee, squeezing the muscle on either side of the cap with those long, dextrous fingers. 'Grey One, you know we must return to the fire, talk with Gleor and Marcán.'

Liath Luachra turned to the *bandraoi*, unable to hide the cynical twist that had formed upon her lips.

'We have to work with *Na Lamhraighe*,' Bodhmhall persisted. 'They are our allies and we need them.'

Liath Luachra snorted and turned away. Bodhmhall said nothing but waited and, after a while, the woman warrior exhaled then gloomily nodded her head. 'Very well. But not just yet. I cannot speak to them yet. I ... I ...'

Her voice trailed off. Bodhmhall nodded sympathetically.

'Of course. Recover your strength, *a rún*. When you are ready we will devise a strategy to salvage this situation.'

The woman warrior looked at her despondently, her expression a complex combination of affection and utter despair. 'And, afterwards,' she said, 'we can sing our death songs around the campfire together.'

***

They held a war council on the flat ground between the stone circle and the cliffs to the right of the waterfall. Here, an array of irregularly-shaped boulders sheltered them from the worst of the waterfall's thunder, muffling it to a distant roar. The other members of the Company watched from the campfire at the far side of the stone circle, waiting in hushed and downcast silence.

The war council was a small grouping comprised only of Liath Luachra, Bodhmhall, Gleor Red Hand and Marcán. All sat close together, cross-legged in a roughly square formation. Seated directly across from the *rí* of *Na Lamhraighe*, the woman warrior stared at the ground, struggling to hide her scorn at their inclusion in the decision-making now that it was too late to do anything.

As leader of the Company, Gleor opened the council. To everyone's surprise, he didn't commence with the ritual evocation of their ancestors but with a bitter, if somewhat oblique, accusation directed at Bodhmhall.

'It seems Tréanmór would see the bones of his own daughter bleached in the sunlight of this lonesome valley.'

131

The *bandraoi* gazed back at the grey-haired *rí*, the skin on her forehead forming into a tight series of furrows. 'Such thorny plotting is not typical of my father,' she countered. 'It's possible this machination is not of his doing.'

'It was your father's message that drew us to this location.' Gleor's eyes dropped to the ground but then rose almost immediately to confront her with smouldering intensity. 'Only to arrange our murder on its cold slopes.'

Surprised by the severity in Gleor's voice, Liath Luachra also raised her head and stared at him. For all his faults, acrimony was not a characteristic she associated with the leader of *Na Lamhraighe*. She could only imagine that his attempts to soothe his warriors had not gone well.

The truth has cut deep.

'Perhaps the betrayal lies with the messengers,' Bodhmhall suggested. 'We have but the word of the *techtaire* that the message was dispatched by my father.'

Gleor gave a sour smile. 'You forget *an t-urra*. I cannot speak for the surety you received at Ráth Bládhma but that provided to me could only have come from Dún Baoiscne.'

Bodhmhall conceded the point with a shrug. 'I do not dispute that the message originates from Dún Baoiscne, I suggest merely that it could have been sent by someone other than my father.'

Gleor snorted. 'And who else would have the knowledge to send such sureties?'

Liath Luachra noted the slight stiffening in the *bandraoi*'s posture and felt some sympathy. Gleor had a point. The surety provided by Cargal Uí Faigil could only have come from a select few members of the *Clann Baoiscne* hierarchy, a group restricted to Tréanmór, his *conradh* Cathal Bog, and the new *rechtaire* Lonán Ballach. Naturally, there was also Becán the *draoi* to consider. Another acolyte of Dub Tíre – the original *draoi* at Dún Baoiscne – he'd reportedly taken on the advisory function of his instructor following the latter's demise.

There were other potential sources for the information used as the basis for *an t-urra*. Bodhmhall's close friends or her immediate family, for example, although the latter seemed particularly unlikely. Her mother had died shortly after childbirth and, of her two brothers, Cumhal was dead, killed during the ambush at Cnucha. Crimall was said to be in hiding somewhere in the lands to the west but no-one had seen him for many years.

Bodhmhall and Gleor started to argue until Marcán surprised them all by holding up his hand, cutting the discussion short with a surprisingly display of determination. When they had fallen silent, he eyed both individually. 'This is not a time for casting recriminations,' he reminded them. 'This council must focus on a more pressing objective: survival.'

Bodhmhall and Gleor looked suitably abashed but it was the *rí* of *Na Lamhraighe* who made the first concession. Clearing his throat, he spat out of the side of his mouth then turned to look Bodhmhall directly in the eye. 'Marcán has the right of it. We allowed our frustrations to distract us from our goal and I was probably most culpable in that regard. I apologise to you all.'

He looked around at the others. Marcán nodded his satisfaction. Bodhmhall raised one hand and made a conciliatory gesture. Liath Luachra shrugged.

The stiffness in Gleor's bearing eased perceptibly. 'Very well. Let us then address the danger that threatens us. If Liath Luachra has the right of it and an ambush awaits us further up the valley, is it possible to force our way back through our original point of entry, the eastern entrance from the flatlands?'

There was a brief silence as they considered the suggestion. 'We could attempt to smash through this very night,' admitted Marcán. 'They might not expect an attempt so soon and we'd have the advantage of darkness.' He turned his eyes to the warrior woman, unusually keen to hear her opinion. She was, after all, the only one of them who'd actually seen the force that opposed them.

Earlier, while the others had been arguing, Liath Luachra had removed her sword and was in the process of repairing the leather thong that was wrapped about the hand grip. A moment earlier, she'd also grabbed a handful of grass stalks and popped them into her mouth to chew on but, sensing the weight of Marcán's gaze, she now spat them out again. 'We could break through,' she admitted. 'But we'd take heavy losses. The entry point is narrow and the *fian* are well placed. They're also carrying many javelins.'

Her forehead creased in thought. 'Even if we were to succeed, the noise of battle is likely to carry in the confines of these ridges. The enemy force up the valley would hear our attempt to break though and pursue us across the flatlands. With Muirne and Demne slowing us down, it'd only be a matter of time before we were overtaken.'

Gleor clenched his fists, annoyed at her dissection of his proposal. 'Do you have a better suggestion to offer?'

Liath Luachra pondered the question in silence for several moments. 'We should consider the course of action that benefits us most.' She looked around at her three companions. 'What advantages do we have over the enemy?'

There was another ponderous silence as they chewed over her question. 'They do not know we are aware of their plan,' suggested Marcán.

Liath Luachra nodded. 'Yes. And neither do they know that Bodhmhall is amongst our company.'

Gleor frowned. 'I fail to see the advantage of Bodhmhall's presence might offer.' He offered an apologetic glance to the *bandraoi* who dismissed the matter with a careless wave of the hand.

'You forget Bodhmhall's *Gift*.'

The two men looked at her blankly.

'She can help to identify the trap before we step into it.' She momentarily considered adding 'again' but then decided against it.

Gleor nodded in belated comprehension. 'Of course. *An tíolacadh*. The *Gift*.' He glanced at Bodhmhall with fresh respect before turning back to Liath Luachra. 'But that does not deal to the fact that it is a trap and prevents us from continuing westwards. We have enemies to our front and to our rear. The *fian* at the eastern entrance are also likely to join the fray if they hear the sound of battle.'

'They cannot join the fray if we prevent them from doing so.' Liath Luachra gestured towards the stone slab traversing the two banks. 'You yourself claimed this bridge could be held by two men. If we remove the slab, the river could be held by a single man left in hiding with sufficient javelins.'

Gleor looked to where the stone slab lay strewn across the surging waterway then tested the suggestion by looking at Marcán. The big warrior briefly considered the proposal before nodding. 'Between us all, we should be able to shift it. As the Grey One says, though, we'd have to leave a man behind to prevent the *fian* from constructing another means to traverse.' He chewed silently on a fingernail before giving an indifferent shrug. 'Still, if it prevents eleven enemy warriors from attacking our rear, the loss is one I can live with.'

'Very well. But what then of the trap?'

'We trip the trap,' said Liath Luachra.

Gleor gave a bleak smile. 'And then?'

'We run.'

Both men considered her, their expressions stern. Gleor's lips drooped into a frown. 'And where would we run?'

She raised a hand to point at the stone circle. 'Back here. The stones form a defensible position of sorts and can provide some protection against javelins. The slabs are set close together and abundant blackthorn grows off to the side that can be cut to fill the remaining gaps.'

'A refuge of last resort.' Gleor Red Hand gave a pained expression. 'I am not convinced.'

'We face superior forces on unfamiliar ground. A defensive position of our own choosing is the only combat advantage we can hope for.'

As night's dark cloak covered the silent valley, the arguing and discussion continued. By the time the final battle plan was agreed upon the only illumination remaining was the weak light from the stars and the flickering of the campfire. Groaning at the stiffness that made his limbs creak, Gleor called an end to the council and rose to his feet. The others, too, stood up and accompanied him back to the campfire where the other members of the Company waited in nervous expectation. Here, as battle leader, Marcán was asked to outline the plan to his men and did so in his usual blunt manner. When he was finished, there was a brief silence following which questions were answered, duties assigned and final responsibilities made clear.

With the key decisions made and a defined plan of action to follow, the *Lamhraighe* warriors seemed noticeably reassured. The tension about the fire began to diminish a little and a renewed spirit of conviviality was introduced. Soon, even an occasional laugh could be heard.

Seeking to raise the morale of his men even further, Gleor moved about and jested loudly but, for the most part, his efforts at joviality fell flat at his feet. Undeterred, he redirected his efforts to where he felt a greater chance for success.

'Bodhmhall, I have a riddle for you.'

Sitting quietly, grey cloak wrapped about herself, Liath Luachra watched as the *bandraoi* looked up, her curiosity piqued despite the other more pressing matters that occupied her thoughts. 'Yes?' Bodhmhall answered warily.

Honing in on that guarded enthusiasm, Gleor drew closer as his smile grew wider. 'This is my riddle. I am loved by some, disliked by others. When you say my name you kill me. When I am no longer there you long for me most. Who am I?'

'You are "Silence".'

There was a single subdued cheer from one of the warriors. Bodhmhall trivialised her success with a brief toss of her head but it was clear that, secretly, she was pleased with the accuracy of her guess. 'Your riddle is too easy,' she told Gleor.

Undaunted, the *rí* laid down a second challenge. 'This is my riddle. I have a mouth but I have no throat. I run but I have no feet. Who am I?'

'You are a river.' Bodhmhall smiled triumphantly in response to Gleor's expression of faux dismay. 'Do you have another?'

The *rí* pondered silently to himself. Finally he raised his eyes. 'This is my riddle. I have one eye but my view is blinkered. My curly hair does not conceal my head. I lead and all men follow but -'

'You are a penis.'

Gleor paused, looking somewhat taken aback by the speed of her response. Marcán and the warriors roared with laughter, a welcome if brief respite from the remaining tension. Unlike the others, Muirne Muncháem did not laugh but squirmed in annoyance. 'Men!' she snorted. 'You are all alike. Driven by little more than the prod of your love stick.'

135

'Come now, *a stór*,' the *rí* of *Na Lamhraighe* countered.

'This is a temper of conversation I would expect from the likes of Fiacail mac Codhna and his foul tongue. Not from the leader of a great nomadic tribe.' With this, she rose in a sharp rustle of folds and creased layers and stalked from the fire. Behind her, she towed the unfortunate Demne who'd been enjoying the campfire conversation up to that point. The boy resisted at first, dragging his feet and scowling until, accepting the inevitable, he allowed himself to be hauled away.

'You are harsh!' Gleor called angrily after her. 'You forget too easily how Fiacail mac Codhna fought to save you at Ráth Bládhma.' Wrapping herself in the cloak of darkness beyond the fire, Muirne did not deign to reply so he turned instead to Bodhmhall to argue his case. 'Is this not so, Bodhmhall?'

'Fiacail is a great warrior,' she conceded. She pulled back a little from the fire as though distancing herself from the conversation. 'But a poor husband,' she added, her voice so low only Liath Luachra could hear.

'Indeed.' Gleor growled absently, preoccupied with his efforts to distinguish his woman through the gloom. With a sigh, he returned his attention to Bodhmhall. 'Where is Fiacail now?' he asked with sudden curiosity. 'Did he not return to Ráth Bládhma with you?'

'He did. But he did not stay. Seiscenn Uarbhaoil had a call on him for he has a new wife there.' The *bandraoi* went quiet. Beside her, Liath Luachra stared into the flames and kept her thoughts to herself.

'A shame,' the grey haired *rí* mused aloud as he ran his fingers through his beard. 'I had believed the combination of your two unique characters would create a relationship of great power in your clan.'

Bodhmhall shrugged, unwilling to discuss the matter any further. Liath Luachra raised her head to glance at the *rí* of *Na Lamhraighe*, startled by his uncharacteristic lack of tact. Distracted once more in his attempt to discern Muirne, he did not notice her scrutiny.

Perhaps there is something of Fintán in his father after all.

She turned her gaze across the campfire to where Gleor's son was sitting, only to find that he was staring straight at her. Caught by her abrupt switch in attention, he guiltily averted his eyes and she was suddenly certain that he'd been watching earlier when she'd washed at the edge of the cliff. Wearied and disheartened by the events of the day, she found herself completely unable to care.

After some further conversation, a fatigued hush gradually spread over those gathered about the fire. One by one, with the exception of the sentries, they drifted off to their beds, laden with thoughts of the forthcoming battle. Liath Luachra accompanied Bodhmhall back to the trees where she'd placed their bedrolls. As they lay down together, she shuffled closer and raised her lips to the *bandraoi's* ear. 'Bodhmhall.

Tomorrow, when the fighting starts you must be prepared to react to events.'

The *Cailleach Dubh* rolled over to face her. By the light of the moon, Liath Luachra could see one eyebrow raised in wary curiosity. 'React to events? What would you have me do?'

Liath Luachra told her.

'The -!'

The Grey One's hand covered her mouth, muffling the exclamation. Leaning over, she brought her face close so that their eyes were no more than a finger's width apart. 'You and I have never sweetened the bitter taste of truth, *a rún*. What I ask is the only option that offers any hope of surviving this trap.'

Releasing her hand, she outlined her proposal in more detail. As she listened, Bodhmhall's face remained aghast, growing even whiter in the moonlight. 'But what of the plan?' she interrupted at last. 'The stand at the stone circle.'

'It cannot succeed.'

'Wha-?'

Once again, the woman warrior's hand stifled her cry. This time however, Bodhmhall's eyes blazed in anger at the abrupt handling and she wrenched the hand away. 'Don't do that. I'm no yapping cur to be stilled in such a fashion.'

Stung by the reproach, Liath Luachra flushed but she acknowledged the *bandraoi*'s wrath with an acquiescent nod. Furious, Bodhmhall sat up on her bedroll, obliging the woman warrior to duplicate the movement.

'The stand at the stone circle was your suggestion,' Bodhmhall continued, her voice still stained with anger. 'And yet now you speak of failure?'

The warrior woman shuffled uncomfortably. 'Yes.'

'Yes?' Bodhmhall stared at her incredulously before brusquely gesturing for her to continue.

'If the Adversary has a *fian* of eleven men to block the eastern entrance to An Glenn Teann, the force waiting by the pass in ambush is likely to far surpass that. No plan can change the reality that our opponent has more warriors and a better battle position. We'll be overcome by sheer numbers, no matter what plan we use.'

'You did not think to share this with the council?'

Liath Luachra shook her head. 'You saw the effect our predicament had on *Na Lamhraighe*, Bodhmhall. Their warriors were demoralized. Even Gleor was disheartened. They needed leadership, they needed a plan. Otherwise, on the morrow they'd have fought like defeated men.'

'But you've just told me the plan you suggested will not succeed.'

'True. But at least this way, they will not roll over and die.'

137

Bodhmhall lapsed into a horrified silence. Although she made no movement and no flicker of emotion traversed her features, Liath Luachra could almost visualise the activity of her intellectual processes, flushing possibility and counter-possibility through her head as she assessed and evaluated everything she'd just heard. After a time she turned her eyes to the woman warrior. 'What you are asking me to do will result in the same outcome.'

'No.' Agitated, Liath Luachra reached over to rest one palm against the *bandraoi*'s cheek. 'I have thought this plan through.'

'It is not a plan. It is an act of utter desperation. Or defiance.'

'The Adversary has chosen his ground, Bodhmhall. He has arraigned his forces, set his trap and you can be certain he's spent time making contingencies for our most likely responses. Our only hope is to respond in a manner he has not anticipated.'

'But, Gods, Liath Luachra. Such a response!'

Liath Luachra paused for a moment, unable to deny what the *bandraoi* was saying. '*A rún*, I have seen what those men do to the women they capture. That's not a fate I would have you suffer.'

'So you would have me die in a less traumatic manner.' The *bandraoi*'s response was not a question but a statement, spat out with uncharacteristic venom. Stunned by her vehemence, Liath Luachra looked helplessly on as Bodhmhall's shoulders slumped and she began to weep. In the milklight of the moon, her tears slid down the pale tautness of her features. The woman warrior struggled vainly for some offering to console her, cursing her own inability with words. 'All is not lost, *a rún*. Perhaps this act of courage can save us.'

'Us. And what of Demne?'

Liath Luachra looked at her silently.

The *bandraoi*'s features twisted in fresh despair. 'Gods, you wish him to accompany me.'

'There is no other option.'

'And the others?'

'Shit on the others.'

The sheer vitriol of her own response surprised Liath Luachra even more than the *bandraoi*'s earlier exclamation. Nevertheless, she could not deny a dark satisfaction at letting the truth out into the open, revealing her true feelings towards their 'allies' at last.

'*Na Lamhraighe* are the instruments of their own downfall. Gleor and Muirne's ambition led them into this pit of woe. And worse, they dragged us in there with them.' She shook her head repeatedly as though to bolster her own resolve. 'No. If we act, there is some hope. For us and for Demne. The others ...' She paused. 'We must leave the others to their own fate.'

The *bandraoi* remained silent for a long time. As she sat there, one hand on the other woman's shoulder, Liath Luachra knew she would be reassessing their situation once more, considering it from every angle in an effort to find some workable alternative.

Finally, Bodhmhall's shoulders sagged again and the woman warrior knew she'd come to the same conclusion she herself had arrived at some time earlier. Bodhmhall released a long, despair-lined sigh, slowly inhaled and exhaled several times. Liath Luachra saw her jaw tighten, a perceptible straightening of her back and shoulders as she struggled to control the dread that withered her insides.

'Very well, *a rún*. What you propose goes against every instinct but I will do it.' She regarded the woman warrior who, unable to meet her eyes, turned away to stare into the darkness.

'For my nephew's sake,' continued Bodhmhall, I will find the courage to do as you ask. I ...' She paused suddenly, shuddered, and struggled to regain her calm. Lifting one trembling hand, she considered it intently. 'You see how my own fear weakens me. I'm no warrior like you. Acts of physical valour do not come naturally.'

Liath Luachra squeezed her hand. 'Which only makes your courage all the more impressive.'

Bodhmhall gave a sad smile. 'And what of you? What do you do to draw such courage?'

Liath Luachra went quiet then suddenly reached over to stroke the *bandraoi*'s cheek. 'I think of you, dear one,' she said. 'I think of you.'

Chapter Eight

Liath Luachra woke before dawn, roused by an instinctive urgency born of a lifetime in the Great Wild. Unwrapping herself from the bulk of her cloak, she sat up and looked towards the campsite. Many of *Na Lamhraighe* were already up and about, stoking the fire, making preparations and, no doubt, doing their best to ignore the same pre-battle queasiness that soured her own stomach.

It was a leaden morning, a dreary murk that promised little comfort for the coming day. Through the gloom she saw that late night showers had soaked much of the ground while she slept. Sheltered by the thick canopy of the oak tree, she'd fortunately avoided such damp discomfort.

Despite the strain of the previous evening's discussion, Liath Luachra had slept surprisingly well, her fatigue bludgeoning her body's usual alertness to the stillness of stone. Now, although her leg muscles retained some stiffness from the rigours of the previous day, for the most part she felt recuperated.

Beside her the *bandraoi* stirred and rolled onto her side. Cracking open one bleary eye, she stared up at the woman warrior. The women regarded each another for several moments but neither spoke. Then, as though by mutual consent, both turned their gaze away. A moment later, Bodhmhall rose to her feet, wordlessly nodded to the other woman and wandered down in the direction of the campfire.

Staring silently at the patch of earth between her feet, Liath Luachra bit her lip in mute despondency. The stricken expression on the *bandraoi's* face was a dismal reminder of the previous night's resolution, of intentions too painful to contemplate in the grey light of day.

With death's cold fingers on your spine, all options are considered. Even those most abhorrent to us.

Feeling increasingly deflated, the woman warrior could empathise with the *bandraoi's* inability to face her or speak to her. Everything that could be said had already been said. Now there was nothing left, nothing but the struggle and the conflict to come.

***

When she'd pulled on her battle harness and finished packing her meagre belongings, Liath Luachra also headed downhill to the campsite where Bodhmhall and Demne were preparing a breakfast of porridge sweetened with slivers of honey. Marcán was pulling the warriors to the south of the campfire but, of Gleor and Muirne Muncháem, there was no sign.

Kneeling to warm herself against the flames of the campfire, she suddenly caught sight of them, two half-shadows engaged in agitated discussion at the far side of the stone circle. Intrigued by their heated behaviour, she continued to observe them. She couldn't hear them at that distance but from the sharp hand gestures and the tense postures, they seemed to be arguing vehemently.

Whatever their differences, they apparently resolved them for the Flower of Almhu abruptly reached over to caress the older man's face with great tenderness. Startled by the intimacy of that gesture, Liath Luachra turned away in confusion. Despite the time they'd spent travelling together since leaving Ráth Bládhma, she'd never seen any evidence of affection between the *rí* of *Na Lamhraighe* and his extremely trying woman. Her assumption, in fact, had always been that the relationship was little more than a mutual convenience: an exchange of sexual intimacy for a position of elevated status within *Na Lamhraighe*. Catching this rare expression of unmistakeable fondness, she realised that she'd completely misread them.

She sat back on her haunches, bemused by her own reaction. To discover the existence of such genuine warmth in people she disliked so intently had left her feeling confused and oddly uncomfortable.

Turning away, she hurried to join the other warriors and busied herself carving thick sections of blackthorn from the northern slope then using them to plug the gaps in the stone circle. By the time the sky had cleared, the spaces between the granite standing stones were sealed tight with a dense barrier of sharp thorn clusters and the ancient structure had taken on a more formidable martial appearance. Despite its more secure aspect however, one obvious weakness remained - a sizeable gap in the northernmost edge resulting from the absent slab.

Marcán was quick to discount this, assuring his men that the break in the defensive structure was intended as an entry point for the retreating warriors once they'd disengaged and withdrawn from the enemy. When everyone was inside, he insisted, a large mass of blackthorn branches bound with flax fibres would be hauled into place, sealing the breach behind them.

His men, no fools, understood that it was hardly an optimal solution but, assured by the strength of his conviction, they seemed to take him at his word and accept the dubious logic of what he was telling them. Standing apart from the others, Liath Luachra did not partake in the discussions but observed the break in the defensive circle and said nothing.

With the fundamental fortifications completed, the *Lamhraighe* warriors returned to camp to eat. Liath Luachra, however, remained by the ancient monument, fretting over the events to come and the strange sense of detachment that had settled over her and undermined her ability to concentrate.

I am not ready for this battle. None of these men are ready for this battle.

The extent of her own aloofness disturbed her. If the Company – herself included – was not fully committed to the fight there was a real risk of losing focus; in which case, the day and all those they loved, were lost. A cold trickle of fear ran down her spine and she shivered, suddenly regretting that Fiacail mac Codhna was no longer with them.

This surprising and unanticipated notion was sufficiently bizarre to rouse her from her uncharacteristic dejection. Troubled, it took her several moments of introspection to work out what had prompted it.

The *Lamhraighe* men.

Cast into disarray by the recent misjudgement of their *rí*, the *Lamhraighe* warriors were unsettled, feeling exposed and uncertain and urgently needing a battle rousing. That particular responsibility should have fallen to Gleor or Marcán but, for some reason, neither seemed capable of stepping to the fore. Because of her gender and her own emotional disconnect from Na *Lamhraighe*, she too was an unsuitable candidate for such a task, however someone like Fiacail mac Codhna ….

She sighed. Think what she might of the Seiscenn Uarbhaoil warrior, she couldn't deny he'd always been undeniably effective in that regard.

Beset by these disturbing considerations, the woman warrior took little interest in Marcán Lámhfhada's slow approach until he was almost standing at her side. Turning to face him, she watched the big warrior clear his throat then spit the accumulated phlegm from one corner of his mouth. Epiglottal ablution completed, he handed her a bowl of steaming porridge. 'Here. You'll have need of this.'

Surprised by the offering, she accepted it with a curt nod then used her fingers as a spoon to scoop out a portion and stuff it between her lips. The porridge was gloopy and had the texture of snot but it was hot and tasted surprisingly good. Scoffing it down, she handed the bowl back. Wiping her lips with the back of her hand, she regarded the warrior who continued to stand, silently observing her. 'I haven't killed Muirne Muncháem,' she said at last.

Marcán's response was a bray of coarse laughter. 'Not in a physical sense, that's true. Mind you, I've seen your face when you look at her. In your head, I'm sure she's died a hundred times.'

Despite herself, Liath Luachra released a hearty snigger. Taken aback by this rare expression of humour, the one-eyed warrior began to chortle as well and for several moments the two of them stood together guffawing loudly.

When the laughter eased, Liath Luachra was startled to realise that she was breathing heavily and that the physical expression of mirth had helped ease the tension knotting the muscles of her neck and shoulders.

'What do you want, Marcán?'

He blinked at her.

'Come now, we've shared a jagged laugh but I know you have reason to seek my company beyond that.'

142

He shrugged, acknowledging her acuity. 'Battle leader,' he said.

This time it was Liath Luachra's turn to look surprised, albeit in her own blank and expressionless manner. The one-eyed warrior shifted his weight from one foot to the other and rested a great paw on the pommel of his sword.

'I like you Liath Luachra. You have gumption and demonstrated battle skill. But …' he paused. 'There can only be one leader.' He threw her a cautious glance but her absence of expression pressed him to continue. 'You are who you are, so I understand you'll feel tempted to interfere, to propose alternatives to my directives. I am asking you to still such urgings. I will need to retain my focus and, besides, my men will not follow you.'

She considered him silently then gave a careless toss of her hand. 'I like you too, One-eye. You're not so much the fool I thought you were.'

'Such praise.' Marcán shook his head slowly in faux amazement. 'In truth, I had expected a more visceral response. Has my request not vexed you then?'

She thought about that for several moments before responding with a slow shake of her head. 'No. In this battle, it makes no difference who leads or who doesn't. The outcome will not change.'

The *Lamhraighe* warrior frowned at that, his brown eyes sparking dangerously. 'My sword will determine the outcome of this battle, Grey One.'

Liath Luachra looked deep into those serious, scowling eyes and behind the vigour of his refutation, she saw it.

He knows. He knows the outcome as much as I.

Despite, or perhaps because of such insight, Marcán continued to hold her gaze, glaring back at her with unwavering rejection. Liath Luachra said nothing but she was impressed. There was fire in the old dog. Despite everything, he was resolved to fight, determined to stem and turn the course of battle. She had to admire the old warrior for that.

Seeking to change the topic, she pointed at the great weapon weighing down the scabbard at his side. 'That's a very big sword, Marcán Lámhfhada. Too much weight, too much momentum. If you miss your swing, it'll veer helplessly by your opponent's head.'

He grinned at that. 'As you say, Grey One. It is a very big sword. As such, I will not miss.'

***

The clouds closed in as the Company made final preparations. A fine drizzle sprinkled the campsite, producing an oddly calming patter from the leaves of the surrounding trees but, by the time they'd gathered west of the campsite, it had already dwindled away again.

Wiping the moisture from his face, Marcán outlined his proposed formation, explaining his intention to lead as advance guard with the warrior, Craon. The main body of the company would follow ten paces to the rear, Bodhmhall at the fore, flanked by Liath Luachra and the warrior Tutal. This would give the *bandraoi* ample view to utilise her *Gift* to best effect. Gleor, Fintán and the remaining warriors meanwhile would cluster close behind, ready to respond to her, or the battle leader's, call.

Despite Marcán's earlier warning, Liath Luachra felt no need to keep silent counsel. The big man was experienced and battle canny and, besides, she and Bodhmhall had their own scheme, independent of the *Lamhraighe* plan.

The sun was an indistinct smudge above the cliffs to the east when the Company finally started up the faint trail to An Bearna Garbh. Advancing up the gentle incline, Liath Luachra could not help noticing the great difference in the comportment of her fellow travellers. The light-hearted banter of the previous days was markedly absent. In fact, nobody was talking at all. Focussed on the potential threat lying ahead of them, all eyes were feverishly sweeping the distant woods and trees, sweating palms nervously adjusting their grip on the weapons they carried.

Several hundred paces from the campsite, Liath Luachra stepped off to one side of the trail and turned to look back, surprised to discover that they'd already gained an appreciable height. From her viewpoint, the large stone slab that had been stretched across the waterway now made a rectangular shaped patch on the grass, thirty paces from the western bank. The stone circle, meanwhile, despite its substantial reinforcement, still looked dispiritingly inadequate as a defensive redoubt. This, apparently, was an opinion shared by the *Lamhraighe* warrior assigned to remain behind. He was working frantically to bulk up the thorn barrier between the stones on the eastern side. Liath Luachra noted how, every now and again, he'd pause to raise his head and stare anxiously down the valley for any sign of the *fian*.

Don't worry. They'll come soon enough.

Her eyes drifted to the shadows thrown down by the eastern stones, where Demne and Muirne sat huddled amongst the wicker baskets and backpacks containing the Company's supplies. It had been Liath Luachra's suggestion that they remain behind in the relative safety of the stone circle, a suggestion that the others had immediately supported. As non-combatants, everyone knew the woman and child would be of little assistance in the impending battle and, during the anticipated flight back, it was unlikely they'd be able to keep up with the running warriors.

As Liath Luachra continued to watch, she saw the boy unravel the sling from his arm, using the same manoeuvre she'd originally taught him. The sight prompted a strong swell of emotion but the sensation was fleeting, gone before she'd fully perceived it and leaving nothing behind but a melancholy softness in the pit of her stomach.

Turning away, she cast her gaze several steps further up the sloping path where Bodhmhall had also come to a halt. Unaware of Liath Luachra's scrutiny, she too was staring intently at the ancient monument below. The drizzle had created a fine net of minute diamonds that glittered in the body of her hair and across her freckled face. At that moment, the *bandraoi* had never looked so beautiful to Liath Luachra: so striking, so exquisite, so utterly perfect.

She felt a sudden great compulsion to approach the other woman, to brush those drops away with her fingertips but before she could act on the impulse, the *bandraoi* had turned and started back up the trail. Watching the *bandraoi* walk away, Liath Luachra felt her throat constrict and it was suddenly very hard to breathe. With an immense effort, she focussed her attention to minute adjustments of the javelin quiver strap then, finally, followed the others up the incline.

The trail leading to An Bearna Garbh continued to steepen, twisting sharply at irregular intervals so that for a long time it was almost impossible to catch a clear glimpse of the mountain saddle. Eventually, the valley straightened out again although the cliffs continued to edge closer and woods and foliage clogged the lower sections, constricting the trail even further.

The Company advanced slowly, displaying greater caution than they had at any other stage over the course of their travels. Watching the hunched, wary movement of the advance guard, Liath Luachra experienced a sudden flush of fury.

Anyone watching will know we are conscious of their presence.

Taking a deep breath, she attempted to calm the blaze of frustration inside her. She knew she was being unreasonable, even irrational. It was exceptionally difficult to feign indifference when the real threat of imminent danger was present. Had she herself been in Marcán and Craon's position, it was doubtful she'd have acted any differently.

With a muted sigh, she glanced over her shoulder, back down along the trail they'd already covered. A long period of time had passed since leaving the campsite and the increasing distance between them and the stone circle made her uneasy.

Bodhmhall halted abruptly, so abruptly that the woman warrior, absorbed in her own thoughts, walked straight into her, her nose contacting painfully with the back of the other woman's head. Despite the appreciable collision, the *bandraoi* made no exclamation for her attention was fixed completely on the route ahead. Gleor stopped beside them and glanced at her sharply.

'What is it, Bodhmhall?'

Bodhmhall's rigid stance did not change. When she spoke her voice was terse. 'I ... I'm unsure.' She continued to stare straight ahead to a point where thick scrub and trees had spread in from the base of the cliffs, reducing the width of the visible trail to a space of about ten paces in length.

Marcán, observing the lack of movement from the main party, tapped Craon on the shoulder to bring him to a halt then quickly hurried back. 'What is it? Have you seen something, Bodhmhall?'

Gleor nodded. 'She has. Something further up the trail.'

'Really?' The one-eyed warrior turned and stared for a several moments. Beside him, Liath Luachra also took the opportunity to examine the terrain but could see no sign of movement, nothing out of the ordinary. 'What is it?' asked Marcán at last. 'I see no threat.'

The *bandraoi* made to raise her hand and point but then caught herself. Dropping her arm to her side, she nodded her head discreetly in the direction of a cluster of beech trees lying fifty or sixty paces ahead, to the right of the trail. The gradient of the valley was quite steep at that point, sloping down sharply to where the Company was gathered. 'That stand of beech trees. There's nothing there. I see ... nothing.'

Marcán looked at her in confusion. 'Nothing? Do you mean that -'

'I mean Nothing. There is no animal life-light in the trees. No birds, no rodents, nothing.'

Gleor considered her gravely. 'You have no doubts, no -'

Bodhmhall silenced him with a cold, hard stare.

By then Craon Dranntánach too had shuffled back to join them as well. 'Can you see life flames of men, *Cailleach*?' he piped up. 'Muirne Muncháem told us that you could see the fire in the bellies of your enemies.'

Bodhmhall responded with an irritated shake of her head. 'That is not how it is. My *Gift* can be obstructed. If a physical object stands between my line of sight and the life force, I cannot see it.'

'Not much use then, is it?' grumbled Craon.

Liath Luachra subjected him to a withering look. 'If Bodhmhall senses a wrongness, it would be foolish not to pay heed. The absence of wildlife suggests that something has driven it away.'

Bodhmhall continued to stare intently at the beech trees, oblivious or simply indifferent to the discussions taking place around her.

'A decision must be made.' Gleor thoughtfully scratched his beard then turned to look at his battle leader. The grizzled, one-eyed warrior winced, adjusted his grip on the wooden haft of his javelin but then gave a single nod.

Gleor took a deep breath then rose to his feet. '*Ullmhaigí*,' he instructed his men. '*Tá an cath orainn.*' Prepare yourselves. The battle is on us.'

146

For the most part, the rí's instruction was superfluous. Seasoned veterans, the *Lamhraighe* warriors were as ready as they were ever going to be, although several did take the opportunity to ensure their blades pulled freely from their scabbards or tested the metal points of their javelins to make sure they were firmly affixed. Because of the need to leave sufficient missiles with the warrior stationed at the stone circle, most of the men were limited to two. Given the plan to cast both prior to an immediate retreat to the stone circle, this number had been considered sufficient.

Marcán jerked his head towards a cluster of mountain ash several paces ahead, to the right of the trail. The terrain between this stand of trees and the distant beech cluster was markedly less vegetated than other sections along the trail. 'We'll assemble there. The trees offer good protection and if an enemy force truly awaits, they'll be obliged to cross open ground to reach us.' He glanced at the skinny warrior standing beside him. 'Craon, you're paired with Gleor. Do not leave his side. Tutal, you're with Bodhmhall. The rest of you – you know what to do. Hold firm. Draw blood, kill your enemy. Once you've cast your second javelin, follow my signal and withdraw to the stone circle.'

Instructions assigned, the gravel-voice warrior started forwards. 'Calmly, now. We don't want them alerted until we're nice and settled.'

Liath Luachra, keeping close to Bodhmhall, shook her head in agitation. *Probably too late for that.*

The Company advanced along the trail then, at Marcán's barked command, shuffled swiftly sideways, into the cover of the mountain ash. Brushing through waist-high fern that choked the ground beneath the trees, they spread out in a thin line behind the substantial shield of the ash trunks. When all were in position, they stood quietly, staring uphill across the open ground at the stand of beech.

A heavy silence fell over the valley, the only sound the distant swish of wind brushing the trees at the top of the pass. Under the thick canopy of the ash trees however, the air was very still.

'I don't see anything,' a sharp mutter from Craon.

'Shut your beak,' growled Marcán.

The interminable silence stretched on, thick and unsettling. Liath Luachra picked at the bark of the trunk that sheltered her, nervously discarding the detached flakes into the surrounding foliage. Across the open ground, the distant copse of beech remained shadowed and serene. Scanning the branches in the higher sections of its trees, the woman warrior could make out no sign of the usual bird activity she'd have expected.

Bodhmhall was correct.

Casually turning her gaze to where the *bandraoi* shared the shelter of the ash trunk, she raised her eyes to scrutinise the branches above their own

147

heads. These too, she couldn't help noticing, were devoid of wildlife activity. Their hurried invasion had driven the animals from this section of the woods as well.

'Is it truly your intent to make me wait?'

The sudden bellow took them all by surprise. Startled, Liath Luachra instinctively pulled closer to the ash trunk even as her eyes fixed on the distant trees from where the call had seemed to come. As she watched, she saw a section of the undergrowth shudder and part as a tall figure pushed his way out into the open, followed by a youth with long, black hair.

It's him!

She recognised him instantly, the tall, hatchet-faced man from the *fian* attack on Ráth Bládhma. The last time she'd seen this particular individual had been six years earlier, when she'd lain in concealment hoping to avert the assault by dispatching the war party's leader with her sling. That attempt, unfortunately, had been in vain for she'd mistakenly targeted a more brutal looking warrior instead, an error with consequences she still found hard to live with.

The two newcomers entered the clearing with remarkable self-assurance but she noted how they remained close to the treeline running along the base of the southern cliff. Working their way to a point about half-way between the two strands of trees, they came to a stop.

The tall man was strikingly slender and had a narrow, bony face with an unusually long and angular jaw. Dressed in a light leather tunic, he wore a wolfskin cloak draped over his shoulders against the drizzle. The youth was sallow-skinned and had no more than fifteen or sixteen seasons on him at most. He remained slightly behind and to the right of the taller man, taking up position against a tree trunk that had fallen into the clearing. Leaning against it with casual aplomb, he regarded the *Lamhraighe* position with a somewhat bored expression. Even at this distance, Liath Luachra could see that he had strikingly dark eyes. His nose was blunt and short, his mouth prim. His lips seemed too full and sensual, almost feminine, but there was nothing girlish about the deadly looking knife he was using to pick the dirt from his fingernails.

'*Cailleach!*' shouted the hatchet-faced man. 'Give me the boy. It is your sole recourse to leave this valley alive.'

Liath Luachra frowned.

He knows Bodhmhall. He's recognised her.

Beside her, the *bandraoi* stared, her hands balled into fists, fingernails fretfully scraping the flesh of her palms. Despite her earlier nervousness however, a distinct trace of fury now flared in those intense brown eyes. Before the warrior woman could caution her, Bodhmhall had stepped out from beneath the trees, striding purposefully across the clearing to where the two men waited. Taken completely by surprise, Liath Luachra cursed, quickly hurrying into the clearing after her. From the corner of her eye, she saw Gleor direct another of the *Lamhraighe* warriors – Tutal – to accompany her.

Bodhmhall came to a halt, separated from the men by a distance of less than ten paces. She stared defiantly at the hatchet-face man and, despite his apparent nonchalance, the woman warrior could tell he'd been taken aback by the boldness of the *bandraoi*'s approach. As Liath Luachra and Tutal Caol rushed up to take a defensive position to either side of the woman, he regained his earlier composure, amused by their obvious nervousness. He smiled broadly, revealing an odd set of blue-stained teeth.

'I see you, Stranger,' said Bodhmhall. 'And I have seen you before. Outside the walls of my home in Glenn Ceoch.'

The hatchet-faced man's smile did not falter.

'I see you, Bodhmhall ua Baoiscne. Yes, I was there. And I saw you too. Briefly.' His eyes abruptly shifted to Liath Luachra and that smile wavered, lost its grip and slipped from his face. 'Hallo, Grey One. I didn't know you with clothing on your back.'

Liath Luachra channelled her hatred into a cold, completely implacable expression. The tall man held her eyes for a moment or two but with no discernible emotion to latch on to, he curtly transferred his gaze back to Bodhmhall.

'How are you named?' Bodhmhall again. 'And what claim do you make on my nephew?'

He stood without expression for several moments but then abruptly raised a hand to his heart and offered a distinctly sardonic bow. 'I am named Gob An Teanga Gorm [Gob of the Blue Tongue]. I have no claim to make on your nephew *Cailleach*. I have simply been instructed to take him from you, which is what I intend to do.'

Bodhmhall glanced down at the skirt of her long tunic and smoothed a wrinkle with her hands. 'Instructed?' she asked, almost absently.

Gob An Teanga Gorm smiled again: a knowing, humourless leer. 'I am not here to bandy words with you, *Cailleach*. You've obviously hidden the boy but he cannot have left the valley. Return to where he's concealed and send him to me. If you do as I ask, I promise that you and your friends can leave in peace.'

'I have your word?'

'You have my word.'

Bodhmhall's tinkle of laughter caught them all by surprise. Liath Luachra nervously adjusted her grip on the javelin haft, noting how the tall man's features tightened, the earlier looseness of his posture stiffening perceptibly.

'Do you truly consider me so naïve? You've never had any intention of letting anyone leave this valley.'

Gob An Teanga Gorm observed her in stony silence, that cruel face now completely void of any humour. Somehow, without speaking or moving, he exuded a terrible sense of silent menace. Liath Luachra sensed an insane blood-craving barely supressed behind that outer facade of calm.

This man's a killer. I must get Bodhmhall away.

The taut silence was broken by a loud yawn to the tall man's rear. Lounging against the fallen tree, the youth appeared utterly disinterested in the edgy discussion taking place, his attention focussed uniquely on the task of cleaning his fingernails.

'It seems we have nothing more to discuss,' Bodhmhall informed them. 'Come to us at your leisure. We'll be waiting for you.'

She made to turn but a low growl from Gob An Teanga Gorm held her in place. 'Tell Muirne Muncháem that I'll be coming for her.' The tremor of rage in the tall man's voice lingered in the air, underscoring the threat. 'Tell her she'll have cause to regret her decision to spurn me.'

Liath Luachra's eyes flicked to the *bandraoi's* face where a brief, almost imperceptible flicker informed her that Bodhmhall too had recognized the significance of what she'd just heard.

Muirne Muncháem knows this man!

Gob An Teanga Gorm, meanwhile, appeared to redirect his full wrath at the *bandraoi*. 'As for you *Cailleach Dubh*.' His eyes drilled straight into hers. 'You should know I've promised you to my men for their sport.'

The *bandraoi* returned that cruel gaze in silence. Suddenly, she smiled: a bright, confident, unaffected beam that completely undercut the attempted intimidation. 'Who betrayed us from Dún Baoiscne?' she asked. 'Who dispatched you to a lonely death in a shadowed valley?'

'Go back to your people, Black Hag. I won't be long in coming.'

'Well hurry up then, Shit-stain!' Although Gleor Red Hand's roar came from a distance behind them, it echoed resoundingly in the tight confines of the valley. Stepping into the clearing, he glared furiously at the two strangers, his face red, eyes blazing. Clearly, he too had heard the tall man's reference to Muirne Muncháem and had not appreciated it. From his rear, Marcán emerged from the shadows under the trees and attempted to urge his *rí* back into shelter. The old man was having none of it. Shaking off his battle leader's arm, he continued to glare, his anger burning an almost tangible path towards them.

'When people walk this path in times to come, Blue Tongue, blossoms will guide them. Pretty flowers will sprout where you fell, nourished by the blood and *caic* of your entrails!'

'Enough!'

The vapid youth, who'd stood quietly by all this time, abruptly peeled himself away from the tree and whipped out his knife hand. There was a rapid blur of movement and a startled gasp to her left drew Liath Luachra's eyes. She froze, shocked, as she saw Tutal stiffen, the weapon embedded to the hilt in his throat. For one horrific moment, the young warrior stood wheezing, hands pawing desperately at the handle protruding from his neck. Slowly, the horror in that panicked gaze faded, his eyes glazing over. Tutal fell to his knees, toppled over to one side and died.

Everyone, even Gob An Teanga Gorm, seemed stunned by the abruptness, the sheer lethality of the adolescent's knife cast. Liath Luachra was first to react, furiously flinging her javelin to spin through the air. Somehow, her target sensed its approach for he dropped to a crouch and it whirred overhead, embedding itself into the trunk of the tree behind. In an instant, the youth was scurrying into the undergrowth, Gob An Teanga Gorm hot on his heels.

With a terrifying roar, a wave of howling figures surged from the distant beech trees, gruesome screams ringing through the valley as they swarmed downhill towards the two Ráth Bládhma women. Grasping Bodhmhall's arm, Liath Luachra ran, hauling her back towards the *Lamhraighe* position. There, roused by the death of their comrade, Marcán and his men released a volley of javelins over their heads, into the attacking mass of warriors at their rear.

Sliding into the shelter of the treeline, Liath Luachra retrieved her second javelin. As she hoisted it, she roared at the *bandraoi* standing bewildered beside her. Her earlier valour dissipated, Bodhmhall was staring horror-struck at the flood of warriors descending upon them. 'Run, Bodhmhall! Run. Do as we agreed!'

With a shove, Liath Luachra sent the *bandraoi* spinning forwards and turned back to join the fight.

The first thing she saw as she whirled about was one of the charging warriors struck in the thigh by a *Lamhraighe* javelin. The impact tripped him, the haft of the missile snapping in two as he smashed against the ground. Selecting a target of her own, she was momentarily distracted as an enemy javelin glanced off the tree beside her, the haft catching the tip of her ear as it spun past. Ignoring it, she refixed her aim and let her missile fly, experiencing that great, incomparable burst of battle elation when she saw it take an enemy warrior full in the chest.

Despite the success of her cast, she knew it would do nothing to affect the inevitable outcome of the battle. There were simply too many of them. The attacking force had at least twenty to thirty men, more than three times their own number. By forcing the enemy to tip their hand early, they'd avoided a complete slaughter and managed to take down a number of assailants with their javelins but, as she'd suspected, any hope for a structured withdrawal was completely stymied by the sheer scale and swiftness of the attack. The *Lamhraighe* party did not stand a chance.

'Gleor! Fintán! Save yourselves. The rest of you, hold position!'

Marcán's unmistakable bellow indicated that he too had worked out the inevitable conclusion from this engagement. At the same time he'd also recognised that, if the enemy force could be held for just a few moments, some of the others would have enough time to flee. Driven by duty and loyalty towards his *rí*, the one-eyed warrior had just declared his commitment to that sacrifice.

She saw the massive warrior step forward, out of the trees and onto the trail. Three of the incoming warriors immediately adjusted their charge, veering towards him. Unfortunately, in their enthusiasm, they'd advanced with such speed they couldn't check their downhill momentum. All Marcán had to do was sidestep then slash upwards with the great sword *Lámhfhada*. Three men went spinning past the one-eyed warrior, one of them independently from his head.

Grasping the javelin that had struck the tree beside her, Liath Luachra cast it but had no time to see if it was a hit or not for the incoming wave of roaring men was on her. Drawing *Gléas Gan Ainm*, she began to fight for her life.

Two of the attackers engaged her directly: a youth in his late teens and an older, burly figure who looked to be in his thirties, although it was impossible to tell beneath the filth that caked his face. They came at her from both sides, working in unison with a familiarity suggesting they'd used this approach before. The younger one lunged with a spear but she deflected it easily by taking a few steps back, deeper into the trees where the trunks thwarted the coordination of their attack. Even as she edged backwards, she could tell the initial parry hadn't been a serious assault, had been little more than a test, in fact. With rising dread, she realised her attackers didn't really even need to fight her. As long as they kept her preoccupied for a few moments, they could just wait until one of their many comrades came to take her from behind.

Better deal to that.

'Shitface!'

She attacked them.

Lulled by her gender and her initial retreat, they weren't expecting that and although she was momentarily exposed to the younger man's blade, she used that brief second of startled indecision to rush forward and strike the older man. Her opponent was unprepared for how fast she managed to close the distance between them and she succeeded in striking him. Her sword took him across the side of the head but because of the angle, she was only able to use the flat of the blade. As a result, although the blow stunned him and knocked him backwards off his feet, she had no opportunity to follow through.

Almost immediately the youth was on her, jabbing savagely with his spear. Twisting to one side she managed to avoid the barbed metal point that scraped the leather of battle harness. Because he'd over extended himself with the thrust, she was also able to grasp the spear haft. Hauling him forwards, she countered with a sharp jab of her own and the tip of *Gléas Gan Ainm* took him in the upper arm. With a cry of alarm, the youth dropped the spear and backed hurriedly away, clutching his bloody shoulder.

She rushed him. He held up his one arm in a defensive gesture but she slammed it aside as she drove her shoulder into his buffed leather singlet and knocked him off his feet. He hit the ground hard but not as hard as the slam of the sword blade against the side of his head. He was out of the fight.

Turning swiftly, she faced the older man who was now back on his feet, swinging his own sword in tight arcs. Instead of continuing his advance, he paused, waiting for two of his comrades to reinforce him from behind.

Liath Luachra quickly took the opportunity to glance around and assess her situation. To her right, another *Lamhraighe* warrior was down, blood streaming from a huge gash in the side of his head. Two of the enemy were stabbing the prostrate form with spears.

To her left, Craon Dranntánach was also down, bleeding badly from one leg. Standing over the fallen man, another *Lamhraighe* warrior was engaged in furious hand-to-hand combat with a red-haired, leather-clad warrior holding a battle axe.

Further to the left, Marcán was also under great pressure. Although he'd somehow managed to dispatch all three of his initial attackers, their replacements had learned from their comrades' mistake. The huge, one–eyed warrior was now surrounded by three fresh warriors and his arms were coated with blood from several cuts as he attempted to defend himself against the probing spears.

We're lost.

This was the moment Liath Luachra chose to leave *Na Lamhraighe* to their fate. Like Marcán, she'd remained behind to give Bodhmhall the opportunity to flee. Unlike the *Lamhraighe* warrior, she had no intention of staying.

Pragmatic as ever, she wasted no time. Spinning on one heel, she started to run out of the trees, back towards the steeply descending trail. From behind came a startled snarl of outrage but she had no idea if it originated from friend or foe and cared even less. Veering close to the *Lamhraighe* man, she stabbed his opponent in the back as she swept him by. Then she was past, out of the trees, rushing downhill. Back towards Bodhmhall, back towards Demne.

Although the downhill hurtle was extremely precarious, it was also a lot faster than their original uphill plod. Assisted by the steepness of the slope, Liath Luachra found that she was able to make significant distance by using long, extended leaps that allowed her to cover four normal paces at a time. Far ahead, Bodhmhall was already well out of sight, hidden by the winding section of the trail but she could see Fintán dashing downhill, followed closely by his panting father. To her left, a javelin glanced off a rock with a tinny, metallic clatter. Instinctively, she veered right, digging deep for another spurt of speed.

Throwing a quick glance back over her shoulder, she caught sight of another *Lamhraighe* warrior pounding behind her. She recognised him as the eldest of Gleor's bodyguard but, despite being red-faced and panting like a blacksmith's bellows, he was moving with impressive alacrity, spurred by the howling mob of blood-hungry warriors less than twenty-five paces to his rear.

Plunging downhill, she managed to overtake the struggling Gleor Red Hand however Fintán remained steadfastly out of reach. Moving at such panic-stricken speed meant that a surprisingly short time seemed to pass before the distant roar of the waterfall became audible above the yips of their pursuers and the hoarse gasp of her own breath.

Risking another glance over her shoulder, Liath Luachra was relieved to find that they'd managed to extend the distance between themselves and their pursuers. Unlike the desperate *Lamhraighe* survivors, the enemy was in no hurry. They knew there was no way out of the valley, no possible route of escape for their quarry. As a result, they were also happy to leave the more hazardous, risk-taking efforts to their enemies. This approach had already justified itself a little earlier when the *Lamhraighe* warrior behind Liath Luachra had tripped and broken his ankle.

Frantic, the remaining survivors hadn't stopped but left their screaming comrade to his fate. At the time, Liath Luachra had also experienced a brief mental image of Marcán Lámhfhada wading courageously into unbeatable odds back at the cluster of ash trees. An honourable man, a brave man. A noble sacrifice. If he had still been with them, he'd probably have stopped to help his fallen comrade as well.

Fool!

Fortunately, the exertion of flight and the concentration it required flushed such thoughts from her mind. She felt no pride in her actions at deserting the screaming warrior but she wanted to live, she needed to live and his misfortune would buy them a few moments of respite while the enemy took time to kill him.

Liath Luachra almost cried with relief as she took the final bend before the long slope down to the falls. Even as the stone circle came into view however, her eyes were drawn to the ferocious activity taking place on the far side of the waterway. The *fian* warriors had finally made their appearance and, disconcerted at the discovery of the missing stone slab, were now trying to traverse the waterway by means of a makeshift bridge.

The structure they were using – two slender ash trunks strapped roughly together with flax – looked distinctly precarious. The position they'd chosen as their crossing point, below the fortified stone circle, was also proving exceptionally hazardous. As a result of their exposed position, the *Lamhraighe* warrior stationed there was able to ply them with a sustained hail of javelins and with no shortage of missiles and no cover to speak of, this was proving lethally effective. Two of the attackers were already down, sprawled unmoving on the ankle-high grass. A third man was also down but he was screaming in agony, the haft of a javelin protruding from his thigh. Even as she ran down the track, the Grey One saw another warrior attempting to cross the rickety bridge only to be struck directly in the heart. Tottering idiotically, he seemed to stare at the javelin haft in disbelief before his legs gave way and he toppled into the roaring waters. Within an instant, he was gone, whisked out of sight by the frenzied current.

Staggering downhill, Liath Luachra turned her eyes from the violent spectacle at the channel to the cliff beside the waterfall, north-east of the stone circle. In spite of the drenching spray, Bodhmhall and Demne had taken up a position on the ledge at the precipice of the cliff. Muirne Muncháem was facing them and, from her frantic body language, seemed to be arguing violently with the *bandraoi*. At the limit of her endurance, Liath Luachra vainly attempted to push herself even faster.

Don't delay! Do it!

She tried to scream but her lungs, already empty, recoiled at the effort of crying out. Infuriatingly, agonizingly slowly, she drew closer, past the stone circle where Fintán had collapsed against the nearest slab, his body heaving from exhaustion. Ignoring him, she stumbled onwards, following the path down to the falls.

Closer now, she could see that Bodhmhall had backed right to the edge of the precipice, one arm clutched tight about her nephew, the other fending off the Flower of Almhu. The latter had managed to grasp the young boy's arm and was hauling him ferociously towards her with both hands. Demne, horrified and bewildered by the incomprehensible actions of the two women, was screaming in terror, the sound of his cries drowned out by the waterfall's roar.

Both women must have heard or, more probably, sensed her approach for they simultaneously glanced towards her. Muirne Muncháem's eyes, widening with hope, widened further with dismay as she looked over the woman warrior's shoulder to Gleor and the incoming horde of enemy warriors. Bodhmhall's features, conversely, seemed to take on an enigmatic, almost otherworldly serenity. With startling alacrity, she released her nephew and stepped forward to smash one fist into Muirne's face, striking the younger woman with such force that she was knocked clean off her feet.

155

Even as Muirne went sprawling onto the stony surface, the *bandraoí's* eyes locked on Liath Luachra. Skidding on a damp patch of earth to the side of the path, the woman warrior slipped and hit the ground hard. Winded, wounded and struggling to breathe, she somehow found the strength to shout above the roar of the rapidly approaching enemy horde.

'Bodhmhall!'

At the very lip of the ledge, Bodhmhall pulled her terrified nephew to her and hugged him close. With spray diluting the tears from her eyes she looked at Liath Luachra without expression.

And jumped.

A gurgling scream erupted from Muirne Mucháem, one grasping hand outstretched towards the empty piece of sky. Her agony was lost in the thunder of the waterfall and the increasing tumult of the approaching warriors. Javelins were now whirring through the air from both the eastern and western sides of the fortified stone circle, clattering against the stones with a terrible clamour.

Forcing herself to her feet, Liath Luachra stared at the ledge with a thumping heart. The previous evening, a great leap into the pool at the foot of the waterfall had been her proposal. Now, confronted by the enormity of that decision, all confidence in her plan was completely shattered. She stared open-mouthed at the cliff and was still staring when something slammed into her back and sent her spinning forward. As she hit the ground, all reason was forgotten as her natural battle instincts kicked in and she rolled to her feet in a single movement, drawing *Gléas Gan Ainm* from its scabbard. As a bulky shape lunged past her, she realised with a start that she hadn't been attacked but barged out of the way by Gleor, desperate to reach his woman. The old man hurtled forwards, followed closely by Fintán who'd apparently managed to get to his feet again. Although Gleor was bleeding badly from a wound in his arm, nothing was going to stop him from getting to the screaming Muirne Mucháem. Even as the *rí* of *Na Lamhraighe* reached her and desperately embraced her, Liath Luachra saw the old man's eyes flick up to the stone circle and the approaching horde. His face turned to her and those eyes stared deep into her soul. At that instant, she knew he'd understood. He'd have been close enough to see Bodhmhall leap with Demne. He'd have known there was no chance of holding the stone circle and he'd also have worked out the consequences of being captured alive, particularly for his wife. The choices were obvious.

He bundled the woman up off the ground and with surprisingly strength carried her towards the cliff. Sensing his intentions, the young woman wrenched free of his arms, resisting frantically, crying out in fresh dismay. 'My baby, Gleor! Our unborn child!'

But Gleor too was pleading, even as he dragged her inexorably closer. 'If you want the baby to survive you must take his leap. Bodhmhall knew this. Hold my hand, dear one. We will leap together.'

Despite his arguments, the Flower of Almhu continued to fight him and managed to wrench one arm free. As she beat him repeatedly in the face, he turned his head, growling something incomprehensible to Fintán. Whatever it was, his son, pale faced, ran to help him pull Muirne closer to the edge.

Although Liath Luachra's intent had always been to follow Bodhmhall off the cliff, she now found herself thwarted, access to the ledge blocked by the little group in front of her. A javelin whooshed past her ear. Another struck the ground beside her, its point embedded deep in the sodden earth.

Screaming, the woman warrior ran straight for the struggling trio now wrestling under the spray at the edge of the cliff. Building up as much momentum as she could, the Grey One raised her hands wide and slammed into them, knocking them off the edge.

To tumble from the cliff.

Into the watery void below.

Chapter Nine

The river lunged up at Bodhmhall faster than she could scream.

Not that she could scream. The constriction of her throat muscles in the terror of that flailing, weightless plunge prevented anything other than a mindless, winded wheeze. By the time she hit the water she was, literally, numb with fear.

The impact of that great initial smack almost knocked her senseless. The sliver of consciousness she managed to cling to was immediately pummelled by the churning assault of water in her lungs and the downward spin into foamy white.

In the end, it was the coldness of the water that stirred her to action, the physical shock of it spurring her to consciousness and igniting a primal drive for self-preservation. She struggled against the raging eddies, fighting instinctively. Somehow, through sheer good fortune rather than through any measure of skill or intent, her head broke surface and she retched up a lungful of water. Before she could fully breathe in, she was propelled underneath again.

Half insensible with shock, she was vaguely conscious of being tossed around, spilled over and over by the current. Despite the fact her eyes were open, she remained disorientated, unable to see anything other than white wash or to work out which way was up.

Once again she broke surface but this time her instincts kicked in and she gulped a mouthful of air before being driven beneath.

Abruptly, the churning motion eased and her head emerged above water. In a brief moment of stillness she caught a glimpse of her surroundings, a sight that served to panic her even more. Situated mid-stream, she'd already been swept far from the falls and was being swept even further downstream by the power of the current. Through the spray and the white-water rush, she caught glances of grey boulders spinning past on either side and although she had the wit to fear them, it was only by some miracle she somehow failed to hit them.

The waters clashed, splashed her face, blinded her, flooded her throat when she tried to breathe. An accomplished swimmer from years of childhood bathing, those skills did nothing to help her here. In the face of this overwhelming surge, she and Demne were helpless, a tranche of human flotsam as powerless as the piles of wood debris washed downstream with them.

Demne!

Fear for her nephew distracted her from her own terror and instilled her with a greater resolve to fight, to try and save them both. At first, tossed impotently by the surging waters, she thought she'd lost him. It took a moment to realise that although she couldn't see him through the spray, his hand was still locked inside her own, a drowning grip so tight that not even death would release it.

With renewed determination, she attempted to swim, to drag them both through the flow. It took less than an instant to realise she was wasting her time. In the spinning current, her arms and legs were useless: numb, leaden, thrashing rather than pulling against the water. They were completely at the river's mercy. She could no more swim and drag them to the riverbank than she could fly them into the air to safety.

As though to emphasise its dominance, the river chose that particular moment to raise them high on a whitewater wave then fling them forwards into another seething maelstrom. Floundering and drifting, she finally broke surface to find the waters calm, the relentless spray diminished. Although the flow swept them along as rapidly as ever, she was finally able to breathe freely, to clear her head and pull her nephew closer.

Something heavy smashed into her back, wrenched her about and momentarily knocked Demne away. The waters rushed between them and she felt them being pulled apart and only that death grip on his wrist prevented her from losing him completely. As she struggled to draw him close, something whipped her in the face. A hand!

A great, hairy arm tangled about her neck and a horrific white face pressed against her own, dead eyes staring into hers. Although her mind screamed, her body was too spent to react as the ghastly features were, just as suddenly, whisked away again, disappearing into the whitewater and wrenching her cloak with them.

Gods! Gods!

Too panic-stricken to make sense of the encounter, she had no opportunity to recover for, abruptly, they were back in the rapids: sliding between boulders, whipped by the tumbling branches of passing wood debris. Pummelled and half-drowned, she'd almost passed out when she felt Demne's little body strike her chest, propelled inwards by the vagaries of the river goddess. Without conscious thought, she wrapped her limbs about him, clenching him close, to spin and spin and spin.

All of a sudden, the water was calm and, blowing through her nose, she found she could breathe again. Her mind began to clear, dispelling the perilous fog that gathered on her peripheral vision. Although they were still being swirled about, she was vaguely conscious that the flow was slower and smoother and the air somehow brighter. She realised the river, having flushed through a series of tight rocky chasms, was now widening out, its force waning as it extended its spread.

The current nudged them nearer to shore and she kicked weakly in an effort to propel them even closer. Eventually, they were drifting alongside steep earthen banks capped with forest and thick foliage where the odd fallen branch dipped down to touch the water.

As they were swept by, Bodhmhall desperately grabbed for one of these but missed it completely. She tried again with the next branch but her fingertips slithered off the slimy surface. Another branch and then another and, finally, she succeeded in grabbing one firmly. Even as elation filled her heart, the rotten branch snapped off in her hand and they were swept on, the decaying wood no match for the momentum of their combined weight in the force of the water.

Bodhmhall would have cried had she any emotion left. Close to utter despair, she suddenly felt the nudge of grainy silt against the sole of her left foot. The sensation startled her to full alertness, prodding her from the jaded numbness that threatened to overtake her. Infused with fresh hope, she splashed clumsily forward, using her toes as a drag anchor to slow her momentum.

At first, it seemed to make no difference. They continued to be drawn downriver and although her feet occasionally scraped the muddy bottom, most of the time they didn't touch it. Fortunately, as the current swept into a wide bend, she was dragged over a raised section of the riverbed. Here, she managed to gain sufficient purchase to slow the drag and push them closer to the bank where the current was weaker. Finally in a position where she could actually stand upright in waist-high water, she staggered free of the river's grip, out onto the relative solidity of a slimy mud bank.

Lifting Demne awkwardly with one hand, she forced herself to totter forwards, further up the sloping mud. There, completely spent, she fell to her knees and rolled onto her right shoulder.

As the dark shadows of exhaustion crowded in from either side, she drew her nephew close. Her last conscious perception before passing out was the sickeningly slick sensation of the mud in which her right cheek was lying.

But she didn't care. The firmness of the land goddess's bosom had never felt so comforting, the magnitude of her welcome never so merciful.

***

When she opened her eyes, Bodhmhall's body was curled tight in a foetal position, barely able to move. Everything hurt.

Everything.

A faint ringing sound echoed in her ears. Her left arm felt wrong, misaligned, as though wrapped in several different layers of pain. It took an effort to keep her eyes open and focus through her blurred sight.

Lying on her side in the tacky silt, she tried to work out how long she'd been unconscious but it was difficult to think, to make any kind of rational conclusion. There was a fuzzy awareness that it'd been raining the last time she'd taken notice of the weather. When she'd stumbled from the water, her body had been chilled, trembling from cold and exhaustion. Now, conversely, she felt remarkably snug, warmed by a strong flush of sunshine against her back and shoulder.

Sunshine?

Maybe she'd been insensible longer than she'd first thought.

The pleasant sensation of sunbeams on her back was matched by the corresponding warmth of Demne's little frame pressed against her stomach. Despite the heat he radiated, she could feel him quivering like the heart of a startled deer. Ironically, that involuntary expression of suffering reassured her. Her nephew was alive.

Somehow, despite the terrible odds, she had saved him and although it seemed important to acknowledge the enormity of their survival she found the task beyond her. Physically and mentally traumatised from the experience of leaping off the falls and the near drowning, she was barely able to hold two coherent thoughts together.

After a time, the fog in her head began to dissipate but as her mind sharpened, the pain in her left arm intensified and grew increasingly hard to ignore. Attempting to rotate her arm, she found that the pain prevented her from turning it more than a miniscule amount. When she tried to flex her fingers, they were barely able to close together.

With growing unease, she examined the injured limb with greater care and discovered the area above the elbow was badly swollen and a patch of skin bulged slightly, pressed out by a knobbly hardness beneath.

The bone is broken!

She stared at the injury with a subdued mixture of shock and alarm. She had no memory of striking the arm although the impact must have occurred following her leap from the falls or against one of the river boulders while she was being swept downstream. Fortunately, because her body remained in a state of shock, she was spared the worst of the pain but it wouldn't take long before that numbness wore off and the full effect of the injury kicked in.

With a groan, she pushed Demne aside. Holding the injured arm close to her chest, she struggled to her feet.

And collapsed again immediately.

The impact with the ground shot a spasm of agony through her arm. A red mist formed in the corners of her eyes and she hissed in anguish as she struggled to fix parameters to the pain, to wrap it up and pull it in to more bearable levels. Finally, her vision cleared, the excruciating scorch reduced to an aching burn and she stared at her legs in incomprehension, wondering vaguely why they hadn't done as she wanted.

It took several moments for the realisation to sink in that her body was exhausted, still struggling to cope with the immense stress to which it had been subjected. It dawned on her then that she wasn't going to be able to move very far. It would take time for her body to recover. Time she didn't really have.

Trembling, Bodhmhall used her right elbow to raise herself into a sitting position. Closing her eyes, she focussed on her breathing and used an old druidic mind technique to shift the deepening ache in her arm to one side, relocating it to a place where she could temporarily section it off. When the burden of pain had finally been corralled, she exhaled and held the damaged limb tenderly against her chest. For now the pain was tolerable but it was only a temporary respite. It would last only as long as her concentration could keep it contained.

Which won't be long.

With a sigh, she raised her eyes to survey her surroundings. The mud bank where they'd landed was a long, shit-coloured crescent that stretched downriver for fifty paces or more before curving back out into the treacherous waters. Immediately down from where she was seated, a scattered set of scuffed imprints marked the point where she'd emerged from the river and staggered up to the muddy bank to more solid sediment higher up.

Slanting gently upwards from the river, the bank continued to grow increasingly drier and more compact until it reached the treeline where it was immediately swallowed up by the undergrowth. Poking above the nearer tree tops – but situated somewhere far in the distance behind them – Bodhmhall observed the barren summit of a long, grey ridge that appeared to run roughly parallel to the river. Across the surging waterway, on the opposite bank, an identical view confirmed what she'd seen from the waterfall. The river flushed through a narrow, inhospitable-looking gorge with steep forest on either side.

She scraped up a handful of gritty sediment and let it trickle through her fingers.

She couldn't tell how far downstream from the falls they'd travelled but, from her current position, the river seemed to run in a westerly direction. The problem was that, just around the next bend, the river could completely change direction as it followed the topographical features lying in its path. It was impossible to know for certain.

One thing she was certain of however, was that An Glenn Teann was almost certainly unattainable from this location. Even if she somehow managed to work her way back upriver, there was no way she could scale the steep cliffs beside the falls, particularly given the condition of her arm.

The thought of the injury prompted a quick stab of discomfort from the offending limb.

Yes, yes. I know you're still there.

Feeling beleaguered, she turned her eyes upriver and it was only then that she noticed the body sprawled about twenty paces from where she was sitting. Lying half-in, half-out of the water, the lower legs and bare heels were hitched onto the bank's grainy surface, the head and shoulders bobbing gently offshore. Like her, Demne and the other bits of river detritus, it had apparently been deposited at that particular section by the whims of the current.

She considered the body with interest. From the size and bulk, it was obviously male and although the head was mostly submerged, the buffed leather tunic identified him as one of Gob an Teanga Gorm's men. She stared at the padded tunic, tightened at the waist by a leather belt. Her lips turned down in a thoughtful frown.

I can use that belt. A splint tie.

Unwilling to trust her feet, she shifted forward on her buttocks, making for the bobbing corpse by sliding down the bank. Clasping her injured arm tight against her chest to protect it from the worst of the awkward movements, she successfully reached the water's edge then crawled upriver to where the dead man's foot was snagged.

Fortunately, the current helped push the body ashore, the weak flow sweeping it in at an angle so that it ended up lying on its side. Once he was stretched on the bank, parallel to the river, it proved a simple enough task to roll the dead warrior onto his back and she studied the moist, white features in silence. The corpse was that of a young man with twenty years on him at most. The face was pale, bearded and stared unseeingly upwards with empty, lifeless eyes.

She recognised him of course. But then, she was hardly going to forget him. After all, he – or rather, it – had struck her in the river and ripped her cloak away while she was drowning.

With a sigh, she began to rifle through the dead man's clothing. Loosening the belt, she found that it had a knife sheath attached. To her delight, a razor sharp knife with a bullhorn handle had somehow remained secured within. The real find, however, was located deep inside the tunic, wedged down between his ribcage and where the belt had been pulled tightest. From here, she withdrew a sodden little pouch and, opening it, emptied its contents onto the gritty surface of the mud bank: two flints, a previously desiccated chunk of fungus that was now completely sodden and several wisps of hay and heather – also sodden.

A fire-starter pouch!

She stared, hardly able believe her good fortune. Fire meant warmth and the means to cook. Fire meant the ability to keep the darkness at bay. Fire meant life.

Putting the flints to one side, she laid the pouch flat on a stone to dry in the sun. With the exception of the fungus, she tossed the other contents into the river. The fungus, too, was saturated but from experience she knew the porous material would dry quickly. If she could return it to its desiccated state it would serve as excellent fire starter material when no other tinder was to hand.

She took the time to remove the dead man's clothing, using the knife to slice the holdings so that they could be pulled free with one hand. Everything had potential as a resource. Everything could be put to some other use.

Plunder completed, the *bandraoi* pulled back from the body and used her feet to drive it off the mud bank. Crawling into the shallows, she pushed it further out, propelling it towards the deeper part of the river where the current tugged it, twisted it about and spun it off downriver. Within moments, the corpse had drifted around the tip of the mud bank and out of sight.

Bodhmhall stared upriver to the furthest point where the white surge of water was still visible, surging through a wide canyon. There was no sign of Liath Luachra.

Revitalised by the heat of the sun, she tried getting to her feet for a second time and, on this occasion, although her legs trembled, she managed to remain upright. She took some hesitant steps forward and made it to the edge of the trees. Heartened by this success, she pushed further through the vegetation, surveying the edge of the forest floor until she found what she was looking for: three thin deadwood branches, each about the same length as her forearm.

Gathering them together, she leaned back against the nearest tree trunk and set them aside on the ground with the belt, the leather clothing and her other plunder. Holding her left hand out as straight as she was able, she probed the break with the fingertips of her right hand, working out the alignment, judging the length and the pressure she'd need to apply to force it back in place. Her lips formed an involuntary grimace. Mental concentration or not, this was going to hurt.

She took a deep breath.

No point wasting time.

Without further thought, she pressed and twisted down with her right hand, jamming the protruding bone back into position.

Her scream echoed off the walls of the valley for a long time after.

***

164

Demne was sitting up when she emerged from the trees, white-faced and trembling, her arm set and braced with the improvised splints. On tentative, unsteady feet, she made her way towards him, clasping the limb with great tenderness. Her nephew regarded her approach but said nothing. His face had regained some of its colour but his expression was blank, his eyes glazed and distant.

He's still in shock.

Keeping her arm close to her body, the *bandraoi* clumsily shuffled out of her sodden tunic and let it drop to the ground. With her free hand, she unwrapped the material of her loincloth then draped both over a thin, moss-coated beech bough that poked down from the forest to dangle at an angle above them. Heavy with water, the clothing pulled the sagging branch even lower.

She turned to her nephew. 'You too.'

The boy complied, removing his own cloak and tunic without any display of emotion then handing her the damp bundle. She accepted it with her good hand, quickly hanging the clothes next to her own on the drooping bough.

Naked, she turned to face the mid-day sun and despite everything: the horrific leap, the near drowning, the agony of her injury and the growing sense of helplessness that threatened to overwhelm her, she found herself enjoying the rejuvenating flush of heat it shed over her body. She closed her eyes, absorbing the pink glow that filtered through her eyelids and found her thoughts turn, unexpectedly, to Fiacail mac Codhna. Back in the old days at Dún Baoiscne, back when she'd been married to the formidable warrior, she'd regularly teased him for his daily ritual of sun worship, standing naked in some open spot as he talked up at Father Sun. Now, with the feeling of that invigorating touch on her own skin, the odd ritual seemed bizarrely sensible.

With a grunt, she lowered herself onto the bank beside her nephew and wrapped her good hand about him. Although he remained silent, she felt him lean in, trembling, against her.

She hugged him closer, his obvious distress provoking a jaded sense of guilt. She had leapt off the cliff of her own – admittedly reluctant – volition. Her nephew, by contrast, had been carried over the edge, kicking and screaming, by the one person he'd always trusted most to protect him. It was a wonder, she reflected, that he even allowed her to touch him.

'You'll understand all this one day, *a bhuachaill*,' she whispered. 'I promise you. For now, we have the sun on our face, a warm breeze through our hair. We are alive.'

Turning her gaze upriver, she stared at the distant surge of white water. Although she was thinking it, she did not add, 'For now at least.'

***

Fearful of upsetting Demne even further, Bodhmhall hid her concern at Liath Luachra's continued absence beneath a mantle of good humour. The truth however, was that the woman warrior should have been with them by now had she followed them over the cliff as planned.

Unless things hadn't gone to plan.

The *bandraoi* comforted herself with the infinite number of reasons why Liath Luachra mightn't have been able to link up with them. She might simply have been carried past by the current, unable to make it to shore. And by the Gods, they'd had enough difficulties of their own on that score! It was also possible the river might have simply taken her in a different direction along the opposite bank or deposited her further upriver.

There was one other possibility of course. One that she simply didn't have the courage to face at that particular moment. To deflect it, she momentarily focussed her full attention on her arm, gasping at the flare of agony it produced before she was able to thrust it back down to the space where she'd left it. When it had settled to a gnawing discomfort, she forced her thoughts to turn to the more practical tasks to be completed if they were to survive the night and however long else they remained Out in the Great Wild. The sheer scale of that particular challenge was such that, for a moment, she just froze, and had to take several calming breaths. *'Coiscéim,'* she cautioned herself aloud, recalling the old mantra that Cairbre had beaten into her over her early years. Little steps.

Little steps and little gains that lead to large victories.

The tension in her shoulders slowly eased as her earlier calm returned. A fresh stab of pain briefly undermined her efforts but after successfully regaining her equilibrium, she felt ready to confront the reality of their situation.

I am in pain. My arm hobbles my physical ability.

We are lost. I have no knowledge of where this river valley leads.

We are defenceless and have no supplies. We have lost our allies and all those who protected us.

Including Liath Luachra.

Don't think of her.

Don't.

Once again, she pushed the woman warrior from her thoughts before the emotion could latch on and depress her flagging spirit. In the subsequent mental flurry for an alternative subject to fill her head, she surprised herself with the first thought that jumped to mind:

Muirne Muncháem.

She sat up, her back completely rigid. As distractions went, it was – admittedly – effective, even if equally unwelcome. Her last clear memory of the Flower of Almhu was the expression of shock on the younger woman's face when she'd punched her, just before leaping from the falls. She

166

considered that recollection with vague detachment for now it felt as though it had occurred a lifetime ago. Finally, she shrugged. Even now, with a cooler head and candid recognition of the sundered alliance, she felt no regret for that particular action. She derived no specific pleasure from the memory of the blow but there was no point in denying the satisfaction it'd given her at the time.

For, by the Gods, she deserved it!

She grimaced, recalling the discussion with Gob an Teanga Gorm immediately prior to battle. Although she'd somehow managed to disguise it at the time, the extent of Muirne's betrayal had cut deep. Despite all her protestations, all the declarations of innocence, it turned out she'd had an intimate knowledge of their hatchet-faced opponent all along.

Her thoughts returned to six years earlier, back to the day when the Flower of Almhu had first appeared in Glenn Ceoch, pregnant and desperate and pleading for sanctuary. Even at the time, Bodhmhall had suspected the woman of having some knowledge as to why she was being hunted, why anyone would seek to murder her and her son. Preoccupied with the defence of her settlement and the protection of her unborn nephew however, she'd neglected to investigate and pursue those suspicions further.

Until it was all too late.

Afterwards, when they were secreting Muirne to the *Lamhraighe* territories, she'd questioned the younger woman mercilessly during the course of their journey. Made of stern stuff however, the Flower of Almhu had not cracked. At no time had she dropped even a hint that she knew more than what she'd already told them. Now, after all the death and destruction that continued to follow her, there was a need for reckoning.

But that will wait another day.

She funnelled her attention back to their immediate circumstances.

So what to do?

Coiscéim. Little steps.

With this approach, the answer to their immediate issues turned out to be surprisingly easy. For the moment, they would have to remain where they were. They'd missed the better part of the daylight for travel and they were in no fit state to start a trek over such rough terrain. A full night's rest would give them opportunity to recuperate, to recover their strength and prepare for the following day. Although growing increasingly unlikely with every moment, there was also a slim chance that the woman warrior might reappear to join them.

The following morning, if Liath Luachra was still missing, they would leave at first light. The risk of remaining in the same location any longer than that was simply too high. Gob an Teanga Gorm, furious at their escape, would no doubt be dispatching forces to find them. Unless they were willing to jump from the cliffs – something she considered highly unlikely – it would take them at least two to three days to reach this valley.

By which time she wanted to be far away.

She paused, tapping the tips of her fingers together as she thought through the subsequent decisions that would need to be made. To leave the valley, they could follow the river, at least until it drained out of the mountains. If they were lucky, the waterway would continue flowing to the west. If they were very lucky they'd eventually strike *Clann Baoiscne* territory and a landscape with which she was considerably more familiar. The terrain to be traversed until then would be rugged, rough and potentially dangerous but, if they were careful, she was confident she could get them to Dún Baoiscne.

She bit her lip.

The prospect of turning up at Dún Baoiscne alone with Demne, injured and bereft of leverage or influence, was not one that appealed to her. Unfortunately, given her current circumstances, she could see no option other than throwing herself on her father's mercy and hoping that Liath Luachra would reappear.

If she lives.

Don't!

Bodhmhall frowned, absently wiping a smear of mud from the inside of her thigh. Thoughts of Liath Luachra would bring despair and despair was the killer of hope. For the time being, she needed to continue preoccupying herself with other issues. Fortunately, there was no shortage of issues that needed to be considered.

'Snares,' she decided aloud. 'We need snares.'

Demne raised his head.

'I can make snares, *a Aintín*. From those reeds.' He pointed at a section of heavy growth further down the river bank. 'Liath Luachra taught me how.'

The *bandraoi* regarded her nephew closely. The glaze had faded from his eyes and although his features remained vacant she was encouraged by the fact that he'd initiated the proposal. 'Very well. You can make the snares. And set them. But make sure you place them in a rabbit path.'

She waited for him to acknowledge the instruction with a nod of his head and answered it with one of her own. 'Good. While you occupy yourself with the snares I'll gather fuel for the fire. Once we have a blaze going, we can make a start on weapons.'

'Weapons?'

She regarded him with a passive expression that belied her relief. Now, she definitely had his interest.

'The Great Wild holds little respect for those who cannot protect themselves.'

168

'I'll protect you, *a Aintín*. I have my sling.' With this, the boy undid the leather sling lashed around his forearm. He held it up for her to see. 'Besides,' he added confidently. 'We won't have to wait long. Liath Luachra will find us. The Grey One can find anything.'

She peered at the child with sudden weariness, her lifting spirits once again subdued by the woman warrior's absence. Unable to muster sufficient enthusiasm to temper her response, she refrained from speech and settled for a limp smile instead. 'Very well, *a laoichín* [my little warrior]. You can protect me. But first,' she pointed towards the reeds. 'The snares.'

***

Once the sun dropped behind the northern ridge, the shadows crept in quietly, like uninvited guests at a banquet. In the blanching daylight, while Demne fashioned a pair of surprisingly competent-looking snares, Bodhmhall returned to the forest, shambling through the dappled shadows like a clumsy ghost. There the *bandraoi* laboriously gathered firewood from the forest floor, lugging small piles of the collected debris back to the treeline above the mud bank. She was pleased to find that the deadwood was dry for the most part, effectively sheltered from the recent rain due to the thickness of the canopy.

Restricted from carrying out even the most basic of tasks because of her arm, she walked Demne through each step of the firebuilding process: using the knife to dig a sheltered fire-pit, creating a small bird's nest of tow and bark and then, finally, striking the flints together to shave off the sparks needed to ignite the tinder pile.

Unaccustomed to the striking technique, the boy's fingers repeatedly bungled the final step and Bodhmhall was obliged to bite her tongue as he repeated the action over and over again. Eventually, almost fifty strikes later, a lucky blow produced a shower of sparks that tumbled into the tinder, instantly igniting the withered material. Quickly blowing over the smouldering tinder, Bodhmhall succeeded in stirring a small flame into life. With great care, she laid thin strips of dry bark over the resulting flicker, watching as it caught at the woody material, nibbled it tentatively then greedily began to consume it. Within a short time, a small fire was crackling cheerfully in the little hole.

'Well done, Demne. That is good work.'

The boy glowed with pride as he carefully broke a pile of dried twigs into smaller segments and used them to feed the fire.

'Slowly,' she warned him. 'Some of those pieces are big enough to suffocate the flame. Use the smaller pieces. Remember, a fire is like a breast-fed baby. It needs to be fed little morsels before it can gorge on larger solids.'

Amused by the description, Demne giggled and Bodhmhall felt a sudden lightness in her heart at that sound.

Later, while the boy wandered downriver to try his hand – literally – at tickling a trout he'd glimpsed in the shadows of the river bank, the *bandraoi* remained beside the fire, awkwardly cutting a rough leather satchel from the dead man's tunic. While she worked, she kept one watchful eye on the passing river. Like the sunlight, her hopes of Liath Luachra appearing were waning. Despite that, she did not intend to miss the woman warrior if, by some chance, she happened to arrive floating downriver towards them.

After a time, Demne returned with a river trout held up proudly in either hand. Bodhmhall nodded, genuinely impressed by the boy's achievement and her empty stomach rumbled involuntarily at the prospect of food.

Laying the completed satchel aside, she quickly showed him how to gut his catch and wrap them in a smooth layer of river mud. By the time they'd placed them in the ashes of the fire to cook, the shadows were thickening around them and, shivering, the *bandraoi* retrieved their clothes from where they'd been drying. Tossing the boy's tunic and cloak to him she pulled on her own clothing with short, awkward tugs, ruefully regretting the loss of her cloak.

They remained by the fire, stoking the embers and growing increasingly famished as they waited for the fish to cook. To pass the time, the *bandraoi* directed her nephew to fetch two lengths of ash sapling she'd procured from the woods to fashion a pair of basic spears. The boy needed little encouragement and was quick to run off and retrieve the ash lengths in case she changed her mind.

She had Demne hold one of the saplings firmly between his palms while she clumsily used the knife to carve a rough point at the tip, sharpening it as best she was able with a series of graceless hacks and cuts.

Raising the finished weapon, she held it lengthways so that her eye could run along the shaft and noted how it curved very slightly to the left towards the pointed end. This defect, in itself, did not overly concern her. She'd been under no delusions that she could ever cast the spear effectively, particularly with a broken arm. The reality was that concealment and refuge would be their greatest protection over the coming days. The spears were intended as a last resort, a potential deterrent where concealment and refuge failed them. Admittedly, any spear wielded by a one-handed woman or a six year old boy was going to be a limited deterrent but it was the best she could do under the circumstances.

Laying the head of the first spear to harden in the ashes, she immediately started on the second, shorter, weapon following an identical process. When this was completed, she passed it to Demne so that he could assess the straightness for himself, a task he assumed with touching gravitas. Just as he laid his eyes along the shaft, a lonely howl, eerie but distant, echoed in from the surrounding gloom. The boy tensed and stared anxiously out at the darkness before turning to his aunt for reassurance.

'Don't' worry,' she told him as she reached down to pull the fish from the fire. 'The wolves are in another valley. They don't have our scent.' She handed him one of the fish, blowing on her fingertips from the heat of it. Waiting for her own fish to cool, her hunger finally overcame her patience and she cracked the hardened mud layer open with her hands. Sweet-smelling steam gushed from the inside but unable to wait any longer, she stuffed the white flesh into her mouth, ignoring the burning sensation as she ravenously gorged it down.

Later, when they'd finished eating, Bodhmhall guided her nephew to a narrow crack in the earth of the upper river bank, a potential refuge she'd spotted while rifling through the dead warrior's clothing. Accessed via a low gap at knee level, her previous exploration had revealed that it cut deep into the bank for a distance of three to four paces before tapering out. Sliding backwards into the constricted space, Bodhmhall found that by hunching her feet up close, she could pull herself inside so that her head rested about four hand-widths from the narrow entrance. It was a tight squeeze but sufficient space also remained for Demne to wriggle in beside her, onto the moss and fern she'd tossed in earlier.

To further defend the little refuge, the *bandraoi* had Demne haul a thick cluster of blackthorn into the crevice behind him. Wedging the dark bough firmly against the earthen walls, it created a spiny plug that would prevent anything larger than a rat from entering.

Tucking the two spears close to her side in case they were needed, Bodhmhall shuffled around to get as comfortable as possible. Although she was hurting, she didn't doubt that her fatigue would eventually overwhelm the aches and pain and allow her to sleep. Tugging Demne's little cloak over them both, she felt the heat of his body against her own as her eyelids flickered and consciousness began to spiral off. Casting one last look at their blackthorn defence, it struck her that she'd gained at least some value from the ill-fated experiment with the stone circle back in Glenn Teann. All she could hope was that, this time around, the outcome would be more favourable.

***

The night passed without incident and they slept soundly. So soundly, in fact, that they overslept, screened from the first light of dawn within the darkness of their refuge. When Bodhmhall finally pushed the blackthorn screen aside, the sun was already above the eastern ridge. With a curse, she wriggled forwards out of the hole, wincing each time her arm came into contact with the side of the little burrow. Rising to her feet, she brushed the accumulated debris from her clothes and stretched the stiffness from her limbs, pleased to note that her head felt markedly clearer.

Rousing her groggy nephew, she urged him from his bed for a breakfast of watercress and the scraps of fish that remained from the previous night's meal. Afterwards, as he sat yawning on the river bank, she washed herself in the shallows before casting one last lingering glance at the waters flowing down from the rocky passage further upriver.

Nothing.

Without dwelling on it further, Bodhmhall turned to pick up her spear and carefully hung the makeshift leather satchel over her shoulder. The discouraging lightness did little to improve her mood. It held nothing more than the fire starter pouch, the knife and scabbard, Demne's snares, and the remains of a rabbit found in one of those snares that very morning, but she knew it could have been a lot lighter.

She looked to her nephew. 'We must be brave and cautious now, *a laoichín*. We have no-one to help us but ourselves.' With this, she turned and started walking.

Leaving the mud bank, they headed west, keeping as close to the river as the landscape permitted for over the next few days they'd be dependent on that body of water, not only as a physical guide through the territory, but as the main source of their food and water.

At first, following the waterway was simple enough. The route alongside the treeline was relatively open and regular and on those occasions when the bank dipped too steeply, veered sharply out into the river or was simply obstructed by heavy vegetation, they could clamber inland for a time, work their way parallel to the waterway and, eventually, return to intercept it again.

Despite Bodhmhall's arm, they made relatively good progress and by early afternoon the *bandraoi* had noticed the ridges push further back as the river gorge widened and the steeper mountains eased down to foothills. The prospect of release from the confines of the narrow gorge heartened her for it provided them with additional space in which to move or hide should the need arise. It also meant that they were less restricted in the paths they chose, an important point if Gob An Teanga Gorm's men came looking for them.

Sometime later, they were able to take advantage of this new expanded freedom when confronted by a heavily vegetated section of the river bank that obstructed any direct passage. Heading inland, they made their way through the thick forest at a diagonal to the river but made sure to keep the waterway in earshot for fear they'd lose their way. By then, Bodhmhall's arm was throbbing incessantly and although she'd managed to fashion a sling to strap it close to her left breast, the pain had caused her to break into a sweat. She focussed her attention on the forest floor, hoping to catch sight of some herbs she could use to dull the pain.

She was still scouring the ground ahead when they cut through a swathe of trees and walked straight into a large clearing. Startled by the sudden brightness, Bodhmhall lifted her head.

And froze.

Directly ahead, in the centre of the sun-laced clearing, a pack of five wolves was feasting savagely on the shredded carcass of a deer. Startled by the sudden intrusion, the animals raised bloody muzzles and stared, black eyes fixed unblinkingly at the involuntary intruders. Slowly, very slowly, Bodhmhall started to back out of the clearing, pressing Demne behind her. The wolves observed their retreat with menacing intensity, muzzles peeled back in hideous full-fanged snarls. Fortunately, reluctant to leave the remains of their feast, they refrained from following.

As soon as they were in the trees, Bodhmhall turned and pushed Deme ahead, hurrying the two of them back towards the river. Here, after some anxious searching, she managed to locate an alternative route that, although steep and treacherous, allowed them to bypass the clearing.

Despite making as much distance as possible, Bodhmhall spotted one of the wolves again later that afternoon, observing them coldly from the shadows in the undergrowth off to their left. Although she was shaking with fear, the *bandraoi* made a brave show of ferociousness, shouting loudly and waving her spear until the wolf retreated, casting a sullen look in its wake as it slunk back into the shadows and disappeared.

Alerted now, Bodhmhall used her *Gift* to monitor their surroundings and, almost immediately, caught sight of another wolf trailing them through the trees to the rear. This time, she made no attempt to scare the animal away but increased their pace, keeping a wary eye open for any other sign of the animals.

After a time, this second wolf also disappeared from sight and even with her *Gift*, she was unable to detect any further evidence of the animals. Bodhmhall breathed a tight sigh of relief. Presumably, the animals had moved on, drawn away by the prospect of less formidable looking prey, a misjudgement for which she was exceptionally grateful.

Coming across a sunny, flower-filled clearing where a wide stream flowed into the main waterway, they paused to rest and slake their thirst. They also chewed on some edible roots the *bandraoi* scavenged from a section of the riverbank and although the fare was hardly satisfying, it was enough to stop the worst of the grumbling in their stomachs. She thought longingly of the rabbit inside her bag but knew such a luxury would have to wait until later that evening. For the moment, they had to continue until they found a more defensible refuge for the night. It was more than possible that the wolves might change their mind and return to stalk them after all.

With a groan, Bodhmhall got to her feet, the ache in her arm somewhat diminished by the sight of her nephew rising to join her without complaint. Leaving the pretty clearing behind, they headed away from the river once more, following the tributary upstream until they were able to find a suitable crossing point. This took them a surprisingly long time and they'd travelled some distance towards the western foot hills before they found a shallow ford. On the opposite side of the stream they were fortunate to hit a recent deer trail that seemed to lead back towards the river and offered a much less arduous route through waist high fern instead of thick woods and gorse. Wary from their experiences with the wolves, Bodhmhall used her *Gift* to keep a watchful eye on their surroundings but, shortly after leaving the ford behind, the terrain changed abruptly once more, the fern growth subsiding and the forest opening out to sparse woodland with low shrubs and ankle high undergrowth that provided little shelter for stalking predators.

'*Coinín!*' [Rabbit!]

Her nephew's excited howl took Bodhmhall completely by surprise and she gaped in heart-pounding confusion as he bounded forwards into the woods, his spear held high. Several paces ahead of him, she caught a brief flicker of a white bob tail as the pursued rabbit fled for its life.

Flustered, she called after the youngster but, consumed by the chase, he didn't hear her and quickly disappeared into the trees after his quarry. Cursing, she increased her own pace, stumbling in pursuit as fast as she was able with the injured limb. Hurrying through the scattered trees, the topography funnelled her into a wide grass-lined passage between two low, heavily-vegetated mounds. Anxious, she was about to call out a second time when she spotted him further along the grassy channel. Standing at the base of the eastern mound, he was angrily poking the head of his spear into a hole where the rabbit had clearly taken refuge.

Breathing heavily, the *bandraoi* finally caught up to him and although she had intended to berate him for his reckless flight, the comical expression of vexed frustration on his face was enough to syphon the anger away. She sighed and released a quiet chuckle.

'Don't worry, *a bhuachaill*. There'll be plenty of others for you to hunt. Besides, when we get to Dún Baoiscne, you can always –'

She stiffened suddenly, her nephew's carelessness forgotten as her eyes flickered towards the top of the eastern mound. A distinct sound was coming from somewhere on the summit, a sustained shuffling or brushing of foliage as though something was forcing its way through the undergrowth.

The wolf pack!

Alarmed, Bodhmhall glanced up and down the passage. The steepness of the slope behind them restricted their options for flight to either continuing along the grassy channel or returning in the direction from which they'd come. Conscious that the latter route would trap them between the river and its tributary, she quickly urged the boy forwards. 'Hurry', she hissed. 'We have to find refuge.'

Jamming the spear under her right armpit, she staggered after her nephew, following the trail as it continued to curve around the base of the eastern mound. Suddenly, on the summit ahead, the bushes shuddered and a stout figure in a dark, hooded robe pushed his way out into the open. Bodhmhall and Demne stumbled to a halt. The *bandraoi* stared up in shock.

Not a wolf!

Oblivious to their presence, the newcomer halted, apparently confused to find himself confronted by what, from where he was standing, must have resembled a long ditch. As he stared across towards the western mound, the bushes behind him shuddered again and another, smaller figure emerged from the undergrowth to join him. This individual, too, was dressed in a cowled robe and although, at first, Bodhmhall thought it was a child, the unusual posture suggested something other than that.

By then, the stocky man's gaze had turned down along the passage to fall on the two travellers below. Bodhmhall saw his posture stiffen, apparently as startled by their appearance as they were by his. For a moment, both parties stared at each other with the usual distrust that characterised such encounters in the Great Wild. The stocky figure looked from her to the boy then back along the trail as though checking to make sure they were alone. The smaller figure tugged insistently on his taller comrade's sleeve and as the latter leaned down, his eyes still on Bodhmhall, he whispered urgently in his ear.

Bodhmhall grasped her spear nervously. Although relieved that they weren't facing a pack of wolves, engaging with strangers was always a risky business in the Great Wild. And these two, although not physically formidable, provoked a distinct sense of unease. She considered the options available to her. From their current position, it was at least thirty paces to that point in the passage where the two newcomers could still descend and intercept them. By retreating, although she was confident they could lose the strangers in the undergrowth – they looked even less physically capable of speed than herself and Demne – they'd be cut off from escaping the river valley. She twisted the grip of her spear once more. It looked as though her best option might be to brazen it out.

She cleared her throat.

'I see you, Strangers,' she called.

'I see you, Woman.' The stocky man, pulled down his cowl. Although still too far away to make out the full detail of his features, she was immediately struck by the fleshiness of his face and the pendulous jowls beneath his jaw. 'It is a pleasant day for a stroll is it not.'

The voice rang hale and hearty but an unsteady undercurrent gave it an oddly forced sound. Bodhmhall shifted uneasily, glancing up the trail.

'Forgive me for startling you, travellers. I am named Regna of Mag Fea. And this ...' He jerked a hand to indicate the smaller figure. 'This is Olpe.' The fat man now turned his gaze to Demne. 'And how would you be named, little man?'

The boy returned that stare with guarded reticence. Like his aunt, he too had sensed something odd about the strangers.

'Are you from these parts?' the heavyset man tried again. 'From this wilderness?'

Bodhmhall took the opportunity to move up and place a hand on her nephew's shoulder. 'My son has been instructed to speak only with faces that are familiar. But, yes. We have a holding upriver.' She urged the boy a few tentative steps forward by applying pressure to his shoulder. Two, three then four more paces.

'So this is your son.' The man eyed her with a blank expression.

She considered him warily, wondering at the oddness of the question given what she'd just told him. Loath to encourage further conversation, she simply nodded, her eyes scanning the trail ahead. She could now see that the passage culminated at a copse of beech trees, a distance of fifty paces or so. If they managed to reach that green embrace they would be safe.

'Ah, yes I see the resemblance.' Suddenly, the fat man was all smiles again. 'It's in the lips, isn't it? And a tight narrowing at the bridge of the nose. I would say he has your good looks.' Despite the apparent playfulness of his words, his voice was flat and, now that she was closer and could see him better, so were his eyes. Flattery was clearly not something that came naturally to him. 'But, wait! I see you are injured. Will you not rest a spell to let me help? I have some skill with herbs.'

Bodhmhall attempted a half-hearted smile and made a generic gesture of regret. 'Alas, my man and his brothers await us. He is not known for his patience so we dare not tarry.'

She kept moving forwards while she was speaking, edging her way up the trail with intentionally unhurried steps. This time however, the movement prompted Regna of Mag Fea to move forwards as well, one step down the rise towards them. It seemed a casual movement but Bodhmhall couldn't help reading a certain menace into the action.

To her surprise, the overweight man suddenly held up his hands, palms turned outwards in apparent acquiescence. 'An impatient man? In that case, you'd better continue. I will never stand between an impatient man and his woman. Travel well.'

The casual nature of Regna of Mag Fea's farewell did not fill her with confidence but she felt a certain relief when she saw him lean against a tree with his arms folded. He nodded benevolently as they passed directly below him and hurried onwards, gradually increasing the distance between them.

Eager to leave the two robed figures behind, Bodhmhall pushed the boy ahead but continued to keep her eyes on them, watching for any sign of treachery, any attempt at pursuit. It was this committed focus to her rear that prevented her from perceiving the ambush ahead. She was still looking backwards as they approached the beech trees so her only forewarning was the sudden snap of a twig and a start of alarm from her nephew.

Swinging about, she attempted to bring the spear to bear but before she could complete the turn, the head of the shaft was knocked aside and the weapon wrenched from her limited grip. A shadow lunged up out of the woods in front of her but she was grabbed from behind and lifted clean off her feet in an enormous bear hug.

Yelling in outrage, she struggled to free herself but the grip was too tight and she was unable to break free. To her right, Demne, too, was struggling ineffectually, in the grip of a tall, bald man with black robes.

The strangers! More than two!

She continued to fight, kicking back with the heels of her feet. Whoever was holding her however, had thighs of iron for her blows bounced off with no effect. Changing her tactics, she targeted the groin area with both feet and was immediately rewarded with a bellow of pain. The great arms loosened and she fell to the ground, slamming into the earth with her broken arm.

A devastating sear of agony flushed through her entire body and, for a moment, she passed out. When she came to her senses, the pain was still present but, thankfully, not as intense. Opening her eyes, she looked up from where she was lying and saw another robed man rummaging through the contents of her satchel. Disgusted at the meagre findings, he snorted and haphazardly tossed the bag, contents and all, into the bushes.

Rolling onto her side, she found Demne sitting beside her, held down by the tiny figure last seen on top of the mound. The stranger's hood had fallen back from his face, revealing the startlingly withered features of a very ugly old man. Somehow sensing her scrutiny, he turned and stared at her with an intensity that was decidedly unnerving.

She was struggling to lever herself off the ground with her good arm when Regna of Mag Fea's distinctive voice sounded from behind. 'Futh, if you please.'

Somebody grabbed her roughly by the hair, using the thick, brown locks to haul her painfully to her feet. Terrified, she twisted around to face her assailant: a brawny bald man with a glacial expression. Over his substantial shoulders, she saw another face that was identical in almost every respect.

177

Her heart sank.

Liath Luachra's Man Pair.

That half of the Man Pair who was holding her forced her head around to where the obese fat man was waiting. Up close, he looked even more physically repugnant. The folds of his cheeks almost obscured the spider tattoo on the side of his face and quivering lips were repeatedly moistened by a darting tongue. A pair of black eyes, completely void of empathy, drilled directly into hers and a tremor of fear ran through her.

Chomh dubh le croí an préachán. As black as a crow's heart.

Regna of Mag Fea stroked a surprisingly hairless chin. 'Very good. You've met my travelling companions.'

'Who are you?' she demanded, feigning a confidence she certainly didn't feel. 'Why do you accost us?'

'Accost?' He looked at her with a mocking smirk. 'Accost?' He shook his head. 'No. We are hardly accosting you, young woman. We are merely inviting you to dinner.'

Chapter Ten

The journey to the strangers' camp was long, arduous and extremely painful. Too tall to walk upright while the big man – Futh – insisted on dragging her by the hair, Bodhmhall was obliged to scuttle alongside in a contorted, humiliating crouch while desperately trying to keep sight of with her nephew. On several occasions, she stumbled and the resulting jolt to her arm caused her vision to flush white in agony.

Most of the journey passed in an aching blur. By the time they finally reached their destination, she was weeping and almost incoherent with pain. As a result, she barely noticed when they stopped and Regna called out, to be answered almost immediately by another gruff male voice.

She was vaguely aware of entering a short box canyon with mossy walls and a shallow cavern at the closed end. Thirty stumbling steps into the canyon, they came to a halt before a small fire with two deadwood logs drawn up on either side. A metal cauldron sat on the ground alongside, waiting to be hung from the wooden frame constructed over the fire pit.

A noisy buzzing drew Bodhmhall's jaded attention to a wicker basket lying just beyond the metal container. Even in the fading light she could make out the stains in its lower section, the dried leakage around its base. A cloud of flies hovered over the puddle.

Without warning, Futh released her. Caught off balance, Bodhmhall collapsed to the ground, her head spinning, her captors' conversation a background hum that competed with the buzz of the flies. Slowly, the haze in her head cleared and she raised her eyes, peering groggily at the old man approaching from the direction of the cave, a distance of fifteen paces or so. Dull from pain, she felt hope kindle inside her at the sight of the bushy eyebrows and wrinkled features so similar to those of Cairbre, her old mentor. As the elder drew up alongside however, that same hope dwindled for his cold grey eyes expressed little other than callous indifference. After completing a rapid and unsympathetic appraisal of the prostrate *bandraoi*, he turned his attention to Regna.

'What's this? You bring us a new dinner guest?'

'One dinner guest,' the fat man responded and, with a flourish, pulled Demne out from where he'd been concealed behind Ruth's bulky frame. 'And one acolyte.'

'One ...' The old man stared hard at Demne. His eyes flickered back to the smirking Regna of Mag Fea. 'Is ... is that him?'

'Olpe has confirmed it so.'

The old man stood wringing his hands, his complete attention fixed on the boy. 'All this time.' His voice was a quiet murmur, his face an expression of bewildered delight. 'All this time. And … it's true.' He raised his head sharply, dark eyes fixed on Regna. 'But how?'

'The boy walked into our hands as we scouted the trail Olpe suggested. He has certainly earned his reward.'

Sprawled at their feet, Bodhmhall struggled to push the pain aside so that she could make sense of what she was hearing. The men were talking over her as though she wasn't even there, revealing subtle, tantalising details that she couldn't quite grasp.

The old man shifted position and although she'd turned her face down in an effort to avoid attracting their attention, she could feel the full weight of his gaze upon her.

'And this one is a dinner guest?'

'Yes.'

On the ground before her, outlined by the dying sun, the older man's shadow gestured towards the wicker basket. 'We have everything prepared for tonight's repast.'

'Then tomorrow night,' Regna retorted. 'In the Great Wild, guests are hardly so easy to come by.'

Bodhmhall shivered, sensing an undertone that she didn't understand but instinctively knew boded ill for her. The old man's response, meanwhile, was a soft grunt. 'We should begin the initiation immediately.'

'As you will, Rogein.'

'Shall I prepare the boy, then?'

'Very well.'

'No!' Bodhmhall succeeded in pushing herself, one-handed, off the ground, facing her captors in furious defiance. 'Leave him be.'

The older man's eyes bulged as though astounded by her insolence. Regna of Mag Fea clicked his tongue in irritation then spoke over her head. 'Futh. Make our guest comfortable.'

Bodhmhall didn't see the big man coming but she certainly felt him as he caught her by the hair and jerked her violently to her feet. Dragging her towards the cave, he yanked her forward, using her own momentum to drive her into the rocky grotto. Unable to slow her forward movement, she crashed into a protruding section of rock just inside the entrance, striking her head against its lumpy granite surface. Half-stunned, she slid to the ground.

Outside, her tumble resulted in a gale of raucous laughter. Through slitted eyes, she saw the little man clap his hands with glee, nudge the stricken Demne and point cheerfully at her.

Shivering on the cold granite floor, Bodhmhall drew on every last reserve of focus she retained, again utilising her training to deflect the worst of the pain. The cave swayed violently as she attempted to get to her feet.

180

Her eyesight darkened at the peripheries but she managed to lever herself onto her knees, grasping the rock wall for support.

The cave in which she found herself was a shallow space, little more than a hollow in the cliff. Evidence of its use in the far past by the Ancient Ones was visible in the two lintel stones that stood on either side of the entrance. Both bore those spiral markings so common to the many other stone megaliths that still remained.

She squinted outside to where night's dark mantle was settling over the world. The robed men were crowding around her nephew, examining him with interest, but he didn't otherwise look to be in any immediate danger.

Blood dripped down the bridge of her nose from a gash where her forehead had slammed into the rocky wall. Smearing it away, she caught a blur of movement from the corner of her eye and swallowed a quick cough of alarm. Regna of Mag Fea was approaching the cave.

With heavy footfalls, the portly man joined her just inside the entrance, folding his not inconsiderable bulk onto a smooth boulder beside the spot where she sat crouched. Frightened, she attempted to back away but he whipped out one foot, catching her behind the ankle and knocking her off balance.

'Stay down, *Cailleach*. You have no need to stand.'

He knows who I am.

Bodhmhall eyed her flabby captor, frantically trying to work out how best to respond. This Regna of Mag Fea was an unknown quantity. Harsh, petty, and undeniably cruel, it was difficult to guess what might appease him. For one brief, ludicrous instant she imagined the scene had Liath Luachra been present. The woman warrior would almost certainly have bludgeoned her way out of the situation for Regna of Mag Fea was no warrior.

But Liath Luachra wasn't there and in her present physical state, Bodhmhall knew that even this obese creature was a match for her, to say nothing of the five other men who remained between herself and the canyon entrance.

No. Her only chance at survival was to use her head and for that she needed to understand his motivations.

'What do you want?' she asked. She kept her voice even, neither confrontational nor compliant, closing no potential avenues for negotiation.

Regna's dark eyes studied her with a chilling callousness. Every time he drew breath, she could hear a slight wheeze, his paunch rising and falling as though recovering from some great exertion. He clasped and unclasped his hands, suddenly reaching down with fingers thick as cow udders to brush a strand of hair away from her face. Bodhmhall recoiled, pulling her head out of reach.

181

'From you, *Cailleach*? I want the truth.'

'The truth.'

She repeated the words as a statement rather than as a question, hoping to draw some further clarification from him.

The truth,' he confirmed. 'I have heard it said that Bodhmhall ua Baoiscne was a woman of great potential, daughter of the *rí* of *Clann Baoiscne*, acolyte to the renowned *draoi* Dub Tíre, a uniquely successful practitioner of the *imbas* ritual.'

Bodhmhall continued to watch the obese man, silently attempting to gauge his intent. Clearly, he was intrigued about aspects of her background and some of the more fanciful tales associated with her. It seemed a slim hope but this curiosity was something she could potentially use as leverage to negotiate a better position.

She turned her gaze outside to where Rogein and Temle had Demne sitting on one of the long logs beside the fire, secured in place by the tall man's hands. The boy looked helpless and very scared, particularly when the old man pulled a short-bladed knife from beneath his robe and started to sharpen the blade with a whet stone.

Forcing herself to mask her mounting desperation, Bodhmhall turned a serene face to her smiling captor. 'I can tell you some of what you wish to know,' she said, her voice a gentle affectation of complete equanimity. 'But, first, I would ask you not to hurt my son. He's a child. He poses no threat to you.'

Regna exhaled slowly, like a tolerant man borne to the limits of his patience by an inane request. 'It is not our intention to hurt the boy.' The smoothness of his voice changed abruptly, taking on the hardness of steel. 'Besides, he is not your son. Do you take me for a fool?'

Confounded by the fat man's daunting insight, Bodhmhall stared, hopes for a negotiated release for herself and her nephew foundering. How could he possibly have known!

Regna took a deep breath, clasped his hands together and then unclasped them again. 'The boy is the offspring of Tréanmór's son, Cumhal, and the daughter of Tadg mac Nuadhat of Almhu. Do not attempt to obscure the truth with mists of falsehood, *Cailleach Dubh*. You'll find they wither before me like ghosts in the light of dawn.'

Bodhmhall swallowed. Despite her earlier intention to present a confident facade, she couldn't help glancing over at the campfire where Rogein had taken the knife to her nephew's hair, slicing the thick, blond strands and tossing them into the flames. 'What are they doing?' she blurted, her reserve routed at the sight of the knife so close to her nephew.

'They are merely cutting his hair. It is part of the preparation for his initiation.'

'Initiation?'

Regna sighed.

'You nephew will be bound to us, become a member of our brotherhood.' He saw the blank look on her face. 'We are a brotherhood of Gifted Ones, seekers of knowledge, of forbidden truths.'

Although she managed to keep her face placid, the *bandraoi* struggled to hide the true extent of the cold hatred gushing up from deep within her. Knowing she could not completely repress it, she channelled it instead, using the anger to counter her fear.

'We are not as different as you would like to believe, Bodhmhall ua Baoiscne.' Regna raised both hands in an expansive gesture. 'Surely you've been tempted by the prospect of aligning with others of your kind, like-minded souls, friendly faces who understand how and what you are.'

'You are no friendly face.'

'Oh I don't know. A fair thing like you. It's possible we could become very friendly indeed.' With this, he reached over and placed a hand like a swollen starfish on her thigh, provoking an involuntary shudder that made him chuckle. 'Fear not, *Cailleach*. We are men of refined tastes. As such, with the single exception of Olpe, we tend to pleasures of the flesh ... in other ways.'

She trembled but said nothing in dread of probing any further. 'You cannot hide what you truly are,' she said at last. 'Your twisted flame betrays your true intent.'

'Ah, yes,' he nodded knowingly. 'I've heard tales of your *Gift* for reading a man's internal flame. And yet, Rogein can read the stars just as you read such flickers. As for me, I have the ability to taste lies, Temle feels the weight of a person's eyes when they rest upon him and even little Olpe has his Gift. In some ways, his is the most powerful of all for he can smell the presence of other Gifted Ones like himself. He is better than any bloodhound. It was he who directed us to you.'

'That stunted beast is not a Gifted One. He is Tainted One.'

'Gifted, tainted – it's all a matter of perspective.' Regna dismissed her argument with an airy wave of his hand then settled back, distributing his weight more equally on the boulder as he paused to enjoy the spectacle by the fire.

Bodhmhall refrained from comment, using the momentary respite to reclaim her shattered composure and contemplate her next course of action. She could not, however, draw her eyes away from the sight of Demne's head being shaved. Soon, like their captors, the boy was completely bald, the absence of long, blond locks making him look even more fragile.

'Rogein's *Gift*,' Regna returned to their earlier topic as though he had never paused. 'It provided us with the knowledge of the boy's birth legacy, of his ultimate potential.' His fingers traced the pattern of the spider tattooed on his right cheek. 'We have sought him out for a very long time.'

Although she burned to ask why they were seeking him, Bodhmhall could tell from the manner in which he was observing her that such a query had already been anticipated. Loath to give him the satisfaction, she refrained from doing so.

Finally losing patience at her continued silence, Regna of Mag Fea shifted his weight and grunted. 'I have questions for you, *Cailleach*. You have my word of blood the boy will remain safe if you tell me what I wish to know.'

She considered that for a moment. Yet another man's word. So easily offered, so poorly adhered to.

Despite her scepticism, she made the decision to play along. She was in no position to disagree and there was no advantage in doing so straight off. Initial acquiescence, at least, might give her some temporary room to manoeuvre. 'Very well,' she said.

'Very good. But do not forget that if I taste a lie, you will taste the knife.' He stared at her, long and hard, to make sure she understood and she was obliged to nod in confirmation before he finally continued. 'Now, the *imbas* ritual. Is it true you were successful?'

Although she'd been anticipating the question, Bodhmhall couldn't help the involuntary shudder. 'Yes,' a reluctant whisper.

'You truly achieved *imbas*?'

'Only … only once.'

Regna stroked the lower of his double chins and considered her with grudging admiration. 'And yet, despite all that great potential, you murdered your mentor, left your clan and kin to flee to the furthest corners of the Great Wild.'

Bodhmhall returned his stare, her flinty expression giving nothing away. Regna probed a little further. 'I've heard it said that the *imbas* ritual … changed you. Some secret knowledge accessed from the ritual compelled you to murder your teacher, the *draoi* Dub Tíre.' He waited and when no response was forthcoming, he leaned back and idly tapped his fingers along the side of the nearer lintel stone.

'Did you really kill him?'

Bodhmhall's face showed no emotion. After a moment, she grudgingly dipped her head a single time.

'And what *imbas*, what forbidden knowledge did you attain that meant Dub Tíre had to die?'

'Dub Tíre's death had nothing to do with the *imbas* ritual.'

He looked at her closely, doubtfully, but her answer must have satisfied him for he continued. 'I don't understand. If it wasn't the *imbas*, why did you kill him?'

'He had cold hands.'

Regna of Mag Fea stared at her in confusion then sudden comprehension filled his eyes. A harsh guffaw erupted from his lungs. 'You mean he was rutting you?'

She regarded him coldly but his response was another jagged, mocking laugh. 'Oh, but there's a bitter story hidden behind the chill of those eyes, isn't there?'

Ignoring the bait, Bodhmhall said nothing. Undeterred, Regna continued with his enquiry. 'Your romantic dalliances matter little to me, *Cailleach*. I care nothing for your murder of the *draoi*. My interest lies uniquely with the *imbas* ritual you say you successfully completed.' He paused and regarded her keenly. 'Did you connect with the Great Mother? Did she truly reveal herself to you?'

'Yes.'

He took a deep breath, making great efforts to remain calm but when he spoke again his voice was strained. 'What did you learn? What forbidden knowledge did you gain?'

'I learned only that the Great Mother doesn't care. She has as little interest in the actions of humankind as we have in the activities of the ants that crawl beneath our feet.'

He observed her closely, peering carefully into her eyes. Finally, he drew back and released a sigh. 'You're telling the truth.' He grunted softly, clearly disillusioned by what he'd just heard. 'In essence, you learned nothing. No *imbas*, no useful knowledge of any kind that could be applied.'

He released a heavy sigh.

'Well, that is disappointing. Despite all the stories, all the legends …' He shook his head and looked her directly in the eye. 'People so rarely live up to their reputations.'

He tapped one blubbery lip with his forefinger and his gaze turned inwards. Finally, he seemed to make his mind up about something for, with a fresh wheeze, he rose up off the boulder. 'Get up,' he said. 'And come with me.'

Bodhmhall regarded those cold, black eyes and realised, with a sinking sensation, that she had suddenly become extraneous. Regna of Mag Fea had no further interest in her.

Although her arm was inflamed and swollen to the point where she could barely touch it, the *bandraoi* managed to get to her feet. Holding the sling in place with her free hand, she stumbled out into the night behind him.

The fat man waddled brusquely towards the fire where the others were gathered, seated around the crackling flames in subdued discussion. Demne had been set amongst them, squeezed between Temle and Olpe, his eyes to the ground and one hand silently rubbing his bald head as though unable to believe the absence of hair.

They all glanced up at the heavy tread of Regna's feet. Seeing his aunt appear out of the gloom, Demne's eyes lit up and it was everything Bodhmhall could do not to run towards him. She averted her eyes, heart close to breaking for she knew she could offer him no hope. There was nothing she could do to protect him.

Regna cranked one crooked finger at the vacant end of the nearer log. 'Sit there.'

She sat, withdrawing into herself and willing herself invisible.

In this respect, she was unsuccessful for the robed men regarded her with open curiosity while Rogein, stirring the metal cauldron, considered her with surly bemusement. He turned a questioning glance to his fleshy companion. 'And?' he asked.

'There is nothing,' the fat man responded. 'A waste of time. Now it is only for Olpe to claim his just reward.'

It was something in Regna's smile that alerted her to the fact that her life was forfeit. Before she could even try to make a break for it however, Futh had come up behind her, heavy paws slamming down on her shoulders to hold her fast.

Across the fire, Olpe stared first at Regna then, with rising glee, to Rogein. Finally, clapping his hands and giggling insanely, he transferred his gaze to Bodhmhall, leapt to his feet and scurried around the flames towards her.

Terror and fury gave Bodhmhall renewed strength. She bucked and struggled, kicked out at the little man with such ferocity that he barely managed to step back and avoid the swing of her heel. Despite the surge of strength stimulated by her desperation however, that of the bald man holding her was that much greater and she was unable to get free from the log. One great hand released her shoulder and reached around to clamp her jaw, holding her head in place so that she had no choice but to watch Olpe slip onto the log beside her.

Clearly enjoying her mounting terror, the little man pulled a razor-sharp boning knife from beneath his robe and held it up before her. Leaning in, he laid the flat of the blade against her face, making her shudder at the touch of cool metal against her skin. Adjusting the angle of the blade, he ran the tip of the weapon down her cheek, applying just enough pressure to leave a fleeting depression where it passed but without breaking the surface of her skin.

He paused for a moment to make an odd gurgling sound then slid the knife down the side of her throat and into the curve of her shoulder. Here, the weapon caught where it encountered the smooth material of her tunic. With a twist of his wrist, the little man snagged the point of the blade into the soft leather then, using the resistance of her clothing against the blade, slowly drew it down towards her belly, slicing the front of her tunic open like the distended belly of a gutted pig. Unable to contain himself, he reached forward, grabbed the slashed edges of the tunic and ripped the remaining material open wide.

There was complete silence from the other men gathered around the fire. Oblivious to their stares, Olpe dropped the knife from his hand so that it fell, embedding itself in the soft earth at his feet. With a deranged giggle, he reached up one gnarled hand to cup her left breast, bent his head to take a nipple in his mouth and began to suck on it with a hideous slurping noise.

Suddenly the *bandraoi* thrust her head downwards, clamping her teeth around the tip of his ear. She bit down hard.

The wizened creature's shriek was a satisfying mixture of pain and startled outrage. She felt the tear of meat as he frantically wrenched himself backwards off the log. Sprawled on the earth, he stared up at her in disbelief and raised one wrinkled hand to his right ear. It came away bloody.

Futh's arms clamped even tighter about her, pushing his full weight down on her shoulders. Meanwhile, a terrible hatred burned in Olpe's eyes. Completely immobile, she watched as he slowly got to his feet, retrieved his knife and started towards her. Reclaiming his seat on the log, he grabbed her breast with one hand, raised his knife and ...

Stopped.

Suddenly, mercifully, the little man had stiffened, an expression of complete bewilderment smeared across his face. Pulling away from the *bandraoi*, he stood up and spun about, staring towards the darkness in the direction of the little cave. The other men stared, dumbfounded by their comrade's odd behaviour. 'What is it Olpe?' asked Rogein. 'What is it you see?'

A strangled groan creaked from the ugly little man's throat. He continued to stand, gaping at something beyond the fire that nobody else could see. He groaned again and this time he called out in a fearful, high-pitched whine: 'Who are you? Who watches me? Show yourself, Old Hag.'

Bodhmhall released a shuddering breath, realisation hitting her with the force of a thunderclap.

I can taste you suckling a large child. And yet I have tasted no birth.

The Hag from Tobar na Guthanna.

I have just saved your life, Bodhmhall ua Baoiscne. Do you believe me?

That sudden insight did little to calm her or help her comprehend what was happening. Like the others, she continued to stare, astounded, at the little man who was now screeching insanely into the darkness.

In the end, it was Regna who brought things to a close. Coming up on Olpe from behind, he grabbed him by the shoulder, spun him around and proceeded to slap him violently across the face until he'd stopped shrieking. Finally, quietened, the little creature was released and slunk away to the cave entrance where he slumped morosely, sulking.

Regna turned to stare suspiciously at Bodhmhall. His lips parted as though to ask a question but then he seemed to think better of it. Instead, he approached and instructed Futh to release her. She gasped with relief when the big man's weight came off her but the respite was short-lived as Regna grabbed her by the neck of her tunic and started dragging her in the direction of the cave.

'Hallo the fire!'

The sudden call took the little group completely by surprise. Everybody stood, or sat, frozen in shock, staring into the darkness from where the voice had seemed to come. Regna of Mag Fea reacted with startling alacrity for his bulk. Concealed by the shadows away from the fire, he fastened one hand about the *bandraoi*'s mouth and manhandled her backwards into the darker shadow of the cave, striking her injured arm and causing her to momentarily black out from pain when she tried to resist. Olpe quickly hustled inside to join them and, pushing her to the ground, both men held her firmly in place.

Back at the fire, Temle placed one hand on Demne's shoulder to prevent him from moving and slipped a long knife inside his sleeve. Rogein glanced nervously towards the cave as though seeking instruction but, when none was forthcoming, his face took on a determined look and he rose to his feet.

Advancing past the fire, the elder peered into the gloom in the direction of the canyon entrance. Futh and Ruth followed him wordlessly, taking up position on either side, wooden staffs at the ready.

After that initial burst of activity, the night was suddenly very quiet. Beyond the flickering circle of light thrown out by the fire there was no sound but a soft fluttering of leaves brushing against each other in the breeze. The darkness made it impossible to distinguish anything.

Inside the cave, unable to break her captors' grip and with Olpe's filthy hand smothering her mouth, Bodhmhall desperately used her *Gift* to scan the woods, quickly pinpointing a distant flicker of human life in the trees left of the canyon entrance.

Her heart sank. A single individual was hardly going to be of much assistance.

The stranger's voice called into the canyon again: male, confident, and difficult to distinguish clearly with the slight echo from the rocky walls and yet, oddly familiar. 'I see you, Strangers. May I approach? The glow of your campfire is a welcome sight on such a lonely night.'

The bearded elder stepped forward, coughed and cleared his throat. 'Approach in safety, Stranger.'

The shadows at the edge of the campsite shifted, reformed and a tall, broad-shouldered figure stepped into the yellow circle of light thrown out by the fire. He was a young man, handsome with a full moustache and a thick mane of black hair tied up in a number of braids that exposed the tattooed patterns on his left cheek and forehead. A green wool cloak hung draped over his right shoulder and on his back he carried a wicker backpack covered in a heavy cloth. 'I see you, Old One. I am named Fiacail mac Codhna.'

Fiacail!

Bodhmhall again struggled against her captors but Regna lay across her, squashing her with the weight of his bulk and driving the breath from her lungs. Olpe, meanwhile, used both hands to stifle her cries.

Over by the fire, Rogein had raised a hand in greeting. 'I see you, Stranger. I am named Rogein.' Fiacail raised a hand in return. 'Hallo, Travellers. I come in peace.' His eyes flickered between each of the Man Pair. Although both men stood poised with their staffs ready to leap into action, he displayed no signs of being overly disturbed.

'Forgive our caution,' said Rogein. 'But the Great Wild is full of dangers.' He coughed and cleared his throat. Rogein waved his right hand and the Man Pair lowered their weapons. Slowly, keeping a wary eye on Fiacail, they retreated to their seats on the log by the fire.

'Now, welcome to our campsite, Fiacail mac Codhna.' The old man gave a smile. 'Would you care to eat with us? There is not much but we are happy to share.'

The big warrior glanced curiously at the steaming cauldron then advanced further to stand close by the fire. He held his palms above the flames then brusquely rubbed them together. 'The nights grow cooler. The end of summer draws near, I think. Good food and company would certainly help to warm the night.'

With this, he took a seat on a small rock set back at an angle from the two logs on which the others were seated. As he sat down, he adjusted the weight of the wicker backpack then removed it completely and set it on the ground alongside him. Apart from the knife in his belt, the warrior didn't seem to bear any weapon although the odd shape under the cloth held the potential for something more lethal.

Fiacail! Please! Gods, help us!

Inside the cave, despite her best efforts, Bodhmhall remained unable to break free of her two captors. Breathless, in pain and close to despair, she helplessly watched the warrior nodding sagely as Rogein outlined his preparations for dinner. 'It's a simple stew,' Rogein was saying. 'Nevertheless, I will add some extra ingredients, we will let it simmer until the flavours seep through and it will not take long.'

Fiacail smiled gratefully, watching with interest as the old man retrieved a leather pouch near the fire, withdrew a pinch of some brown looking herb and dropped it into the little cauldron. The old man stirred the meaty stew with a wooden ladle, releasing a cloud of steam that dissipated up into the night air.

'This particular herb adds a unique flavour. I'm sure you'll find it interesting.'

Bodhmhall saw Fiacail's eyes wander around the little campsite, pausing to rest where Futh and Ruth had reseated themselves. Both continued to regard him with hostility and the warrior made a point of resting his hand on the handle of his knife, an action that did not go unnoticed by Rogein.

'I hope my comrades do not cause discomfort,' said Rogein. 'They look fierce but, in truth, they are gentle souls. Some find their demeanour fearsome and treat them unkindly but their appearance belies a kind pair of hearts.'

Fiacail nodded in sympathy. 'I bear no ill will to any Man Pair.' He addressed the two silent men. 'Besides, I, too, have a pair of my own.'

Rogein put the ladle aside and took a seat opposite the Seiscenn Uarbhaoil warrior. 'You do?' He considered Fiacail with surprise. 'You did not strike me as a family man.'

The warrior reached out his right hand and snatched off the cloth that shrouded his backpack. Beneath the fibrous material, two smooth wooden hafts, tipped with black leather, poked up in an 'X'- shape above the sides of other basket. At the sight of the weapons, the older man gave an involuntary start. Their guest however, did not appear to notice for he grasped both handles and whipped a matching pair of axes free. Wrists enclosed by fixed leather thongs in the base of the hafts, he held the weapons firmly out before him. Both hafts were about a foot and half in length, tipped with large black blades that were offset by a similar, but smaller, blade on the opposing side.

'These are my twins,' said Fiacail mac Codhna. 'Bloodnamed, of course. He hefted the weapon in his right hand. The metal blade gleamed dully in the firelight. 'This is *Folamh Dearg*. And here is his brother *Dord Fiacail*.'

Rogein stared at the deadly looking weapons. Fiacail's attention was completely focussed on his blades for he did not appear to notice his hosts' apprehension or the tense hands creeping closer to their own weapons.

With a sudden, double backhand swing the warrior gracefully sheathed his weapons. This resulted in an immediate lessening of the visible tension about the fire. The robed men seemed to ease back on their seats. Rogein exhaled deeply as though he'd been holding his breath. 'From where do you hail, Fiacail mac Codhna?' he asked, his voice decidedly creaky.

'From Seiscenn Uarbhaoil. It is a pleasant settlement. Good, flat land near a river. Pasture, cows ...' He paused and stared into the fire. 'Women,' he added.

'The name has a ring of familiarity.'

'Perhaps you know of it because of my association. I'm famous for my deeds of valour. Have you heard the song chant *Blood Defender of Ráth Bládhma*? That was me.'

Rogein rubbed his beard. 'I've heard the song.' He frowned. 'But I had understood the Blood Defender of Ráth Bládhma was a woman.'

'Bah. You know how these tales are twisted over time.'

'If I recall the words correctly, the Blood Defender led the invaders to their death in the marshland by drawing them away with her nakedness.'

'*Ráiméis!* Nonsense! There was nakedness of course but that is only because I battered the invaders to death with my great truncheon of a cock.'

This produced a low rumble of coarse laughter. When it ebbed, the big man looked around at the other members of the party. 'Rogein, you still haven't introduced me to your comrades.'

'Oh,' the old man looked startled. 'Forgive me. I am a poor host.' He pointed to the Man Pair. 'These are Futh and Ruth. They are brothers.' He gave a wry grin. 'But you may have already noticed the family resemblance.'

Fiacail smiled politely, nodding a formal greeting which the two men returned although their features remained terse and unfriendly. Rogein however, had moved on to the tall figure with the cowl. 'This is Temle'.

Temle lowered his cowl and nodded. 'Welcome, Fiacail mac Codhna.'

'And finally,' said the old man, gesturing to where Demne sat shivering at the far end of the log. 'This one is our newest recruit. He is named Demne.'

'Hallo, Little One.'

Inside the cave Bodhmhall squirmed, the stink of Olpe's filthy hand close to suffocating her more than the lack of air reaching her lungs through those clasping fingers.

Muirne's son, Fiacail! Gods! The name is hardly common.'

Even as she watched she felt a sudden surge of hope for the big man was frowning, leaning forward to regard the little boy more closely. He raised one hand and thoughtfully scratched his chin as his eyes drifted across to where Rogein was watching.

Yes, Fiacail. Yes!

'I am curious, Rogein.'

'Oh?'

'Your newest member has no hair. He looks freshly shorn. In fact none of you have any hair. Have you suffered an infestation? Has the scurvy come upon you?'

191

Fiacail, you stupid cur!

A muted tremor of amusement rolled through the shoulders of the robed men. Off to Fiacail's left, shielded from the warrior's view by Futh's expansive bulk, she saw Temle roll his eyes in a mocking manner.

'Nothing like that,' Rogein was quick to reassure his guest. 'A bare scalp is a sign of true commitment to our brotherhood. A bare scalp and this spider you see tattooed on our left cheeks.' He raised his finger to touch the marking. Fiacail studied it, his response a non-committal grunt.

Temle, meanwhile, had shifted position, moving around Futh, then down the log so that he too faced the Seiscenn Uarbhaoil man directly. 'Friend, Fiacail. If you come from Seiscenn Uarbhaoil then you have travelled a great distance.'

'That's true. I am on the hunt.'

'So far from home?'

'It is a blood hunt. A *geis* [obligation] of vengeance placed on me by my sister.'

'A *geis* of vengeance?' The tall man maintained his stare but his eyes had taken on a suspicious glint.

The warrior gave a rueful shake of the head. 'A *geis* is rarely a matter of choice. My sister seeks vengeance on one who has stolen something precious from her. I am merely the instrument of her intent. As a result, I must now hunt the land and draw blood to set the balance right.'

'And who is the focus of this hunt?'

'A dangerous will of the wisp. Someone who follows untravelled trails, who lays down in the night and leaves unseen every morning.'

Temle looked at him and rubbed the fresh stubble on his skull, clearly intrigued by the story. 'That is a fascinating tale. Do you have a name?'

Fiacail shrugged. 'I have no name.'

'But without a name how can you possibly locate your quarry?'

Fiacail tapped the side of his nose and gave a knowing smile. 'I am a very good tracker.'

'But,' Rogein interrupted, 'the Great Wild is … great.' The elderly man looked somewhat abashed.'

'And wild,' added Fiacail. 'Yes, I know.'

'But in all this vast wilderness how can you possibly succeed in finding the tracks to guide you?'

'I do not follow the tracks of my quarry. Instead I have decided to work out their intent and travel ahead of them. There I will wait and when our encounter takes place I will draw blood.'

Rogein blinked. 'This individual must be very worried.'

Fiacail shrugged. 'Unlikely. From what I gather, I am not chasing the brightest star in the sky.'

Fiacail and Temle looked at each other across the fire and chuckled for what, to Bodhmhall, seemed like two very different reasons. When the laughter had faded, the big man shivered and looked around. 'You choose a strange place to set camp. This is a place of the Old Ones. My people say such sites are haunted and should be avoided.'

'Do they?' The warrior's opinion seemed to surprise the older man. 'And yet I find such places comforting. It gives me some pleasure to sit and dwell on the achievements of the Old Ones. Whoever they were, the impressiveness and splendour of their structures and monuments cannot be denied.'

'I'd be more impressed if they were still around to explain what purpose they served.'

Within the cave, Bodhmhall had feigned unconsciousness while listening in on the conversation but, in truth, the pretence was not difficult to maintain. She *was* close to passing out from the pain and the lack of air, restricted as it was by Olpe's hands over her mouth and the tightness of Regna's arm about her windpipe. However, apparently reassured by her continued stillness, and presumably also intent on listening into the fireside conversation, they gradually let their hold on her relax a little. As soon as she felt their grip loosen, Bodhmhall whipped her head free and just had time to release a stifled cry before Olpe managed to clamp his hands around her mouth again.

As the little man wrestled her face to one side, she caught a glimpse of Fiacail mac Codhna. The warrior's head was up and he was staring in her direction. 'That's a woman!' she heard him exclaim.

He twisted his head to regard the startled Rogein then his face broke into a sly grin. 'You have a woman secreted here? All this time and you've said nothing. Brotherhood, indeed. Crafty devils.'

Inside the cave, Bodhmhall wailed silently and died a little death.

Flustered by this new development, Rogein stared at the warrior speechlessly, his jaw hanging loose in consternation. 'She is ... a slave girl,' he stammered at last. 'Not one of our brotherhood. We could not tell if you were alone or intent on violence so we kept her hidden.'

Fiacail nodded in sage approval. 'Wise. Ah, yes, very wise. So many men out there who can think of nothing further than the tip of their *bod*.' He reached out to accept the wooden bowl that Rogein hurriedly handed to him, watching silently as the older man ladled in a dollop of stew. Raising the bowl to his nose, he closed his eyes and inhaled dreamily. 'Aah, by the Gods! Yes, friend Rogein. You spoke the truth. This smells delicious.'

He looked down at the bowl, stirring it thoughtfully with his finger as though struggling with some inner conflict. 'Forgive me, Rogein ...'

The elder man glanced at Temle but the taller man remained expressionless. 'Yes,' he said carefully.

'Returning to the subject of your woman. Would you trade for some time with her? It's just that ...' He paused. 'It's just that this sword's been sheathed for far too long.'

Rogein stared, completely confounded by the question. 'No,' he managed at last.

'If it's a question of trade, I have fresh venison in my backpack. Or a good hunting knife?'

Rogein shook his head. 'I don't think - '

'I have a good voice,' Fiacail persisted. 'I can sing you *Blood Defender of Ráth Bládhma,* just for a few moments alone with her.'

The old man took a deep breath and exhaled slowly. 'Perhaps we can eat first and discuss the matter on a full stomach.'

'Of course, of course. That makes sense,' the Seiscenn Uarbhaoil man agreed. 'Besides, it would be poor form to rut on an empty stomach, would it not?'

Bodhmhall's own stomach lurched as she saw him raise the bowl to his lips.

No!

The *bandraoi* bucked and, with one last frenzied effort, managed to twist her head free. Taken completely by surprise, the little man immediately attempted to cover her mouth again but this time she snapped her teeth around his forefinger, biting down with all her force, right through to the bone. Olpe screamed in agony as a warm flush of blood flooded the inside of her mouth, yanking his hand free but leaving shreds of flesh between her teeth. Spitting the meaty pulp from her mouth, Bodhmhall managed to cry out 'Fiac-' before Regna had her down again, stuffing a cloth halfway down her throat to muffle her cries.

Despite their fury, her captors were unable to harm her any further because their proximity to the fire and the noise produced by such actions would have even further troubled their guest. As it was, all eyes were now turned towards the cave and it was only as the cave grew silent once more that the robed men turned back to assess Fiacail's reaction.

Surprisingly, the warrior looked completely unfazed. Having consumed the contents of his bowl, he wiped his hand across his lips and winked at Rogein. 'By the Great Father's Balls, she's a feisty one, your slave girl.' With this, he looked sadly down at his empty bowl. 'Friend Rogein. You will make some woman very happy one day with this cooking of yours. Perhaps another serving?'

'Of course, of course.' Flustered, but greatly relieved by the warrior's eccentricity, Rogein gave a watery smile. Rising to his feet, he picked up the ladle and bent forward for Fiacail's bowl. Taking it in his hand he was about to pour when he stared into the wooden container and, suddenly, his body went rigid.

The Seiscenn Uarbhaoil man lunged like a starving river eel, swinging up the knife that he'd apparently palmed while the others were distracted by Bodhmhall's scream. The blade connected with the old man's throat, sending a scarlet spray over Ruth and Futh, who were seated closest to him. With a strange gurgling sound, the old man staggered about. His comrades stared in horror at the blood gushing out of the jagged gash beneath his epiglottis and spilling down the front of his robe. Rogein collapsed like a sack of rocks released from a great height.

Temle leaped to his feet. Fiacail reached for the axes. The weapons were barely clear of his backpack before the Man Pair were on him. Bodhmhall was startled to see that a metal blade had appeared at either end of the wooden staffs as cylindrical wooden tips were discarded. The weapons had suddenly become ten times more lethal than they'd first appeared.

While Temle attempted to staunch his fallen comrade's wounds, the two brothers closed in on Fiacail, working in unison to take him from either side. The big man stepped back, using the leather wrist thong in the hafts to swirl his axe in controlled loops that greatly extended the reach of the weapons. For a moment, his opponents paused, slowing their advance to take the measure of their enemy. In that moment, Fiacail must have realised the danger he was in for he suddenly, unexpectedly, resorted to a desperate and exceedingly dangerous manoeuvre.

Whipping the axe in his right hand up in a powerful underarm swing, he let the weapon fly. Not expecting such a foolhardy move, it caught Futh completely by surprise, the metal end smashing into his head just above the ridge of his nose.

The big man staggered and fell, just as his brother, snarling, launched himself at the warrior. Fiacail backstepped with impressive dexterity, although not impressive enough to avoid the blade end that whipped past and sliced the flesh of his upper right shoulder. The warrior gasped, more out of surprise, Bodhmhall suspected, than pain. Fortunately, he was ambidextrous enough to toss the axe into his left hand and use it to defend himself.

Bodhmhall felt Rogan's weight shift then lift from her back as he rose and, with Olpe, scurried from the cave to assist his comrades. As they ran she saw them both pull long knives from beneath their robes.

Temle too, realising that there was nothing he could do to save his friend, also rose to his feet and went to retrieve Futh's bladed staff from where the fallen man had dropped it.

Four to one.

Although she had no idea how she could possibly help and her left arm was numb from sheer pain, Bodhmhall pushed herself onto her knees, then her feet and stumbled out of the cave. Demne was still sitting at the edge of the log, transfixed by the fight and paralysed with fear. She tottered towards him as quickly as she could, stopping only to scoop up the boning knife that Olpe had dropped.

By now, Temle and her two captors from the cave had joined Ruth, all forming a ragged half circle about the beleaguered Fiacail. Fortunately for the Seiscenn Uarbhaoil warrior, the truth of the matter was that he was facing only two serious opponents: Ruth because he was clearly a very able warrior on his own merit and Temle who – although not a warrior – was able to use the extended staff to make lethal thrusts while Fiacail was otherwise preoccupied. Regna and Olpe with their knives were merely a distraction, albeit a potentially lethal one.

Despite this, the odds were significantly against Fiacail so, hushing her terrified nephew, she staggered up behind the engagement, edged her way towards Temle and plunged the boning knife deep into his back.

The scream from the tall man was so loud that it served to distract his three companions and momentarily offered an opening to Fiacail's left where the less skilled fighters were located. The big man didn't hesitate. Stepping forward, he whipped the axe-head outwards, smashing Olpe in the head.

The little man dropped without a sound, the side of his head a bloody mess of pulp and bone. Regna screamed in dismay and fury but, surprisingly, it was Ruth who took matters in hand.

'Get the boy,' he roared. 'I'll deal to this shit-pig!'

With that, the fat man stepped backwards and out of the fray. Spinning about, his eyes immediately fell on the trembling *bandraoi* and she didn't need her *Gift* to see the great flare of loathing in those soulless black eyes.

Springing forward with surprising speed for a man of his bulk, he ran at Bodhmhall. Terrified and without any means of defending herself, the *bandraoi* attempted to run but, in her panic, stumbled over the prostrate Futh.

She hit the ground hard and, once again, the agony of her inflamed arm washed over her. She was barely conscious of the fast man's approach, the bulk of him as he loomed over her and raised his knife.

The blow that smashed his head in took them both by surprise. One moment, he was slavering pure venom, screaming his utter hatred at her, the next, an expression of complete astonishment filled his eyes and his head was wrenched around to reveal a bloody hole in the left forehead. He toppled backwards, hitting the ground with an almighty thump.

Bodhmhall slowly sat up and stared at the quivering corpse, rolls of fat still jiggling under the robe from the force of the impact. Using Futh's corpse as support, she raised her head and looked behind to where Demne was standing, bald head gleaming in the firelight, inner flame blazing bright enough to light the entire forest for those who could see. With fading eyesight, Bodhmhall stared at him, unable to understand what was

196

happening as consciousness increasingly leeched from her brain. Somewhere in the distance, there was a sound of metal striking metal, the grunt and bellows of fighting men but in front of her was her beautiful nephew, illuminated in a dazzlingly ethereal inner glow.

Like the glow, her consciousness subsided but just before she passed out, in his hand she saw that he carried Liath Luachra's sling, the weapon that had been strapped about his arm all this time, apparently unnoticed. Despite herself, despite everything, she smiled.

Chapter Eleven

Later, Fiacail would tell her that she'd slept for two full days. From the grinding ache in her back she'd have no trouble believing him.

The first thing she was conscious of was the cheery twitter of bird song, an erratic background punctuation to the ongoing throb of pain that had become such a large part of her existence. Both sound and sensation gradually intensified until she was finally ready to open her eyes.

She awoke on a bed of crushed fern and heather in the shelter of the cave. It was mid-day and the canyon outside was bathed in sunshine although a threatening tinge of grey cloud was visible above the lip of the canyon wall. The campfire still smouldered, puffing intermittent streaks of greasy smoke into the air as the gusting breeze sporadically tugged it. Demne was sitting to one side of the fire pit, humming a wordless tune to himself as he worked on a new spear similar to the one he'd made with his aunt.

There was no sign of the robed men.

She was still pondering their absence when she fell asleep again.

She dozed on and off for the rest of the afternoon in this manner, waking for brief moments of clarity during which she looked outside and tried to make sense of things before sliding back into the comfort of unconsciousness once more. Even at the time, she understood her body had taken control so that it could heal properly, shutting down her self-awareness to prevent her from doing anything that might interfere with its recovery. It was a strange feeling for her to be relegated to the role of passive bystander to her physical self yet, at the same time, it also felt oddly comforting.

Towards early evening, she was stirred from slumber by a soft shuffling movement within the cave and a more indistinct sloshing sound that seemed further away. Opening her eyes, she saw a thick curtain of rain outside the cave mouth, obscuring her view of the canyon beyond.

With a stifled grunt, Bodhmhall raised her head and sat up, wincing as her injured arm made its presence known. She glanced at it, surprised to find that the loosened splints had been replaced, the supporting bandage tightened.

She turned her eyes to the cavern wall where Fiacail mac Codhna was busily arranging a set of javelins, his back turned towards her. To the warrior's left, Demne was feeding a small fire set just inside the cave mouth where it was sheltered from the rain. A small metal pot had been hung over the flames and a strong smell of broth pervaded the enclosed space.

'Fiacail.'

The Seiscenn Uarbhaoil warrior looked over his shoulder. The tanned, tattooed face split into a toothy grin when he saw her sitting up. He got to his feet and stood before her, thumbs hooked loosely in a horse-leather belt, filling the limited space in the cave.

'Bodhmhall ua Baoiscne. You return to us.'

She stared at him, suddenly feeling strangely awkward and upended by the unexpected appearance of someone with whom she was so familiar in such an unfamiliar environment. His presence had an unsettling quality about it for the sight clashed with her memories of him back at Ráth Bládhma and, much earlier, during their life together in Dún Baoiscne.

'Fiacail, what are you doing here? How did you find us?'

'Are you up to such discussions, Bodhmhall?' He gestured with his hand, indicating the small fire and the pot just inside the cave mouth. 'Eat first. Fill your belly and we can talk.'

Her stomach growled at the prospect of food but when she stared at the pot her shoulders tensed.

'It's venison,' he reassured her. 'And the pot is from my own backpack.'

With this he turned away, leaving her sitting quietly, watching in a daze as he poured the broth into a wooden bowl then returned to hand it to her. Although initially reticent, she raised the bowl to her mouth. As soon as her tongue touched the smooth, salty texture, any concerns she had melted away and she began to scoff it down.

Fiacail eased himself onto the floor of the cave beside her and sat patiently while she devoured the broth. As she was eating, she stared at him, intrigued. Five years had passed since they'd last exchanged words, since the warrior had set off by himself from the gateway of Ráth Bládhma. At the time, he'd told her he was headed back to Seiscenn Uarbhaoil but she hadn't quite believed him for she knew he'd lost any sense of connection with that settlement. As she watched him walk away alone, into the Great Wild, she'd been genuinely saddened to see him leave but knew his decision was best for both of them.

In a physical sense, the warrior had changed little over those intervening years. The lines beneath his eyes had become more pronounced but he was still as handsome as ever, still moved with that cocky, ostensibly nonchalant ease that could snap into focussed action at a moment's notice.

At the same time, she also sensed a difference about him, some alteration that she couldn't quite put her finger on. He was still all brash vivaciousness of course but beneath the layers of bravado she sensed a trace of weariness, a rough-edged fatigue of the soul. Without thinking, she utilised her *Gift* and saw that although his internal flame was still as vibrant as ever, there was a paleness to the edges that hadn't been there before.

'It swells this heart to see you, *a chara*.' Even as she said it, Bodhmhall realised how much she meant it. True, part of her reaction was a result of the immense gratitude and relief she felt at finding such a trustworthy protector, but this reunion was much more than that. Even though he infuriated her at times, she'd missed the warrior's gregarious company more than she'd ever have cared to admit.

Fiacail smiled, clearly touched by the words although he responded with none of his own. He took the bowl she handed back to him and put it to one side.

Bodhmhall's hand dropped to her chest and, with a start, she realised that the central tear of her tunic had been stitched up and overlain with another strip of leather that had also been stitched on. The end result was by no means a thing of beauty but it was certainly practicable. She looked up to find Fiacail grinning at her.

'It's true I'm a fine man with a needle when the need arises, be it battle wound or tunic tear. But the truth is, it was a good opportunity to see your breasts.'

She considered him wryly. No-one could ever accuse Fiacail mac Codhna of practicing deceit.

'Aaah!' He gave a sad sigh as he stared long at her bosom. 'It was truly pleasant to rediscover two such long-lost old friends.'

Bodhmhall's eyes closed and her gaunt cheeks puffed out in a wounded smile. 'How did you know where to find us?' she asked again, too quickly. She looked out at the empty canyon. 'Where are …?' She paused, unable to find the words to suitably describe the terrifying individuals who'd had such horrific designs on her and her nephew. 'Are they ..?'

'Deader than an old man's cock.' He gave a self-satisfied nod. 'I dragged the bodies outside the canyon. Wolves found them on the second night so …' He shrugged. 'I didn't get that giant with the quarterstaff, though. He made a run for it. Truth be told, I was happy to let him go for he may have had my measure.' He scratched his stubbled jaw with a dirty hand. 'It was fortunate you brought his tall comrade down. I see now that I underestimated them. I thought this band operated uniquely by guile but evidently they had strength to call on as well when it was needed.'

'Fiacail, how did you know we were here?'

'I didn't know you were here. I was seeking these …' He made a contemptuous gesture with his hand. 'Bald Ones. You heard the conversation? About the *geis*, about my sister?'

'I didn't even know you had a sister. I …' She forced herself to stop. 'Yes, I heard.'

'She's more of a half-sister really but we've grown close the past few years.' He sniffed and started to finger the edges of his moustache. 'She took a man at Seiscenn Uarbhaoil, a man called Sárán an Srón. When he didn't return after a hunt she asked me to find him. Fortunately, I knew the trails where he was headed so I was able to find some tracks that hadn't been swept away by the weather and follow them to where he encountered a group of travellers. After that, there were no more tracks.'

He released the moustache and a troubled expression crossed his face.

'When I searched about, I found a small pit with his bones and a few other bits and pieces. They'd eaten him. No doubt that was to be your fate as well.'

Bodhmhall shivered.

'I lost their trail but when I told my sister what I'd found, she put me under a *geis* to obtain vengeance, to cleanse the insult and kill the men who'd murdered him. It was difficult to find their trail by then but stories were starting to come in of other solitary travellers who'd also disappeared. Always, it seemed that the stories were based further and further west so that was the direction I took.

Several days ago, I encountered a Great Wild woman whose father had gone missing. That confirmed my suspicions. Familiar with the terrain as I am, I knew they'd have to make their way through An Bearna Garbh eventually so I travelled ahead and waited on high ground to watch for their fire. I was waiting for several days. You know the rest.'

Bodhmhall was silent, numbly thinking of the fate she'd escaped through the big warrior's intervention. 'What was in the bowl?' she asked at last.

'The bowl?'

'Before you cut that old man's throat I saw him stiffen when he looked into the bowl. He saw something in there that frightened him.'

'You truly wish to know?'

'Yes.'

The big man grunted as he reached back to grab his backpack. Fishing about inside, he withdrew a leather pouch and tossed it to her. She caught it in her right hand, undid the securing string with her teeth and emptied its single content – a small fleshy object – onto the ground. She stared at it for several moments before she realised what it was.

'A nose?'

'Yes.'

Bodhmhall picked it up and sniffed before replacing it on the ground. 'It's pickled.'

'My sister's wish. Apart from bones, that's all that remains of her man. Part of my *geis* was to show it to his murderers before I killed them.' He grinned. 'She desired "balance".'

With this, he reached forward, picked up the swollen proboscis and studied it closely. 'Sárán an Srón. You can see how he got that name.' He shook his head sadly. 'I told him once that we could plough a field with that nose.'

He replaced the fleshy object in the leather satchel and repacked it.

'But enough of me. You have stories of your own. Your doting nephew …' He gave her an amused look. 'Demne, told me the greater part of your adventures: the visit of the *techtaire*, the journey through the Great Wild for Dún Baoiscne, the ambush, your great leap from the falls and your subsequent capture by the … Brotherhood of Bald Ones.'

The Seiscenn Uarbhaoil man yawned abruptly and rubbed his eyes. Ignoring his evident fatigue, he continued. 'What the boy could not tell me clearly however, was why. Why did you leave the safety of Ráth Bládhma? Why were you travelling to Dún Baoiscne on such an isolated route in the first place?'

Bodhmhall bit her lip. In hindsight, Fiacail's questions made their actions look very foolish.

'It was a deception. A deception put into play by the Adversary to draw us away from Ráth Bládhma and into an ambush. He lured Muirne and Gleor with the bait of a potential association with *Clann Baoiscne*.'

Fiacail stared at her in astonishment. 'They fell for that?' He shook his head in disbelief. 'Clearly Muirne still thinks her arse shines like silver. And as for Gleor Red Hand, he should know better. Since taking that woman to his bed, he's obviously been balls deep in bad ideas and poor notions.' Disgusted, he turned his head and spat into a shadowed corner of the cave.

'It may be a mistake they paid for with their lives, Fiacail. And besides, it wasn't completely their fault. The *techtaire* provided *an t-urra*, a surety only one from Dún Baoiscne could have known.'

Fiacail's eye widened. 'So a traitor feeds from the fat of Tréanmór's house.' The Seiscenn Uarbhaoil warrior lapsed into silence, tapping his fingertips as he thought things through.

'I struggle to make sense of these events, Bodhmhall. I recall your claim of some mysterious Adversary five years ago but at the time I lacked full conviction. Now, I think your suspicions hold substance.'

She glared. 'You certainly gave the air of one who had conviction.'

'I had conviction I could win you back but that was before...' He sighed. 'But these are old stories, Bodhmhall. Best forgotten.'

He leaned back on his haunches as though physically distancing himself from the topic. 'What does this Adversary want from you that he would go to such extremes? First the attack on Ráth Bládhma, now this ambush and the lure of treachery from within a clan of recognised reputation. And where does he find all those warriors?' He shook his head. 'These are things beyond my understanding. Do you know what this Adversary desires?'

'I don't know.' The lie tasted sour to her so she added. 'For certain.'

Fiacail gave her a sideways glance that lingered, slowly transforming to an insistent stare.

She exhaled deeply. 'They want Demne,' she said, lowering her voice so her nephew couldn't hear.

Fiacail glanced over his shoulder to where Demne was trying to sharpen the tip of his spear. He turned back to the *bandraoi*. 'Muirne's brat? Why?'

Bodhmhall glared at him and made a downward movement with her hand.

'Why?' he repeated in a whisper.

'There is something ... unusual about him.'

'What?'

'I don't know. But even those robed men knew of it for they were seeking him with a ferocity equal to that of the Adversary.'

Fiacail's gaze turned inward and he was silent for a long time. Suddenly, he swivelled around and called to the boy. 'Demne Maol [Demne the Bald], put your stick aside. Come sit here by me.'

The boy looked up in surprise, scowling as he realised what Fiacail had called him, but proceeded to do as he was told. 'It's a spear,' he mumbled as he settled down next to the warrior.

Fiacail raised one cryptic eyebrow and eyed the child carefully. 'What's a spear, Demne Maol? That twisted stick you were playing with?'

'It's a spear,' the boy insisted stubbornly although his voice was growing thick with emotion. 'And don't call me Demne Maol. That's not me.'

Bodhmhall, sensing the boy's distress, was about to intervene but found herself pre-empted by a sudden change of tack from the big man.

'Very well, little man. I will do as you ask. And don't fret. It's a very fine spear. I would hate to be on the receiving end of that. Even more so if it was sharper.'

Demne looked at him suspiciously, unsure if the warrior was being facetious or not.

'I saw how you felled that fat creature,' continued Fiacail. 'Six years of age! I've seen seasoned warriors who couldn't have made such a cast.'

The boy's fists tightened until the white of his knuckles shone. 'He was going to hurt Bodhmhall. I couldn't ... I ...'

'Easy, boy. That man deserved your bullet and your aunt was fortunate that you were so proficient. Who taught you the skills of sling cast?'

'Liath Luachra.'

'Huh.' The big man grunted, his fiery enthusiasm abruptly dampened. 'It matters not. Now, your aunt tells me it is your intent to follow the warrior path, to train as a *gaiscíoch* – a warrior.' Behind the boy, Bodhmhall furiously shook her head but he ignored her completely. 'Do I have the right of it?'

The boy nodded enthusiastically.

'Very good! Well, you've already demonstrated one of the key characteristics of the *gaiscíoch*, the bravery and heart of a boar. Your actions show you are fierce and not afraid to stand your ground, to protect your territory. But to be a superior *gaiscíoch*, you must meld a piece of fox and a piece of rat with that boar, eh.' He tapped his head. 'Cunning and slipperiness. You understand?'

Demne nodded but it was obvious he had no idea what Fiacail was talking about.

Despite her mounting irritation, Bodhmhall continued to observe their interaction, surprised to find that Fiacail was demonstrating a hitherto unknown facility with children. True, any little boy like Demne would be awed to be in the presence of such a renowned warrior, but still ...

Using her Gift, she studied her nephew, noting the fierce glitter of his internal flame. Although nowhere near as intense as it had been when he'd cast his shot and saved her from Regna of Mag Fea, it was still disturbingly unusual. The more she stared, the greater the impression she had of watching an ember glowing in a restocked fire, a seed waiting for the right stimulus to germinate and burst out onto the world.

'Demne, we will need more firewood. Go out to the closer trees and gather some.'

Man and boy turned as one, surprised by her interruption. Her nephew looked at her, turned his eyes to the plummeting rain outside then eyed her again.

'Best to do it now,' she said without sympathy. 'Rather than when it grows dark. Take your cloak and hurry. There's shelter in the lee of that canyon wall. The wood should be dry there.'

Knowing better than to argue with his aunt when she was in this frame of mind, Demne pulled on his cloak with a sigh and ran out into the rain.

Fiacail watched him go, continuing to study him as he disappeared into the gloom. 'Interesting lad, that. Hard to believe such a child sprang from the Flower of Almhu's womb.' That particular thought seemed to rekindle some distant recollection. 'Mind you, do you recall the night of his birth?'

Bodhmhall nodded, knowing she was unlikely to ever forget it. That delivery had been particularly arduous for her as she'd had to deal not only with the physical practicalities of a panic-stricken mother but the reflection of that panic through the flames of Muirne's life-light and that of her increasingly stressed unborn child.

'He was noisier than two pigs fucking,' Fiacail recalled aloud. 'All that screaming and squealing. He'd have woken the dead.'

The *bandraoi* clucked her tongue in disapproval. 'Come now, Fiacail. You must be used to the braying of children. You've probably left a trail of infants in your wake wherever you tarried.'

'True. That's most likely true. But never a we'an with the one woman I wanted to have a child with.'

Bodhmhall shifted uncomfortably, the movement provoking a fresh shot of pain through her arm. She winced, drawing Fiacail's attention. He caught the expression in her eyes.

'Don't fret, Bodhmhall. I haven't saved you just so I could burden you with romantic notions. You know I'd travel one hundred days if you had real need of me but you made your decision clear. You've always stood on the brutal side of honesty and I respect that.'

He edged back into silence and with the tip of his forefinger absently tapped the bowl he'd given to Bodhmhall earlier.

'I will not lie, Bodhmhall. It's been five years since I left Ráth Bládhma and not a day has passed that I didn't have to fight the urge to run back and seek you out.' He shrugged. 'I know such thoughts are fruitless dreams. I know your heart is with another. That is why I travelled so far and stayed away. I truly did not think I'd see you again.'

He lapsed into silence. In the orange light of the fire, his face has taken on a gentler hue, softening the harshness of his features.

Bodhmhall reached over and took his hand in hers. It was a funny thing to see that large hand with its dirty, broken fingernails enfolded in her fine fingers, that same hand that had once held her.

'You will always be my dear friend.'

'Ah, yes. Dear friend.' He sniffed and his left foot tapped a nervous cadence against the wall of the cave.

'My friendship then is so unappealing?'

He gave her an exasperated look. 'When you sit at the feast and find yourself limited to scraps and morsels then, yes, it is unappealing.' He shook his head in agitation. 'Let us speak no more of such things. Tell me of your plans.'

'My plans?'

'You are a clever woman Bodhmhall. I know you must have had some plan.'

Bodhmhall felt her shoulders slacken, unsure what to say. 'In truth, my sole plan was to try and survive until we got to Dún Baoiscne. Once there, I had hoped to fall on my father's mercy.'

'And now?'

She paused in thought. 'My preference is to return to Ráth Bládhma. That is the only place I can truly assure a defence of my nephew.'

'Then to Ráth Bládhma we will go. I have fulfilled my *geis*. I will escort you and the boy there safely.'

Bodhmhall shook her head.

Fiacail frowned. 'What now?'

'I must continue to Dún Baoiscne. *Clann Baoiscne* need to be warned of the traitor in their midst and I would use the visit to seek information on the Adversary. Our family is linked to him – of that I have no doubt. I just cannot work out how or why.'

'You are so certain the Adversary stands in the shadows of this ambush?'

'Yes. The leader from the assault on Ráth Bládhma also led the *fian* that ambushed us at An Bearna Garbh.'

Fiacail stiffened, his eyes regarding her with heated intensity. Having fought those forces so furiously on the battlements of Ráth Bládhma, this was a subject of deep personal interest to him. 'What?' he asked. 'You mean that tall turd with the odd face?'

Bodhmhall bit her lip. For a moment she considered telling him of Muirne's unexpected involvement with this deadly individual but then decided against it. In hindsight, despite her own feelings, her instincts were telling her that there was more to the matter than she'd first believed. She wanted more time to mull it over.

'Yes. He is named Gob An Teanga Gorm. He seems to act as some kind of servant to the Adversary.'

Fiacail cursed. 'That pig rutter.'

Bodhmhall stared, somewhat taken aback by the angry reaction.

'While I was waiting for the Bald Ones to appear,' he explained, 'I saw the *fian* who ambushed you travelling towards An Bearna Garbh. Naturally, I didn't know they were looking for you.' He shook his head as though furious with himself. 'I kept out of sight but I caught a glimpse of some of their warriors. I saw some *Clann Morna* men but I certainly didn't see that man. If I had, I'd probably have left the Bald Brotherhood for another day.'

This time it was Bodhmhall's turn to express shock. 'It was a *Clann Morna* fian?'

'No, no.' He shook his head. 'It contained some *Clann Morna* warriors I'd encountered in the past but no more than two or three. One of them was Cónán Gruagach, son of Aodh. Nasty little bastard, that one. A penchant for knives and so volatile he's considered an outsider, even amongst *Clann Morna*.'

Bodhmhall thought of the boy and the knife protruding from Tutal's throat. She nodded but said nothing, for the warrior's revelation prompted a heightened sense of urgency and, despite the pain in her arm, she felt a sudden spur to action. 'We should rest,' she decided aloud. 'We can leave early in the morning.'

Fiacail shook his head with a firmness that brooked no contradiction. 'We will not be travelling for several days. Your arm is broken, dear one. All that mistreatment from the Bald Ones has inflamed it badly. If you don't rest and keep it still to let the inflammation settle, you may lose the limb.'

'Gob An Teanga Gorm will have men out looking for us.'

'This canyon is well concealed and wildlife teems in these woods so our bellies will be full. Besides, if they do find us, I will protect you.'

The *bandraoi* grimaced, infuriated and frustrated not only by the time they would lose waiting for her arm to heal but by the realisation that once again, she was dependent on others to protect her. It was a bitter recognition for one who'd been so independent for so long. Eight years. Prior to that, as a woman in a brutal world dominated by male violence, she'd been dependent on others for her safety. First, her father at Dún Baoiscne and later, when she'd distanced herself from him, Fiacail and her brother, Cumhal. Negotiating her departure from Dún Baoiscne and taking up residence at Ráth Bládhma had been her first active step to independence although, even there, she'd had Liath Luachra as *conradh* to defend the settlement.

Too hard. My head spins.

She suddenly felt very tired. Her legs were stiff, her arm ached.

'I don't know. There is so much to do and the risks of discovery are significant.'

'I said I will defend you.'

'Ah yes,' she snarled, unable to keep the vitriol from her voice. 'Of course. For you are Blood Defender of Ráth Bládhma.'

'I bloody am!' Fiacail's voice rose an octave in response. 'I *was* the defender. I led the defence, I fought on the wall, I held the people together.' He glared at her. 'And do you think I am remembered? Do you think I get my own blood song? Oh, no! But Liath Luachra does. Just because she ran around with her arse hanging out!'

Bodhmhall stared furiously at him but then slowly, the corners of her mouth twitched and wrinkled into a smile. She sighed. 'I think Liath Luachra made her fair contribution.'

The fuming warrior turned his head away, staring outside at the pouring rain until it had sufficiently cooled his temper. 'Ach, I know she deserves the blood song,' he said at last. 'But, honestly! What kind of way is that to fight? If I'd known I could get a blood song out of it I'd have divested myself of clothing every time I went into battle.' He grinned 'Of course, I have the unfortunate disadvantage in that my member presents a target that is difficult to miss. I realise Liath Luachra doesn't suffer such … '

He paused in sudden realisation, raising his eyes to observe her quietly. 'Bodhmhall, in all this time you have not once mentioned Liath Luachra. Where is she?'

With this, any good humour the *bandraoi* had managed to regain, evaporated into the air and it felt as though a shard of steel had suddenly embedded itself in her chest.

'I don't know,' she said.

***

The story will continue in Book Three: The Adversary.
If you would like advance notice of when the next book in the series is available please sign up for 'New Releases' at irishimbasbooks.com

Pronunciation Guide:

Characters:

Sárán:
Saran is pronounced 'Saw-rawn' in English (something like 'Sauron' in the Lord of the Rings)

Liath Luachra:
This is pronounced 'Lee-ah Luke-rah' in English

Bodhmhall ua Baoiscne:
This first name is pronounced 'Bough-val' (the 'mh' in Irish produces a 'v' sound). There's really no easy way of pronouncing 'Baoiscne' for non–Gaelic speakers. Please just check out the audio guide at irishimbasbooks.com

Muirne Muncháem:
This is pronounced roughly as 'Mir-neh' and 'Mun – cawm' in English. I'd recommend checking the audio guide at irishimbasbooks.com for the closest approximation.

Fiacail mac Codhna:
This is pronounced as 'Fee-cull mack Cow-nah' in English.

Gleor Red Hand:
Gleor is pronounced like 'glore' in English (rhymes with 'bore').

Placenames

Ráth Bládhma:
This is pronounced 'Raw Blaw-mah' in English (the 'th' and the 'dh' are silent. Irish speakers love long silences – not!)

Dún Baoiscne:
'Dún' sounds like 'Dune' in English. Again, for 'Baoiscne' I'd recommend you go to the audio guide at irishimbasbooks.com.

Seiscenn Uarbhaoil:
Again, quite difficult for non-Gaelic speakers. Seiscenn sounds like 'shesh-ken' but best to check this out at the website pronunciation guide.

Author's Historical and Creative Note:

As mentioned in the foreword, this novel and its predecessor draw heavily on the twelfth century manuscript *Macgnímartha Finn* (The Boyhood Deeds of Fionn) and various other texts from before or after that.

Working with such source material has several advantages and disadvantages. The key advantage is that the original text is very concise (the *Macgnímartha Finn,* for example, has about 2500 words although the only remaining version of the text is incomplete and finishes rather abruptly). This allows a writer a lot of scope to develop complex characters and plot lines while still adhering to the narrative core.

The main disadvantage of using an old source manuscript however, is that it will often contradict or have different elements in it that don't align with other source materials for the same story. This could be as a result of 'artistic licence' by the original authors but, more likely, it's due to local variations of the core narrative being developed over the centuries and subsequently recorded. As a result, key characters will often end up having different roles in the different manuscripts. Bodhmhall, for example, is cast as either a *bandraoi* (female druid) or a warrior woman depending on which text you read. Liath Luachra is one of Fionn's original guardians (Demne, in case you haven't worked it out, was Fionn's original name) in the *Macgnímartha Finn* but, later, also turns up as a male enemy warrior who was the first to wound Fionn's father at the battle of Cnucha. Working through this complex web of intertwined storylines to produce a coherent contemporary narrative can be something of a challenge.

Finally, I should add a note on the 'Brotherhood of the Bald' (as Fiacail calls them) who turn up in this particular book. In the original *Macgnímartha Finn* this group was summarised as follows:

> *Later he (Demne) went with certain cairds (men of art) to flee from the Sons of Morna, and was with them about Crotta. These were their names: Futh and Ruth and Regna of Mag Fea, and Temle and Olpe and Rogein. There scurvy came upon him, and therefrom he became scald-headed, whence he used to be called Demne the Bald. At that time there was a robber in Leinster, Fiacal, the son of Codna. Then, in Feeguile, Fiacal came upon the cairds, and killed them all save Demne alone.*

The use of the word 'cairds' (from *aes cerda* meaning craftsmen) is an unusual one and their description of baldness suggests that this group were some kind of druids or 'Gifted Ones' as the latter were known for the practice of tonsuring their heads (in fact 'The Bald' was a common epithet used for druids in ancient literature. You may also note that, here, Fiacail turns up, not as the husband of Bodhmhall but as a simple bandit.

Naturally, I wanted to keep this episode, not only because I felt it was important for the authenticity of the story, but because I saw the 'cairds' dramatic potential. Needless to say, the whole variation of 'Gift' and the cannibal element is entirely my own invention.

Brian O'Sullivan

See Brian's blog and website at *irishimbasbooks.com* for contact details and updates on new and upcoming titles.

Fionn: Defence of Ráth Bládhma:

[The Fionn mac Cumhal Series: Book 1]

Ireland: 192 A.D. A time of strife and treachery. Political ambition and inter-tribal conflict has set the country on edge, testing the strength of long-established alliances.

Following their victory at the battle of Cnucha, Clann Morna are hungry for power. Meanwhile, a mysterious war party roams the 'Great Wild' and a ruthless magician is intent on murder.

In the secluded valley of Glenn Ceoch, disgraced female druid Bodhmhall and her lover Liath Luachra have successfully avoided the bloodshed for many years. Now, the arrival of a pregnant refugee threatens the peace they have created together. The odds are overwhelming and death stalks on every side.

Based on the ancient Irish Fenian Cycle texts, the Fionn mac Cumhal Series recounts the fascinating and pulse-pounding tale of the birth and adventures of Ireland's greatest hero, Fionn mac Cumhal.

Beara: Dark Legends

[The Beara Trilogy – Book 1]

Nobody knows much about reclusive historian Muiris (Mos) O'Súilleabháin except that he doesn't share his secrets freely. Mos, however, has a *"sixth sense for history, a unique talent for finding lost things"*.

Reluctantly lured from seclusion, despite his own misgivings, Mos is hired to locate the final resting place of legendary Irish hero, Fionn mac Cumhal. Confronted by a thousand year old mystery, the distractions of a beguiling circus performer and a lethal competitor, Mos must draw on his knowledge of Gaelic lore to defy his enemies and survive his own family history in Beara.

Beara: Dark Legends is the first in a trilogy of unforgettable Irish thrillers. Propulsive, atmospheric and darkly humorous, *Dark Legends* introduces an Irish hero like you've never seen before. Nothing you thought you knew about Ireland will ever be the same again. *[irishimbasbooks.com]*

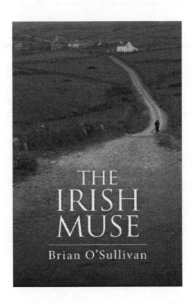

The Irish Muse and Other Stories

This intriguing collection of stories puts an original twist on foreign and familiar territory. Merging the passion and wit of Irish storytelling with the down-to-earth flavour of other international locations around the world, these stories include:

- a ringmaster's daughter who is too implausible to be true — despite all the evidence to the contrary

- an ageing nightclub gigolo in one last desperate bid to best a younger rival

- an Irish consultant whose uncomplicated affair with a public service colleague proves anything but

- an Irish career woman in London stalked by a mysterious figure from her past

Made in the USA
Middletown, DE
15 January 2022

58783055R00132